From inside the boathouse came a faint creaking, timed to the brief gust of wind that whirled snow dust, and rattled the ice-dry reeds along the bank. Tessa thought the wind was causing something inside the boathouse to swing gently, to creak, and then be still again.

There was a small door in front of her. The handle was dented, blackened brass. Because she couldn't turn away she grasped it and pulled.

Warmer air engulfed her. And the most terrible stench.

She had screamed in panic before the flashlight beam jerked upwards in her hand and caught the hanging figure, tattered, decayed. Teeth, eye sockets, lank hair. She was screaming as the torch fell from her hand, into the boathouse, rolling forward to where one dangling foot was locked solid by the ice.

About the Author

Thomas Dresden was born in London. He began writing as a scriptwriter in Canada and the United States. He is the author of *Talking to a Stranger*, which introduced Detective Superintendent Jack Abbeline, 'the great grandson of the Scotland Yard detective who worked on the Jack the Ripper case.'

Thomas Dresden became interested in the Jack the Ripper investigation as a boy when his grandmother used to tell him how, as an eighteen year old barmaid in Spitalfields, she narrowly escaped being one of the Ripper's victims as she made her way home through the notorious Mitre Square during the autumn of terror, 1888.

Missing

Thomas Dresden

CORONET BOOKS
Hodder and Stoughton

Copyright © 1995 by Thomas Dresden

First published in Great Britain
in 1995 by Hodder & Stoughton
A division of Hodder Headline PLC

Coronet paperback edition 1995

10 9 8 7 6 5 4 3 2 1

British Library Cataloguing in Publication Data

Dresden, Thomas
Missing
I. Title
823.914 [F]

ISBN 0 340 63756 0

Typeset by Letterpart Ltd, Reigate, Surrey.
Printed and bound in Great Britain by
Cox & Wyman Ltd, Reading, Berks

Hodder and Stoughton
A division of Hodder Headline PLC
338 Euston Road
London NW1 3BH

To Marie-France

PROLOGUE

Later, the police were able to reconstruct in part the movements of Beth Naylor, the twenty-seven-year-old American research student at Cambridge University, on the first Saturday in November, the day on which she was judged to have disappeared.

At just after ten o'clock on that morning, she left the rooms she rented in the Market Place and walked across to the Midland Bank where she withdrew £3000 of the £3795 she had in her account. While in the bank she met an acquaintance, another American research student named Sylvia Ziemcka. The bank security cameras show that meeting. Beth Naylor is completing her transaction at the counter. She is tall, with dark brown hair cut close to her head. She wears a dark roll neck sweater, a beige padded jacket and dark plaid skirt, and boots. Sylvia Ziemcka, further along the counter, waits until Beth Naylor is finished. The camera shows the two young women talking and laughing before they leave the bank together. Sylvia Ziemcka's statement records that they parted a few minutes later at the King's College end of St Edward's Passage.

At some time shortly before midday Beth Naylor was seen at the laboratory building off Pembroke Street where she conducted her research. She removed some things from her locker but she did not enter the laboratory itself.

Shortly after two in the afternoon she was seen again, this time by a market trader whose Saturday stall was opposite the entrance to her flat. She was seen to lock her front door and begin crossing the Market Place carrying a large canvas bag.

Beth Naylor was last seen that day in the forecourt of a house on Trumpington Street where she parked her red Escort F393 GFA on

1

a long-term arrangement with the house owner. It is not possible to determine whether she loaded any luggage into the car before she drove away.

Nor is it known, after leaving her parking space, in which direction she drove.

It was Tessa's husband, Carter, who had said it first in what Tessa thought of as his New England, carefully calculated, *guilt-inducing* way . . . 'How long is it since you've heard from Beth? Nearly two months? Is it that long?'

In the kitchen, cooking supper, she had nodded carefully, not looking up.

He had put down the pile of books he had brought in from the car and said slowly, mature adult slowly: 'My God, Tessa, two months – and you haven't even called her? Your sister could be missing, even dead by now.'

A familiar wave of guilt passed over her. How was it he could make her feel like this? And so easily, Tessa thought. Like pressing buttons.

'She hasn't called me either, Carter,' is what she said.

He'd walked through the conservatory to look into the small paved yard, before turning. 'If she's missing, Tessa, more especially if something more serious has happened to her, I don't have to point out that she could hardly have called you.'

Weird, she thought. The man I'm married to is *weird*. She looked up from her lasagne. Did he have a point? Talking to Carter it was always self-doubt she couldn't keep at bay. Maybe she *had* left it too long.

All the same, she didn't call. And she hung it out until nearly the end of November until she wrote:

Cambridge, Massachusetts   *25 November*

Dear Beth,

You were never in the running for any 'regular correspondent of the year' award but nearly two months since your last letter is a record even for you! It's a small feat of memory to recall what you wrote – although I know where I was when I read it. I was sitting in the sun on the porch of the house at Cape Cod, feeling better, truth to tell, than I have since I was ill. The September sun, Bethkin. Mid-September I seem to remember. You sounded in great spirits. How would you sound now if you wrote? Cambridge, Mass., is bracing itself for the first snow – Cambridge, England, I guess, is deep in November mists. My spies here tell me it's colder 'n cold there in those old rooms with no heat beyond smoky peat fires – and guttering candles to read by. How come the place has such a reputation for DNA research? And what news of the boyfriend? Laurie, is it? Do you still see him? Or have things moved on apace? (One sister can ask another surely). When do we get to meet him on this side of the turbulent pond? Listen, Beth – I'm serious. Write! I really miss hearing from you. Write now!

Tessa

That was it. She'd written. Got Carter off her back. They were peaceful days. Carter was busy finishing the proofs on his book on Jacobean minor dramatists (another book on Jacobean minor dramatists) and Tessa was back at work after four months of . . . what? Holiday? Convalescence?

She asked herself how do you describe a depression that reduces the mind and body to total inertia? Escape, is the way you describe it, Tessa, she told herself as she sat in her car, in a traffic jam on Harvard Bridge, listening to the reports of coming snow. Escape from yourself. When what you surely should be thinking about is escape from Carter.

In the first week of December he began again. 'Rob Castle called in at my office today.'

Tessa had nodded, waiting. Rob and Sonnie Castle had met up with Beth in England during the summer. It was they who'd reported on the boyfriend, Laurie Woodward. A pretty poor report as a matter of fact – 'a louche, long-haired hippie'. Didn't sound like Beth but there it was . . . Rob said if Beth were his sister he'd want to keep pretty close tabs on her.

'I have written,' Tessa said.

'How about the phone?'

'I haven't called.' She knew Carter was right. 'I'll call,' she said.

That evening Beth's clear, precise voice crossed the Atlantic.

'You've reached Beth Naylor, Cambridge 77077. I'm afraid there's no one to take your call at the moment. Please leave your name and number after the tone.'

And Tessa had left her message.

'Beth, this is Tess here. Please call me, honey. I'm getting a little worried. Okay, not very worried. More curious about what's going on. Call me. Do it tonight, there's a good little sister.'

But now doubt was beginning to form in Tessa's mind as she sat stalled on the Charles River crossing each day. Beth had never been this long without making contact. She was also a girl who particularly did not like putting herself in the wrong. Preferred to laugh at Tessa for playing mother-hen than to have to admit she had given cause for concern. Around this first week in December, a feeling began to grow in Tessa, sometimes even to the point of a sharp twist in the stomach, that all was not as it should be. Not that she really knew anything yet. She decided to call again.

'You've reached Beth Naylor. Cambridge 77077 . . .'

'Beth – Tessa again. I want you to call me, Bethkin. Early morning as you like. But call this weekend. Love you. But call, dammit.'

And again a few days later.

'You've reached Beth Naylor. Cambridge 77077 . . .'

'Beth . . . Beth . . . I've been calling you all week. Just call me, please. Right away. Okay?'

By then it was a call she put off no longer:

'Cambridge City Police. Good morning.'

'Good morning. My name is Tessa Wilson. I'm calling from Cambridge in the United States. I have a sister, Beth Naylor, who is a research student in chemistry at Pembroke College. You know the college?'

'Yes, of course.'

'My sister has not been in contact for two months or more. I've made innumerable phone calls to her apartment . . .'

'Well, the university has gone down for the Christmas vacation, miss. Your sister could quite easily be off staying with friends.'

'I suppose . . . but it doesn't explain why she hasn't written.'

'Does she live in the college?'

'No, she has an apartment in the town. In the Market Place. I've called there a dozen times in the last few days.'

'Okay. Let me suggest you contact the Bursar at Pembroke and if you don't get any satisfaction we'll send someone round to where she lives to look into it.'

'Thank you. Thank you very much. I'll do that.'

'Let me give you the number to call . . .'

'Cambridge City Police. Good afternoon.'

'Hallo. Did I speak to you earlier? It's Mrs Tessa Wilson . . .'

'Calling from America? Yes, you did, Mrs Wilson. Sergeant Blyton here. Did you have a word with the Bursar at Pembroke?'

'Yes, he wasn't really very helpful. Well, I guess he was as helpful as he could be.'

'What did he say?'

'He said Beth, my sister, had not been seen in college since before the end of term. That wasn't strange in itself because her research fellowship doesn't require her to be in Cambridge throughout the term. Apparently she spends time liaising with people doing similar work at other universities.'

'There you go then.'

'The Bursar said a couple of people had commented on the fact she hadn't been seen around. He also felt it strange for her to have left without saying goodbye to anyone.'

On the other end of the line the sergeant grunted.

'It's very unlike her not to have been in contact. To let us know whether she plans to come back for Christmas, for instance.'

'Is there any friend of your sister's we can get in touch with? Any other member of your family?'

'I believe my sister has a man she sees regularly . . .'

'Do you have his name and address?'

'*I have his name only. It's Laurie Woodward.*'

'*Laurie Woodward . . .*'

'*Does the name mean sometimes to you?*'

'*It rings a bell. I'll ask round the station.*'

'*Is that all?*'

'*No. We'll send someone round to her rooms, Mrs Wilson. That ought to sort things out. Which number the Market Place is it?*'

Was she really worried, or was she still doing this for Carter, to persuade him she was a responsible adult? It was an ugly thought. But Tessa had been sick, she accepted that. When . . . when she had miscarried, she had been assailed for months with a sense of dreadful inadequacy. So it was perhaps not surprising that, coming back home in the evening, stalled again on the bridge, watching the falling snow make sparkling cones beneath the street lamps, she asked herself again and again, was she proving something or was she really worried for Beth?

Yes. She was worried. And why should the name Laurie Woodward ring a bell with the police in Cambridge?

The call came from England when Carter was eating breakfast. To Carter breakfast time was sacrosanct. He ate toast, he drank orange juice. He allowed himself one cup of weak coffee and he studied his notes for that morning's lecture.

'*Hallo . . . I'd like to speak to Mrs Tessa Wilson. This is Cambridge City Police.*'

'*This is her husband, Carter Wilson. Cambridge, England?*'

'*Yes, sir. Sergeant Blyton.*'

'*Is it bad news? Perhaps you ought to tell me first.*'

'*I'd sooner talk straight to Mrs Wilson, if you don't mind, sir.*'

'*I'm her husband. You can tell me if it's bad. My wife has not been well lately. She's in no condition to receive bad news about her only sister.*'

'*It's not bad news about her sister, sir.*'

'*Then I can hear it anyway.*'

'*Mrs Wilson, if you don't mind, sir.*'

'*Jesus . . . It's the British police for you, Tessa. They won't speak to me.*

'*Hallo. Tessa Wilson speaking . . .*'

6

'This is Sergeant Blyton, Mrs Wilson. I've checked on the name you gave me, Laurie Woodward. I'm afraid there's bad news there. Mr Woodward came off his motorbike at a particularly nasty bend just outside Cambridge . . .'

'You mean he was killed?'

'Yes. The accident was immediately fatal.'

'When was this, Sergeant?'

'During the early hours of November the fourth to fifth.'

'Was my sister informed?'

'No. The police had no reason to inform her. We had no knowledge of your sister's relationship with him.'

'What about people at his work?'

'He was apparently some sort of travelling carpenter.'

'A carpenter?'

'Yes. Does that surprise you?'

'No . . . no . . . I suppose I'd assumed he was someone in Beth's own field. An academic maybe.'

'A travelling carpenter was our information. But no one came forward to claim the body. He had no assets, or none visible. He was buried, let's see, I've got it here, on December the first. On the parish.'

'What does that mean? At public expense?'

'Yes.'

'When my sister finally discovered he was dead, perhaps even several days later, after the funeral, that would have been an appalling blow . . .'

'It might have been. It depends how close they were.'

'When you went to my sister's apartment, was everything as it should have been?'

'Yes, I would say so.'

'Nothing to suggest where she might have gone?'

'No. No, nothing like that. We checked with her neighbours. Do you know the flat, Mrs Wilson?'

'No, I've never been to England.'

'It's over Thatchet's, the chemist's shop. The landlord, Mr Thatchet, keeps a set of keys. Our officer went in with him.'

'No signs of trouble of any sort?'

'None at all. Books and papers were all stacked neatly. No mess, *no sign of a disturbance. every indication that she'd been away for a reasonable amount of time. Plenty of mail behind the front door dating from beginning of November. She's staying somewhere over Christmas after the tragedy, looks like.'*

'After Laurie Woodward's death, you mean.'

'If she was attached to Mr Woodward, that seems to me a natural thing to do.'

'What about the landlord? Did she say goodbye? Wish him Happy Christmas?'

'No, she didn't.'

'Someone else she didn't say goodbye to, then.'

'Yes. But there's nothing conclusive in that. If she was upset, even very upset . . .'

'Not upset enough to call her sister and tell her what had happened.'

'These are family matters. I wouldn't know about that, Mrs Wilson.'

'What about her car? Where does she keep it?'

'Not on Market Hill, Market Place as we call it. But she does have a car, a red Ford Escort.'

'Where is it now?'

'It's in a parking space she rents from the sister of her landlord, a Mrs Taylor, on Trumpington Street.'

'The car's there?'

'Yes.'

'Have you looked in it?'

There was a faint note of exasperation in the sergeant's voice. 'We have, Mrs Wilson. It's empty. We checked the boot.'

'Boot?'

'The trunk, you call it. No sign of any disturbance. Tank half full. Engine turns over.'

'So she left without her car?'

'Looks that way. Could she have gone back to America for Christmas? Staying with friends, without letting the family know? It sometimes happens.'

'I can't imagine that.'

'Perhaps you'll phone around to her friends in Boston, Mrs Wilson?'

'Will you be making any other enquiries?'

'Not as things stand. People have a right to disappear. What I mean is, it's not always that people want others to know where they've gone.'

'You think I'm over-reacting.'

'Mrs Wilson, I know nothing about the family set-up. All I know is that in our experience what you've told me doesn't warrant further enquiries at the moment.'

'At the moment?'

'Not unless any disturbing new features come to light.'

'Sergeant, my sister is missing . . .'

'She is and she isn't, Mrs Wilson. I realise it's worrying that you don't know where she is, but technically she's not missing. We can't really spare anyone to do much more at this stage. I think you'll find she's staying with friends.'

'I see. The police overload, is that it?'

'Same here as it is over there, Mrs Wilson. We've left a message on the door for her or any friend that might be dropping by. That's all we can do for the moment. If I hear she's back, I'll contact you immediately.'

In the traffic jam on the bridge that evening, Tessa moved forward twenty yards at a time, mesmerised by the rooster tail of snow-slush produced by the pick-up in front of her. Clear Carter from your mind. Are you worried about Beth? If you were Beth, would you want your sister to do something? Something decisive?

'Logan Airport. British Airways reservations.'

'Good afternoon. My name is Tessa Wilson. I'd like a seat on the earliest flight to London you have.'

What do you wear in England in December? What do you wear to look for a missing sister? Taking off like this, was she just showing off? she asked herself as she packed. Or was she just getting away from Carter for a few days or weeks? Or did she really, really think her brilliant younger sister was in trouble? She shrugged. All three reasons rolled into one, perhaps. Only lovers, her father used to say with a smile curling his lips, only lovers believe that when we act, we act for one single, compelling reason.

CHAPTER ONE

Tessa Wilson felt her eyes gritty and her legs heavy as she came through immigration and customs, loaded her two bags from the carousel on to a trolley and wheeled it forward to just beyond the barrier. From here she was on her own. She experienced a sudden lost feeling after all the directed movement of the journey. Through body checks and baggage checks and ticket checks and customs checks until she stood here, alone among all these people, uncertain in which direction her next step should take her, feeling younger and more lost than she had for a long, long time.

Carter, of course, had warned her this would be the case. The adrenalin, he'd said, will carry you there, carry you all the way across the Atlantic. And then what? And then what will you do, alone and feeling increasingly helpless?

'Listen,' she'd said across the dinner table. 'Before we met, before we were married, I got up in the morning, I showered, I went to work, I took vacations and I didn't slip, slide, suffer accidents – or at least no more than anybody else doing the things I was doing. I once even took off walking in the Himalayas. Alone.'

'With the Mountain Travel Company.'

'Okay, they're good but they're not nursemaids.'

'I'm not trying to put you down, Tessa,' he'd said. 'On the contrary, I don't need reminding, you need all the building up you can get . . .'

She had jumped up and run from the room. Mark up another petty domestic victory for Professor Carter Wilson.

People flowed back and forth about her. So here she was. In England. Not on holiday. Not on a business visit. In England, for the first time, and looking for a missing sister.

11

There was reality to face. She knew that. Police stations, red tape, maybe even worse. She wasn't unfamiliar with it from her hospital work. The sinister formaldehyde smell. The unctuous manner of all morgue attendants in the presence of relatives . . .

She pushed her trolley slowly towards the exit, then turned and pushed it back again. In the middle of the concourse at London Airport, Tessa thought hard about her sister. Everybody admired her. Even Carter admired her. Maybe a little more than that.

Strange, Tessa thought, how they'd turned out, the two sisters. Or, to cite the more important relationship, the two *daughters*. Because that's certainly what they were: two daughters and only incidentally two sisters. Two daughters of Quentin Naylor, philanderer and genuine nice guy. Competition had made them what they were. Competition for their father's affection or esteem was the crucible. For Beth that had meant an arrow-straight academic line: Radcliffe, a year at the Pasteur Institute in Paris, and now a prestigious research fellowship at the other Cambridge. On this side of the Atlantic. Cambridge, England.

And Tessa herself? She had stayed around the house after their mother died, had looked after their father as he aged elegantly. Not looked after him in an old maid, house-keeping sense. No, she had pursued her career in hospital administration. Pursued it with some success. But it was true she had only married, in a hurry, at the age of thirty-four, less than six months after her charming old devil of a father died.

The present swept down upon her again. She was in that exhausted, up all night, light-headed state where impressions hit hard: the tang of fresh newsprint and coffee, suddenly cut by the sharp scent of the two well-dressed Arab men passing her, and as they moved on, other impressions . . . the large number of Asian women either passengers or airport workers; in a more or less secluded area between an Information desk and a Hertz stand, a group of men and women on their knees in silent prayer. She expelled air across her upper lip and decided she would find the coffee shop and sit for a few minutes thinking about the best way to go about doing what she had come here to do. Just a few minutes out of the fortnight she had before she returned to work as Assistant Personnel Director of Boston's largest hospital complex. A few minutes out of a whole fortnight of minutes couldn't be too extravagant, she thought to herself light-headedly.

She moved towards the aroma of coffee. The group on their knees between Information and Hertz began to pray loud and clear.

In another part of the arrivals building two uniformed members of the London Airport Police stood on a high landing and watched Detective Superintendent Jack Abbeline start up the carpeted steps towards them. Quickly they exchanged a glance. When Sergeant Bragg and his partner had been told that Abbeline had once played quarter-back for London University, they had automatically given him extra girth, extra years, created an Abbeline in their own image of a balding, beer-drinking, two hundred-pound fifty year old, who would lumber, head held low, up the steps towards them and stand puffing on the landing before he spoke.

He wasn't at all like that, moving smoothly up the steep staircase, a slim build, not yet forty, his head raised, his eyes on them.

The two men on the landing looked at the woman with Abbeline. Red spiky hair, pert mouth, short skirt and high heels – looking more like a tart, they separately concluded, than a detective inspector. 'Looks like he picked up something on the road,' one uniformed man whispered to the other.

Abbeline caught the tone rather than the content. 'Share your thoughts with us,' he said drawing level with them. He was tall. His blue eyes seemed to lock on to them. 'No?'

The two officers straightened under his silent stare. 'I'm Abbeline,' he said after an uncomfortable moment. 'This is Detective Inspector Janet Madigan, Special Branch.' He pursed his lips as if to underline the words. Then turned and led the way into a long narrow ante-room, pictureless but with several functional, overbright sofas along one wall and a black and white floor of hard vinyl that clicked under Janet Madigan's heels.

Abbeline was no stranger to the layout of the detention area. He glanced at the four numbered doors occupying the wall opposite the sofas. 'Where are you holding him?'

'Number Three,' Bragg said.

'What was his reaction?'

'Difficult to say, sir.'

'Was he surprised, resigned, angry . . .?' He looked across at the second man who shook his head, not prepared to volunteer an opinion either.

'Very hard to say, sir.'

'I saw some video footage of him when he was arrested once in America,' Jan Madigan said. 'That fucker's out on his own heath.'

The men from Airport Police looked at her, grateful for the support, shocked at the terms it was couched in. 'There you go, sir,' Bragg said. 'half the time you're not quite sure whether he's speaking to you or God Almighty. When we told him he was being detained pending Scotland Yard instructions, he just spouted out for two or three minutes on end. Biblical stuff. Old Testament.'

Abbeline nodded. 'Has he asked for anything? Or anyone?'

'No, sir, no requests. Hasn't even mentioned a lawyer.

'Right, you know the form. Let's have him.'

Bragg opened the door and held it wide. The man rising from the single chair made Abbeline think first of all of a large, ragged-winged crow. He was tall, taller than Abbeline, but young-faced beneath untidy thick black hair. Somewhere in his early thirties. He wore a neat tweed suit and knitted tie and over that a black trenchcoat which, although long, seemed barely adequate in the sleeves. Large wrists and red-knuckled hands splayed from the black material of the coat. Abbeline's first impression was of an over-large, over-earnest young man who might have just taken life from a comic strip.

His youthful face was reminiscent of a woodcut, long with a broad well-shaped mouth. But the eyes were small and furtive. Somehow Abbeline had imagined the eyes of a leader of a far out religious cult would be luminous and compelling. But the eyes of Leonard Passmore, below thick, turbulent dark eyebrows, were small and insignificant.

Not so the voice. When he spoke it was in a deep, tobacco rich, mid-Western voice with an additional trace of an accent Abbeline couldn't make out. 'I demand to know by what law or statute I am held, locked for hours without my Bible . . .'

'The door was not locked, sir,' Abbeline said. 'You are not a prisoner. You have been detained less than thirty minutes and you made no formal requests for anything or anybody.'

Passmore glared at him. 'Interfere with the Lord's word,' he said, in a low voice, 'and you are damned. Damned, you understand the word? Personally and individually damned. We have no soft words for our enemies.'

'Evidently,' Abbeline nodded equably.

'No soft words. We would deal with our enemies as Oliver Cromwell dealt with his at the battle of Worcester.'

' "God made them as stubble to our swords?" ' Abbeline grimaced. 'I think Cromwell's bark was worse than his bite. He wasn't all bad.'

Passmore stared at him. The airport Police Officers exchanged tight smiles. Janet Madigan clicked around the vinyl floor on her high heels. Liverpool Irish by extraction, she wasn't happy to hear Oliver Cromwell come in for praise, even if it was faint and pretty back-handed. She would take it up with Abbeline in the car on the way back to the Yard.

Abbeline held up his hand. 'Come through, Mr Passmore. You're entitled to make a statement of complaint.'

'I have a volume of complaint.'

'No problem there. I'm aware of no legal limit.'

'Am I being refused entry to the United Kingdom?'

'No, not at all, sir.'

He drew back his head, lifting his whole ribcage and extending his arm like an actor about to declaim: 'Deportation. Like a common criminal. This is deeply shocking to me.'

'Let's not play games, Mr Passmore,' Abbeline said briskly. 'Nobody has mentioned deportation. I am Superintendent John Abbeline of Special Branch. My office is responsible for foreign diplomats and eminent visitors. You come under the latter category.'

Passmore glared. 'Is this then the mat of welcome?'

Abbeline stretched out his arm and Jan put the folded papers into his hand. 'There's no need to detain you long, Mr Passmore. I have a number of questions to ask you. A number of questions to ask you about your last visit to England which was, let's see, just last week . . .'

'Ask your questions.'

'I regret to have to tell you that you, personally, are the subject of an accusation by a London woman . . .' he read from the paper. '. . . Mrs Cynthia Copeland . . . that you are responsible for the abduction of her daughter and that you know her whereabouts.'

'I have just arrived from America, Mr Abbeline. From Bloomington, Indiana. How could I possibly know anything about the abduction of a girl in the United Kingdom?'

'One of the mysteries we have to clear up, Mr Passmore,' Abbeline said. 'Sit down, will you, and allow me to explain?' He waited while Passmore settled like a malevolent bird on one of the armless sofas. 'I'm going to ask you a few questions. You're going to refuse to answer them. I am then going to caution you and you could very well be held on suspicion, your case admittedly being reviewed every six to nine hours, for up to thirty-six hours.' He paused, looking down at Passmore. 'Or . . . we can talk sensibly about this accusation and possibly get the whole thing over in fifteen minutes?'

Passmore's face fell into its woodcut lines.

'The girl's name is Rosemary Copeland,' Jan said. 'This is a photograph of her.' She took from her briefcase a picture of a young girl posing in a bikini.

Passmore hissed through his teeth. 'I have never heard of this Mrs Copeland. To my knowledge her daughter is not, nor ever has been, a member of my church. Now can I go? I have members of my flock waiting downstairs for me.'

Abbeline handed over the papers that Janet had given him. 'This is Mrs Copeland's statement.'

Passmore unfolded the statement, making the paper crackle in his huge hands. He achieved the unfolding in four or five completely separate, jerky movements. Then he lowered his chin and backed his head on his long neck to achieve a comfortable focus.

Watching him, Abbeline was aware of the pure theatre of his movements. Did he know it? Was he just a gifted poseur, a TV performer who had impressed many influential people in different countries of the world? Or was he a natural? A convinced prophet of the Lord?

Passmore went through the four pages once and started over

again. Abbeline waited no longer. 'Have you ever met Rosemary Copeland?'

The eyes were on Abbeline, from under the shock of black hair.

'Have you ever met her, Mr Passmore?'

'It's possible,' he said carefully. 'I don't believe so.'

'So you've never even heard of Rosemary Copeland?'

'I just told you.'

'You told me you'd never heard of her mother. Have you heard of Rosemary Copeland?'

'No. Never.'

'Your church runs a mission to the poor in Soho.'

'In King's Cross and Soho, yes.'

'Mrs Copeland, as you see, claims that her daughter spent many evenings helping to give out soup in your canteen there.'

'It's even possible she did. I still wouldn't necessarily know her name.'

'Mrs Copeland's statement says her daughter came under your influence. The statement makes the point that the girl, Rosemary, came home on several occasions and described conversations she had had with you personally.'

Passmore mused a few moments. 'This girl is aged seventeen, I see. Legally under age.'

'Yes.'

'The Millennium Church has had some recent problems with parents complaining that their sons and daughters have somehow been unreasonably persuaded to follow the ways of God.' Passmore's tone had changed, lost its declamatory note. His small eyes creased at the complaint, his brows furrowed.

'I thought most of the problem stemmed from the fact that the sons and daughters had been persuaded to hand over their inheritances?' said Jan.

Abbeline gestured to her to be quiet. 'What are you saying, Mr Passmore?'

'I'm saying that an inventive seventeen year old who wished to spend her evenings in Soho might well tell her mother she was working in a soup kitchen for the homeless.'

'She might,' Abbeline conceded. 'I can see she might.' He beckoned to Jan Madigan to walk with him further down the

17

gallery. 'What d'you think?' he said, keeping his voice low.

'Hold the fucker,' she said. 'Bang him up. Cromwell's his hero – he must be guilty of something.'

'Jan . . .'

'Sorry, sir. Only a joke. Nothing to go on, I'd say. We can always pick him up later.'

They returned to Passmore. 'You'll leave the address of your church here in England, Mr Passmore. I understand your people are not very forthcoming about addresses.'

'It's true we don't publicise the address of our prayer centre. There's no law in this country that says we have to. I'll leave you an address where you can reach me, personally. And now I would like to be released.'

'You were never in custody, Mr Passmore,' Jan said cheerfully. 'Our unit is here to prevent anything like that happening to eminent American gentlemen like you.'

'The arrogance of office . . .' Passmore breathed the words into the air and turned to Abbeline. 'There was a Passmore born in Roxwell, Essex, who figured in the Poll Tax lists of 1381. There was a Passmore who fought at Tewkesbury, another who drowned opposing the Armada. In the seventeenth century we were preachers until expelled to Massachusetts under James II. We have a place in this country, Superintendent.'

'You're free to go, Mr Passmore. I'm sorry to have detained you. I shall put your denial to Mrs Copeland. Perhaps she'll accept it.'

'If not?'

'I'll need to talk to you again. If she withdraws her accusation that will be the end of Scotland Yard's interest in you and your church's activities. You'll hear no more of us.' He paused delicately. 'And I hope we'll hear no more of you.'

Passmore's heavy lower lip jutted, showing even white teeth. Capped, Janet Madigan thought. Very expensively.

'If you expect to hear no more of the Millennium Church,' Passmore intoned in his preacher's voice, 'you will be massively disappointed. Just look into the eyes of those people at prayer, waiting out there on the airport concourse, Mr Abbeline. You saw them?'

Abbeline shook his head.

The denial meant nothing to Passmore. 'They'll tell you,' he said. 'Their very presence will tell you that you will hear more of us, Mr Abbeline, and more yet. For our church is poised at the very threshold of a great beginning.'

Tessa stood in the open phone booth, one hand on her luggage trolley, the other holding the receiver to her ear.

'You must come and stay the night with me in London,' Laura Portal said. 'It's on your way. You can hire a car or take a train to Cambridge tomorrow. You need someone to talk to, Tessa. I can imagine how worried you must be.'

Tessa felt better. She thanked Laura, told her she would be there in less than an hour and put down the phone. Trundling her trolley across the concourse she passed the group at prayer and was struck by how ordinary they looked. There were no beards, no beads. Only twenty or so men and women of all ages, quietly dressed, making no attempt to impose themselves on passersby. She remembered afterwards that she was quite impressed.

But she was also relieved she was no longer entirely on her own. Laura Portal was an old friend of the family; her daughter Sally had been at school with Beth in Boston. To spend the night at Laura's, even though Sally was away in India, offered comfort, a familiar voice, and someone who would be genuinely, personally worried about Beth.

CHAPTER TWO

Within a few minutes of arriving at Laura Portal's house in Barnes, Tessa knew there was something wrong.

'Did Sally say anything about a man Beth was seeing?'

'Yes.' Laura hesitated. 'Yes, she said Beth had met someone. Woodward? Laurie Woodward.'

'Did you know that he was killed in a motorbike accident early in November?'

'No.' Laura shook her head vigorously. 'I haven't heard from Beth since Sally left for India. This happened in the last few weeks?'

'Laura, what did Sally have to say about Laurie? Did she meet him?'

'Yes. I'm sorry, Tessa, but Sally's impression of the man is that he is . . . was . . . thoroughly unsavoury. Immensely talented, apparently. But frankly, weird. Sally couldn't imagine what Beth was doing with such a man.' She took a deep breath.

'It's pretty much what colleagues of Carter's, Rob and Sonnie Castle, thought when they called on Beth while on vacation over here. Woodward was there. They didn't take to him.'

'No.' Laura Portal looked down at the carpet. 'If only Sally were in London,' the older woman said, I'm sure she could help.' She gave Tessa an uncharacteristically furtive look.

'Have you something to tell me, Laura?' Tessa said in one of the long awkward silences while Laura made tea.

'Yes.' The Englishwoman hesitated. 'Yes,' she said again. 'Something that's very painful for me to say, but I have no choice now.'

Tessa waited.

'Let's take our tea through and sit down.'

Laura Portal steadied the Worcester teacup in its saucer and placed it carefully on the table beside Tessa. She was one of those Englishwomen to whom the 1960s seemed never to have happened. In both dress and manner her contempt for ruling fashion was evident. She was tall, grey and in her late-fifties, what would once have been called a handsome woman.

In her childhood Tessa had found her formidable when the Portal family, Sir Robert, Laura and their daughter Sally, had made one of their visits to the Naylors in Boston. But the years had changed that. Since Robert Portal's death, Laura had come to Boston often, especially when Sally was doing her undergraduate degree at the same school as Beth, and as time had softened the age difference between Laura and Tessa, they had become friends.

'I'm only sorry Sally isn't here to be with you,' Laura Portal said. 'By now she's somewhere between Delhi and Nepal. There's no chance of calling her back. I'll do all I can . . . and obviously if you need somewhere to stay in London?'

Tessa shook her head. 'I have to start in Cambridge,' she said. 'What is it you have to tell me?'

Laura sat uneasily in the upright Louis XV chair opposite Tessa. 'You really do believe she's missing? There couldn't be some explanation? Life's full of things like that. Could Beth have left for somewhere and simply forgotten to tell anyone?'

'No . . . that's Carter's story. And the Cambridge police. But I don't buy it. You know Beth, Laura, that just is not her style. As I see it at the moment there's more than one possible explanation. A lot depends on how close she was to this man Laurie Woodward. Some sort of breakdown is not impossible when she heard of his death.'

'More than one possible explanation, you said?'

'Laurie Woodward might have played no particular emotional part in her life,' Tessa said. 'In which case, Beth's simply disappeared. She's missing, whatever the police say. And attractive young women who are missing in this world are usually in some sort of very big trouble. Now you've got something to tell me, Laura?'

'Yes. But I'd like to start at the beginning, during the summer when Beth arrived from Paris. She had time to spare before she had to go up to Cambridge. Sally's flat is minute so I put Beth up here.'

'How was she then?'

'Fine. Looking forward to starting her work in Cambridge.'

'Did she call you after that?'

'Sally spoke to her a couple of times. She was busy preparing for her Indian trip. There were a dozen permissions she had to get to visit some of the sites she needed to see for her doctorate, but she did visit Beth once in Cambridge. That would have been towards the very beginning of November.'

'How did Sally find her then?'

Laura Portal looked anxiously out of the window where there were traces of snow in the air. 'The things I have to tell you, Tessa, I should perhaps have told you before. Let me start with the weekend Sally stayed in Cambridge. She found Beth very strained. She thought it was the work, the research not going well or something. But that proved not to be the case.'

Tessa was sitting forward on the edge of her armchair. 'What *was* the case, Laura?'

'Sally couldn't find out.'

'Was Laurie Woodward there?'

'The boyfriend? No. He'd gone away for the weekend but Sally didn't get the impression it was man trouble.'

'How did she describe Beth? Depressed?'

'No, not really. "Desperately preoccupied" was Sally's phrase.'

Tessa shrugged. 'I guess we've all seen Beth like that.'

'This was more than usual. Much more. Introverted. Staring into space.'

'All weekend?'

'More or less. Sally said Beth didn't want to talk about anything. Cambridge . . . the people she'd met, even Laurie. So Sally began talking about the time they were undergraduates together, right back to when they were children and Robert and Sally and I used to come and stay with you.'

Tessa saw the shadow on Laura Portal's face, the tightening of the shoulder muscles, saw her hands close on the slender arms of her chair. 'What is it, Laura?' she asked.

Laura took a deep breath. 'Would you like a drink?' she offered.

Tessa shook her head.

'You don't mind if I do? This is going to be rather difficult for me.'

She went through the double doors into the dining room and returned a few moments later carrying a tumbler containing an inch of Scotch.

'What do you have to tell me?' Tessa asked as the older woman sat down opposite her.

For a few moments Laura was silent, then she looked up at Tessa. 'You know how our two families met, don't you?'

Tessa nodded. 'Sally's father was something at the British Embassy in Washington, and with Dad's British connections – isn't that it?'

'Part of it.'

'But only part?'

Laura nodded. 'Your father was a dazzling man, Tessa, when I first went to Washington.'

Tessa kept her eyes on the still handsome patrician face. 'And . . .?' she said deliberately.

'I think you've guessed. I went to Washington to stay with my fiancé – and I immediately began an affair with your father.' She laughed shortly. 'Oh, he knew how to make it easy. He was . . . let's say . . . something of a philanderer. I suppose you know that?'

'I knew he liked being around women.'

'More than being around. He charmed them, seduced them and betrayed them. But they still loved him. I know I did.'

'You were in love with my father but still you married Robert?'

'Yes. I gave myself a good talking to. Told myself I'd been taken to bed by a pastmaster of the art of seduction. That's all it was.'

'And was it?'

'No. No, it wasn't. A month after my marriage I was in your father's bed again. I was hopelessly infatuated. He was marvellous to be with, very *considerate* of Robert who, of course, knew nothing. And I was appallingly weak. I let it go on and on . . .'

'Until?'

'Until one day I discovered I was pregnant.'

'By my father?'

There was a long silence. Laura took a huge gulp of her Scotch. 'I simply didn't know.'

Tessa looked at her. 'You don't know?'

'I was living the normal life of a young married woman with Robert – and at least once a week I was spending an afternoon in

24

bed with your father. When I discovered I was pregnant, I felt literally suicidal.'

'Did you tell Dad?'

'Yes.'

'What did he do?'

'He proposed a solution which was calm, sensible, and I suspect suited him to the ground.'

'Which was what?'

'He proposed we should end our affair. Remain good friends. Continue to see each other but only when Robert was present. And let the ardour fade naturally, as he put it. I suspect the truth was that he was already wooing another young woman.'

'The child was Sally, of course?'

Laura nodded briefly.

'Does she know?'

'Yes. She does now.'

Tessa picked up her cup, stared down at the tea and put it back again on the saucer. 'Maybe I'll join you in a drink after all. Do you have any wine?'

'White?'

Tessa nodded.

Laura went out of the room.

For a few moments Tessa stared out of the window across trees and gorse bushes sprinkled with snow. She felt a strangely mixed reaction to what Laura Portal had just told her. A mixture of shock and a curious, nervous admiration for her father seemed uppermost. Then she thought of Laura's husband, Robert, knowing nothing. And her own mother, guessing perhaps, on some level, but too wrapped in her Bible readings to enter the real world where ordinary men and women committed adultery daily. In her mother's world only monsters of lust would do such a thing – thus by definition not her husband. So she remained deliberately blind.

Laura came back and handed Tessa a glass of chilled wine. She picked up her own glass and took a sip before sitting down. 'The reason I'm telling you this, Tessa, is not because I've suddenly come over irrepressibly confessional. It's to do with Sally and Beth at Cambridge last month and, God knows, it might just have some bearing on Beth's disappearance.'

'What makes you say that?'

'I had never told Sally,' Laura Portal said carefully. 'But after her father died last year I did, quite deliberately, drop a few hints. I intended to create a situation where, without forcing the information on her, I would give Sally an opportunity to ask – if she wanted to.'

'She never did?'

'No. I think she preferred not to know. But at Cambridge that weekend with Beth, somehow the whole thing came up. Sitting talking about their childhood, the visits we used to make to your house in Boston . . . that sort of thing.' She paused. 'Anyway one night on that weekend, very late – it was after midnight – Sally rang here.'

'And asked you?'

'She asked me outright – was it possible she was Quentin Naylor's child?'

There was silence in the room. Tessa couldn't take her eyes off the face of the woman opposite her, the pale skin just surplus to the fine bone structure, the china blue eyes no longer clear as in youth, the hair now passed almost imperceptibly from blonde to a creamy white. 'You told her on the phone?' Tessa said. 'You told her Robert wasn't her father *on the phone?*'

'My God,' Laura said. 'I had in a sense invited the enquiry, I couldn't duck it then – though I'd never thought she might ask me on the telephone.'

'So you told her?'

'Laura shook her head. 'I told her it was possible. It was all I *could* tell her.'

'How did Sally react?'

'Badly.' She paused, remembering. 'Pretty badly. I know now what I should have said.'

'What's that?'

'Either yes or no. Perhaps it didn't really matter to Sally which. But to say I just wasn't sure . . .'

'What happened?'

'When she came back from Cambridge, her face was like thunder. I couldn't blame her. I felt the same as she did: it was disgraceful her mother couldn't say for certain who her father was.'

'And Beth?'

'Beth, apparently, was horrified. Sally said she took it very badly. Went almost totally silent for the rest of her time there. My God, Tessa, I feel so horribly ashamed. Of not *knowing*, more than anything. Are you shocked?'

Tessa ran her hands through her hair. 'No,' she said slowly. 'Or perhaps a little at first. But tell me more about Beth? Did she call Sally after that?'

'No. She called me. She asked me, not very politely, to tell her again what I'd told Sally. I did and she put the phone down on me.' Laura gestured hopelessly. 'I never imagined it might affect you or Beth like that. Sally I could understand.'

'Did you and Sally make it up? Before she left for India?'

Laura stretched a smile. 'More or less. It's not really something you make up.'

'But Sally was okay?'

'It was Beth I was worried about. And then you phoned with the news she was missing. And I knew I must tell you everything straight away.'

Tessa sat numbly. Beth had idolised her father. Was it possible that the discovery of his affair with Laura had affected her balance in any crucial way? Could this story from a quarter of a century ago really have any bearing on whatever happened to Beth at the beginning of November?

CHAPTER THREE

Streetlamps were reflected in the blank windows above the chemist's shop. Tessa rang again, leaning heavily on the bell. She knew it was useless, knew it was not suddenly going to produce an open door with Beth, flustered but pleased to see her, drying her hair or apologising for not having heard the bell over the sound of Wagner in full flood. But she kept on ringing all the same.

Behind her she could hear the rumble of the waiting taxi's diesel engine. She rang one last time, stepped back to stare up at those blank windows and turned away. Creating her own story-board of a traveller from afar let down by some feckless male, the woman taxi-driver was sympathetic. 'The Pelican Inn,' Tessa told her, accepting the driver's sympathy because it was easier than explaining.

She stood in darkness. Just enough light from the streetlamp outside came off the snow-laden roofs to illumine the room. The beams, which she knew were dark brown oak, showed as thick black ribs across the plaster ceiling. The wardrobe, angled slightly to the right, was a huge black box. The bed, a fourposter, stood as a stark frame hung with diaphanous curtaining, through which she could make out the heavy bronze bust of a Roundhead or Cavalier on the far side of the room. Tessa shivered slightly within her warm robe. She was behaving, she knew, like a child: deliberately giving herself what she and her sister as kids used to call the jitters. She crossed the plain boards and opened the casement window. A gust of cold air whipped past her head. Flecks of snow brushed her cheek. She had somehow not imagined that England would be so cold. But then she had not imagined, coming from the snow drifts of Cambridge, Massachusetts, that this Cambridge would be deep in snow, too. Unlikely, people who knew had said, unlikely to find snow in the fen country before January or February. Bitterly cold winds straight from Russia, yes, blowing across the North Sea and the German-Polish plain, unchecked by any range of hills between here and Moscow. But snow? That was for later in the winter, they said.

When Tessa passed through the saloon bar of the Pelican ten minutes later, heads turned. She found herself cheered by that. Consuming the last years of her thirties far too fast for comfort, she found she fought an unending series of losing skirmishes with the scales. She knew she couldn't be described as heavy, much less as fat, but she wasn't really fashionably thin either. She was tall enough to carry some excess, but knew that excess was just teetering on the edge of being excessive. Carter had said he'd prefer it if she put on a little more. But, contrarily, she no longer admired his taste in women.

Yes, she still turned heads. Her dark-blonde curling hair was well brushed. She wore her usual restrained amount of make-up. And her long black fitted coat and leather boots, gave her, she thought, a certain style. Of course they did, she told herself, catching a passing glimpse of herself in a pub mirror. She smiled her thanks as the locals dropped back and allowed her to reach the bar.

George Pringle, the publican, was on duty. 'Good evening, Mrs Wilson,' he said, polishing glasses. 'Can I get you anything before you brave the cold?'

'No, but I'd like to make a phone call if I may?'

In the big apartment on Massachusetts Avenue Carter Wilson walked with long strides into the living room – plaid shirt, jeans, white socks, no shoes. Automatically he smoothed his thinning hair before he picked up the phone. 'Hi,' he said. 'Where are you?'

'Where I'm supposed to be, Carter. I stayed the night with Laura Portal in London and I'm now here. In Cambridge, England. Right?'

'You made it, then?'

'I made it.'

'Good on you.' Frontier accent.

'Carter. I'm a thirty-six-year-old perfectly competent woman, and I can find my way from Cambridge, Massachusetts to Cambridge,

England. Even though the train from London was stalled without heat for two hours in deep snowdrifts.'

'My God. But you're okay now?'

'At the Pelican Inn as planned.'

'At the Pelican. That's great.'

She knew he meant '*That's astonishing*' and found she didn't know how to keep the snarl out of her voice. She tried. 'Stop worrying, Carter, okay? I'm here, I'm warm, I'm comfortable, and I've got an appointment to see the Dean of Pembroke College in less than half an hour.'

'How far's the college from the inn?' he asked.

'Carter . . .' She was not far short of snarling now. 'Pembroke College is maybe two hundred yards away. I could hop there in time on one snowshoe.'

'Sorry. But you've got to let me worry a bit about you. You're a long way away and I really wish I was there with you.'

She softened, reluctantly. 'Yuh, okay.'

'I just don't like you being there alone.'

'I know that.'

'Maybe if I had a word with Max he could fill in for me.'

She didn't answer. She was thinking. Should she tell him what Laura Portal had told her? No . . . Beth hadn't gone missing because she suddenly found out Sally Portal was also a child of their father. No, that didn't make any sense.

'Tessa, I said I'd talk to Max.'

'We discussed all this, Carter. You have a course of lectures to prepare. Stay put and do it and I'll get on with what I have to do here. Just stop worrying, okay? I'm hanging up now or I'll need that other snowshoe.'

'What?'

'Forget it. A joke. Love you, Carter. I'll call you.'

'Tessa . . .'

She hung up and walked back into the warm, smoky, Christmassy atmosphere of the bar. Love Carter, love her husband? That had been a long, long time ago.

Sergeant Ken Russell was fifty, overweight, drank too much beer and had become aware, of late, that he waddled a little as he walked. His wife hadn't mentioned it, but Jan Madigan, his immediate boss, had. Several times.

In New Scotland Yard, Russell collected up his notes and left his office thinking of Jan Madigan. Never thought he'd get along with her, but he had. At first slowly coming to like her, then finally to think of her as the sort of friend you worried about. Bad luck for her that, to fall for her boss just six months after she got married to someone else. Not that Jack Abbeline had noticed the way she felt about him. Or if he had he'd been clever enough not to recognise it. Once it was out in the open Jan would have to be transferred to another team. And that would break her heart.

He knocked on Abbeline's door and ambled in, his shoulder thudding against the jamb.

Abbeline, eyes closed, jacket off, was sitting with his feet up on his utterly clear desk.

'I'm not interrupting anything, I hope, sir,' Russell said. 'Like a few quiet moments transcendental meditation perhaps?'

Abbeline pulled down his legs. 'I was just composing a grovelling letter of apology to Leonard Passmore,' he said. 'Mrs Cynthia Copeland has withdrawn all her accusations. Her daughter Rosemary returned in tears this morning, having run off with the manager of a karaoke club.'

'In Soho?'

'Where else? She had been meeting him under colour of false holiness.'

'What does that mean, sir?'

'It means she was claiming to be ministering to the deserving poor of Soho . . .'

'. . . when in fact she was stretched on the manager's horsehair sofa, being given one to the sound of karaoke in the club below?'

Abbeline grunted. 'There's nothing to this Rosemary Copeland case, Ken. But the Commander wants us to keep an eye on Passmore all the same. There have been all sorts of suggestions of undue influence. Usually involving young women. Very often quite wealthy young women. And this is the sixth or seventh visit he's made to the UK in the last few months.'

'It can't be the money. I'm sure he makes a lot more out of his TV appeals to the good folk of Bloomington, Indiana.'

'He claims he's supervising the church's new soup kitchens in Soho and King's cross.'

'He's getting a lot of publicity from them.'

'And recruits.' Abbeline stretched. 'All I'm really saying, Ken, is that this is something to keep on the boiler. As he made the point rather forcibly to me himself – I don't think we've heard the last of the Reverend Leonard Hope Passmore or his Millennium Church of Christ Reborn.'

'Then I haven't been wasting my time after all, sir.'

'What have you got there, Ken?'

'Couple of statements. Informal, unsigned, but I think we can back them up if we have to.' He paused for effect. 'I've spoken to a Mrs Rafaela Mattia of Soho. She says her daughter Linda is being wheedled away from the family.'

'How old is the daughter?'

'No good, I'm afraid,' Russell said. 'She's just turned eighteen.'

'How did you get on to them.?'

'I stayed down on the airport concourse this afternoon while you and Jan went up to question Passmore. His welcome party were down on their benders praying for a miracle or two.'

'I saw them as we left.'

Russell nodded. 'I picked out the youngest, a nice little Italian cockney girl named Linda Mattia, and asked her what she thought she was up to.'

'You mean you bullied her? Made it sound as if she was guilty of soliciting in the grounds of Buckingham Palace?'

'That sort of thing. The kid's young but spunky. Started in immediately having a go at her mother. Said if the old lady had been complaining to the police again it was time she minded her own business. She was eighteen now. An adult. And since when was saying your prayers breaking the law? I took her home address and went straight over to Soho to see her old lady.'

'Mattia . . . they're going to be Catholics, aren't they?' Abbeline mused. 'How did young Linda get mixed up with a Protestant fundamentalist group like Passmore's? Boyfriend?'

'I think they put a lot of effort into recruiting. They first approached Linda at a disco. A very nice young man, Signora Mattia thought he was. Until he started talking about sacrificing everything for the Lord. By then Linda was spending seven nights a week at the Soho soup kitchen. Three weeks ago she disappeared to prayer camp. That was the last Mrs Mattia saw of her daughter.'

'Do we know where they hold the camp?'

'No. That's what's worrying Linda's mother. East Anglia was mentioned but they're very secretive about where exactly they hang out. If there was a big meeting scheduled, Linda was picked up in a cafe or on a street corner. She never knew where she was going.'

'What about contributions to the cause. Had they asked her?'

'Linda used to work at Marks & Spencer. Six weeks ago she stopped giving her mother the few quid she normally turned over for board and lodging. A week later she was on the elbow, trying to borrow her bus fare.'

'You think the brothers cleaned her out?'

'Signora Mattia certainly does.'

Abbeline nodded slowly. 'Well, as you say, it's good background. She's not going to do a Mrs Copeland on us?'

'Not this one, sir. You won't be writing any grovelling apologies because Mrs Mattia's pulled out.'

Abbeline nodded. 'Okay, Ken. Well done. Now, clear off and let me grovel in peace.'

From the corridor outside the office there came a sudden crash of shattering teacups and the sound of raised voices. A woman's voice pierced the hubbub and faded, cursing.

'I'll take a look.' Russell ambled towards the door.

'If it doesn't concern me, I don't even want to hear about it,' Abbeline said as the door closed behind his sergeant.

He swung round in his chair and picked up the phone, buttoned a number and waited.

A woman's voice answered. 'Hallo, Jo Saunders.' It was a warm voice, deep and modulated and more than a little actressy.

'How many times have I told you to answer the phone without giving your name?'

'But I *like* dirty phone calls.'

'You wouldn't if you ever got one,' he said curtly.

'No, I'm sure I wouldn't. Sorry. It was me being tasteless as usual. Let's start over. Hallo, darling, how are you?'

'Fine. What is it now, eight o'clock? I'm finished for today. How about you?'

'Name the place.'

'The wine bar.'

'Fifteen minutes.'

'I'm on my way.' He hung up. He was on his feet, reaching for his jacket, when the door opened and Jan Madigan came in, quickly closing it behind her.

Abbeline slid his arms slowly into his jacket, his eyes on her face. 'What is it, Jan?'

'I'm sorry,' she said.

He frowned. 'About the commotion outside? Was that you?'

She shook her head then shrugged quickly. 'Well, partly. It was Rhoda, I'm afraid.'

The colour drained from Abbeline's cheeks then mounted, heightening to a flush across his cheekbones. 'What have you done with her?'

'Ken's got her in an interview room, end of the corridor,' Jan said. 'I told her she was out of order, coming here, where you work.'

He buttoned his jacket. 'Thanks, Jan.' He stood, his fingertips splayed on the clear desktop. 'What's she looking like?' he asked with an effort.

Jan shrugged again.

'Not good?'

'Few drinks.' She paused. 'Only a couple of clerks saw her on this floor.'

He nodded. 'I really shouldn't be thinking about my own dignity, should I? But it's hard not to.'

'There's no need for you to see her,' Jan said. 'It's blackmail, you know that. She wants money. Kick up a fuss about you being a big noise here at the Yard and you'll drop her a few quid to keep her quiet. She knows that, Jack. I bloody know she knows it.'

'I'll see her,' he said.

'Don't.'

He hesitated.

'Leave it to me,' she said. I'll give her the few quid, tell her she'll be arrested if she tries this again.'

'Christ, no.'

'Or I'll tell her you don't work here anymore.'

He shook his head. 'No. I'll see her.' He walked to the door, tension creasing his face like an older man's. 'But thanks, Jan.'

CHAPTER FOUR

Two of the customers leaving the Pelican had volunteered to walk with Tessa to the gates of Pembroke College and the three of them set out into a fine cold moonlit evening. At the end of the lane, not two hundred yards through snow that crackled underfoot, they came out on Trumpington Road almost opposite Pembroke. Here her escorts left her and she walked towards a high arch that opened directly off the pavement. From the porter's lodge set into the arched entrance she crossed a court with low medieval buildings on either side and a later, perhaps nineteenth-century, building in front of her. 'We like to think of Pembroke as a small college, madam,' the porter said. 'Small, but not short of distinguished men. William Pitt the prime minister was here. And Gray, who wrote Gray's Elegy. And, of course, bishops and churchmen galore . . .'

They had passed through a second archway and now stopped in a small courtyard facing a low Tudor building. 'That's the staircase, madam. Go up to the first floor and Mr Butler's rooms are directly in front of you.'

She thanked him and passed through the low stone entrance. The staircase was heavy black oak, uncarpeted. The walls were panelled to shoulder height and lit by a cream globe hanging over the staircase. Tessa stood for a moment, wondering whether she was making a complete fool of herself. At the back of her mind was the memory of a conversation with her father a year or two before his death: 'Beth's temperament,' he had said, 'is a pendulum. You've seen her since your mother died, swinging from indifference about her studies to intense concentration. She's been through, as we all know but don't mention, a period when any good-looking young

37

guy would do, and shortly afterwards a period of almost puritanical self-denial. We've seen her silent for days, then elated and *bavarde* beyond belief . . .'

'She's over all that now,' Tessa had said.

'You mean that was a reaction to your mother's death? It lasted some.'

'These things do. In Beth's case into her late-teens. But she picked herself up. She became the Beth we know now. A very cool, self-possessed, highly successful young woman.'

Her father had nodded, his white hair reflecting the deeper gleam of firelight. 'Yes. But all those movements of the pendulum cause fraying of the cord, Tessa. Promise me you'll keep an eye on your kid sister? I'd like to be assured that one or other of us will be around if the cord ever snaps.'

Now Tessa climbed the stairs, brushing snowflakes from her shoulders. At the door in front of her – England's first floor, she realised, was the second floor in American usage – she knocked and listened as music (classical, unfamiliar) was turned down and footsteps approached.

The door was opened by a man in his late-forties, in a dark sweater with just the rim of a blue denim shirt collar visible beneath. His thin, intense face was oddly anchored by a long neck to a slender but short-legged frame. He gave the disquieting impression of having been intended by nature to be an immensely tall man in his upper half, and a rather short, solidly based figure from the waist down. Even so, he was three or four inches over six foot. He bent towards her, bringing his head down level with the low door. 'Mrs Wilson?' he said. 'I'm Will Butler. Come in, won't you?'

She thought, removing her coat and handing it to him, that she might have left the black dress back in the Pelican and worn jeans and a thick sweater with her boots. Butler himself with his thick baggy cords and boat-shaped shoes was sartorially a mess. The rooms he occupied were an untidy scatter of books, teacups, newspapers and academic magazines. But the stone fire surround was, she saw, Tudor. Not that she could have dated it herself beyond recognising a vague Renaissance outline, but it carried a date, 1570, flanked by a pattern of small birds.

'Martelets,' Butler said.

She looked at him.

'The birds – they're martelets. from the coat of arms of the Countess of Pembroke, Marie de Valence, who founded the college.'

She nodded towards the stone fireplace. 'In 1570, I presume?'

He smiled. 'No, over two hundred years earlier. But I mustn't seem too boastful. We're not by any means the oldest college.'

They sat down and she was given sherry. 'Now what can I do to help, Mrs Wilson?'

'First,' she smiled, 'I'd like it if you called me Tessa. Is that okay?'

'Why not? And I'm Will.' His head bobbed on its long neck. He sniffed his sherry and sipped it, pursing his lips as he swallowed. 'You've got questions for me?' he said, looking up at her.

She nodded. 'I guess I'm a little confused by what you told me on the phone. You said you didn't see Beth for the last week of term?'

'The last few days, I think I said.'

'Is there no formal requirement that she turn up each day?'

'No, not really. Let me explain first that I'm the Senior Tutor of the college. That's probably quite different from most American Deans. I teach of course but my main function is really welfare officer to our undergraduates. And I offer any help I can to new research students like Beth.'

'I see,' Tessa said, not sure that she did. 'So maybe I should be talking to whoever it is who oversees her work?'

'I don't think that would help you much. I've called Dr Thomas and he tells me Beth very much runs her own research programme. That may mean she needs to be in the lab on such and such a day, or perhaps she feels she needs to consult a colleague somewhere. A visit to Oxford or Edinburgh, for instance, where there are people working along very much the same lines.'

'I see this might be more complicated than I thought.'

'It might also mean that there's less need to worry than you imagined.'

'Beth's not being here for the end of term doesn't have too much significance, you mean?'

'Not *too* much. Though I'm perhaps a little surprised if she's

39

taken off for Christmas without dropping in to say how she's getting on.'

'Or even just to say Happy Christmas.' She saw a frown disguised by his nod and thought: To hell with it, I need answers – even if it means treading on toes. 'Do you mind if I ask,' she said, 'do you get on well with Beth?'

He paused. 'I like to think so.'

She found this type of Englishman particularly difficult to understand. What was he saying – he didn't like Beth? Well, ask him. 'Do I understand by what you say that you and Beth *don't* get on well?'

He looked shocked. 'Oh, no,' he said. 'We are good, very good, friends indeed.'

'I see.' Tessa very deliberately drew out the words.

He was blushing. 'I must be careful not to suggest there's something between us. There isn't.' He drank some more sherry and this time she followed suit. She was surprised at its rich, powerful taste. 'It's very good, isn't it?'

He cocked his odd-shaped head towards her. 'Very good.'

A silence fell between them.

'Have you heard of a man named Laurie Woodward?'

He inclined his head. 'I've also recently learnt that he died in an accident on that dreadful Granchester bend.'

'Did you know him?'

'I met him once or twice, not often.'

'He was some sort of travelling carpenter, is that right?'

'He was a good carver of genius.'

'Ah . . . moving about, working wherever he was needed?'

'He did repair work of an incredible standard on furniture or carved screens for colleges, country houses, churches . . . Before he died he was working at the Fitzwilliam Museum – a long-term project, I believe.'

'He and Beth . . .' she began cautiously.

'I believe, of late, they became very close.'

Tessa could almost hear the pain in his voice. The unrequited lover. And likely to remain unrequited with his long, clerical neck and bobbing head. At least as far as someone like Beth was concerned. 'How close?'

'I don't think I should be answering that.'

'I believe Beth is *missing*, Mr Butler.'

His eyes filmed. 'Of late I believe he has sometimes been staying at the Market Place.' He stood up and circled the room, running his fingers down the spines of books in the shelves.

'You didn't approve of Beth's relationship with Woodward?'

'Nobody would.' The small mouth snapped closed.

'Tell me.'

'Woodward was a man of great talent. Perhaps he was attractive to women, I can't say. But he was a braggart, violent, an ugly individual . . .' He was shaking.

Tessa allowed his anger, frustration, whatever it was, to pass.

'I think I need to find out more about him. If he had family or friends Beth might be staying with. How could I find out more about him?'

He stood uncertainly. 'I know the director of the Fitzwilliam employed him a great deal.'

'The Fitzwilliam Museum. Is that far?'

The question calmed him. 'Just across the road. Nowhere's very far in Cambridge.'

'All right, I can make a start there tomorrow.'

'Anything at all I can do to help . . .' He stood helplessly in the middle of the room.

'There is something more I'd like to ask you.'

'And that is?'

Tessa hesitated. 'Would you say Beth was her normal self in the last week or so you saw her?'

'No,' he said firmly, 'I would not.'

'Go on.'

'I wouldn't say Beth was her normal self for several weeks before I last saw her, in fact. She was finding it extremely difficult to concentrate. Her mind was quite evidently not on her work. This I have from Dr Thomas.'

Tessa made an effort not to smile. She wanted to say it was called being in love. But so far as Will Butler was concerned it was also called being in love with someone else.

'There were outbursts,' he said. 'On several occasions recently.'

'Outbursts against you?'

'Not particularly against me. Friends or colleagues generally. I thought I ought to add that, Mrs Wilson . . . Tessa . . . in case you thought here was a rather poor fellow who couldn't see what was happening under his own eyes, namely that Beth was in love. And regrettably not with him.'

Tessa flushed – and made a resolution not to take Cambridge dons for granted. They were the same breed as their confrères across the Atlantic: otherworldly until they showed their teeth. She stood up and took her coat. 'I'm sorry,' she said.

He smiled tightly as he helped her into the coat. 'I hope I've been of some help. Perhaps, if you think it's appropriate, you'll let me know where she is?'

Out in the snow-covered courtyard she stood in silence, her eyes on the bowed line of the rooftop opposite and the moon glittering above. Strangely, she found her thoughts were not on Beth, but on the special nature of the people who live the academic life. Her husband, Carter, for instance.

CHAPTER FIVE

She was wrapped in a dark coat and the sweetness of breathed alcohol filled the room. Her hair was blonded grey and she lay stretched on the bench seat in the narrow Scotland Yard waiting room, asleep.

For a moment Jack Abbeline stood looking at her before he closed the door quietly behind him. His eyes moved slowly from the woman herself to the handbag and the patent leather high heels dropped next to it on the floor. One shoe lay on its side. There was the beginning of a hole in the leather sole.

'Rhoda . . . Rhoda, wake up.' He was ashamed of the fact that he didn't want to lean over and shake her. Didn't want to touch her. 'Rhoda . . .'

Grunting, the woman raised her head, shook hair from before her face and rubbed at her chin. For a moment she sat staring ahead, not turning.

In profile a small, straight nose and a finely shaped mouth dominated her features. The blonde-grey hair was tangled and the forehead permanently furrowed, but in profile and the soft lighting of the room there were still signs enough of her earlier good looks. When she turned to face him and smiled the lines creased around her mouth but her teeth were still good. 'Hallo, Jack,' she said.

'Rhoda.' He took out a packet of small cigars.

'Can I have one of those? They're supposed to be better for you than cigarettes.' She had a well-modulated voice formed fifty years ago in Miss Somebody's Preparatory School for Girls.

He handed her one and lit it. He knew what the problem was going to be. It was always the same. 'Is there trouble with your room?' he asked her.

'I've been thrown out. No notice. On to the streets.'

'Were you behind with the rent?'

'Rent? It's nothing to do with the rent. It's the other women there . . .'

'A hostel.'

'Rooms, just rooms. But the women there are all thieves. It's the way they exist, stealing from other people. And when there's nothing left to steal they go out on the streets, tapping or tarting, it's all the same to them.'

'Where are you living now, Rhoda?'

'They steal – or play the tart the moment a man appears.'

'A hostel, is it? Not the Salvation Army?'

She would never say where she was staying. 'They're appalling women, Jack. Leilia said as much to me the other day.'

He forced himself not to ask who Leilia was.

'She said women like that ought to be locked away . . .'

'Rhoda, you mustn't come here, you know that.'

Her eyes narrowed. 'Why is that, Jack? Why can't I look up my son once in a while? It's not every day, is it?'

'It's not every day,' he conceded.

'And your father won't help, you know that.'

'He'll do anything for you . . . Listen, Rhoda, do you need any money?'

'Stole the lot. My last Giro disappeared from under my eyes.'

Abbeline took money from his wallet, five ten pound notes. She stretched out a grey hand and took the money. He remembered when those long fingers carried rings and bright finger nails. 'Yes,' she said, 'I know who did it. Leilia told me. I said to her: My boy's Scotland Yard. He'll sort it out.'' They didn't believe me. I told them you'd come down straightaway and sort them out.'

Abbeline's face was impassive. 'When did this happen?'

'Last week.'

'You should have reported it straight away.' He was going through the motions. He knew that if it had happened, it was probably months ago. And the witness Leilia would probably be a drunk, or maybe just a sad middle-aged lady with a neurotic, unfocussed memory.

'Will you come down there now with me?' she pressed him. 'You could sort it out in minutes.'

'I can't, Rhoda, now.'

'Ten minutes in a car.'

'No, Rhoda.' He used his usual tactic. Perhaps she saw through it, perhaps not. 'That hostel I found for you in Richmond, have you been to see them?'

She looked down sullenly.

'It's a good place, Rhoda. Your own room . . .'

'Regulations. That booklet you showed me. Rules and regulations as long as your arm.'

'I'm happy to drive you down there.'

'I'll go down by myself. When the weather gets better.'

He stood up. 'I've got to go now, Rhoda. If you want me, call me at my flat. You've got my number.'

'You're never there.'

'Evenings. Call me then. But never come here again.'

She smiled. 'And say I need you quickly?'

'Leave a message on my answerphone. Tell me where you're staying.'

'No. If you knew where I was, your father'd have the men in white coats round the same day.'

'Have it your way, Rhoda. Listen, I want to buy you a Christmas present. How about a new coat?' He took out his wallet again. There was a £50 note left. 'Will you do that, buy yourself a warm coat?'

She took the money. 'What are you doing at Christmas? Going somewhere nice? The Bahamas? Tenerife, of course, would be much too unsmart for you. Are you going to marry that actress? I'm against it, Jack, I don't mind saying. The woman has a distinct air of the trollop about her.'

'It's the part she plays on television, Rhoda. Don't pretend you don't know that.'

In Markham's Wine Bar most of the customers were stealing covert looks at the woman with the dark amber-coloured hair and smoky green eyes who sat alone in the corner with a glass of champagne on the table in front of her. Few people at the other tables were unaware that her name was Jo Saunders, and that she played Mollie Parkinson, the most popular character in *The Scattersby Inheritance*, Britain's most popular running serial.

Jo thrummed her carefully manicured fingernails on the table. She could sense the atmosphere. If Jack didn't arrive in a minute or two there were at least three tables on the verge of moving in on her. Not all men. The two middle-aged women in the far corner were exchanging nudges that would bring them across the room within minutes: 'Excuse me for asking, but aren't you Mollie Parkinson' – a self-deprecating laugh – 'I mean Jo Saunders of course.'

Jo kept her eyes down now, glancing occasionally round the room through long lowered lashes, wondering if the two women would break cover before the well-dressed elderly man at the bar. She didn't really complain. She knew this was the price of her particular job. But she did wish like hell that Jack would remember she hated sitting alone waiting for him.

If the women came over she would smile, be polite, and tell them quickly she was waiting for someone. There was a noise near the door. She looked up, into the eyes of the elderly man. He smiled and began to stand up. At that moment the door opened and Jack came across the room towards her. Looking past him she saw the elderly man struggling back on to his barstool and the two women cease speaking as they savoured the first glimpse of the face of Mollie Parkinson's – sorry, Jo Saunders' – companion.

Abbeline bent and kissed her on the lips. 'I'm really sorry, darling. Rhoda turned up.'

'At the Yard?'

'Very nearly at my office. Jan intercepted her.'

He sat down and signalled to the barman for a glass of white burgundy.

'How is she?'

He shrugged. She knew he didn't want to talk about it.

Jo stretched out and touched his hand. 'If we could get her into some sort of hostel with maybe some supervision, medical supervision . . .'

'She won't have it, you know that, Jo. I have to accept it, I suppose. She wants to be in Soho, drifting from pub to pub, sponging drinks off all those failed artists of the seventies.'

'Where is she living?'

'Nowhere at the moment. Thrown out of her place again. Not paying the rent, or drunk and disorderly I suppose. She sees it as the usual persecution.'

'She's still drinking as much as ever?'

'I'm sure.'

'No hope while she's on the bottle.'

'Not really. Perhaps if I could get her to agree to treatment, she might be rescued. Rousseau had this crazy idea that people must be forced to be free. He should have met Rhoda before he shot off his mouth.' He stopped. 'Tell me about you. How did it go today?'

She was silent, nursing her drink.

'Jo . . .?'

'You know we're about to sell the programme to Australia?'

'The residuals should be good.'

She nodded. 'The deal is we shoot half a dozen location shows to break them in. Me and maybe a couple of the others on a trip to look up family in Sydney.'

'I knew that was the plan.'

'It's been pushed forward,' she said quickly. 'We're to leave earlier than I expected.'

'Before Christmas?'

'Yep. Darling, they've cancelled this week's shooting here. The new executive producer wants us to leave for Australia day after tomorrow.'

He was silent.

'I was looking forward to Christmas,' she said, 'My mother, your dad.'

He smiled at the thought. 'Maybe we've been saved a disaster. How long will you be away?'

'They want some publicity appearances too. Away maybe two months.'

'Jesus. A long time.'

She nodded. 'A long time for a relatively new relationship.'

'Not that new. We've been together nearly a year.'

'Not without our little local difficulties.'

'No,' he admitted. 'You think a two-month separation could give us trouble?'

She drank some wine. 'No, not in the normal course of events.'

'What's a nice girl like you doing with a phrase like that?' he said.

'You may think this trip doesn't fall within the normal course of events, that's all.'

'Look, Jo – we both know the deal we have. If you fall for some heavily muscled, and of course bright and charming, Australian wine grower, I won't like it – Jesus, I'll hate it – but . . .'

'I'm free to take risks, we both are.'

'That's what we said.'

She put her hand over his. 'I'd be a lot happier not even taking the risks. I don't *want* to lose you. Dammit, I'm not going to.'

'So? What's the problem?'

'Leo will be on the trip to Sydney.'

'Jesus Christ! Did you arrange that? Is that what you're telling me?'

'Jack . . . darling . . . Yes I did, and no I am not.' She stopped. 'I want you to take a deep breath and *believe me*, for Christ's sake.'

'Okay – a deep breath . . .'

'You know Leo hasn't played a decent part for three years. The last thing he had was a Noël Coward that never made the West End.'

'The reason your ex-husband doesn't work is that he suffers delusions of adequacy. He'll turn down any part that falls short of Hamlet. When you were up and coming he used to cavort around, sneering at every walk-on you were given. Now they've seen through him. They know he's second-rate. *I* know he's not just second-rate, he's a bastard. I know he used to come home and knock his wife about from one room to another. Ending in the bedroom. You remember telling me that.'

'I remember.'

'So what the hell are you doing even *talking* to the guy? Let alone getting him a job. That's what you did, isn't it, you got him a job?'

'A small part. Something he could pass off as a guest appearance. Even had that credit in his contract. Then . . .' she shrugged.

'Then . . .?'

'The Australian sale came up. They decided Leo would just fit the Australian second cousin's role.'

'Your second cousin?'

'Yes.'

Abbeline pursed his lips. 'And what happens when you finally meet? I mean you, *Mollie Parkinson*, finally meet your slightly raddled but still attractive second cousin?'

Jo swallowed.

'You have an affair?'

She winced. 'I couldn't possibly have guessed they'd write it that way. Believe me, Jack.'

He held out his hands, palm upwards, not sure himself what the gesture meant.

'Do you believe me?'

'I know enough about the business, *your* business, to know that almost nothing is planned in advance – and when it is it seldom works out as intended. So I believe you. But I still *really* hate the idea.'

They were silent for a few moments. 'Why is Leo the only man you're jealous of?'

'I'm not jealous,' he said.

'You sound jealous.'

'He doesn't deserve you as a friend, for Christ's sake. He never did. Even though you think you owe your career to him.'

'In a sense I do, Jack. I was a secretary in a publishing house when I met him. He persuaded me to believe I was better than someone who spent their time picking other men's flowers, that I could do something *myself*. I would never have even thought of applying to RADA if it hadn't been for Leo.'

'Don't you think you paid him in full, over the next few years?'

'Yes,' she said slowly, 'in my head I know I did. But he can still make me feel so sorry for him. It hurts. So I do something.'

'And the lucky bastard ends up having an affair with you in Australia.'

'On screen.'

He pushed back his chair. 'Do you really leave day after tomorrow?' he said.

'Yes.'

'Then we're wasting time,' he said quietly. He stood up. 'We ought to be at home with our arms round each other or drinking wine in front of the fire.'

'Whose home – yours or mine?'

'Doesn't matter,' he said, 'as long as we're there together.'

She got up quickly and took his hand. 'I love you, Jack,' she said, standing close. 'But you're crazy about Leo.'

'As long as you aren't,' he said.

Standing there, they kissed. The two middle-aged ladies in the corner seat were too riveted even to exchange glances.

CHAPTER SIX

The morning light was subdued and misty through the floor to ceiling windows of the Curator's office at the Fitzwilliam Museum, but a wood fire burned in the marble fireplace and heavy brown radiators supported its efforts from the back of the room.

Tessa shook hands to her mild surprise (she had found herself expecting a man in his fifties) with the Curator, a large and very blonde Dutch woman, still in her early-thirties. She wore a well-cut dark pinstriped suit and black leather shoes with a medium heel. Only ten years ago she would have been the Senior Curator's secretary.

'I shouldn't be surprised,' Tessa said. 'But it's very hard not to be.'

Anna van Gelden laughed. 'I'm used to it. And, to tell you the truth, still rather flattered by it.' She spoke English with a pronounced American accent. 'Sit down, Mrs Wilson, how can I help? I should say quickly that my field is Old Master drawings. If you're wanting to talk Greek coins or Renaissance medallions I'll have to call someone else in.'

Tessa shook her head. 'No, my questions aren't at all academic. Your assistant didn't tell you . . .'

'I only saw her for a moment outside the door.'

'I'm over from the States looking for my sister. I understand she spent time with somebody who frequently worked here at the Fitzwilliam – Laurie Woodward.'

'You're Beth's sister, then?'

'You know Beth?'

'Yes.' Anna van Gelden's big face tightened in a frown. 'You say she's missing?'

'I'm not sure if missing's the right word, but she hasn't been seen since before the end of term.'

Tessa looked at the other woman's expression. 'What is it?'

'You're aware Laurie Woodward was killed in a motorbike accident at the beginning of November?'

'Yes. About the same time Beth disappeared.' Tessa paused. 'What was he like, Laurie Woodward?'

'His work was incredibly in demand. He was . . . eccentric. He lived an itinerant life working his way round this part of the country. His home was his work truck, I suppose.'

'Except when he stayed with Beth.'

Anna van Gelden shrugged.

'Eccentric, you said?'

The Dutch woman hesitated. 'Well, yes, a little highly strung at times.'

Tessa lifted her head. 'What does that mean exactly?'

'He was a very committed young man. Put his heart and soul into whatever he was doing. Ninety-five percent of the time that was great. During the remaining five percent Laurie could be . . . well . . . difficult.'

'Argumentative?'

Anna van Gelden shifted uncomfortably behind her desk. 'I'm not really happy talking about someone like this, Mrs Wilson,' she said awkwardly. 'But, yes, somewhat arrogant. Argumentative. He knew he was not just another woodcarver.'

She didn't like him, Tessa thought. Nobody liked him. So why did Beth? 'This truck he used . . . he kept his tools there?'

'Lived in it, kept his tools in it. It had more locks than Fort Knox.'

'Very valuable tools, then?'

'I would say so, yes.'

'Yet the police told me he had no assets. He was buried at the public expense.'

She nodded. 'I understood that his truck was never found.'

'Isn't that curious?'

'Perhaps. At the time I didn't really think about it. The sequence of events was like this. Laurie stopped coming in for work. Nothing too unusual about that. Then perhaps a week later someone on the staff drew my attention to a report of the accident. By that time he was buried. I assumed his family had taken charge of things. I called Beth but couldn't get her. I called perhaps a couple more times and I'm afraid, left it at that. Laurie wasn't any sort of special friend. Beth neither. I went to her room for drinks a couple of times.'

'Did you meet Dr Butler there?' Tessa wasn't quite sure why she was asking.

'Will Butler, from Pembroke? Yes, he introduced me to your sister. He took me out a few times before transferring his attentions to Beth. Without any success, I'm afraid.'

Tessa nodded. 'What's clear,' she said, 'is that Beth disappeared at almost exactly the time Laurie Woodward was killed. Without a word to anyone. Which leaves me very worried.'

'Understandably,' the Dutch woman said slowly. 'It's why I'm answering your questions. But if all this turns out to have a perfectly innocent explanation, I'm relying on you to forget we ever talked like this.'

Tessa nodded. 'That's a deal.' She smiled. 'It really is a deal.'

The other woman nodded. 'I believe you.'

'I think,' Tessa said slowly, 'I have cause to be worried. Maybe very worried.'

Anna van Gelden took a deep breath. 'Okay, I'll jump in with both feet. Laurie Woodward was an artist but a thoroughly undesirable human being. I can't begin to imagine what your sister was doing with him.' She hesitated. 'Did she do drugs?'

'She swung back and forth on most things but I think she stayed pretty firm on drugs. What about Woodward?'

'He'd come to work here in the morning glassy-eyed. I'd guess that when he hit that bend outside Granchester at three in the morning he was carrying a cocktail. I wondered if that was his connection with Beth?'

'You mean he was her dealer?'

'It makes sense. But I don't have any evidence.'

'Where was he coming from – or going to – at that time of night?'

'Dealing?' Anna van Gelden shrugged. 'I don't know. But I'm sure it wasn't only drugs Laurie was into.'

'You think he had a record?'

'He was about as unsavoury a character as I'd like to meet. I can only think Beth was in some sort of trouble *before* Laurie died. Whether his death helped things or made them worse, I can't guess. And nor can you.'

Tessa stood up abruptly. 'I shouldn't even be trying,' she said. 'This is for the police to handle.'

'That's not information I'm supposed to divulge, Mrs Wilson,' the sergeant said in the small interview room at Parker's Piece.

'I don't know the law, Sergeant Blyton, but I believe I have the right to know. Did Laurie Woodward have a criminal record?'

The sergeant gnawed on his lip. He nodded.

'What for?'

'Torture.'

'What!'

'He was found guilty of torturing a young man last year.'

Tessa found her heart beating faster. 'He was trying to get something out of his victim . . .'

'Blood,' the sergeant said laconically. 'He was doing it for pleasure, Mrs Wilson. He was doing it for fun.'

'Jesus – and you're still not taking my sister's disappearance seriously.'

'Laurie Woodward's dead.'

'My sister disappeared about the same time. That might mean before he died.'

'You're suggesting Woodward had something to do with your sister's disappearance?'

'Yes.'

'No,' he said. 'The last record of your sister we have is very early on the morning following Woodward's death when she removed her car from the place in Trumpington Street where she used to park it.'

'Why didn't you tell me on the phone?'

'The owner of the parking space only came forward yesterday. Mr Thatchet, your sister's landlord at the Market Place, arranged for her to park there. After our visit he called Mrs Taylor in Trumpington Street and suggested she give us a ring. A very public-spirited man, Mr Thatchet.'

'I see. I would still like to file a Missing Person's report. I have the feeling you think that's premature.'

'Missing person's is the one area the police would like to duck out of altogether, Mrs Wilson.' Sergeant Blyton looked out over the large square of snow-covered, treeless grass known as Parker's Piece. 'Apart from missing children, of course. We find most adult missing persons turn up within a week or two, very indignant about the fuss.'

Tessa nodded slowly. 'But you do take steps?'

'We take what steps we can. What steps seem appropriate.'

They eyed each other across the desk. Blyton was the first to break eye contact and look down at the form he was completing.

'Are you telling me you don't find my sister's association with a man with a torture record pretty surprising?'

'There's plenty of pretty surprising stuff goes on that'd still be within the law, Mrs Wilson.' He nodded regretfully.

'Can we go ahead?'

'We'll need the name of any friends she has in England. anybody she might be visiting.'

'I wouldn't know the names of any friends she might have made since she arrived. Except Laurie Woodward.'

Blyton nodded.

'There's one old friend she has in England – a girl named Sally Portal. They shared an apartment when they were at Harvard together. Sally was studying archaeology. She's in India now.'

'Have you contacted her family?'

'Yes. It's weeks since Sally or her mother was in touch with my sister.' Tessa hesitated, wondering if there was any point in going into the whole Quentin Naylor, Laura Portal story. His hair was thick, grey, slightly crinkled. He raised his head, his brows knitted in a heavy frown. She decided this wasn't the time to talk about Sally's visit to Cambridge.

'No other names come to mind?' Blyton asked.

'No.'

'Okay, Mrs Wilson. I think I have all the details. We know where you're staying . . .'

'So what steps will you be taking?' Tessa said. 'What steps, in your phrase, seem appropriate?'

Blyton put down his pen and rubbed the palms of his hands together. He was heavily built, a dark five o'clock shadow already apparent under the skin of his cheeks. His hands, she saw, were gigantic. 'There are no signs of anything amiss at her flat. None that I can see.'

'You couldn't say the same for her work. She does seem to have left very suddenly, without saying anything to anybody at the lab or her college.'

'That's true.' Blyton slowly clasped his hands together. 'But frankly it doesn't amount to much. Perhaps that's a good thing,' he said in an attempt to be reassuring.

'What will you do?' she asked bluntly.

'I shall complete this Missing Person's Report . . .'

'And?' She sat on the edge of her chair.

'And I'll talk to my inspector.' He paused. 'I'm going to be frank with you, Mrs Wilson . . .'

'You already have been,' Tessa said shortly.

He took her point with a sharp inclination of the head. 'If your sister is simply missing,' he said, 'it's not a cause for police concern. If she's run off with a Roman Catholic bishop, or sunk her life savings in an expedition to the South Pole, it's worrying for you, but not for us. Our concern is with what we rather quaintly call foul play. And foul play in nine times out of ten means a body. That's the way it is, I'm afraid.'

'You're saying without a body there'll be no police investigation?'

'I'm sorry, Mrs Wilson. I know you've come a long way. But at this stage, you're not going to get a great deal of help from the police. I very much hope the point is never reached when you will.'

'You're saying I'm on my own.'

He shrugged apologetically. 'Unofficially, I'm afraid I'm saying exactly that.'

CHAPTER SEVEN

In the offices of the *Cambridge Daily News*, the young, red-bearded journalist placed a large cream folder on the desk. A white sticker, Tessa saw, was pasted across the upper edge: Woodward, Laurie.

'I'll leave you while you read through them,' the journalist said.

Tessa drew the cuttings from the packet. There were about a dozen, mostly *Daily News* but one or two from national papers, the *Times* or *Telegraph*.

'Cambridge Man accused of Torturing Victim' was the headline above the story of Woodward's arrest. On an early-summer evening last year police had been alerted to a fire burning in Silverton Woods. Arriving there they had found a large party in progress. Many of the party-goers had run off into the night; a youth of nineteen had been found hanging from a tree in an improvised velvet neck harness, naked but for a red silk cloak. He had been beaten and had suffered severe loss of blood. He had been cut down just in time to save his life. Laurie Michael Woodward, 35, a journeyman carpenter of no fixed address, had been arrested and charged with malicious wounding.

The red cloak and the hanging had caused a minor press stir but when the case came to trial it was clear that the young man was not quite the victim he presented himself as. He had attended the party willingly, had volunteered to take part in sexual games. He claimed he had never realised that hanging was to be part of the game. The jury had chosen to believe him and Woodward had been sentenced to six months.

All but two of the other clippings covered this story. These two recounted the events of another night, some months before the hanging incident, when Woodward and Peter Howard Mason, 27, unemployed, were arrested for assault on a woman. The magistrate dismissed the charge on the grounds that the woman advertised herself as available for sexual experiment in certain magazines, and had thus invited the events that followed.

Tessa turned to the young journalist. 'Nothing on Peter Howard Mason?'

He shook his head. 'He's not from around here.'

'Have you ever met Woodward?'

'I've seen him around. Cambridge out of term isn't a very big place. And you couldn't miss a face like that.' He pushed a photograph across the table. It showed, head and shoulders, a long-haired man in his thirties. Scruffy, unshaven. A thin mouth and mean eyes. 'He looks like trouble, and he was,' the journalist said. 'I think he'd go for anything.'

'What does that mean?'

He shrugged. 'I heard him in the pub a few times, boasting. He was a psycho. The Granchester bend did us all a good turn. You're writing a story on him?'

'On his woodcarving.'

'Strange that, isn't it? People say he was a genius.' He pulled on his beard. 'I still say that Granchester bend did us all a good turn.'

In the small back room of the chemist's shop at 7 Market Place Tessa watched incredulously. The old man had taken a sheet of thick white paper and a fountain pen from a drawer, had folded back the sleeve of his white coat over a plump hairless wrist and written, in an elegant copperplate hand:

Recognising that I, Mrs Tessa Wilson of Cambridge, USA, have represented myself to Mr Albert Thatchet, chemist of the town of Cambridge, England, and recognising that I have explained to the said Albert Thatchet the great urgency of the matter, he has therefore delivered the spare set of keys of my sister's flat to me, and disclaims all responsibility whatsoever, in which disclaimer I concur.

'Better,' Mr Thatchet's round face turned towards her, 'safe than sorry.'

'Sure,' Tessa said. She watched him wave the paper carefully from side to side to dry the ink. There was only limited space in the small room lined with mahogany shelves filled with chemist's preparations, bottles and packets and boxes of sachets. In his small pudgy hand, the paper floated from one side of the room to the other. The sense of another century was reinforced by a strange musty odour in the atmosphere.

Mr Thatchet placed the paper on the sloping mahogany desk. 'Now if you'll satisfy yourself that you are prepared to sign, Mrs Wilson . . .'

Tessa pretended to read the lines with the degree of attention she knew he considered they warranted. 'Yes,' she said, after a moment, taking the pen. 'Very thorough. Elegant,' she added, biting her lip.

Mr Thatchet smiled modestly. 'In my family, I tend to be the one they turn to if they have need to put pen to paper on an important, perhaps *quasi-legal* matter.'

'Yes.' Tessa stood.

'The keys then are here.' He extracted a bunch of keys from several hanging inside his white coat. 'You go outside, Mrs Wilson, unlock the green door next to the shop and simply continue up the stairs.'

'Let me ask you, Mr Thatchet, when do you think you last saw my sister?'

'Noon on Saturday, November the fourth.'

'You've no doubt about that?'

'None. I recall it was the day after the high pressure system moved rapidly south and was replaced by a front which brought mist and a sudden drop in temperature. Freezing fog.'

'Can you date it that precisely?'

'I confess I contribute to a country matters magazine under the *non de plume* of Old Abraham. I tend to remember these things.'

Tessa stood thinking. 'Before I go up,' she said at the door which led into the main shop, 'may I ask you – it was you who arranged for my sister to park her car at Trumpington Street?'

'It was.'

'Presumably you know the owner of the house?

'Mrs Taylor. My widowed sister.'

'Would you say that memory is a family strength? That her memory is, let's say, as sharp as your own?'

He described a circle with his hands. 'No, I'm afraid not. My sister is known, just within the family, as *Dotty*. The soubriquet does not originate entirely from her forename Dorothy.'

'So when she told the police that my sister picked up her car early on the morning of November the fifth . . .'

'When Dorothy gives that evidence six weeks after the event, there's no knowing within a week either side. I have already remonstrated with her. I have asked her to go back to the police and tell them she can't be sure of the date. She's thinking about it.'

They stood in silence for a moment. Tessa found herself gaining an increasing respect for the little chemist. 'May I ask you, Mr Thatchet, were you aware of any change in my sister, any change in her lifestyle, in the last month or so?'

He allowed his round head to roll to one side on his shoulder. '*Oh Cupid, Cupid, Prince of gods and men!*'

'I beg your pardon? Ah . . .' She nodded slowly. 'Mr Woodward?'

'Precisely.'

'He sometimes spent the night here?'

Eyebrows were raised and lowered. 'How often I could not say.'

'Did he live here?'

'Definitely not. You may be sure I would have known. But he was here quite often. During September, two or three afternoons a week, I remember. There would be others too. Young men and women. There would be *lively* discussions. And singing.'

'Singing?'

'Of a religious nature.'

'Would it be possible, Mr Thatchet, that Mr Woodward was not exactly a boyfriend? You understand what I mean?'

'I understand. But . . .' His pink tongue played at his lips.

'You're trying to say that if he wasn't a boyfriend, what was he doing staying the night?'

'Indeed.'

'Do you know how long my sister had known Mr Woodward?'

'It was, as far as I know, a recent friendship.'

'And, as far as you're aware, they were getting on well.'

He hesitated as she tried to produce a facial expression to urge him on.

'Am I being indiscreet?'

'No, most certainly not, Mr Thatchet. You're being very helpful.'

Reassured, he said: 'On one occasion there was certainly tension. Raised voices. A certain number of thumps and bumps. My wife and I were working late.'

'When was this?'

'In the last week of September. We were stock-taking. At midnight Mr Woodward came thundering down the stairs, shouting up to Miss Naylor. Rather unpleasantly. She had clearly . . . refused him.'

Tessa nodded slowly. 'Well, thank you, Mr Thatchet. And thank you for the key. I'll return it during the day.'

He inclined his head in a half bow and she walked through the shop and out on to the snowy pavement.

The Market Place was crowded with Christmas shoppers and the quickest glance revealed at least three Father Christmases at different points of the square. Tessa turned towards the green door and let herself in.

Two or three pieces of mail underfoot, the rest had been placed aside in a large pile, presumably by the police. Brown envelopes with glassine fronts. Bills. A very narrow passage, a narrow stair, a single modern Tiffany lampshade on a low wattage bulb. Clean, cheap and grey haircord carpet. Walls a duck egg blue, a large brown and white reproduction of The Stag at Bay hanging inconveniently at shoulder height. The decorator's eye of Mrs Thatchet, Tessa decided.

She climbed the steep staircase and unlocked the door at the top. Pushing it open she was flooded by light. There was no hallway. She was standing in a single large room, its bow windows overlooking the Market Place, its ceiling of extraordinary rococo exuberance where nymphs fled from visibly rampant gods while cupids serenaded the chase of flute and lyre.

'Oh Cupid, Cupid, Prince of Gods and men.' Mr Thatchet's line ran through her head as she brought her eyes down from the remarkable ceiling to the unremarkable furnishings of the superb room. They were mostly a mixture of hand-me-down Edwardian tables and sideboards. Two newer armchairs flanked a gas fire in a plain wooden surround. A daybed occupied the space below the window. The carpet was Mrs Thatchet's serviceable dark grey haircord with a Mexican rug which Tessa remembered from Beth's room at home many years ago.

There were books in shelves and piled in corners, hi fi equipment, and two panelled doors around which plump putti frolicked in plaster vineyards.

She crossed to the first door and opened it on to a small hall with a bathroom beyond. To the left, off the hall, she pushed at a door and revealed a small kitchen. Then came back and opened the other door. The bedroom was of slightly less magnificent proportions than the sitting room. The original eighteenth-century ceiling had at one time collapsed and been replaced by modern plasterboard and skim. The bed was large, double, with a simple pine headboard. There was a wall of fitted cupboards, a white chest of drawers and an ugly white table. Outside, in the back yard, Tessa could see that it had started to snow again.

Now that she was here in Beth's apartment, she wasn't sure what to do. She wandered back and forth from room to room, stopping, letting her eyes rest on a book, a sweater thrown over the back of a chair, a CD of *The Messiah*. She would have to start searching desk drawers, opening briefcases, reading letters. She frowned, feeling for a moment as inadequate as the woman Carter liked to portray her as. She opened the middle drawer of the Edwardian desk in the sitting room and looked helplessly down at the unsurprising collection of writing paper, envelopes, biros, paper clips, scotch tape. There were two letters, both from Tessa herself, written back at the beginning of the autumn when Beth was just settling in. A third letter without an address and signed by someone named Alan was an invitation to spend the weekend with him at Oxford. Dated early-October. From one or two references, fellow researchers' in-jokes, she could guess Alan was in the same field as Beth. Then:

My grandmother thinks you're a darling and in fact it was she who put me up to the idea. I know it's ridiculously early but I'm going to stake a claim for Christmas. My parents have a villa outside Antibes and I'm getting together a party to go down from Oxford – maybe a dozen of us. Will you come, Beth? OK, I know your bossy big sister (she sounds a complete cow) is going to require your presence back in the US – but just say no. You can do it. Come to Antibes with us/me.

Alan

Tessa felt her mouth dry. She walked across the room holding the letter. 'Your bossy big sister'. Was that what she was? 'She sounds a complete cow'. Tears swam into Tessa's eyes. She swallowed hard and gasped for breath. She remembered her father saying: 'Never read someone else's letters unless you're prepared to face the shock of discovery. They're not called private letters for nothing.'

She refolded the letter and put it in her pocket. What she needed was a drink, a friend. She stood in the middle of the magnificent room and looked slowly around her. What was she achieving here in England? Oh Christ. Tears rolled down her cheeks.

She had to do something before she returned the keys. It was all too humiliating otherwise. She would walk out on to the Market Place having done nothing but deliver herself a body blow that still twisted at her stomach. How could Beth talk about her like that? What had she said about Tessa to justify this man's parenthesis: 'she sounds a complete cow'.

She threw off her coat and walked quickly into the bedroom. Opening the wardrobe she began to go through the clothes. Many of Beth's that she recognised, some in plastic film from the dry cleaner's . . . A leather jacket that didn't seem to be the sort of thing Beth might wear, big, tan leather . . . Laurie Woodward's?

She turned away from the wardrobe. Photographs, would they help? For a few minutes she searched through drawers for any record of Beth and Laurie's time together.

But there was nothing. As the police had said there was no sign of struggle, of hurried departure, no detail really to cause alarm.

And yet she *was* alarmed. And miserable. And very much on her own.

For no good reason she returned to the bedroom wardrobe and looked at the big tan jacket. What could Beth have seen in the man? She reached out and began to slide her hand into the jacket pockets. Most were empty, but the inside fob pocket revealed a plastic card. A membership card for the Research and Development Club in London. On the back, Woodward's name. And an address: The Old Boathouse, Granchester. Whose address? After all, Laurie Woodward was a travelling cabinet maker. He lived out of his truck. Nobody had yet suggested he possessed an address.

Mr Thatchet's sister's house on Trumpington Street was set back to give enough parking space, in the gravelled front garden, to several cars. As Tessa stood on the front steps looking back, there were three cars below her, a white Fiat saloon, a red Ford Escort and an old Peugeot estate, rusting now round the rear door.

Inside, Mrs Taylor's home had the air of another century. 'During term,' she said, 'I have four undergraduates. Nice young men . . . very nice young men.' She paused. 'Mostly.'

Tessa followed her into an overfurnished sitting room. She was a jowly, comfortably built woman in her late-fifties. There was a nervousness in the way she bustled about, straightening chairs, thrusting newspapers under cushions, that made Tessa think of what Mr Thatchet, the chemist, would have called her soubriquet.

'How long has my sister rented a parking space from you, Mrs Taylor?' Tessa asked her when they were both finally seated.

'Since the beginning of Michaelmas term. I let the spaces a term at a time. My brother suggested it. Like that I can discontinue undesirables.'

'Undesirables?'

'Young people who want to roar in with their music playing at two in the morning. I sleep in this room, you see, dear. You wouldn't think it but the sofa you're sitting on is my bed. So I can't have comings and goings all night. I should soon lose my beauty sleep.'

'And my sister Beth, she's a good tenant for a space?'

'Very good. Simon, my brother, recommended her.'

Tessa turned her head to glance out of the window. 'And that's Beth's car, the red one?'

Mrs Taylor became visibly agitated. 'Yes,' she said. 'Now are you going to start doubting me like my brother? I said what I saw, Mrs Wilson. Simon says I didn't. Or didn't see when I thought I did . . .'

'That's okay, Mrs Taylor,' Tessa said easily. 'Now will you just tell me what you saw? And when you saw it?'

'Very well. First the date. Now Simon says I'm wrong . . .'

'It doesn't matter for the moment what he says,' Tessa said soothingly. 'Just tell me what you saw.'

Mrs Taylor nodded. She was not going to be diverted. 'I had just got up. Still in my dressing gown, with the kettle on for tea. Now I always sleep with the open curtains and I draw them again in the morning to get dressed.'

'And what time is that?'

'Seven sharp on weekdays and Saturdays.' She giggled. 'Half-past eight on Sundays, I'm afraid.'

'So it was half-past eight when you drew the curtains.'

'*The Week's Good Cause* on Radio Four. That's how I know it was Sunday.'

'But it needn't have been any particular Sunday.'

'I was getting ready to ask one of my young gentlemen to leave. Another young man in his room all night.' She frowned. 'If it had been a town girl I would have turned a blind eye. Times change, I'm aware of that, Mrs Wilson . . .'

'You mean, you wouldn't forget the Sunday you had to ask someone to leave?'

'Exactly.'

'And that was the first Sunday in November?'

'Yes.'

'Okay,' Tessa said. 'So you went to the window to draw the blinds, and what did you see?'

'Your sister. She was wearing a polo neck sweater, a beige anorak, and I think a tartan skirt.'

Nothing wrong with your memory, Tessa thought.

'Miss Naylor walked across the front driveway. She was holding her keys. She got into her car and she drove away. And I will not have my brother claim that I saw anything different!'

Tessa glanced again out of the window. 'But her car's still there.'

'Then she brought it back.'

'You saw her?'

'No.'

'When do you think she brought it back?'

Mrs Taylor shrugged. 'I don't know. I dressed. I drew back the curtains. By then it was full daylight. And . . .'

'The car was back in place?'

'Yes, yes, yes.'

'Okay.' Tessa raised her hands. 'You're saying she took it out and brought it back, all within, say, ten minutes?'

'Simon thinks I'm dotty. That's my name in the family, you see. Dorothy, Dotty.'

'Was the parking space full when Beth took the car?'

'Chockablock.'

'No spaces.'

'None. And it was definitely your sister who took the car, Mrs Wilson.'

Afterwards Tessa walked down and stood for a long time looking at her sister's car. There was nothing unusual about it. No marks she could see. The interior, when she peered through the window, was clean and neat. It sat there, smugly almost, knowing the answer to the highly improbable, but apparently indisputable, fact that Beth had driven away for the last time early that Sunday morning. Yet ten minutes later, Beth – someone – had returned the car. And that's where it had sat ever since.

CHAPTER EIGHT

The ball point pen in Sergeant Blyton's large hand travelled speedily across the page. As he finished writing he looked up at the American research student across the desk from him in the interview room at the station at Parker's Piece. 'So you saw Beth Naylor leave the bank . . .'

'We left together,' Sylvia Ziemcka said.

'Ah, yes, sorry.' He consulted his notes. 'Then walked down St Edward's Passage to King's Parade?'

'Yes.'

'Do you have any idea how much she withdrew while you were in the bank?'

'I saw several packets of bills. Ten pound notes. Twenty pound notes perhaps. Maybe even fifties.'

'Did she realise you'd seen the withdrawal?'

'I think so because as we walked down towards King's Parade she told me about the skiing holiday. That she had to pay for it that morning.'

'You were a close friend?'

'No. An acquaintance. Our work sometimes touched in the laboratory.'

'Is that where you heard she might be missing?'

'Yes. Dr Butler from her college, Pembroke, came over to the lab this morning. Asked us if anyone could help. Which is why I'm here.'

Blyton looked up from the pad he had covered with tiny, neat handwriting. 'In the last weeks before the day you were in the bank together, did you think there was anything different about her? Was she behaving differently?'

Sylvia Ziemcka looked down at Blyton's hands. 'Her work had fallen off. We all knew that. She was in the lab less and less often. Frankly we put it down to Laurie Woodward's being around.'

'Not a good influence?'

'I think we could agree on that, Sergeant. The last thing you might want to call Laurie Woodward was a good influence.'

The message to go over to the police station had been waiting for Tessa when she returned to the Pelican Inn. On this visit Sergeant Blyton ushered her into an interview room. She wondered if it meant Beth's case had been upgraded.

'A small piece of information you can help us with perhaps,' he said as they sat opposite each other. 'Do you know a young American here named Sylvia Ziemcka?'

Tessa shook her head.

He told her of Sylvia's meeting with Beth in the Market Place bank and the large sum of money Beth had withdrawn. 'Apparently it was for a skiing holiday.'

'Do we know where? Which company?'

He nodded his head slowly. Tessa thought the sergeant looked unhappy. 'I rang around,' he said. 'She had booked to go to an Austrian resort with Cambridge Skitours. Even paid the deposit during October . . . But she never paid the rest of the money on November the fourth.'

'So when she disappeared she had a considerable sum of money on her?'

'Unofficially I had a word with the bank. On that day she withdrew most of the money in her account. She was carrying nearly three thousand pounds.'

'Three thousand pounds? Getting on for five thousand dollars.' Tessa sat back, shocked. 'Far more than she'd need for any skiing holiday.'

He nodded. 'So she was walking around on November the fourth with three thousand pounds in her pocket. That much we know.'

'So her disappearance could involve robbery?'

'Don't jump to conclusions, Mrs Wilson. Your sister withdrew a large sum from the bank. She didn't use it to pay for a skiing holiday. That's all we have so far.'

'No, Sergeant. we have more than that. My sister's missing.
Nobody knows where she is. She has been missing since just before
or just after Laurie Woodward's death.'

'We've dealt with that one, Mrs Wilson. Your sister was definitely seen alive on the morning after Woodward was killed.'

'Definitely seen by a woman whose memory is so uncertain she's
known in her own family as Dotty. I've been to see Mrs Taylor.'

'You have?'

Tessa nodded. 'I admit she seems very certain that she saw Beth
on Sunday morning.'

'That's good news then, isn't it?'

'If it's true it's very good news. But my guess is Mrs Taylor's a
pretty obstinate woman. Doesn't like to be seen to be wrong.'

'That doesn't *make* her wrong.'

'No, but it means I don't think we have any grounds for ruling
out an involvement of Laurie Woodward in my sister's disappearance.'

The sergeant scratched his head with his pen.

'She's missing in circumstances that are beginning to look
increasingly strange, Sergeant. I think you should recognise that.'

He stood up. 'We're treating it seriously, Mrs Wilson.'

She pushed back her chair and stood beside him. 'How many
men do you have working on my sister's disappearance?'

He grimaced.

'Just yourself?'

He paused, then nodded.

'Part-time?'

'I can call in help if . . .'

'. . . it seems justified?'

He walked with her into the main hall. 'I know where to find you,
Mrs Wilson. I'll do my best to keep you informed.'

She smiled bleakly. 'Thank you, Sergeant. But I think I should
warn you I'm not just going to give up and go home.'

'No.' He smiled grimly. 'I didn't really imagine you were.'

'You didn't mind my calling you?'

'Not at all,' Anna van Gelden said. The Curator looked around
the Blue Boar dining room. 'No one I know. Good. So Beth drew

69

out three thousand pounds from her bank before she disappeared?'

'Much more than the amount she owed Cambridge Skitours. I've just been in to see them. They confirm they have seen or heard nothing of Beth since she paid the original ten percent deposit. The rest of the money wasn't due until immediately before the party was due to leave in December. So whatever Beth withdrew the money for, was nothing to do with paying for a skiing holiday.'

'Earlier you went to her apartment?'

'First I had to get past the chemist. Albert Thatchet is Dickensian! He made me sign a document before he handed over the keys.'

The waiter arrived and they ordered a bottle of Buzet and a mozzarella salad. 'Did you find anything?'

Tessa found it hard to keep the tears out of her eyes. 'No new discoveries about the present,' she said. 'More than I bargained for about the past.' She swallowed hard and told Anna about the letter from Alan.

'And that was a blow?'

'I always thought we got along just great. She's a younger sister, seven, eight years younger, so I was maybe a little heavy-handed with my advice. But all that was a long time ago.'

'Perhaps that's all the letter suggested.'

Tessa shook her head. 'No,' she said firmly. 'Maybe I haven't quoted it word for word. But what this man wrote certainly reflects something present and very powerful about the way Beth feels towards me.'

'Think about it,' Anna said. 'These things between children usually come from competition for the parents' affection. It can happen that the more secure child is relaxed and confident in the love of the parents.'

'And the other?'

'I think a lot of bitterness can be building up there without anybody seeing it. Without, at first, the insecure child understanding anything of what's happening to her or him.'

'Go on,' Tessa said slowly.

'You mean I've scored?'

'You could be close. Beth was always pretty strong on the "you don't love me" tantrums when she was a kid. After our mother died, she stopped the tantrums, but became quiet, very reserved. At least at home.'

'Whose affection was she competing for? Both parents?'

'No, my dad's. Exclusively. He was a pretty charismatic figure. And a very, very nice guy. Mostly,' she added, thinking of Laura Portal.

'But Beth felt she never got a fair share of his affection?'

'If you say so.'

'What do you think?'

Tessa paused. 'Dammit, I think you're right.' She drank a large gulp of wine. 'I know you're right. Thing was, I wasn't that secure myself as a very young kid. I think I was jealous of Beth. I remember clearly enough times I tried to squeeze her out, belittle her in some way. I was a child, a teenager. I thought I could make my mark with my father without it affecting Beth.' She poured wine for both of them as the salad arrived. 'Very wrong.'

'What will you do?'

'Apologise to her. When I find her.'

'Okay,' Anna van Gelden said, smiling sombrely. 'So let's just concentrate on that, shall we?'

Tessa nodded. 'Laurie Woodward is the key to this, I'm beginning to be certain about that. I don't think he was in any sense living with Beth. I don't even think he was really a boyfriend.'

'So what was he?'

'I don't know.'

'Frankly, Tessa, they were a pretty odd couple.'

'Something bound them together. It couldn't be religion, I suppose?'

'Why? Is Beth that religious?'

'No . . . It's possible she has become more interested in the last year. Mr Thatchet, the chemist, thought he heard hymn-singing coming from upstairs when Laurie Woodward and a few others were there.'

Anna put up both hands. 'You can count Laurie Woodward out of that equation,' she said. 'He was a long, long way from the ways of the Lord.'

'Okay.' Tessa thought for a moment. 'When I went through the clothes in the closet I found a man's leather jacket. This was in one of his pockets. Looks like membership to a club of some sort.' She took the plastic card from her pocket and laid it on the table.

Anna picked up the card and frowned. 'Beak Street. An unusual address for something called the Research and Development Club,' she said. 'Beak Street, W1 is in the heart of Soho. There are more strip clubs than debating clubs there.'

Then suddenly she smiled as she turned the card and examined it.

'What is it?' Tessa said. 'Something I've missed?'

'Maybe.' Anna pushed the card across the table. 'See here on the back – *Recommending member: Brn. de Charlus.*'

'Yes?'

'You don't read Proust?'

'*Remembrance of Things Past?*'

'Yes. Isn't Charlus the exhibitionist gay Baron that Swann meets at the Guermantes mansion?'

'So this is an in-joke?'

'Looks like it. My guess is that the Research and Development Club is some sort of gay massage parlour.'

'What about the address?' Tessa turned the card over. 'The Old Boathouse, Granchester. Not Woodward's?'

'I wouldn't think so. As far as anybody knew he didn't have an address.'

'Then it's got to be worth looking into.'

For a moment they sat in silence. 'I'm feeling something of a fool, Anna,' said Tessa. 'What the devil do I know about Beth's life in Cambridge? She must have known what sort of man he was. Everybody else did. Maybe she never *intended* me or anybody to know where she was spending Christmas. Maybe flying the Atlantic to the rescue of a kid sister who doesn't need rescuing is just the sort of action that makes Beth describe me as a pain in the ass – "a complete cow" as her friend Alan interprets it. Dammit, I feel like hiring a car, driving straight to London Airport and taking the first flight back.'

'Don't do that,' Anna said slowly.

'Why not, for God's sake?'

'Because I think your first instinct was on track – I've no idea what, but I think there *is* something desperately wrong.'

Outside they walked slowly back along King's Parade towards

the Fitzwilliam Museum. The streets and pavements had been cleared of snow but there was still a thick layer on the roof of the classical pediment of the museum. 'I've a spare bedroom,' Anna van Gelden said. 'Several in fact. The Fitzwilliam supplies accommodation sufficient for a Curator and his large Victorian family. Their sexism never imagined a *femme seule* occupying the post. Pick up your bags this afternoon and move in. I think you might need some support over the next couple of weeks.'

CHAPTER NINE

There was still another hour of light when Tessa, in Anna van Gelden's black BMW, drove out along the Trumpington Road to the riverside village of Granchester. The Old Boathouse address she had found on the membership card of the Soho Club was on the far side of the village. As she drove through she looked up at the church clock and remembered vaguely the nostalgic lines from the English war poet Rupert Brooke:

> *Stands the church clock at ten to three?*
> *And is there honey still for tea?*

There had, she thought, been better poets in the English language. But curiously enough the clock *was* still stopped at ten to three.

A narrow lane took her down towards the River Cam. The grey sky and frozen droplets of mist seemed to merge here. She saw gaunt trees, and crows lifting and circling above them. Stopping the car, she could see, among the trees, a ramshackle wooden boatshed perched over a frozen creek which joined the river fifty yards or so below. Tessa got out of the car, frowning. She couldn't easily imagine anybody living in the old place in summer – in winter the idea was out of the question.

An iron gate carried a small painted sign: '*To the Old Boat-house,*' and Tessa, still puzzled, pushed it open and began to follow the path through the trees. The snow was thinner here, sitting high on the mounds of marshgrass and the tops of rhododendron bushes that obscured the track ahead.

Only after a further thirty or forty yards into the wood did she see that the timber-planked boathouse was not the only building. A short distance higher up the creek, almost obscured in the mist, stood a small brick and flint boatman's cottage. Who, she wondered, had Laurie Woodward known well enough to give their address as his?

Tessa passed through the wooden gate and approached the front door of the cottage. It was dark green, chipped. To her surprise she saw it was standing open a couple of inches.

She stopped, pluming breath into the cold air. There was no sound from within. In fact, she registered now that the curtains were drawn. She walked forward, her footsteps crunching on the frozen snow. The brittle crackling underfoot seemed to emphasise the silence around her. She stopped again. Looking down she realised there were no footprints in the snow on the path ahead, or on the steps up to the open door. A nervous chill passed up her back. No one had been here since it had snowed heavily this morning. Perhaps for much longer.

The part-open door now looked infinitely menacing. She knew it was pointless but she called out nevertheless: 'Is anybody there?'

Crunching forward over the virgin snow she climbed the steps and stood with her gloved hand flat against the door. She pushed. It swung back with a whispering creak. 'Is anybody at home?' She raised her voice but she was aware of its nervous reediness.

She waited, listening. The hallway in front of her was dark. She could just make out a flight of stairs. She reached out and flipped the light switch but nothing happened.

She took a step backwards. Carter would say at this point that common sense demanded she get out of this cold, musty house. But then Carter would patronise her for ever if she did.

She pushed the door wide open. Snow, driving through the part-open door into the hall, had left a black stain on the wall where it had melted. On the boarded floor it glistened wet. She called out again, strongly this time, waited and then stepped forward into the hall. On her left there was a door. She took the handle and turned. It opened into complete blackness.

For a moment it was a shock. Even thick curtains let in a little light at the join or the edges, but in this room she could not even make out where the window was. She closed her eyes hard and opened them again. A little borrowed light from the hallway behind her filtered into the room and allowed her to see the outline of a sofa and two armchairs. She stepped between them and reached the far wall. Curtaining moved under her hand. She grasped a handful and pulled sideways.

The grey misty light from outside took on a religious brightness as it flooded past her. She turned and saw the room clearly at last. It was a small cottage room but a wall had been demolished to connect it to the old stone-floored cottage kitchen. Together they made a narrow but decent-sized room.

In the sitting-room part, books in well-built bookshelves occupied large stretches of the wall space. The furniture was all fine, local auction house finds of Regency carvers and early Victorian oak chests and tables. The floorboards had been sanded and polished.

She opened a small door in the back wall. In the half light she could see several pieces of furniture, part dismantled, drawer fronts held in a heavy vice, rows of tools in racks along the walls. She was certain she was in Laurie Woodward's workshop, a place undiscovered by the police or press who described him as having no fixed abode.

She came back into the hall and climbed the stairs, stumbling in the darkness of the landing. There were two bedrooms, the curtains here already drawn back to show each room furnished similarly with auction finds, the polished floors covered with worn but good quality kilims. But the pictures on the walls made her pull in a sharp breath. They were photographs from all over the world. News pictures of a young Chinese being shot in the back of the head, an Arab woman being stoned to death, pictures of young Jewish girls lined up naked for the bath house at Auschwitz or Treblinka. Several photographs of young Arab boys being beaten by a European with a long cane. A disgusting picture of a circumcision operation being performed on a young African girl.

Tessa felt her stomach turn over.

She was anxious to leave now. It was somehow enough to have been here, to have entered an empty house. These were things she could tell Carter, tell Anna. She was about to leave the main bedroom when she saw the faint movement of a door to a built-in cupboard. She was pretty sure that it was her own displacement of

77

air as she walked quickly past that had moved it. She stopped, wheeling round, not in fear but in something less strident, a mounting apprehension. Her eye flicked towards the window. The grey of the afternoon was changing to real darkness, the darkness of night. She stepped forward quickly and wrenched at the door. It opened and she sucked in air in relief. Clothes hung there, a golf bag stood in the corner . . . What had she expected? She tried to smile wryly at herself, but it didn't work. No smile came.

She was looking more closely at the contents of the cupboard. The clothes were all dark-coloured, black or deep red. They were all of silk.

She backed off a step, her eyes on the strange garments. Each was, she saw, a sort of long caftan or short medieval tabard. She peered into the depths of the cupboard. From the golf bag protruded handles bound with twine. She reached in and pulled at one. The bag fell towards her. In her hand was a short leather whip; on the floor at her feet were a series of scattered objects, silk hoods, blindfolds, yellow nylon cord, brass instruments that were maybe thumbscrews . . . giant realistically detailed penises in latex . . .

She reared back in distaste. Her heart was beating hard. The hand that held the whip was shaking. She threw it back into the cupboard and walked quickly out of the room. On the landing she stopped. Years of Bostonian good manners came back to still her shaking hands. She was in someone else's house. Perhaps it was not Woodward's. If whoever owned the house kept this stuff in his cupboard that was his concern. Not hers. The thought calmed her. She went back into the room, picked up the whips and masks and instruments that had fallen from the bag and put them back in the cupboard. Then she went out on to the landing and back down the stairs.

The kitchen was the only part of the house that didn't look as if a cleaner had been through it. Here were two used wine glasses and an overturned bottle of Bordeaux, the red wine having leaked on to the stone floor and congealed in a panhandled dry stain. She bent down and sniffed at the neck of the bottle. A powerful smell of vinegar arose. So it had stood there some time. Well over a week. Perhaps more.

For a few moments Tessa looked from the bottle to the stain. So someone had knocked over a bottle. Nothing very unusual in that. But why hadn't they stood it up – surely that was the straightforward reaction?

She moved over and opened the refrigerator, expecting to find it empty. Instead it was full and smelling badly of decay, the electric supply to it working no more than the light. She forced herself to examine the contents: white wine, two cartons of taramasalata, one opened and dry-crusted; rillettes de canard in a jar, open, half eaten and with green fingers of mould on the surface of the fat; a carton of skimmed milk, sour; and a few cold-dried pieces of camembert and Brie. Finally, eggs in their own cupped compartment, and celery and carrots, limp and unappetising.

So someone was living here up until a few weeks ago. Woodward – until the night of his death. It would explain the sour taramasalata, the mouldy rillettes, the abandoned milk. But it wouldn't explain the partly open door.

It was rapidly getting dark. The sky outside seemed unchanged – a heavy metallic grey. But the light in the room was failing. She would go to the police – ask them to come and take a look. Try and persuade them to establish whether Beth had ever been to this house.

Outside she could hear the wind sough through the trees. She watched the river mist lift around the rotting planked boathouse at the end of the creek. The front door whispered on its hinges.

The phone rang. Her stomach turned over in the first milliseconds of intolerable noise. She stood rooted to the spot. From the kitchen she could see, on a scratched brown desk, the dark green modern telephone, its high warble demanding attention.

She took two steps forward and hesitated. Another two, uncertainly, towards the phone and was stopped dead by a loud click. She had not registered the answerphone on the shelf behind the desk. staring at it, she listened to Woodward's voice. It was light, with a slight fenland accent: *'This is Laurie Woodward. Can't come to the phone now – leave your name and number, I'll get back to you soonest.'*

A click, a whirr and a bleep before a laughing male voice came on: *'Laurie love. Surprise, surprise! Lulu's back in town. I'll be in*

*Cambridge by seven, seven-thirty. See you then. Lots and lots to tell
you, as you might very well guess. And you to tell me, no doubt!
Sayonara.'*

The machine clicked. Tessa's heartbeat slowly returned to normal. She pulled the curtains and fumbled her way back into the
hall. For a moment she stood undecided in the open door. Then,
leaving it as it was, she walked carefully down the steps and
retraced her footprints down the path. The greyness of mist and sky
had melded now so that she could barely see the outline of the gate
into the lane.

Seven to seven-thirty. Tonight presumably. Tessa found the car
and got in. Immediately she was enclosed in that exaggerated sense
of security that cars so notoriously induce. The nervousness of a
few minutes ago drained from her. She would come back in a
couple of hours – and meet the man who had called. Someone, she
suspected, who knew more about the below the surface life of
Laurie Woodward than either one of his employers like Anna, or
her sister, Beth.

'Carter,' Tessa said patiently, but with her knuckles showing white
on the hand that held the phone, 'Anna van Gelden is Senior
Curator of the Fitzwilliam Museum, one of the most important in
Britain. She is not running a white slave organisation, nor, to my
knowledge . . .' she raised her eyes to where Anna was sitting on
the sofa on the far side of the large room, '. . . is she the Ms Big in
British drug distribution. She has simply been astonishingly kind to
me. In other words, Carter, you can put your mind at rest.'

'Yuh, yuh,' her husband said on the end of the line two thousand
miles away in Cambridge, Mass. 'I was just asking whether you
knew the woman? You don't just move in with anybody who invites
you.'

'You're right, I don't.'

There was a long silence on the line. 'Tessa, I worry about you,
okay?'

'Okay.'

'And you're getting nowhere.'

'I wouldn't say that. Not entirely. I've seen the police. I've
tracked down Laurie Woodward's house. I've found out a lot more

about him that I wouldn't mind betting Beth herself knows . . . Some of it not that nice. No, Carter, I've a feeling I am getting somewhere. This evening I may be getting even further.'

'What happens this evening?'

'I have a date with a friend of Laurie Woodward's. The friend doesn't know it yet, and he obviously doesn't know Woodward's dead. He thinks he's seeing him tonight. But when he turns up, it'll be me waiting.'

'For God's sake!' Carter said. 'Where is this meeting to take place.'

'At the Old Boathouse down by the River Cam.'

'Are you quite crazy?'

Tessa bridled. 'What does that mean?'

'It means are you crazy? It means are you crazy enough to go down to some no doubt deserted boathouse and meet some unknown?'

'Carter, I'm here to find Beth.'

In the kitchen in the apartment on Mass. Avenue panic rose in Carter Wilson's chest. He was finding it difficult to breathe. No, he was breathing too much, too quickly. He was hyperventilating. Christ, that's what he was doing. He was hyperventilating. 'I've got to go,' he said, and slammed down the phone.

Tessa replaced the phone and sank down in an armchair. 'Oh, hell,' she said. 'I should just say, nothing is happening, the police are investigating and I've moved in with a great bunch of nuns. Write me care of Sister Anna . . .'

Anna got up and carried the wine bottle across the room. She jiggled it over Tessa's glass.

'Please.'

Anna poured red wine and walked back to her chair. 'He's a worrier, uh?'

'That's one side of it.'

'And the other?'

Tessa sipped her wine slowly. 'I think he's determined I shouldn't get credit for anything. Afraid maybe I will.'

'How long have you been married?'

'We're not a long-running act. Until my early-thirties I was a career woman. I was personnel director for a group of hospitals in

Boston. Then I met Carter and then I wanted a baby. Or was it the other way round?'

'What does Carter do?'

'He teaches English Literature at Boston University. We met at a party. He seemed solid, stable, uncompetitive, unaggressive. I thought he must be for me. He's also very good-looking, though worried about his hair thinning.'

'So did you have the baby?'

'We married three years ago. I was pregnant maybe a year later. And six months after that I caught a bad skid on the Massachusetts Turnpike and crashed into a tree.' She looked across the room, over Anna's head to the gilt oval mirror and the yellow silk curtains reflected in it. 'I lost the baby,' she said. 'I was fine, not a bone broken, hardly a scratch. But I lost the baby.'

'I don't know what to say.'

'Nothing. I'm sorry. I was really telling you about Carter. I guess what happened after the car crash was that I felt I couldn't go back to work – or I didn't want to. I felt very low and my confidence was at rock bottom. I didn't need a psychiatrist to tell me that I felt guilty for walking clear of the crash.'

'This is when Carter took over?'

'I think it was from real concern. He began to look after me, guard me from things, ordinary daily difficulties. I was feeling so low, so lousy, so inadequate, I let him. In two years I deteriorated from go-getting executive to pudding. I put on weight. I sat around watching TV. I cried a lot. It was the most active thing I did.'

'How did you start hauling yourself out of it?'

'I think it was when Beth came back from some trip to Peru last Christmas and started in with the same "there, there, don't worry" line as Carter. I remember I ran upstairs, looked in the mirror and didn't have to fish around for a New Year's resolution. January the first I called my old boss and asked for a job – I'd take any grade. He was good. He slid me back in, not where I was but close. The last year has done wonders for me.'

'And how does Carter feel about that?'

'Whatever happened to the girl I used to know? He's still adjusting.'

'Will he make it?'

Tessa looked at her. 'The jury's still out – I think.' She got up. The carriage clock on the table beside her said six o'clock. 'I must go,' she said. 'Are you sure it's okay if I use the BMW?'

'Take it,' Anna said. 'You don't want me to go with you?' She smiled. 'I'm not playing Carter.'

'No, I know. But I feel I'll get further with Laurie's pal if I'm alone. Or maybe I just need to tell Carter I did it myself.'

She stood up as the phone began to ring. Anna took it, listened and handed it to Tessa.

'Hallo . . . Carter? Something happened? . . . Carter?'

In the apartment on Mass. Avenue Carter Wilson made several passes with his hand across his thinning scalp before he spoke. 'I had to come to a decision, Tessa. I don't apologise for it.'

'What decision?'

'You have influence on that side of the Atlantic. Your family has. Your name.'

'Oh Christ! You haven't done anything, Carter?'

'I made a call.'

'Damn you, Carter.'

'I made a call to someone I know in the State Department.'

'I told you before I left. I told you I didn't want my father's name in this.'

'I don't apologise,' Carter said stubbornly. He listened, thinking she'd hung up on him. 'D'you hear, Tessa. I'm doing it for you. I don't feel the need to apologise.'

'You should, Carter,' she said quietly. 'You really should.'

CHAPTER TEN

Commander Keith Loverell gestured Abbeline to a seat and slipped a cassette into his player. 'A little bit scratchy, I'm afraid, Jack. But it was first recorded best part of sixty years ago.'

The tape began to crackle. In the background there was the sinister howl of an air raid siren and the thud of distant anti-aircraft guns. Then an American voice:

'As London braces itself for its third air raid tonight, on what will be its 53rd consecutive night of air raids, I am standing on a rooftop in Fleet Street. Behind me the whole of the City of London seems engulfed in smoke and flame around the outline of St Paul's Cathedral. In the street below, fire engines race across fallen masonry and broken glass . . .'

Loverell fast-forwarded the tape and lifted his finger for the peroration. Among the scream of bombs and the echoing crump of explosions, the bells of fire engines and the hollow clangour of the guns in Middle Temple and Lincoln's Inn the low, powerful voice wound up:

'What Mr Churchill and the British people need now is more than just words of encouragement from across the Atlantic, more than cries of "Good luck" or "Keep going!" What the British need today is the might of the United States firmly at their side. The losses of the last few months have been horrendous. If we cannot send soldiers, let us send tanks. If we cannot send airmen, let us send planes. This is a battle in which, whether we yet know it or not, every American is already involved.

'*Last year in Berlin I met many members of the German air force. Those pilots I met were, as men, not so different from the pilots of the RAF. But the Luftwaffe is something more. Today it represents a philosophy which is in direct opposition to those ideals that founded the United States of America. American War Aid to the beleaguered forces of Britain is the only way to keep those ideals intact.*

'*This is Quentin Naylor, reporting the Battle for London, the night of December third, 1940.*'

Loverell switched off the machine, poured Abbeline a glass of Scotch and water and crossed to hand it to him. 'Quentin Naylor,' he said, 'did more to state Britain's case for US aid than anybody short of Winston Churchill himself. At the end of the war he was given an honorary knighthood and Churchill's word that if ever he or his family needed anything Britain could supply . . .' He looked down at Abbeline. 'You've got the picture?'

Abbeline nodded slowly. 'I've got half the picture.'

Loverell stood, one hand in his trouser pocket, his own glass of Scotch held to his chest. He rocked back and forth on his heels. 'What's the workload look like at the moment, Jack?'

'I was going to have a word with you about that. Not a lot on at the moment. I've got a long-term surveillance in place on a suspected drug warehouse which one of the Pacific Rim embassies could well be running . . . that sort of thing.'

'Quiet time, then?'

'I was even thinking of applying for twenty one days' leave.'

Loverell raised sandy grey eyebrows. 'To go to Australia?'

'You should have been a detective, sir.'

Loverell smiled, pleased with himself. 'Big picture of Jo in last night's *Evening Standard*. Story speculating on her likely effect on red-blooded Aussie beach boys.'

Abbeline grunted, aware that Loverell was avoiding the issue. 'What needs to be done about Quentin Naylor?' he said at last.

'Naylor's dead. Died a few years back.'

'And . . .?'

'The State Department called the Foreign office who called . . . you know how it goes. It landed on my desk. This tape and a note from the PM: "Action this day". Churchill's phrase, deliberately chosen.'

'What action?'

Loverell went round to sit at his desk. 'Quentin Naylor had two daughters. One's supposedly here at Cambridge studying biochemistry. Beth Naylor, research student. Very bright lady. Last Sunday her elder sister, a woman named Tessa Wilson, decided to take a plane over to look for Beth.'

'Is she missing?'

'Probably not. Chances are she's off skiing. But we need someone senior and tactful to reassure the old dear. She's not happy about finding her way around this side of the Atlantic. Her husband's not happy about her pottering about aimlessly trying to rescue a sister in non-existent distress. I called the husband, a man named Carter Wilson. Seems a decent chap. More worried about his wife than his sister-in-law. That was the picture he gave.'

'You want me to see her?'

'Pat her hand. Give her a Martini or two and a good lunch. Give her a shot of the Abbeline charm.'

'Yes, sir.'

'And . . .'

'Just one small thing.'

'Yes, sir?'

'We've had a call from that man Passmore, the Reverend Leonard, telling me he appreciated your letter.'

'It was grovel from start to finish.'

'Well, it seems to have done the trick. He's invited you to go over to Soho or King's Cross to see the church in action.'

'To go to a service?'

'No, to what he calls their ministry to the poor. He'll be at King's Cross now. Pop over and cast a glance at the sort of thing they do. It may even be that he's not as bad as we thought.'

'If you think so, sir.'

'Then you're free to bugger off to Australia.' He paused. 'That's all, Jack. Give my love to the beautiful Jo. Incidentally my wife's furious with you.'

'Me?'

'And me. She's desperate you bring Jo round to dinner. She'll brook no excuses. From either of us.'

'The week we get back.'

'I'm counting on you, Jack.'

Jo Saunders pulled her blue Mercedes off the road, turned down the ramp and drove into the place reserved for her in the dimly lit garage. 'This is where you get out,' she said to the man in the passenger seat.

Leo Bannerman half turned towards her. 'You're not going to make me walk home in the rain?'

'I offered to drop you off at your place. Stop playing games, Leo.'

'Give me a drink before you turn me loose to face the elements.'

'No drink, Leo.'

'Then I shall have to molest you here in the garage.' His left hand came over her leg and ran up the inside of her thigh before she grabbed his wrist. 'For Christ's sake, Leo,' she twisted his hand away, 'I said stop playing games.'

'One drink and I promise to leave.'

'Jack's coming over in half an hour. I'm in enough trouble with him as it is over Australia . . .'

'He doesn't want you to go? Afraid of what you and I might get up to?'

'Leo, we've been divorced two years. I've never let you think there's *any* chance of us getting back together.'

He smiled, a smile he'd used in a dozen scenes. One that worked terribly well, directors always said. A little wry, a touch amused, not at the situation in hand but at life generally.

'Take that silly smile off your face, Leo. You haven't just rescued me from a fate worse than death, you've just tried to shove your hand up my skirt. Now get out of the car. I'll see you at the airport tomorrow. For Christ's sake, don't forget.'

'One drink. And I'll go quietly. Be a sport.'

There were probably fifty people standing in line. Of all ages, both sexes, but mostly white, they shuffled forward towards the trestle tables where sausage and mash and a cup of tea was handed out on a styrofoam tray.

Standing next to the brightly lit servery van with *Millennium Church Mission* in big letters across its side, Abbeline watched for a few moments then turned as he saw Leonard Passmore coming towards him. The preacher wore the same black trenchcoat and a thick black muffler but was hatless, his thick shaggy black hair speckled with snow. He smiled an even-toothed boyish smile. 'Hi, Mr Abbeline,' he shook Abbeline's hand, 'gracious of you to come.'

'Gracious of you to ask me.'

'I appreciated your letter. A man who can admit an error . . .'

Abbeline smiled tightly. It wasn't *his* error he'd been admitting, it was the error of Rosemary Copeland, the girl who's run off with the karaoke joint manager. But he let it pass. 'You do good work here, Mr Passmore.'

'You can call me *Dr* Passmore without exaggerating my qualifications, Mr Abbeline. I hold a doctorate from the Nathaniel Bell University, Indiana, a small but exacting college of theology.'

Abbeline had a sudden image of Passmore as a basketball player, the huge hands and red wrists reaching up . . . 'Dr Passmore then,' he said reluctantly, and gestured to the line moving slowly forward. 'It's tragic we have so many people in need in this weather.'

Passmore nodded gravely. They walked the length of the line and turned. The servery had been set up in a street behind the station goods yard and trucks queued to pass through the main gate, the drivers leaning out to talk to the mini-skirted girls who stood in twos and threes beneath the street lamps.

'I, in turn, have an apology to make to you, Mr Abbeline. At the airport I was ugly, threatening. I should have spoken more moderately. I become overwrought. It's a failing, I know it. I pray to God nightly to help me suppress my anger.'

Snow was floating down through the streetlights; from one of the queuing trucks a radio blared 'Jingle Bells'; the hookers laughed and shouted crude responses to the drivers. Abbeline looked towards the Mission truck. If you really were a man of God, he thought, there could be cause enough for anger here, in the street, where fifty or more people line up for sausage and mash to eat out in the open.

'I suppose "American television evangelist" conjures up many undesirable images to you, Superintendent? There were many scandals, it's true. But nobody in the church works for profit, Mr Abbeline. I pay myself an allowance which is barely enough for the necessities of life. These clothes are not an affectation. I have no Swiss bank accounts, no secret mistresses or private mansions.'

'You must have some sort of central church?'

'Yes, we have a prayer centre here in England. A retreat, we call it.'

'Where is that, Dr Passmore?'

'In the country. I don't disclose the whereabouts. It's a retreat after all and journalists, you know, can make life impossible.'

'Journalists and policemen?'

Passmore smiled. 'Perhaps.' He extended his hand. 'Accept my apology, Superintendent. The world's wrongs cannot be righted by anger, any more than they can be by any of the other sins of man.'

'Is that what you're here for?' Abbeline gestured to the line of people at the truck. 'To right the world's wrongs.'

'We have a task, a role that goes even deeper than loneliness or hunger, Mr Abbeline,' he said reasonably. 'The Millennium Church is here to guide mankind through the horrors of the Apocalypse to come.'

'Ah.' Abbeline looked at Passmore's eyes. They were suddenly different. Small as they were, they somehow now seemed to dominate his face.

'The Apocalypse, Mr Abbeline,' Passmore said with a curiously reasonable-sounding passion. 'You must look to us for guidance. There really is no one else.'

Abbeline walked slowly back to his car. There were two thousand cult churches like this in the United States, probably several hundred in Europe. Guidance through the horrors of the imminent Apocalypse. Salvation if you entrust yourself to me. It sounded good enough to some to make them abandon family, friends . . . As ever, Abbeline thought, it was the vulnerable who were most vulnerable.

Pleased with his modest *bon mot* he looked towards a girl in a short sheepskin coat who was leaning against his Jaguar, smoking a cigarette with exaggerated pouting of the lips as she plumed smoke into the cold air.

'You come with me, darling, and I'll fix you up for the night,' she said.

'You come with me, darling, and I'll fix *you* up for the night,' he told her amiably. 'In King's Cross Police Station.'

She stepped back in alarm and he opened the car door. 'Get in,' he said.

'What?'

'Get in.'

The girl's mouth dropped open. 'Are you taking me in?'

'I'm taking you for a ride round the block.'

'I see,' the girl said.

'No, you don't. Just jump in. I'll take five minutes of your time, no more, I promise.'

'How short can a short time get?' the girl said. She swung herself into the car and Abbeline rounded the bonnet and got into the driver's seat.'

'What is it you're after?' the girl asked as Abbeline drove off.

'These holy rollers, do you have anything to do with them?'

The girl pulled down her leather miniskirt and grinned. 'They're not the best set of customers you could hope to find parked on your doorstep.'

'Have you ever come across Passmore himself?'

'The mad doctor?'

'Why do you call him that?'

The girl lit a cigarette. 'Is this why you're giving me a ride around the block? To pump me on Passmore?'

'I'd like to know more about him, yes,' Abbeline conceded.

'He's a great one for an under the eyebrow look at a miniskirt or big pair of bangers.'

'So are a lot of men.'

'But he claims to be different, don't he? Well, he's not is what I'm saying. It became a bit of a game with the girls last time he was here to give him a bit of a wiggle as they passed. You should see him redden up.'

Abbeline shook his head. 'Why do you call him the mad doctor?'

'Okay . . .' The girl waved to a pair of friends as Abbeline slowed for the traffic light. 'Because he's got a rare temper on him, I'll tell you that for nothing.'

'Have you seen him explode?'

'Not me. Janice, my friend, did once. He was here with his people and got caught short. So he popped down the alley for a piss. She followed him round, more or less for a giggle but you never know, and offered him a quick one.'

At the corner Abbeline turned left again bringing him again to the street lined with girls. 'How did Passmore react to the offer?'

'I could hear him shouting and raving from where I was outside the phone box,' the girl said. 'Went for her.'

'You mean he hit her?'

'Back handed her across the head. She ran for her life, Janice. In this business you get to recognise them.'

'Recognise them?'

'The serious crazies. It's a rule among all us girls that you never persuade any man too hard. If he wants it, he'll buy it. If he doesn't, he won't. In between there are a few who are terrified of it – and desperate for it at the same time. Those are the ones you never want to catch in a dark alley. Like Janice did.'

CHAPTER ELEVEN

She had brought a flashlight. She had run the BMW past the house, almost down to the river, and parked at the entrance to a watermeadow. In the mist rolling over the river banks it would not be seen, even in the headlights of a car approaching the boathouse.

Leaving the car she had walked back with the torch shaded by her free hand, showing just the yard or two of frozen grass and mud in front of each step she took.

At the gate marked '*To the Old Boathouse*', Tessa paused. There had not been too many times in the last year she had thought Carter might be right. But retrospectively she wasn't too sure at the moment. The wind, though light, was enough to move the mist over the river, the fantastic swirl and roll revealed by a moon which peered through the skeins of cloud. During dark periods when the moon was totally obscured, the wind seemed to drop, the frost deepen in intensity until all that could be heard in the darkness was the cracking of the knuckled ice on twigs and branches.

Tessa opened the gate, the torch pushing a yellow light out along the path. Once into the rhododendrons she directed the beam more freely about her. Down by the creek was the boathouse itself, the low timber building crouched like a dog's kennel above the frozen water.

Higher up, the boatman's cottage was dark as she had left it. She turned on to the path, took a few steps up and stopped. She had heard a sound from the house. Not loud, not easily identifiable. Yet clearly a noise.

At the red light on the embankment, Abbeline buttoned the Cambridge number Loverell had given him and waited until a woman's voice answered. 'Mrs Tessa Wilson?'

'No. This is Anna van Gelden, Tessa Wilson's staying with me. Can I take a message?'

She liked the sound of the classless male voice at the other end of the line. 'This is Superintendent Jack Abbeline, I'm calling from Scotland Yard. But no need for alarm,' he added quickly. 'In fact I was calling to ask Mrs Wilson to have lunch with me. Will she be back later this evening?'

'If you call in say an hour or so . . .'

'Or perhaps she could call me on this number?'

He gave his mobile number, thanked her and hung up.

Scotland Yard. Superintendent Jack Abbeline. Anna pursed her lips. Tessa's father's name must be enough to haul a good deal of weight.

She had been wrong. Nothing showed through the thick black curtains of the main room of the boatman's cottage, but a light, presumably coming from that room, gleamed dimly at the transom above the door.

She stood still at the beginning of the path. She could hear nothing now beyond the distant whine of a car engine somewhere in the village. There were footprints on the snow of the path. Her own there and back and one further set, a man's. This afternoon's caller who had come earlier than his promised seven to seven-thirty?

She swung the gate and walked boldly up the path. The chipped green door was closed. She knocked loudly.

Now the silence was complete. The snow-covered garden and hedges seemed to create their own deep hush. The moon appeared and disappeared. She stood on the doorstep, suddenly uncertain.

There was no doubt that whoever was inside, if they were still inside, heard her knocking. No doubt at all about that. The thought induced a quick burst of determination. She hammered with her torch on the door, waited a few seconds and opened it and walked in.

The burn was fading. She was close to running. She stepped forward and pushed open the door to the main room. Light flooded into the narrow hall.

A man stood before her, slender, poised like a forest animal to run. He wore black leathers, heavily studded and decorated with chromium badges. His blue eyes blazed in the light. He was holding a big plastic bag in one hand. 'What the fuck!' he said.

Tessa stayed in the doorway. She could see behind him the wreckage of the room: drawers had been pulled out; papers scattered across the floor. The man had not moved. 'You're a friend of Woodward's,' she said. 'I want to talk to you.'

'Best of luck.' Even in those brief words she could recognise the light, accented voice of the man who had called Laurie Woodward and left the message that afternoon. She could see on his face some mix of anger and fear she couldn't begin to fathom. 'I'm Tessa Wilson,' she said. 'My sister Beth is missing. She was a friend of Laurie's.'

The man responded with bared teeth, not in a smile or even a snarl. An exhausted animal baring of the teeth.

'You're a friend of Woodward's. You can help me,' she said, coming forward.

He stared at her, jerked his head back, surveyed the room quickly and made to walk past her to the door.

'You're the man who called this afternoon, aren't you? Left a message . . .'

'Oh, Christ!' He dropped the bag and turned on her. As she dropped back he moved past her, frantically grabbing at the answering machine on the desk. Opening it, he tore out the tape.

'Who are you, for God's sake?' Tessa said.

'You think I'd tell you?' He was down on one knee, pushing the tape into the plastic bag. She could see his hands were trembling violently.

'All right, don't tell me,' she said. 'But what are you afraid of? At least tell me that.'

He jerked a thumb over his shoulder.

'Is someone out there?' Tessa looked towards the window.

He laughed with an edge of hysteria in his voice. 'Nobody that's going to do you any harm.'

'Where?'

He moved towards the door, gesturing outside, towards the river.

She stood in his way. 'What is it, for God's sake?'

He moved to push past her.

'What are you talking about?' She tried to block his way but he shouldered her easily aside. At the door he swung round. 'I'm talking about what's in the boathouse. Go and see for yourself, you stupid bitch!'

Standing on the doorstep, Tessa saw clearly the small white car as the man drove fast up the land and headed for the village.

When the engine noise faded, she found herself alone in another world of sensation. A world different from any she knew. The moon floated in a sea of patchy cloud. Cold, fear, an awful sense of vulnerability, made moving, simply putting one foot in front of the other, a complex balancing which she guessed might be the way invalids walked, victims of a recent stroke perhaps or sufferers from Menière's Syndrome which temporarily suspends the gyroscopic function of the middle ear.

She stood swaying in the snowbound luminescence of the small cottage garden. The Old Boathouse was directly in front of her now. Beyond it she could see the reflection of the moon on the still unfrozen water of the River Cam.

She drove her steps forward. Down the path, through the gate.

The boathouse sat at the end of a narrow creek, the snow thick on its roof like a white thatch. The stream was frozen out from both banks, locking rushes and broken branches in the grip of the ice. The leafless trees swayed silently.

A path led along the bank above the creek. She flashed her torch in front of her, though the moon still stood starkly clear of cloud. By the side of the boathouse she stopped. Close to, she could see that the planking was no longer aligned, iron nails having rusted away to let individual planks slip out of line.

Close to, she could catch the almost warm dank smell of rotten wood, stirred on each rustle of wind.

Close to, there was something else. She felt beyond fear as she listened.

From inside the boathouse came a faint creaking timed to the brief gusts of wind that whirled snow dust and rattled the ice-dry reeds along the bank. She thought of the wind causing something inside the boathouse to swing gently, to creak, and then be still again.

There was a small door in front of her. The handle was dented, blackened brass. Because she couldn't turn away she grasped it and pulled.

Warmer air engulfed her. And the most terrible stench.

She had screamed in panic before the flashlight beam jerked upwards in her hand and caught the hanging figure, tattered, decayed. Teeth, eye sockets, lank hair. She was screaming as the torch fell from her hand, into the boathouse, rolling forward to where one dangling foot was locked solid by the ice.

CHAPTER TWELVE

Abbeline came back from the bar of the Chelsea Potter with a glass of white wine and a long orange juice.

Jan Madigan, sitting in the corner bench seat, her crossed legs exposed to the crotch, caught his glance. 'What are you looking at?'

'Your knickers,' said Abbeline. 'You're here to talk business. You're not here on the pull.'

'Sorry, guv. If it offends you . . .' She took the hem of her leather skirt and wriggled on the seat. 'There, that's better.'

He smiled, pushed the white wine across to her.

'You're not drinking,' she said.

'Later.'

'Cheers.' Jan raised her glass. 'What's the good news?'

'For me, it's that I'm off to Australia.'

Her face fell. 'Secondment?'

'Two weeks' holiday.'

'Ah.' She forced a smile. 'I thought you might be leaving us, for a moment there.'

Abbeline looked at her as she switched her glance away from him and openly studied the two young men who had just entered. She was a difficult girl to come to terms with, he was thinking. Liverpool Irish with a natural hostility to authority, and yet his first choice for deputy when he was asked to form the Foreign Nationals Division at Scotland Yard. Less than six months married but still flashing her legs at any man in sight. Most liked it, despite Jan's spiky red hair and the rather thin-lipped mouth that promised an earful to anyone who stepped out of her somewhat unpredictable line.

'A lad like that should wear a codpiece for his own protection,' she said, turning back to Abbeline.

He lifted an eyebrow. She took her black notebook from her bag. 'So you'll be away two weeks?'

'Three altogether. What have we got on the agenda?'

'All sleepers. We're waiting on information on that French Embassy business. Ken's working on a bit of background on Leonard Passmore.'

'I've just seen him at his King's Cross soup kitchen. I *think* he's on the level. Claims all the money collected is for charitable purposes. I somehow don't think we'll have any trouble with him. What else?'

'There's the long-running saga of possible drugs in Middle Eastern diplomatic bags. And I'm keeping an eye on that diplomat's son.'

'Brazilian . . .'

'Bolivian,' she said. 'Claims to have been mugged three times in four weeks.'

'Another candidate for a codpiece if I remember.'

'I wasn't going to give him to Ken. Put temptation in his way after twenty-five years' blameless service.'

'You've got a heart of gold.' Abbeline drank some orange juice and twisted his lips against the sharpness. 'There's something else.'

'A new job?'

'I fell for it tonight. A woman named Tessa Wilson in England looking for a sister who seems to have gone missing.' He reached for his briefcase, unlocked it and took out two stapled sheets of paper. 'I wrote up the notes.' He handed her the pages. 'I'm having lunch with her tomorrow. Just to reassure her the police are doing all they can, pat her hand, that sort of thing.'

'What's her pull?'

'You'll see in the notes. Her father was an old friend of this country. Her husband phoned someone for help. FO passed it on to us. I've already checked with Cambridge Police who are handling it. They're going through the usual motions – visiting the girl's place, putting out an Interpol description. She's probably gone skiing – Austria, France, Italy.'

Jan was scribbling notes. She looked up. 'What do you want me to do?'

'Slip over to FBI, US Embassy, when you've got a moment. See Rod Keating . . .'

'Always a pleasure.'

'Ask him to do a little background on this young woman, Beth Naylor.'

'I'll do that. Nothing else?'

He shook his head.

'We haven't had a caseload as light as this since last Christmas.'

'That's why I'm heading for Bondi Beach.'

'If you're expecting to see all those Aussie girls stretched out topless, it don't work that way anymore. They cover each tit with a mountain of suntan cream these days. You'll have to plunge in there and wriggle about to find what you've got in these days of high incidence of skin cancer.'

'There's an innate romanticism about your cast of thought, Jan. It must have done wonders for your love life.'

'My love life hasn't been so bad,' she said, suddenly defensive.

'No . . . anyway, no time for plunging after elusive tits. Jo's filming over there for a couple of weeks.'

And there's nothing elusive about her tits, Jan thought. She nodded. 'Okay,' she said. 'When do you leave?'

'The flight's at six-fifteen tomorrow. I'll just have time to have lunch with the blue-rinsed Mrs Wilson, write up the notes for you, pack my bags and *go*.'

'I wish I was coming with you.'

He smiled. 'Stay here and look after hearth and home.'

Jan winced.

Jo Saunders lived in a small block of mansion flats behind the Duke of York's Barracks off Lower Sloane Street. Two flats, one above the other, had been linked by a spiral staircase, to make one very spacious apartment. The fact that it had two front doors, one on the third floor, one on the fourth, was, as the estate agents had claimed, a feature worth something in the current state of the market.

It was the fourth-floor door that Jo had designated her front door and the one Abbeline fumbled at with the key she had insisted he keep. 'If you don't have a key my mother'll think you're a one night stand,' Jo had said, 'and you wouldn't like that.' Abbeline, thinking of the large and formidably upper-class Mrs Haywood-Saunders, had agreed, and very happily taken the key.

He heard Leo Bannerman's voice as he opened the door. That unmissable theatrical voice 'projected' in order to carry across the stalls or the room, demanding attention but getting far less now than in his heyday just a couple of years ago.

He heard the stage whisper. 'Good God, it's Scotland Yard. I shall be nicked for being alone with you.'

'For God's sake, Leo,' Jo's voice said, seconds before she appeared in the hallway. Abbeline was taking off his coat. She closed the door to the sitting room. 'Leo is here,' she said. 'Came up for one drink only. I'll get rid of him straight away.'

She was wearing jeans, a dark blue silk shirt and a thin gold necklace that gave an extraordinary richness to her auburn hair; very little make-up. He took her shoulders and kissed her hard on the lips.

'That I like,' she said.

Bannerman pulled open the door. 'Abbeline,' he said. 'Don't skulk about in the hall. Come in. You don't need a warrant here.'

'Leo!' Jo's voice was tense with anger. 'This is *not* your flat. You are *not* mine host. I'm sorry, Jack.' She turned anxiously to Abbeline.

'What for?' He put his arm round her. 'I'm feeling in a particularly good mood tonight.'

She relaxed. 'Good news?'

'Could be!'

'A drink first,' she said.

'I'll get it.' He crossed the room and poured himself a glass of white Mâcon. Her glass was full. He didn't even look at Bannerman's.

'Leo is just going,' Jo said.

'Good.'

'Going? So I am. Packing to do.' He turned to Abbeline. 'Looking forward to this part. The irony, I suppose.'

'Irony?'

'Didn't Jo tell you?'

'She told me you had a part in the Australian episodes.'

'Leo, just finish your drink and go, will you? I have things to talk to Jack about.'

'The irony,' Bannerman said, ignoring her, 'is in the part. I play Jo's ex-husband who returns and they . . . uh . . . you know, get on rather well.' He finished his drink in one gulp. 'Must go. Airport tomorrow, Joey. Don't be late.'

He winked at Abbeline and walked out into the hall. Putting on his coat, he looked back into the room. 'Life's full of little ironies,' he said. 'Sorry there won't be much sun, sea and sex for you pounding the beat in London this Christmas.' He lifted his hand and turned quickly for the door.

'He's insufferable,' Jo said. She faced Abbeline. 'I'm sorry, darling. I should have told you about the part.'

'You did.'

'I didn't tell you *what* part. That the second cousin has become the ex-husband. But we don't come together with a big bang or anything.' She took a quick breath. 'It's true that Ben Eliot, the writer, has made it a bit more doe-eyed than the draft I originally read. But there's no hanky-panky. No physicals.'

'I'll have to keep an eye on things all the sane,' he said gravely.

She looked at him. Saw him smile.

'What does that mean?' she said, breaking into a smile herself.

'It means what you've just guessed it means,' he said. 'It means I'm coming to Australia. British Airways 6.15 you said.' He felt in his inside pocket. 'I have a seat booked.'

She gave a yip of pleasure. 'You lovely, lovely, lovely man,' she said, her arms round him, her body grinding into his. He eased her away and slipped his hand into the front of her jeans, feathering her stomach down to the hair line with the back of his fingers. When the phone rang it took a moment for both of them to orientate themselves.

'Dammit,' she said, and took her arms from round his neck.

'It's my mobile. In my briefcase.'

He found his case in the hall, flipped the catches and picked up the mobile. 'Abbeline.'

'Superintendent Abbeline,' Anna van Gelden's voice was low, 'I'm calling for Tessa Wilson. She asked me to contact you.'

'Yes?'

'She's making a statement at Cambridge police station now,' Anna said. 'Half an hour ago she found her sister's body. The police here think it's murder.'

CHAPTER THIRTEEN

In Cambridge Police Station interview room Tessa sat sipping hot, sweet tea. Anna van Gelden sat beside her at a plain vinyl topped table, pocked with cigarette burns. Opposite them, note pad and tape recorder beside him, sat Inspector Ray Rose of Cambridge CID with a female detective sergeant.

The tape recorder was running.

'So your distinct impression was that this man you found in the house was engaged in robbery?' Rose lifted his dark eyebrows at the end of the question. There was still a strong trace of a Yorkshire accent in his voice.

'I think the bag he had was full of things he'd taken from Laurie Woodward's cottage,' Tessa said. 'To tell you the truth, I'm not thinking too straight at the moment. Your doctor gave me some medication. It's making me feel pretty muzzy . . .'

'But you're quite sure about the room being neat and tidy when you went in the afternoon?' the sergeant said.

'Absolutely certain. I remember noticing the two used wine glasses and the bottle on its side and thinking they were the only items not stowed away.'

'Okay.' Rose leaned forward, locking thick, stubby fingers together under his chin. 'Now the man, Mrs Wilson. He left and ran down the path?'

'Yes.'

'And you believe he had a car stashed in the bushes?'

'Just after he left the house, I heard an engine start up. I was standing on the doorstep by then, I think.'

'You saw him?'

'I saw a car roar down the lane. Without lights.' Tessa forced herself to concentrate. 'Yes, he went down the lane towards the main road at a tremendous speed.'

Rose and his colleague exchanged a glance. 'Let's go back to when you were in the house,' the woman detective said. 'You are sure the man you saw there was the man who called himself Lulu on the answerphone?'

'I never imagined his name *was* Lulu. "Lulu's back in town". It's what . . . a line from a song?'

'It's also the name of a rent boy who works the Cambridge area,' said Rose.

'Rent boy?'

'Homosexual prostitute.'

'I'm out of my depth,' Tessa said. 'Could we take a break now?'

Rose nodded to the sergeant. She leaned closer to the tape recorder. 'The time is 21.16, December the fourteenth and this interview is halted at Mrs Wilson's request. For resumption later.' She stabbed at the off button.

Rose stood up. 'We'll leave you for a few minutes, Mrs Wilson.'

'Thank you.'

'You need cigarettes or anything from the canteen? Tea?' the sergeant asked.

Tessa shook her head.

'Sorry we can't offer you a drink,' she said. 'You could probably do with that more than anything.'

Tessa nodded.

'Fifteen, twenty minutes then.'

'Just give me time to catch my breath.' She paused. 'Inspector, where is the body now? Where is my sister's body?'

Rose's dark features compressed in a frown. 'It'll be where you found her,' he said. 'I haven't got down there myself yet. Photographers, scene of crime officers . . . everybody's got a lot to do before the body is moved.'

'I see.'

'You okay with Dr van Gelden – or do you want me to send a policewoman in as well?' The inspector pushed in his chair under the table.

'No. No, I'm fine.' Tessa's face was drawn, her eyelids dark and heavy. She turned her head sharply. 'Oh my God,' she said, and lifted her hands to her face.

For a moment or two Rose and the woman sergeant watched her before silently leaving the room.

'Anna,' Tessa withdrew her hands from her face. 'Anna . . . I can't describe what I'm feeling. As if in the last few hours I've stumbled into a pit of madness. Nothing makes sense to me.'

Anna reached out and held her hands. 'It's your guarantee of sanity,' she said.

'Maybe.'

For a long moment Anna watched her. 'What is it, Tessa?'

'I don't know. There's something forming in my mind. It's hope, I suppose.'

'What?'

'When I think hard about it, I realise, in a moment like that, at the boathouse, your senses aren't working normally . . .'

Anna watched her. 'Just go on.'

'What I mean is, I think I saw what I thought I was going to see.'

'Say that again,' Anna said gently. 'You think you saw what?'

'I mean, when I ran down to the boathouse. When I stood at the door . . . I could hear something swinging back and forth. I think I decided then what it was. That it was Beth.'

Anna took a pack of cigarettes from her pocket. 'Are you sure you won't have one?'

'Yes. Maybe.' Tessa accepted a cigarette and a light. 'I haven't smoked for twelve years.' She exhaled. 'But it's good. It feels good.'

'What were you saying?'

'Grabbing at straws. I don't know. When I pulled open that door I was thinking of that young boy I'd read about in the newspaper office. I knew I was going to see Beth hanging there.'

'And you did.'

'I saw something more horrifying that I could possibly have imagined. A scarecrow of protruding bones and lank hair.'

'Don't, Tessa.'

'But I couldn't possibly *know* it was Beth.'

Anna lit her own cigarette and looked across at her.

Tessa stared back. 'I must know,' she said. Suddenly she stood up, crushing out the cigarette in the tin ashtray. 'I must go back there, Anna. I must find out if it was Beth.'

'I'll tell the inspector.'

'No.' Tessa shook her head. 'No. He'll want us to stay here. To wait for the official report. I can't wait for a report, Anna. I've got to go back there now.'

Anna pulled the BMW in behind the white police vehicles that lined the lane. A spinning blue light on a police van threw cold beams across the crusted snow on the hedges. At the gate, uniformed police stamped their feet and clapped their gloved hands against the cold. Seeing Tessa and Anna coming towards them, one of them moved to block their path. 'I'm sorry, ladies, you can't come through here. You're not press, are you?'

Tessa looked past him to where several floodlights had been set up around the boathouse. Blue and white plastic tape fluttered in the wind. Five or six men were standing there, in uniform of dark overcoats.

'This is Mrs Wilson.' Anna took the policeman aside. 'She found the body.'

'I must go in,' Tessa said. Before either of them could move, she stepped past both policemen and ran towards the group of men outside the boathouse.

She was aware of shouts behind her, of her feet slithering on the frozen path. As she fell, she felt her legs dissolving beneath her. Her cheek, she was suddenly aware, was pressed against a frozen clump of marshweed. Close up she could see each blade of grass was hung with tiny drops of ice, like cuckoo spit, sparkling in the police floodlights. After a second or two she began to hurt.

Anna's voice was speaking, down close to her face. Other male voices seemed to echo around her. With help she was brought into a sitting position. With more help she struggled to her feet. A tall man in a leather jacket had his arm looped round her, his hand comfortingly tucked under her breast. 'We'll get you to the car,' he said. 'You slipped on the ice.'

She knew she hadn't. She stared at him, then past him to the boathouse. She wasn't aware of asking a question but the tall man in the leather jacket seemed to be answering her.

'It's not who you thought,' he said. 'It's a woman but it's not your sister. Too short, wrong colour hair. Who it is, we don't yet know. But it's definitely not your sister.'

She absorbed the fact, shivering.

'I'm Abbeline,' he said. 'Jack Abbeline. Let's get you home.'

CHAPTER FOURTEEN

At nine o'clock the following morning, Dr Sandy Waller, Cambridge CID's pathologist, swung his swivel chair away from his desk in answer to a knock at the door. A young woman stood in the doorway. A singer in a punk rock group? Even one of the more cheerfully exhibitionist students at the university? But not the Scotland Yard woman inspector he had been told to expect. Not with her hair teased out in red spikes, a drop-dead leather mini-skirt and *red* high heels. He stood up.

'Lost for words, aren't you, whack?' she said, grinning. 'Inspector Jan Madigan.'

The young pathologist grimaced cheerfully. 'Scotland Yard? Really?'

'Really,' she said, waving her ID which showed the same spiky hair but in blue black and green. 'And not even undercover. What can you tell me about this hanging?'

'Come in. Can I get you a cup of coffee?' He pointed to the pot. 'Where's your boss? Or doesn't he like path labs? A lot don't.'

'You surprise me. The superintendent's over at the Market Place looking over somebody's flat.'

He nodded. 'How do you want it, the coffee?'

'Black, thanks. The hanging,' she said. 'Give me a general.'

'A general rundown. Okay. Female, white, five foot four inches, blonde undyed, age approximately twenty-five to thirty. Expensive dentistry. Antique ring on the right middle finger.'

'Clothes . . . pockets?'

'Clothes expensive, labelled. Daks, Jaeger, nothing flashy. Good upper-middle-class wear.'

'Time of death?'

Thomas Dresden

'Nothing too precise in the circumstances.' He poured coffee and handed her a cup.

'Parameters?'

He looked down at the file of notes on his desk. He had already forgotten the oddity of her appearance. 'Between six and ten weeks, perhaps. Not very helpful.'

'Once we identify, we can probably tie that down closer with sightings, work attendance. We'll get it down to a few days.'

Waller crossed to a box-file, opened it and carried it to her. 'These are the complete contents of the pockets.' He lifted the lid of the box-file. Inside were two or three plastic envelopes holding loose change and a crumpled Kleenex. The largest envelope contained an open leather money-fold, dry but green from immersion in water at some earlier time. Several £20 notes were visible in the left-hand fold, stained yellow above the stitched rim. Jan bent over the box.

'All the objects and clothing up to just below shoulder level have been in water. Not for long, I'd say. Not long enough to disintegrate the Kleenex. One hour at the most. A few minutes more likely.'

'Up to just below the shoulder level?'

'Shipped in, I'd guess, during the hanging.'

She nodded without speaking.

The pathologist handed her a pair of chromium tweezers. She took them and lifted the wallet from the plastic envelope, then eased out the twenty pound notes and placed them carefully on a sheet of paper on the desk. Spreading them like a fan to ensure they were all the same, she examined the numbers. 'They're new. The numbers might help with the time of death. What about dentals?'

'I'll get full records during the morning.'

'Okay.' Jan paused. 'So . . . cause of death? Asphyxiation?'

'Undoubtedly. Unless she was dead already.'

'In which case?'

Waller pursed his lips. 'How about internal haemorrhage?'

'If you say so. How come?'

Waller took a pack of 10" × 8" photographs from his desk and handed them to Jan.

'Not a pretty sight,' she said, leafing through them.

112

'Look at the last group. The skull.'

They were photographs taken after Waller had cleared away the remnants of skin and hair. He pointed to the damaged skull. Two circular indentations in the bone. 'Two blows to the head,' he said. 'The heavier blow here, in the parietal region. Another in the high right frontal region.'

'Not a bludgeon?'

'No. A hammer perhaps. Several bones in the right hand are also shattered. Here . . .' He selected a photograph.

She examined it. 'As if she was warding off the blows?'

Waller nodded.

'These blows to the head. Were they enough to kill her?'

'Very possibly.'

Jan walked back and forth in the small room. She stopped suddenly, frowning at him. 'So what do you make of the hanging?'

'CID here tell me the owner of the place where she was found liked to play dangerous games. Apparently they found a whole cupboardful of S&M gear. Whips, thumbscrews, that sort of thing.'

'They're suggesting this began as a play session? A hanging game?'

Waller shrugged. 'It doesn't hold a lot of appeal for me.'

'It probably didn't hold a lot of appeal for her. These are usually boys' games. So maybe she wasn't there voluntarily.' Jan shrugged. 'Or maybe she just liked to join the boys.' She stopped pacing. 'So . . . as she jerked on the end of the rope, the ferret, or maybe there were two or three ferrets, all piled in with hammers or whatever . . .'

Waller grimaced.

'It gives a new meaning to the phrase, "a night out with the boys", doesn't it?' Jan said.

'What do you think?'

'I think that our ferret must have been standing in five feet of water when he hit the victim. Which roughly means that we're looking for someone around eight foot six in height. Shouldn't be difficult to find.'

Waller looked at her, bemused.

'I think your CID doesn't know its arse from its elbow,' Jan said.

Waller sat heavily in his swivel chair. 'You've lost me,' he admitted.

'The lesser blow was high on the frontal region. And the heavy blow was to the parietal bone . . .'

'Yes.'

'Both were struck from above, or at least the arc of the weapon rose above her head and came down on her skull.'

'Yes.'

'So unless someone got themselves a ladder and settled it in the water in the boathouse, the blows were struck *before* she was strung up.'

'That's pretty bizarre. You mean the murderer hanged the already dead body?'

'Dead or unconscious,' Jan said. 'I don't understand it either. But it sounds as if it has to be that way. Unless we find a ladder – or a handy eight foot six suspect.'

'In this one, nothing'll surprise me.'

Jan finished her coffee and looked up at him. He was grinning.

'Something you haven't yet told me?' she said. 'Or are you just pleased to see me?'

'I was saving it up for the right moment. The corpse I signed for was not complete.'

She raised her eyebrows.

'Long hair, advanced decomposition, rodent activity to the face – nobody realised at the time that the ears were missing.'

'What?'

'That's it, Inspector. Both ears had been cut off.'

'You do that to a fox, don't you?' Jan said when she picked up Abbeline in the Market Place. 'Don't you cut off the ears after the dogs have caught him?'

'I think you cut off the tail,' he said. 'The brush. And wipe blood across the cheek of the novice huntsmen.'

They walked towards Jan's car. 'You're going to have to get your skates on, boss, if you're going to get that plane to Oz this afternoon.'

Abbeline grunted and climbed into the passenger seat.

'Where to?' Jan said when she was behind the wheel. Looking at his expression, she was sorry now she'd made the crack about Australia. He looked glum, thoughtful. 'Where to, sir?'

'First we'll take a look at this boathouse. I didn't get a chance for a real look last night. We're going to need all your legendary Liverpool tact here, Jan. This is Cambridge CID's murder, not ours.'

'Keep my mouth shut, you mean?'

He nodded. 'Ears cut off . . . what *does* that remind me of?'

She had awoken, and immediately relapsed into a numb, shocked state. The grisly body, creak of rope on the wet beam, above all the stench . . . Tessa threw back the bedclothes and stood up in the cold bedroom. To lie in bed with this image fouling her mind was intolerable.

Downstairs in the kitchen, she sat opposite Anna, a mug of coffee cupped in her hands. 'It's strange the way the mind works,' she said. 'When the Scotland Yard man Abbeline, told me it wasn't Beth last night, I thought: That's all right then. She's safe. I had this ridiculous idea that just because she hadn't been murdered, she was safe. The cold light of dawn quickly changed that. And for the first time I began to think, there's still someone dead, someone who's died horribly. And I still don't know where Beth is, whether she's safe or . . .'

'Listen,' Anna said, 'this is a time to keep a tight rein on your imagination. If you're going to stay in England, you must take things one day at a time. As it happens. No anticipating what might have happened. Very tough but very necessary.'

Tessa nodded and they sat for a moment in silence. 'You said *if* I'm going to stay in England . . . what made you say that?'

'I should have told you,' Anna said. 'After you'd taken the sleeping pill last night, Carter phoned.'

'What did he say when you told him what had happened?'

'He wants you to come straight back home. Today.'

Tessa put down her mug. 'Doesn't he realise what it means, finding the body? Doesn't he realise that, whoever it is, it's mixed up some way with the disappearance of Beth? Doesn't he realise that it almost certainly means Beth is in appalling danger?'

Anna didn't answer her directly. 'He's worried about you, Tessa.'

'I guess so.' She said it without conviction. 'I guess that's it.' She looked at her watch. 'Maybe it's better I call him. Catch him half asleep.' She stood up. 'Do you mind? I'll call collect.'

Detective Inspector Ray Rose of Cambridge CID met them on the path to the boathouse. 'Everybody's finished,' he said to Abbeline. 'No need to worry where you put your feet, sir. Except for places where the timber's rotted. This place hasn't been used as a boathouse since before the war.'

Abbeline opened the door. Inside, a warped planking walkway ran round the walls. Abbeline stepped on to it and moved cautiously to one side to let Jan and Inspector Rose enter. For a moment he stood, letting his eyes become accustomed to the half dark. The boathouse was about ten feet across and perhaps twenty-five feet long. There was no boat and the reeds and rushes, now locked in ice, had grown to the level of the walkway they were standing on. A cross beam ran at head height from one wall to the other. A length of coarse rope, severed at one end, dangled from a pulley attached to the beam. Boat-hooks and paddles rested on nails hammered into the framework; the tattered remnant of an old boat club flag hung on the far wall.

Abbeline looked down at the ice a foot or so below the level of the walkway. A hole three feet across had been hacked in the smooth surface.

'That was to release the feet, sir,' Rose explained. 'One of them was set in the ice.'

'Where do you think she was killed, Inspector?'

Rose looked at him oddly. 'She was hanged, sir.'

'Inspector Madigan tells me she also had a broken skull.'

'Inflicted afterwards, in my opinion. I think this was an S&M happening, myself. Have you seen the picture books we found in the desk? Very nasty stuff,.'

'It's not usual to have a woman involved.'

'No, sir. True, most of these hanging games are between men. But the picture book shows Mr Woodward was into bisexual orgies. Plenty of girls being knocked about as well.' He grimaced his distaste. 'Personally,' he said, 'I don't see why the game couldn't have been played just as well with a girl. If you're into that sort of thing, that is.'

'So you think . . .?'

'She was strung up here and her partner or partners went berserk with the hammer.'

Jan puffed her cheeks in disbelief.

'The other possibility,' Abbeline said carefully, 'is that the dead girl was killed or just rendered unconscious by blows from the hammer, then hauled in here and dragged up by means of that boat pulley.'

Rose shrugged. 'Perhaps. Part of the game? Perhaps, sir.'

'What do you make of the missing ears?'

'The excitement, the frenzy.'

'Has forensic finished at the cottage?'

'Just winding up now, sir. Do you want to go in?'

Abbeline shook his head. 'I've disturbed you enough.' He turned towards the door and Jan and Rose filed out before him. In the crisp, cold air, their breath billowed. 'One thing you could do for me, Inspector . . .'

'Gladly, sir.'

'If there *are* any signs of blood in the cottage, let me know, will you?'

'Of course.' Rose watched Abbeline and Jan go back down the path to where their car stood in the lane. This was the first murder case he'd been handed as his own property. Bad luck to have a senior Scotland Yard man sniffing round his heels.

They sat in a square box of an office, each wall painted bewilderingly a different shade of cream, Abbeline in a suit and tie behind the metal desk, Tessa in her outdoor coat, sitting in a wire-back chair with spindly chromium struts. 'What a truly awful room,' she said.

He nodded. 'The only way to inhabit these boxes is to keep them utterly clear of your own possessions. Try to make them more acceptable by hanging a picture or two, setting up a favourite bronze, adding your own chair, and they make the occupant look ridiculous. They're not rooms that accept the imprint of people. They'll always remain alien.'

'You've thought about this before.' She paused. 'Will you be in charge of the case? Is that how it works?'

'Not entirely. The murder you discovered last night will be handled by the local police here. My field of interest is finding your sister Beth.'

'At the moment they seem as if they might overlap.'

'Yes.'

She was silent. 'How do you go about looking for a missing person?' she said after a moment.

'We begin by creating a framework,' he said carefully. 'Her name and description are circulated to every police force in the country. They in turn are in contact with local hospitals in case of accident or a stress-induced loss of memory. That's much more common than most people think. Then we extend the framework wherever it seems necessary. To the Boston Police Department in this case. And to Interpol.' He paused. 'That's the official framework within which I'll be operating.'

'And?'

'I'll want to check with all her known friends and acquaintances in this country. I'll want to pin-point when she was last seen, where and by whom. I promise you I won't lose sight of the fact that must be uppermost in your mind – that there's a new urgency since last night.'

Tessa sat very still, her eyes on his face. 'I'd like to ask you, Mr Abbeline . . . I'd like to ask you what you are looking for?'

'I'm not sure I understand you.'

'I think you do. I'm asking are you looking for Beth – or her body?'

He got up and went to the window. Outside, across a wide expanse of snow, small black figures walked their dogs on Parker's Piece. The single Victorian lamp in the middle of the open space was alight. It was a Lowry painting. 'I won't insult you by saying I never speculate.' He turned back to face her. 'But I will say that whenever I do, I become even more prone to making mistakes. Let's just content ourselves at the moment with saying we're looking for your sister. That's the important thing.'

She smiled briefly.

'If I were to speculate,' he said, 'I'd admit it doesn't look good. That's what you wanted to hear.'

'No. But if you'd say anything less I wouldn't have been able to trust you again.'

He watched while she smiled up at him. Not a young woman's quick flashing smile. Tessa Wilson's smile was warm, unhurried. Good dark-blonde hair, a full face with a wide mouth and even teeth. Nice eyes. In six or seven years she would be matronly. Not yet. 'I'm going to try to keep you informed step by step in this operation,' he said.

'That's unusual?'

'You know it is, here or at home in the US. Every copper from the beat upwards is terrified of the press. If they choose, they can savage you. Say too much, it's rash. Too little, it's secretive. They make the rules.'

'I understand.'

'I'm proposing a deal.'

'I thought you were.'

'I keep you as fully informed as I possibly can. No holds barred. Bring you in close to one of the team. Almost.'

'In return?'

'You don't talk to the press until it's all over. I'm not trying to gag you . . .'

'You are. But you're doing it in a sort of fair and square way. I accept.' She held out her hand and he took it. Surprisingly warm and living. He wondered about her sister's hand at this moment.

He released her and sat down. 'They're overcrowded here.' He gestured to the station around them. 'Thank God. The local superintendent has asked if I could possibly operate from another base. He'll supply communications and a few extra people to set up an incident room. He's offered me two large police caravans we can set up on Parker's Piece, but I told him that, with every Cambridge college empty of undergraduates at the moment, we ought to be able to do better than that.'

'So you get your wish?'

'To move out of here?' He nodded. 'I've scouts out. You'll be told as soon as I know where we're moving.'

'I'd like to do something practical.'

'You can. Be on tap to answer the questions only you can answer.'

'Such as?'

'I went to the Market Place this morning. To your sister's flat.' He paused. 'For someone researching the Natural Sciences she has a lot of books on religion, comparative religion perhaps.'

'I didn't notice when I was there. In any case they may have been Laurie Woodward's.'

He shook his head. 'Her name's in one or two of them: *The Elizabethan Occult*, Fraser's *Golden Bough*, Fox's *Book of Martyrs*.'

'What are these books?'

'They're something that an educated student of the occult might be looking at, I suppose. Although I can't quite see where Fox's *Book of Martyrs* fits.'

'What is it?'

'A crude seventeenth-century collection of woodcuts of martyred Puritans. In its day it had a Goebbels-like propaganda value.'

'I'm baffled. This must be something new. Something Laurie introduced her to. Martyrs, whips, caftans. Don't they seem to go very much together?'

He gave her a half smile. 'It's not enough though, is it? If they go together we don't know *how* they go together. We know that Laurie Woodward practised the rough stuff, probably mostly homosexual but sometimes with women.'

'You know nothing more about the man I met at Woodward's house?'

'Perhaps.'

'You're behaving like a policeman.'

He nodded. 'Sorry.' He paused. 'When you saw him leaving the boathouse, he took off at speed, you said?'

'Yes. In a white Mini, I think it was. Burning rubber, that sort of thing.'

'He was unwise enough to keep it up. A police patrol car spotted him and gave chase, as they say.'

'Did they get him?'

'Yes. He ran the car up an embankment, got out and tried to run across a disused railway bridge. What he didn't see was that half the sleepers had been removed.'

'He fell?'

'Thirty feet. Broke one leg badly. He's at Addenbrooke's Hospital with his leg set in traction. He won't be going far. Time of accident fits. I'd like you to come with me and take a look at him.'

'Of course.'

'There, you see – I'm not just asking you to hang around.'

'This is all because of my father, isn't it?'

He looked at her. 'It's part repayment of a very large debt this country owes him. There's nothing dishonourable in that, is there?'

'I suppose not. I feel uncomfortable about getting special treatment.'

'But not *that* uncomfortable?'

She thought for a moment. 'No. Not *that* uncomfortable.'

'One more thing.' He took a postcard from his pocket and held it in his hand. 'It's a postcard of the stained glass window of King's College Chapel.'

'King's College here in Cambridge?'

'Yes, one of the biggest colleges. It's got a magnificent chapel with late-medieval stained glass windows. These.' He put the postcard down on the bare table.

She couldn't imagine this was the nave of a college chapel. It soared like a cathedral to intricate fan vaulting. Even in the postcard the colours of the stained glass glittered softly. But across the surface of the picture, as if in child's spite, someone had taken a thick red felt tip pen and scrawled a crude cross.

'Did you find this at Beth's apartment?'

'Yes.'

A chill passed through Tessa. 'Laurie Woodward's?'

'Perhaps.'

'What does it mean?'

He turned the card over. 'Is that Beth's writing?'

Tessa read: *But for 13s 4d!!!*

'There's not really enough to go on,' she said. 'I couldn't be sure.'

'We can have it analysed,' he said. 'We've got examples of both their writing.'

'I don't know what it means. 'Thirteen *s*, four *d*.' She looked up at him, her brows knitting in a question.

'It's British pre-decimal currency,' he said. 'Thirteen shillings

121

and fourpence. Before 1973 there were twenty shillings in a pound. Twelve pence in a shilling.'

She frowned. 'So thirteen shillings and fourpence is a very odd sum?'

'Yes. Except . . .' He paused. 'Yes . . . thirteen and fourpence is exactly two-thirds of a pound.'

'Does that help?'

'Not me,' he said. 'I'm a post-decimal lad. I'm going to have to ask my elders and betters. I wonder who she or Laurie Woodward planned to send it to?'

'I can't see Beth scrawling red crosses over pictures of superb buildings.'

'No.' Abbeline stood up. 'Let's get out of this box. Let's take a look at this young man in traction at Addenbrooke's.'

Jack Abbeline stood looking down at the man in the bed in the private ground-floor room at Addenbrooke's Hospital. 'Lulu, you call yourself,' he said.

'I'm in no fit state to talk,' the man complained. 'I'm still suffering from the effects of the anaesthetic. Anything I say won't be admissible as evidence. I want a lawyer.'

'Have you finished?'

'I didn't kill him. I didn't kill Laurie.'

'You didn't.'

'I swear to you . . .'

'I said, you didn't. It wasn't Laurie. He came off his motorbike on the Granchester bend about six weeks ago. Only he wasn't as lucky as you.'

'You mean he copped it?'

Abbeline nodded.

'Jesus . . . Then who was it in the boathouse?'

Abbeline examined the man's right leg, raised in a traction apparatus and heavily encased in plaster. He tapped the foot. 'Perhaps you'd like me to be the first one to sign it?' he said.

'Very funny.'

'In a couple of minutes I'm going to bring someone in here. I want you to behave yourself. Answer questions politely and clearly. Understand me, Mason?'

The man in the bed stiffened. 'How do you know who I am?'

'Peter Howard Mason. Fingerprints on the answering machine. Once arrested with Laurie Woodward for assaulting a prostitute. Three convictions for robbery of men you'd picked up. You're an ageing rent boy, a thief and a bit of a tearaway. Remember, behave yourself.' Abbeline turned and opened the door.

Tessa was standing across the corridor talking to the policeman on guard. Crossing towards Abbeline, she paused in the doorway.

'Come in, Mrs Wilson.' Abbeline waited for her to come forward, then closed the door behind her. 'This is the suspect, Peter Howard Mason.'

'What am I suspected of?'

Abbeline looked at him and he fell silent. 'Is this the man you saw in Laurie Woodward's house last night, Mrs Wilson?'

He looked very different in hospital pyjamas. They stared at each other. His blue eyes glittered. 'Yes,' she said.

'What were you doing there?' Abbeline asked him.

'I went to meet Laurie, that's all.'

'How did you know him?'

'Met him in a club in Soho, about two years ago.'

'A homosexual club?'

He shrugged. 'Laurie played it all ways. Knight and squire – lady and skivvy. As long as there was someone to rub their nose in it, he didn't care whether it was girl or boy.'

'You partied at the boathouse?'

'Ideal. Out of the way. Nobody to hear the yelps.'

Tessa looked at him with baffled distaste.

'Who attended these parties?'

'No shortage of bents in a town like Cambridge. He'd have a few people round. Bit of a rave up.'

'Girls too?'

'Sometimes. Laurie liked to mix it.'

'When did you last see him?'

Mason hesitated. 'Before I went inside last time. Two months ago. So that lets me out, right? I was doing time when whoever it was was strung up.'

'We're not sure yet how long ago it happened. You're not off the hook yet.'

Mason bit his lip, staring at Abbeline from under his brows.

'Did you know an American woman he was seeing from time to time?'

'Beth, yes.'

'Did she ever attend the parties?'

Mason watched Tessa stiffen, and grinned.

'Did Beth Naylor ever attend the parties, Mason?'

'Never saw her there,' he said.

'But you met her?'

'Couple of times in the street. He introduced me as his cousin.'

'So she didn't know he was bisexual?'

He paused. 'She knew something.'

'What do you mean?'

'She wasn't very friendly.'

Tessa leaned her back against the door jamb. She felt slightly sick. She was not sure she understood all Mason was saying, but could Beth really have chosen a man like Laurie Woodward, knowing anything about him at all?

'Do you have anything you think you should be telling me?'

'What do you mean?'

'It would be a serious mistake not to come clean now.'

'I was inside when anything happened. I'm in the clear. Nothing to tell. Scout's honour.'

'The parties you talked about,' Abbeline said, 'at Woodward's house . . . I'll want a list of the people present.'

'First names only. Charles, William, Robert.'

'For your own sake, let's hope you can do better than that when my inspector comes to take a statement off you. I want you to rack your brains, Mason. Let's talk about girls.'

'I'd rather not!'

'The body you found was a young woman in her twenties.'

'Was it? Was it really? You couldn't tell, hanging up there.' He frowned. 'I didn't think women went in for that sort of thing. Known plenty of boys, but never heard of a girl got her kicks that way.'

'For her it might not have been part of a game.'

'You mean, Laurie forced her?' He shrugged.

'Possible?'

'Laurie liked fun. He'd get it any way he could.'

'The girl,' Abbeline said. 'The dead girl. Natural blonde. About five foot four tall.'

'A scrubber?'

Abbeline shook his head. 'I'd say no. Does that description ring any bells?'

'Not much of a description.'

'At the moment, all we've got.'

'Means nothing to me.' Mason's eyes strayed to Tessa. 'He knows I didn't do it,' he said. 'The only thing that's keeping me in Cambridge is this fucking plaster.'

'There's nothing to stop me charging you with burglary, Mason. When they found you, you had a sackful of Woodward's trinkets on you.'

'All my things I'd lent him when I was in prison.'

'Lifted from his house when you thought he was hanging in the boathouse,' Abbeline went on relentlessly. 'That won't look good in court. He paused. 'Did he ever talk to you about Beth?'

Mason looked at Tessa. 'This her sister? American. Different colouring but a bit similar to look at.'

'About Beth,' Abbeline said.

'All I remember is we had a bit of a laugh sometimes when he first met her. About Americans being so serious about things.'

'What sort of things?'

'Life, sex . . .'

'They sound like pretty serious subjects to me,' Tessa said.

'Did he talk about sex and Beth Naylor?'

'No, no.' Mason shook his head and winced with pain as the movement reached his leg. 'There was no sex. There was nothing like that between them.'

'Then what was the relationship between them?'

'I don't know.' He stopped and looked away.

'What was it between them, Mason?'

He turned his head slowly towards Abbeline. 'I tell you, I don't know. All I know is, Laurie told me she wouldn't so much as let him put a hand on her.'

'You believe him?' Tessa said as they left Mason's room and started down the long corridor.

'I certainly believe that the relationship between Beth and Laurie Woodward was a whole lot different from what you assumed.'

'I have to give you that, Superintendent. What's the next move?'

'Jan Madigan, my inspector, interviews your sister's friends and works on establishing the last sighting of Beth. She'll be staying at the Garden House Hotel. You can contact her there if you need her.'

'And you?'

'I have to be back in London this afternoon.'

Uniformed nurses and young, white-coated doctors passed them. 'Is this the end of the senior officer's involvement in Beth's case?'

Abbeline stopped. 'No. No, it's not.' He paused. 'I just have to be in London for a couple of hours to cancel a trip I was planning.'

'A trip?'

'This is not the end of the senior officer's involvement, Mrs Wilson,' he said crisply. 'It's the beginning.'

She realised then. 'It was a holiday,' she said.

'Yes.'

'Something you were really looking forward to?'

He relaxed and they walked on. 'I'm sorry,' he said. 'I was taking it out on you. I was going to Australia.'

She nodded. 'With someone special?'

'That was the idea.' He opened the swing door into the hospital courtyard. 'I'll buy you a drink at the Pelican before I leave.'

CHAPTER FIFTEEN

Lit up and decorated for Christmas, Harrods was an extraordinary sight to Tessa. Certainly, she decided, Jordans in Boston was not really in the same league. The great halls glittered and the people who streamed through them spoke a dozen languages. The actual products on sale, the leather, jewellery, clothes, furnishings, all seemed to take second place to the visitors, she thought, as if they were assigned a less important role in the extraordinary occurrence that was Harrods.

At least she thought this until she arrived in the Food Hall where she was to meet Laura Portal. Then the sights and smells of the produce assailed her and she wandered in a pleasant, gluttony-induced haze, examining hams from Brabenham, pheasants and partridges, a whole display of the world's cheeses, jars of caviar, of foie gras from Alsace and Perigord, smoked salmon from Scotland and smoked sturgeon from the Caspian . . .

Laura Portal had called as soon as Tessa had got back to Anna's house. There was no doubt about the agitation in her voice. 'Tessa darling,' she said, 'I'm having a twinge of conscience. It's a small thing, I'm sure, but I haven't been entirely frank with you. Would you meet me? In London?'

Harrods had been chosen although Tessa had said she would have no difficulty finding her way out to Barnes. But Laura had insisted. In a voice that veered between shaky and unnaturally firm, she had said: 'I'd like us to meet at Harrods for another reason too.'

'Okay,' Tessa said. 'I'll be there.'

The first few moments of their meeting had been difficult. Laura sounded stilted and cold.

'What is it, Laura? What's troubling you?'

127

She shook her head. 'Will you come with me?' she said, and turned away to lead Tessa to the lifts. 'This morning,' she said, 'I had a phone call from someone here at Harrods, in the travel department. I'd picked up the airline ticket for Sally back in November. Apparently they'd asked me to leave my number.'

The lift doors opened and they entered. Laura dropped her voice. 'The caller this morning asked . . .' Her voice broke.

The doors opened and Tessa guided her out. 'Asked what, Laura?'

They walked towards the travel department. 'The man told me that in certain circumstances Sally could make a claim. I had no idea what he was talking about.'

'What sort of claim?'

'Apparently she had taken out some insurance against not being able to catch her flight.'

Tessa stopped. 'What are you saying, Laura?' Even in this huge store, with its bright, warm atmosphere, she could feel a desperate chill. 'Are you saying that Sally didn't make the flight to India?'

'There could be some mistake,' Laura said. 'There must be.'

It took only a few minutes at the desk. The travel clerk insisted to Tessa there was no mistake. Laura Portal stood slightly to one side as if it wasn't really her daughter they were talking about.

'No mistake, madam,' the man behind the desk confirmed. 'We know that seat was not taken up because it was reassigned immediately before the flight.'

'Either he wants me to carry on digging or he doesn't,' Ken Russell said on the phone to Cambridge. 'If he's no longer interested in the goings on of Leonard Passmore and his bloody Millennium Church, I'd appreciate knowing. Then I can pack up and go home and replace the glass in my greenhouse.'

'Hold on, hold on.' Jan Madigan was using the phone in the reception area at Parker's Piece Station and felt very exposed to the curious glances of the young coppers all around her. Other times she would have revelled in the attention; now she lowered her voice and turned her back on the room. 'Listen, Ken. The boss is still interested in Passmore, but he's got a lot on his plate at the moment.'

'I've been trying to get him all day. Left messages everywhere.'

'I know,' Jan said. 'But this Cambridge job has ballooned, Ken. The American woman found a dead 'un last night. So far unidentified. This whole thing's running faster and deeper than we thought.'

'Okay, I forgive him.' Ken Russell said reluctantly. 'But I still need to talk to him. Put him on, will you?'

'He's on his way to London. He says he'll meet you at the Yard sometime just after seven tonight.'

'Bang goes my greenhouse repairs. Okay, Jan. I'll be there.'

They caught a taxi and rode through the brightly lit streets. There was evidence of Christmas in almost every shop window but for most of the journey the two women stayed quiet, hands clasped on the seat between them.

'I wasn't totally frank with you because I was deeply ashamed,' Laura confessed.

'Tell me now.'

The taxi ran down Fulham Road and over the bridge near Chelsea Football ground. Laura turned her face from the window. 'I wasn't frank when I told you how Sally had taken the news that Robert was not her father. Or, perhaps even worse, was possibly not her father.'

'She was very upset, you said.'

'She was much, much more than that.' Laura nodded slowly, the memory visibly painful. 'We'd always got on so well. We'd always been such great friends . . .'

Tessa waited.

'In fact she came back to London utterly furious. She came to see me in Barnes boiling with anger. She had some pretty harsh words for a mother who didn't even know who'd fathered her child. It didn't help that I agreed with her. I tried to explain that we were not talking about me *now*. We were talking about a young girl, several years less than Sally's age. Totally infatuated by a man who was immensely attractive, intelligent, and above all *famous*. I was immensely flattered apart from anything else.'

'It made no difference to Sally?'

'However much I insisted we were talking about a young girl in totally different circumstances . . . no.'

They left the taxi at Sally's flat in Fulham and entered the communal hallway littered with junk mail. 'She couldn't come to terms with it. She wouldn't take my calls. She left for India . . . or I thought she left for India . . . without saying goodbye.'

She fitted the key into the lock and they both walked into the flat. It was small, a tiny hallway direct into the living room. Three packed cases stood on the sofa. In the bedroom, Sally's passport and airline ticket lay on the made-up bed. 'Oh my God,' Laura Portal said softly. 'What a dreadful world we live in!'

CHAPTER SIXTEEN

The powerful engines howled as the jets took off on the runway on the other side of the road. But once inside the hotel the noise was cut off cleanly.

Abbeline brushed the glittering diamonds of sleet off his shoulders and asked a man in brown Excelsior uniform where *The Scattersby Inheritance* press conference was being held.

He was directed to the McCormack Room to the left of the bar and walked through to find his way blocked by two security men behind a desk.

'Press or cast, sir?' one of them asked.

'Neither.' Abbeline reached into his pocket.

'Only press and cast allowed in, sir. Unless you have an invitation, of course.' He watched Abbeline's hand as it came out of his inside pocket.

'Scotland Yard,' Abbeline said. It was the quickest way.

'Will you be needing assistance?' the security man asked hopefully.

'No. I'm not arresting anybody. At least, not yet.'

'Just straight through, then.' The man pointed to the tall double doors.

Abbeline reached the doors and paused. He felt a vague nausea as he reached for the door handle. Jo would be surrounded by a dozen journalists and photographers. He was going to have to settle for a quick dozen words with her before she was whisked off again. He turned the handle and the door swung open.

One wall of a long room was lined with tables carrying drinks and canapés. Waiters in red jackets circulated among the guests. The distribution of people in the room was unequal. One end was

131

almost empty, occupied by a few couples or groups talking and drinking together, separate from the main group. From the centre of this second, much denser throng, camera lights flashed constantly. It wasn't difficult for him to guess who was in the middle of it.

A publicity girl attached herself to Abbeline. 'Hello,' she said brightly. 'The traffic?'

He frowned.

'The traffic. Held you up? You missed our producer Sepp Lander's briefing on Australia, I'm afraid.'

'I've missed more than that,' he said.

'Ah, no. Jo Saunders hasn't done her bit yet. I've got a copy here for you.' She opened a folder and took out several pink pages stapled together. 'She writes these herself,' the girl affirmed. 'They're not the product of some company PR department.'

'You surprise me,' Abbeline said.

'Oh, yes. Jo's by no means the oversexed bimbo she plays in *Scattersby*.'

'She's a bit old to be called a bimbo, anyway, isn't she?' Abbeline said mildly.

'I'll give you a biog. and get you a drink. I'm Patsy, incidentally, I'm new on the team. And you are . . .?'

'Jack Abbeline.'

'Of . . .?'

'Scotland Yard.'

She laughed. And waited.

'I'm not a journalist, Patsy. I'm a friend of Jo's. I'll do without the biog. – but I'd be very grateful for a drink.'

'Okay.' The girl frowned uncertainly. 'Sure.'

As she crossed the room towards the drinks table, the centre throng began to break up and Abbeline saw Jo over the heads of journalists and photographers. She was wearing a light summer linen suit and a wide-brimmed hat with faint echoes of an Australian bush hat. A life sized model kangaroo stood beside her and two photographers were taking final shots of her with the kangaroo's paws round her waist. As she turned away she saw Abbeline.

She lifted her hand. 'No more for the moment, boys,' she said, coming quickly towards him. 'There'll be a chance later.'

Two or three journalists followed her, asking for comments, but she skilfully brushed them off.

'Hallo, darling.' She lifted her face and he pecked her cheek so as not to spoil her make-up. 'What a bear garden.' She took him by the arm and led him to a window in the corner of the room. The photographers were picking up shots of the rest of the cast. Some of the journalists tried to hang about within earshot but a blank-eyed look from Jo moved them back a few paces.

'The thought of getting on that plane and relaxing for twenty-four hours is absolute bliss.' She looked at him. 'For you too, I'd say. You look tense. Listen, we're going to have a holiday together.'

He was shaking his head.

Her smile faded. 'Oh, Jack.' She turned quickly so that her face was away from any of the journalists. 'Tell me. You can't come?'

He caught the warm odour of a cannabis spliff before he heard the familiar, fruity voice. 'Abbeline.' Leo Bannerman drew deeply on a long, ragged cigarette. The champagne glass tilted in his hand. 'Can't come with us, after all? Catastrophe, old chap. No one to take your place on the beat?'

'Careful,' Abbeline said.

Bannerman took a step back.

'Leo,' said Jo. 'Be a darling. Go and talk to someone else for a moment.'

'Must tell you this lovely story Dickie told me . . .'

'Later, Leo, please. It can wait.'

'Not this one. Apparently Dickie . . .'

Abbeline took his arm and swung him round. His mouth, came close to the other man's ear. 'Find someone else to talk to,' he said. 'Or I'll hold you for questioning on possession of cannabis until the plane's halfway to Australia.'

Bannerman detached his arm carefully from Abbeline's grip, smiled towards the nearest group of journalists, drained his champagne glass and moved quickly away across the room.

'What did you say to him?'; Jo said as he turned back to her.

'I asked him to do the decent thing,' Abbeline said shortly. 'You know old Leo – he couldn't resist it.'

She looked at him for a long moment. 'You're not coming,' she said. 'You're here to tell me something's come up.'

'Yes.'

'Your blue-rinsed American lady?'

'She's not exactly that,' Abbeline said. 'But she's the reason.'

The producer, Sepp Lander, was calling Jo from across the room.

'Kiss me, Jack,' she said. 'To hell with the make-up.'

'And the photographers?' He kissed her lightly on the lips.

'I'm scared,' she said. 'When you told me you were coming, I had the whole thing planned.'

'I'm not following you. You had the whole thing planned?'

'For you and me, I mean.'

'It's not for long. The plans will have to wait till you get back.'

She gave him a tight smile.

'It'll be all right, Jo.'

'I really do love you, Jack. It sometimes comes out in a pretty funny way, but I really do.' She paused. 'Stay out of harm's way, yes?'

'Trust me.'

Sepp Lander's voice rose above the background noise. 'Jo, could we have you over here, please?'

'Call me as soon as you get to Australia,' Abbeline urged.

'I will,' she said absently.

'It looks like this is the only chance we're going to have of saying goodbye without an arch of flashbulbs and three dozen journalists throwing confetti.'

She squeezed his hand. 'I do love you, Jack.'

For a moment they seemed to be isolated from the hubbub around them.'

'I love you too, Jo,' he said.

She looked up at him, a strange, uncertain glance. 'Then ask me to marry you.'

'What here, now?'

'Yes. Here. Now.'

Suddenly he knew she was deadly serious. He shook his head slowly. 'No, Jo. Not like this. I can't ask you to marry me like this.'

She was squeezing tight on his hand. 'Okay then, I'm asking *you*.'

'*Not here, Jo.*'

'I want an answer, Jack.'

He stood there while she slowly loosened her grip on his hand. 'Will you, Jack? Will you marry me?' Her hand fell away from his. 'Will you, Jack?'

'This is not the place, for Christ's sake, Jo! There are a hundred people in this room, most of them with their eyes and cameras fixed on you. If you think I'm going to ask you to marry me here, you're wrong.'

'This isn't a publicity stunt, Jack.'

'We'll talk when you get back.'

She looked at him for a long moment. 'No, Jack,' she said. 'By then it could be too late.' Turning abruptly away, she walked to the waiting group of journalists.

At the door the PR girl, Patsy, stopped him. She offered him a glass of champagne. He stopped and drank it down quickly.

'You're not really from Scotland Yard, are you?' she said. 'Which paper *are* you from?'

'*Psychic News*,' he said, handing her back the glass. 'I've got a bad feeling about this Australian trip.'

CHAPTER SEVENTEEN

Arriving home, Jack Abbeline threw his briefcase into the corner of the sofa, peeled off his jacket and raked his tie undone.

It wasn't a large flat, less than half the size of Jo's, with one bedroom and a second room he used as an office. From the living room he looked through at the blinking light on the answerphone on his office desk. For a moment he stood mesmerised by its insistent blink. Then he slammed the office door on it and poured himself a large Glenmorangie.

Why, in God's name, hadn't he said yes? What was it that stopped him, left the word trembling in the air between them? But left the word, as far as Jo was concerned, unsaid.

She had turned and walked away. And throughout the next minutes, surrounded by journalists, ushered by Sepp Lander on to the dais, she had never once looked his way.

But then, why should she?

Sipping the malt whisky, he tried to imagine being without her. Since they had first met last year there had hardly been a day they hadn't seen each other, sometimes for not more than a few minutes – a cup of coffee in her dressing room as the make-up girl added a few touches to her face or a glass of wine at the wine bar opposite the Yard. Once or twice she had had to do a quick trip abroad for promotional work but in England somehow they'd managed to make sure they saw something of each other almost every day. And almost every night. Almost, because they both consciously rationed the nights they spent together. Neither of them, so he'd thought, had any wish to become an established married couple.

Abbeline put on some Bessie Smith, turned it low and sat on the sofa, savouring the smoky velvet of the Glenmorangie.

He knew Jo Saunders was not just another woman in his life. He knew clearly enough that she was the one he would have to make the all important decision about. But it was a decision he had backed away from. Before tonight it was a decision she had equally backed away from when she saw his own hesitation. For the last year the unmade decisions had remained, binding them together, holding them apart. Until tonight. Until tonight they had been two outwardly confident people afraid of the future. But tonight Jo had spoken for the future. A future to be spent together.

The past was easy. At least, *their* past. They had met the year before when the flat next-door, in Abbeline's modest block, had been occupied by a new tenant. Prem Garcia, an Indian television executive, had suddenly moved out. His place was taken by a woman who used only the old service elevator and who seemed to leave the flat before seven in the morning and return after midnight. The only evidence for Abbeline's mounting curiosity about her was the haze of very agreeable perfume she trailed on the landing and the occasional click of high heels on the Edwardian tiling in the hall of her flat.

Strangest of all in Abbeline's view was Prem Garcia's disappearance without a word. He and Jack Abbeline had been good friends, having a regular drink together, sometimes picking up a late-night curry across the street. So why hadn't he mentioned the change? And had he sold the flat, rented it, or just lent it out? He would have to catch this woman and ask, Abbeline decided.

That February was a busy time. A Greek diplomat had stolen some files from his embassy and was believed to be trying to sell them to Turkish diplomats in London. Tracing the man and discreetly persuading him to hand over the documents had filled Abbeline's thoughts for the best part of the month. The night it was finished he had parked his car in the small car park of Seaton Mansions and walked through to take the lift as he always did. Behind him he was aware that another car had parked and he stood holding open the lift door, waiting for the driver to come through into the small front hall.

No one came. Instead he heard the clash of the grille on the rear service lift and the slow whine of the cage ascending.

He got into the passenger lift and pressed the button, thinking no more about it. As he got out at his floor he heard the slower tradesmen's lift come to a stop beyond the service door. He stood, curious now, deliberately taking his time to find his keys as the footsteps approached and the service door swung open.

What he remembered most from his first conscious glimpse of Jo Saunders' face was her shocked expression.

'I live here,' Abbeline explained, pointing at his own door.

She relaxed and came forward. 'Hi.' She held out her hand. 'Prem told me I'd have Scotland Yard next to me. Jack Abbeline. Is that you?'

They shook hands.

'Prem still owns the flat?' he asked.

'Yes.' She smiled, a warm, friendly, even-toothed smile. 'I'm a temporary occupant.'

He thought she was a very good-looking woman. He also had a vague idea that he'd seen her before.

'Prem asked me to apologise to you when I saw you,' she said. 'He moved out so quickly he had no time to say goodbye. As a matter of fact,' she said, 'I was planning to knock on your door and ask you in for a drink this very evening.'

He smiled. 'I'm not sure I believe you, but I accept.'

'I must remember I'm dealing with Scotland Yard. No little white lies. How about now?'

They had spent an easy evening talking mainly about themselves. She told him she was an actress but realising he hadn't recognised her, said nothing about *The Scattersby Inheritance*. Nothing about the real reason she was hiding in Prem Garcia's flat.

At eight o'clock he suggested they go out to the restaurant across the road.

'How about a pizza?' she said. 'Delivered here.'

'Okay.' He had brought in some Pouilly Fuissé from his own flat and got up to open a second bottle. 'You don't have to tell me what's going on,' he said slowly. 'But we might as well get off on the right footing.'

'What's going on?'

'Prem vacates his flat virtually overnight. A mysterious lady moves in who uses only chauffeured cars . . .'

'How did you know that?'

'However early I leave there's no strange car in the car park. A mysterious lady who only uses the service lift. Who is shocked to run into her neighbour. Who won't even cross the road to a good restaurant and prefers a home delivery pizza . . .'

She laughed. 'Okay. A fair cop.' She held out her glass for him to fill it. 'Have you ever heard of *The Scattersby Inheritance?*'

'Of course.'

'But you've never watched it.'

'No. I'm not going to claim that's because I'm above watching soaps . . .'

'Good. Because I'm not above playing in them.'

'Your face.'

'What's wrong with it?'

'Remarkably little. But it's familiar.'

She smiled. 'Fame at last. I find I like you very much, Jack Abbeline. What good taste of Prem to have a neighbour like you.'

'So who are you hiding from?'

'Partly the press. Partly the husband I'm just divorcing. Leo Bannerman.'

'Ah.'

'You've heard of Leo?'

'Yes.'

'He's a serious actor. He's also a serious drinker. And a serious skunk. But until the story fades off the front page of the tabloids, I have to stay here.'

'Long may it take.'

'Let's drink to that,' she said, 'before you order the pizza.'

By the time the story faded, another one had opened. Jack Abbeline and Jo Saunders were together, tentatively at first as two proud people must be, but very slowly moving towards something permanent. They both knew that even while they both delayed that final decision. Except that tonight Jo had taken it. And he had delayed again.

By eight-thirty Abbeline had drunk three Glenmorangies and listened to all the Bessie Smith, Billie Holiday and Sister Ernestine Washington tapes he could take. Except to get a drink and change the tape he had not moved from the corner of the sofa. The sofa opposite the closed office door.

When his glass was empty again and the ache of missing Jo had been alcoholically diminished enough for him to think about other things, he pushed himself to his feet and went into the office.

The answerphone light gave off a double blink. Two messages. He pushed the play button and sat down heavily behind his desk.

Ken Russell's voice echoed harshly. 'Ken speaking. I stayed on here at the Yard until nearly eight. I'm at home if you need me. Otherwise I'll be in the office nine o'clock tomorrow. I know you'll be there because you're down for a meeting with the Commander at ten-thirty. I think I have something interesting on Leonard Passmore. *I* think it's interesting anyway.'

Abbeline grunted. He had completely forgotten that he was supposed to meet his sergeant that evening. It wasn't hard to hear the irritation in Ken's voice.

The machine clicked and the second message filled the room. A woman's voice, American, subdued: 'Hi. This is Tessa Wilson. I'm in London. At the house of Laura Portal. Please give me a call at 0181-148 3333. I'm sorry to call you at home but it is urgent.'

Abbeline stood up and spun his empty glass in his hand as he looked down at the machine. He had given Mrs Wilson his home number because there was no proper office set-up yet in Cambridge. He hadn't expected her to use it.

He picked up the phone and buttoned the number she had given. A middle-aged voice said: 'Laura Portal' and he explained who he was.

After a few moments of silence, Tessa Wilson came on the line. 'Mr Abbeline,' she said. 'I won't apologise again for using your home number. I really do think I have something that has a bearing on Beth's disappearance. May I meet you tomorrow morning?'

'Of course. Do you want to tell me what it is?'

'I'd sooner tell you face to face.'

'Okay, I'll be in my office from . . . Hold it. I have a meeting first thing.' He knew he had to give Ken time on the Passmore investigation. And then he was due in Loverell's office at ten-thirty.

'You're tied up tomorrow morning,' she said.

'Yes. How urgent is this?'

'God knows,' she said. 'It seems pretty urgent to me.'

'Where are you now?'

'In Barnes.' She dropped her voice. 'But don't come here. Somewhere nearby?'

'Can you get to the Sun Inn? Next to the pond.'

'I'll find it.'

'Half an hour?'

'I'll be there.'

They sat in a corner apart from the pre-Christmas celebrations going on in the main bar. Abbeline had been here several times before with Jo. If not exactly an actors' pub, the Sun Inn is at least a place often used by the many actors who live in Barnes. Several of them friends of Jo.

With an effort Abbeline turned his mind back to Tessa Wilson. She sat opposite him, her face drawn with worry. He pushed the glass of white wine she had ordered towards her, encouraging her to start talking.

'You won't remember,' she said, 'but the name Laura Portal was down on the list of Beth's friends in England, which I gave the police.'

'Laura and Sally Portal.'

'You do remember.'

He nodded. He was silent while she told him, step by step, first what Laura had told her about her affair with Tessa's father, then what had happened in Harrods today.

'And afterwards you went to Sally Portal's flat?'

'Her mother had a key. Her cases were there, packed. Passport and tickets on the bed. She parked her car in a lockup garage round the corner. That was empty.'

He listened, expressionless.

She felt a flash of irritation. 'You're not going to say the fact that Sally didn't catch her flight has nothing to do with Beth's disappearance?'

'I'd be a fool if I did,' he said slowly. 'Two young women who know each other, who were both shocked it appears by the discovery that your father may have been Sally's father as well . . . Two young women who seem to have gone missing at the same time. No, there's a connection there all right. I've no idea what it is – but it's there.' He paused. 'How well did you know Sally?'

'Not very. She was definitely Beth's friend rather than mine.'

He twirled the glass of Perrier until the ice clinked. 'Why did you think the news of Sally not taking the flight was so important I had to hear it tonight?'

She took a deep breath. 'You know why.'

Her eyes were on him. He knew she wanted him to be the first to say it. He said slowly: 'Because you think it was Sally hanging there in the boathouse?'

He thought for a moment she was going to faint. Her face paled, her head moved to one side and he reached out a hand and held her arm. But all she said was: 'Yes . . . God knows why, God knows how anyone can relate that thing hanging there to a living human being, but I know now it was Sally. I'm sure of it.'

CHAPTER EIGHTEEN

From the Sun Inn Abbeline and Tessa called a taxi and rode across the river towards Chelsea.

'Laura Portal has her sister staying with her tonight. She's out of her mind with worry but still hasn't made the connection.'

'The possible connection.'

'The possible connection,' Tessa parroted. 'I couldn't bear to stay there tonight. I found myself avoiding her eyes. I thought she'd see it in my face. I told her I had to get back to Cambridge.'

'I'll buy you dinner then get you a car to take you back to Cambridge. This is a bill the Foreign Office is picking up.'

She shook her head. She told him she couldn't face a real dinner whoever was picking up the tab. 'Tonight,' she said, 'I can't find anything to feel celebratory about. I'll take this cab on to Liverpool Street and catch the train.'

'You're going to have to eat something.'

'On the train?'

'I doubt it.'

She shrugged unhappily. 'I can wait.'

'Listen,' he said. 'I make a respectable omelette. And I have a bottle of Château d'Angludet 1983 that probably should be drunk about now.'

'Isn't this a bit beyond the call of duty?'

'Not really duty,' he said. 'This is not the best night of my life. Not the best of yours. Let's just agree to have an omelette together and drink a bottle of decent wine.'

It was after eleven by the time they got to the flat. She took off her coat and drifted towards the bookshelves while he opened and chopped garlic and parsley in the kitchen.

The shelves, she saw, carried a lot of history and biography. Burke, Napoleon, Madame de Stael, Turgenev, Hitler, Lenin, Oscar Wilde, Joan of Arc . . . It was a good room, high-ceilinged with wide Edwardian windows, the curtains unpulled. There was a mahogany sideboard, two small old pine cupboards, a Chesterfield, and two armchairs arranged around a low dough bin that served as a coffee table. On the walls the pictures were early twentieth-century landscapes and one small head and shoulders cartoon in oils. American abstract expressionism was clearly not for Jack Abbeline.

Through a half-open door she saw an office, an old comfortable swivel chair behind an oak desk.

Her eye caught the small cartoon again and she moved closer. A strong face with mutton-chop whiskers. A well-shaped mouth and eyes that sparkled with a tiny touch of white oxide on the pupils. She turned towards the open door to the kitchen. 'I think he looks like you,' she said.

He looked up from the chopping board. 'Who does?'

'The Victorian gent in the picture here. Is that possible?' She came and stood in the doorway, leaning against the doorjamb.

'Possible,' he said. 'it's my great-grandfather. He was the Scotland Yard detective who didn't quite catch Jack the Ripper. A man of as much mystery as the Ripper himself. The family story is that he knew who the Ripper was and accepted early retirement on a fat pension in exchange for keeping mum.'

She was peering at the bent brass nameplate underneath the picture. 'Frederick *Abberline*,' she said, spelling out the surname. 'It's spelt differently.'

'It's not uncommon for a Victorian family name of the lower orders to pick up or drop a letter on the way. My grandfather settled on Abbeline and it's been Abbeline ever since.'

'What happened to Great-grandfather Fred?'

'As Jack the Ripper's fame grew, Fred's shrank. He retired to Bournemouth and never mentioned the Ripper again.' He whisked the eggs, added chopped girolles and poured them into the pan.

He smiled. 'It all conceals a minor Victorian tragedy. My grandfather says Frederick died an unhappy man. If he did accept a pension bribe from the Police Commissioner, it serves him right.'

For a few minutes she helped him lay the table in the kitchen. 'In case you're really impressed,' he said, 'omelettes are the only thing I can cook.'

They sat down and he poured the wine, swirled it in his glass, drank a little, pulling the wine through his teeth. Then he sat back and lifted his eyebrows.

'Is it okay?' she asked, slightly alarmed at his reaction.

He laughed. 'Sorry about the performance. It's nectar. Before I served a year in Interpol in Lyon, I knew nothing about wine, nothing much about food. But three hundred and sixty-five lunches, discussed, examined, criticised and anatomised by my French colleagues left their mark, I'm afraid. I came back to London the complete wine snob, persuaded as much as they are that France has the best food, the best cooking, and the best wine in the world. I'm brainwashed.'

She smiled. 'It's good of you to ask me here,' she said. 'But I'm thinking about that train. Is there a hotel nearby?'

'Earl's Court is a hotel area. The Hallam's an okay place. There'll be no problem.'

'On your head.' She lifted her glass and drank.

When they finished their omelettes he got out some cheese and French bread. She studied the cheeses – orange rind, black ring – then looked up and saw him looking at her.

'Fill me in a bit,' he said. 'What sort of upbringing did you and Beth have? Were you close? Did you get on well together?'

'Is that an official question?'

'No. Not entirely. But it might help to know.'

'Okay.' She cut herself some cheese and nibbled on it for a moment or two. 'At different times in our lives I guess there was a fair amount of sisterly competition between Beth and myself. For our father's attention, that sort of thing. I thought that was all long past.' She leaned over and picked up her bag. 'Until I found this in her room at Market Place. I suppose I should have given it to you before. You'll want to check out this guy Alan at Oxford. But that's not what I'm showing it to you for.'

He read it quickly and pursed his lips as he came to the end. 'I'd like to keep this,' was all he said.

147

She nodded. 'It doesn't seem to be that important now. When I first read it, it hurt.'

'How did your mother fit into the family?'

'A troubled, sad woman,' Tessa said. 'She died when I was just turned twenty, and Beth was twelve. Drowned off Cape Cod. Maybe she let herself drown, I don't know.'

'Is that possible?'

'She fought a long struggle against instability, depression. She thought she found comfort in the Bible but she read it as a yardstick to measure her own failure.' Tessa paused. 'Sometimes it got too much for her. Two or three times she went to hospital for quite long periods of treatment.'

'She knew about your father's affairs?'

'There were so many he hardly troubled to disguise them in the last few years. He wasn't a bastard or a brute around the house. He was cheerful, fun to be with – he just had affairs and didn't really care if my mother knew.'

'And the knowledge didn't help the family's problems?'

'The affairs took us three different ways. My mother suffered. I revelled in them. Beth pretended they never existed. Even into her twenties, she professed to be ignorant of the facts.'

'And when your mother died?'

'I think it just intensified the competition between Beth and me for our father's time and attention. Things only quietened down in the last years before he died. Less philandering on his part as he got older, our interests moving elsewhere.'

He poured another glass of wine.

Carter Wilson was worried. He had phoned the house Tessa was supposed to be staying at and Anna van Gelden had said she was in London, meeting Laura Portal. He had then phoned Laura and she had said Tessa was meeting someone from Scotland Yard and then taking a train straight back to Cambridge. It was now midnight and he had phoned the van Gelden woman again and there was still no sign of Tessa.

'I'm sure you don't have to worry, Mr Wilson,' Anna said soothingly. 'If her meeting went on late, she's probably taken a hotel room.'

'How can you say,' Carter Wilson said, straining to keep his voice reasonable, 'that I don't have to worry? Her sister's disappeared. Somebody has been found murdered, and now there's no sign of Tessa herself.' His voice rose. 'Of course I have to worry.'

'I mean that if she's with Superintendent Abbeline, there's no need to worry.'

'But we're not sure she's with this man Abbeline. And what would she be doing with him after midnight anyway?'

Anna van Gelden lifted her eyebrows but said nothing.

'This is just not good enough.' Carter Wilson seemed to be talking more to himself than to her.

'I'll get her to call you the moment I hear from her. Probably tomorrow morning now. How will that be?'

'No, this is not good enough. I don't care how late it is, I'm getting on to Scotland Yard. They can get me Commander Loverell's home number or I'll bring the press in. I need Loverell's personal assurance that she's safe. I don't care how many toes I tread on to get it.' He put down the phone.

Anna replaced the receiver slowly. If Abbeline and Tessa were having dinner together somewhere in London, maybe Carter Wilson did have something to worry about. But it was not the sort of worry he had in mind tonight. Or maybe it was.

In the room he used for a study Abbeline was on the phone to Jan. 'I'm getting a dental check done first thing in the morning,' he said. 'But I don't think there's much doubt that we're looking at the murder of Sally Portal.'

'Okay,' she said. 'Question number one from the manual: how did she get to the place she was killed?'

'Her car was not in her lockup garage. So we'll start with the assumption she drove to Cambridge.'

'To see Beth?'

'There's no obvious other reason.'

'Do we have the car's registration?

'No. Her mother couldn't remember it. But we have the make and colour. It's a red Ford Escort.'

'I'm running to catch up,' Jan said. 'Red Ford Escort. Same car as Beth Naylor's.'

'Apparently they bought them at the same time. Shortly after Beth first arrived in England. One owner, ex-company cars. They didn't like bright red but the price was persuasive.'

'D'you get that feeling in your nuts there's something weird here?'

'Don't tell me you do?'

'Ha!' she said. 'But there's something weird. I'll get the car number from the DVLC and let Rose know we need to find it.' She paused. 'How's the American lady taking it?'

'Okay.'

'Is she on her way back to Cambridge?'

'Not yet.'

There was a silence. 'I'll leave you to it then.'

Abbeline put down the phone and went through to the other room. Tessa was sitting in the corner of the sofa, a glass of the Château d'Angludet to her lips. He put his hand on her shoulder and she looked up. 'I can't really believe you're a policeman,' she said. 'When I look around, at the pictures, the books, even just at this room itself, nothing much says "Tough, crime-busting cop".'

She watched him pick up his almost empty glass, swirl it and sniff deeply.

'And when I see you swirling a glass of red wine . . .'

'You make me sound like Oscar Wilde. I'm a copper because I think it's the best work in the world. It's as simple as that.'

'Aren't you ever depressed at what people do to each other?'

'Often. I'm also impressed by the extraordinary guts and plain goodness of a lot of other people.' He shrugged.

'For all your fashionable suits and books and wine, you sound like a very old-fashioned cop.'

'I don't deny that. Like my dad, I believe in the job.'

'I didn't know there were any high-minded cops left.'

He was silent. 'Plenty. The diet of mistrust is difficult to take, but we've deserved that often enough. We have a long way to go, but we'll get there.'

'Not all cops take that view.'

'No.'

'Your father was a cop too?'

Abbeline nodded. 'He gave his health, his marriage, everything to the job. I don't take kindly to cheap sneers at the police, especially from over-paid lawyers. But bent coppers should be shown no mercy.'

'You are a *very* committed cop.'

He smiled. 'Yuh. I'm pretty committed.'

'Do you have a private life?'

'I have a lady who's halfway to Australia at this moment.'

'Are you equally committed to her?'

He looked at her over the edge of his glass. 'Yes. Yes, I'm committed to Jo. I think she's committed to me. I think we're still trying to lock the two commitments together.' He wondered how true a summary of things that really was. Especially after tonight.

She smiled slowly, her eyes looking down at the carpet.

'What did I say?' He crossed the room and dropped down into the other corner of the sofa.

'I wonder if commitment is the whole story,' she said. 'Carter's the most committed husband I know. Very concerned, loving. Too concerned. Too loving. Isn't there a word for that?'

'Uxorious.'

'Yuh. Uxorious. That's Carter. Committed, but committed to the wrong me. It seems to me that a relationship can only really work if the myths we hold about each other coincide with the sort of people we believe we are. Carter sees me as a dependent creature, likely – very likely – to slip on the first banana skin in my path.'

'You don't see yourself that way?'

'I'm learning not to. Here, strangely enough. In the midst of all this horror of a dead friend and a missing sister. Listen,' she said. 'I think I must be very drunk.'

'I'm ahead of you. How about a final glass of Calvados?'

'I think I should call a hotel. It's gone midnight.'

'Stay here if you like,' he said. 'You can use the bed. I've got a daybed in the study.'

'What would Carter say?'

'I don't know.' He laughed. 'I don't really care. You're welcome to stay.'

He watched her uncertain smile, watched it drift away into a firm nod. 'Hell,' she said. 'I'm going to say yes. And that's even when I *know* what Carter would say.'

CHAPTER NINETEEN

At just before midnight, in the US Airbase at Lakenheath, Norfolk, a tall black girl in a US Air Force sergeant's uniform crossed the parking lot of the Education Centre and got into her Toyota. For a moment she sat slumped in the driving seat. Annabelle Wright was tired of the sort of meeting she had just attended. Subject: the music to be played in the jukebox in the Enlisted Men's canteen. Objections lodged by certain airmen: that the music proposed in the list for January was too *black*. Objections lodged by others: that the current list for December was too *white*. For nearly three hours the wrangling had continued while she tried to act as impartial umpire. Why the hell couldn't they all enjoy the same music?

She belted herself in, started the car and drove out through the main gate. At some point on the road to Norwich she became aware of a car that had been behind her for some time.

She speeded up and the two points of light behind her speeded up. She slowed and the lights seemed to slow too. She wasn't seriously alarmed. Her mind drifted to other things. In front of her now was Norwich. As she entered the city the lights turned against her, and as she stopped an old Volkswagen Beetle pulled up alongside.

The driver had seen her of course. Had probably followed her from the base. She pursed her lips. She recognised the car. It belonged to the weirdo she'd first come across a couple of weeks ago, selling salvation like popcorn. Only yesterday morning he had approached her at the main gate. She had been polite then, finally making excuses to go. In the afternoon, she hadn't been polite at all. She had made it clear as the guy had walked along beside her, long black coat flapping like wings, that she wasn't going to stop and talk. Not about Jesus or her immortal soul or anything else. 'Is he bothering you, Sergeant?' the sentry at the gate of the Education centre had said, and the weirdo, Leonard Hope Passmore he said his name was, had veered off with almost a snarl on his face as he raised his black hat to her. From her office in the Centre she had watched him lurking for nearly an hour across the road until he had finally driven off in an old white Beetle.

The one that was beside her now.

She thought first of all of taking a few quick sidestreets to throw off the car behind but on second thoughts settled back with a smile and decided to drive straight to the Café Mozart. Her German boyfriend Karlheinz was waiting. He was over from Germany, her last posting. He would know exactly how to deal with Leonard Hope Passmore.

At this time of night parking was no problem. She pulled the Toyota over outside the all-night Café Mozart. From the driving seat she could see that the place was still fairly crowded. A lot of American servicemen, some with local girls. But in the corner seat they usually took, there was no sign of Karlheinz. Automatically she flicked her eyes up at the mirror. The old Volkswagen was sliding into the parking place behind hers.

She wasn't really frightened. She was within screaming distance of a café full of people, many of whom were friends. She wheeled down the window three inches as Passmore got out of his car and walked forward.

He leaned one large hand on the car and bent over. 'It is essential I talk to you,' he said urgently.

'Anything that can't be said through a three-inch crack in the window?'

'Please let me sit in the car with you?'

'Say what you have to say and go.'

'Jesus saves,' he said.

'You let me in on that one yesterday.'

'You are a young woman of great importance – both to Him and your fellow men.'

'All I have to do is answer a lot of questions about who I am and where I come from and what's my phone number . . .'

'God knows I can see why a young woman should refuse the path of righteousness, the thorns that tear at her fleshly body. You must see this. You must read it with care.' He reached inside his long coat.

'I don't want any tracts,' she said. Then, deliberately, from the safety of the car: 'My trash can is full to here with junk mail.'

He glowered at her. Small strange-coloured eyes. He drew from his inside pocket a leather notecase. 'In here is contained a history . . .'

Coming down the empty street she saw a figure bundled deep in a khaki parka. She knew by the walk it was Karlheinz. 'I don't want to see it, you understand?' Emboldened, she got out of the car and stood next to Passmore. He had straightened up in surprise.

'I am here to save you,' he said urgently.

'I want you to listen carefully, Mr Passmore,' Annabelle said. 'I don't know who you are and I don't want to know. As far as I'm concerned I don't need saving. Now just go, huh? And don't bother me anymore. Or that guy who's crossing the square now will show you he's not a happy man.'

His pale face under the ridiculous black hat, the high cheekbones, the heavy brows that almost obscured the eyes . . . she had never seen such a completely mad face.

'You must hear me,' he said. 'It may be that a path is marked out for you. A shining path. Achievements in this life as great and extraordinary as the resurrection of Dorcas Erbury.'

'What?'

'The raising from the dead of the widow Dorcas Erbury in Exeter Gaol. It was witnessed. It was seen.'

She shook her head in astonishment.

'You're feeling something. I can see it.' His eyes bored into hers. 'The name Dorcas Erbury means something to you? Say that it does.'

Annabelle turned away from him. 'For Christ's sake . . .' she muttered under her breath.

He pulled her back. His breath had a harsh, metallic odour on her face. 'The country road . . . it's all recorded here.' He waved the notecase. 'The crack and rattle of a cart over the frozen snow. The cathedral bells . . .'

'Karl,' she screamed out, trying to push Passmore from her.

'The gibbet,' he said. 'The rope. In a leather bucket she whetted knives to slash at the ears. Oh God, you have suffered.' He was shouting in her face now, but his small dark eyes were looking over her head, speaking to someone out in the ether. 'But you will rise again,' he cried. 'Like poor Dorcas Erbury, you will rise again. In your seed you will live for ever.'

Karlheinz grabbed him by the shoulder as Annabelle screamed again. A young American had come running from the Café Mozart and caught Passmore's other arm. 'Who the hell is he?' Karlheinz asked.

'The one I told you about on the phone, for Christ's sake!' she said, angry now. 'The one who's been following me all day.'

The two young men were holding Passmore, uncertain what to do next. The tall man in the black overcoat made no attempt to resist. He was hunched a little forward. His arms, gripped by the young men, were held straight and slightly behind him. 'I think we call the police,' Karlheinz said.

Leonard Passmore lifted his head. He was taller than either of the two young men and with a sudden eruption of energy threw his arms up, twisting his body back and forth, grunting and crying out until they were hurled from him, sliding across the snow. The two men scrambled to their feet. Breathing heavily, they faced Passmore warily. The girl had reeled away in alarm.

'Please accept my deepest apologies, Miss Wright. My deepest apologies. I become too pressing . . . I was . . . I was *overwrought*.'

All three now, without speaking, watched Passmore step back a pace. And another. Then, while the two men and Annabelle exchanged an uncertain glance, he turned on his heel and walked with raking strides across the pavement to his car.

'She asked you to marry her? Tonight?'

Tessa was making an effort to concentrate through the warm fumes of alcohol that were comfortably fogging her brain. 'And what did you say?'

'What did I say?' Abbeline thought about it. Sprawled in one corner of the sofa, his glass held balanced on one crossed knee, he thought about what he had said. 'Nothing,' he admitted.

'A girl asks you to marry her and you don't answer? You say nothing?'

'No.'

'Nothing at all?'

'No.'

'Jesus. By comparison, Carter has the magic touch with women. You really stood there like a big dumb hunk and said *nothing!*'

'Yes.'

'Why?'

He struggled to sit up in the corner of the sofa. Speech more deliberate, glass used to gesture with, he said: 'I couldn't say anything, Tessa. I just don't know why but I couldn't.'

'You're a phony, Jack Abbeline,' she said amiably. 'I've found you out on our first date. Have you got any more of that Calvados there? I find it has a remarkably soothing effect. The more I drink, the further away Carter seems. Would you call that strange?'

'I'd say you're as big a phony as I am.' He got up and brought the Calvados to where she was sitting.

'Your dad was a cop,' she said, watching him pour. 'What about your mother?'

He stood holding the bottle. 'Very classy, very good-looking – when young. Something of a handful.' He turned away and replaced the bottle with the others.

'For your father? A handful for your father?'

'Uh, yes. A class difference. My ma was from the sort of family we used to call upper-middle-class. My dad was a working-class lad.'

'What happened?'

'She walked out on my dad within six months of finding an armed robber had put him in a wheelchair for the rest of his life. She came back for maybe a month once or twice a year, hugging us both and swearing she'd never leave again. Then one morning she'd be gone again, no word, no call . . .'

'How old were you then?'

'Her reappearing act ran from the time I was about six or seven until I was twelve, I suppose.' He paused. 'She was on the game, of course.'

'You mean on the streets?'

He shook his head. 'No. It was in a fairly high-class sort of way. She'd be invited to diplomatic parties. Something would be left in the pot afterwards. She's spent half a lifetime in the pubs of Soho but I don't know that she ever worked the streets. I doubt it. Anyway, by then I hated the sight of her. I watched that dependence on a woman tear my father apart. By the time I was ten, eleven, he and I were having fights. I wanted him to lock the door to her. Keep her out of our lives.'

'Does your father still see her?'

'He'd still like to, that's the sad thing. She took from him any chance he might have had of coming to terms with what had happened to him. She was there every few months, sweet as pie then gradually changing, jeering at him, flaunting herself in front of him. Then, at some point, she'd take all the money in the house and go. And gradually life would calm down again, and he and I would get on fine. We'd go fishing together, he really liked that. To football matches . . . And then one night, the key would turn in the lock again and my mother would be back for a few weeks of fights and screaming and humiliating my father.' He laughed shortly. 'Before I was eleven I had a plan to murder her. Quite a well-developed plan.'

She smiled. 'You didn't mention that at your initial police interview?'

He shook his head.

'How about now?'

'I see her from time to time. She drinks on Social Security. She lives in hostels, has fights with other people there, gets thrown out. Calls me.'

'You're too bright, too stable, to believe that all women are the same.'

He laughed shortly. 'My fear's different. I think maybe all *men* are the same.'

'You think you could find yourself in the same relationship to a woman as your father? Same dependence he had on your mother?'

'It's all pouring out, isn't it?'

'It's only fair after what I've told you about myself.'

'You haven't. You haven't told me anything about your husband.'

'There's not much to tell. I made a mistake, I know that. Carter is a really nice, intelligent, totally safe husband . . .'

'And what you really want is to sail the seven seas with a pirate with a patch over one eye?'

'Do I, Jack? I don't know. But that's the way I come on to you, uh?'

'I'm probably too drunk to know.'

She put down her glass. 'I think I'd better get to bed.'

'Sure.' He got to his feet. 'I'll just get a couple of things out of the bedroom. My reading glasses, dammit. Do you know, I now can't read late at night without glasses.'

' "Gather ye rosebuds . . ." ' she said, unsteadily.

He looked at her.

She stood stretching, her eyes on him. 'Listen, I have a question for you, Jack. That's to say, I *think* I have a question for you.'

'Go ahead.'

She faced him, her feet slightly apart, hands in her skirt pockets. 'It's not going to be an easy one.'

He considered a moment. 'Okay.'

'I was going to ask you if I could stay the night?'

He frowned. 'Of course . . . I already said . . .'

'Be a big boy, Jack. Stop pretending. I mean, stay. As in, stay in your bed. With you.'

'Ah.'

She smiled. 'Now that's not an easy question, is it, Jack Abbeline?'

'No.' He leaned forward and kissed her lightly on the lips. His hands were on her hips, her hands resting along the length of his forearms. A position that held the tension between them, committing neither to move forward.

'It could even be,' she said, 'a very destructive question.'

He pulled a face, a half smile. 'Not the question. The answer might be.'

They looked at each other. She found his mouth, the expression somewhere between wry and troubled, infinitely appealing. He could feel the bloodrace, feel himself hardening. When the phone rang it broke a long silence between them.

Abbeline picked up the receiver.

'Jack.' Loverell's voice was sharp. Abbeline automatically glanced at the clock.

Tessa moved to pick up the glasses and he stopped her with a movement of the hand. 'What is it, Commander?' He seldom used Loverell's rank, but it was enough to stop Tessa in the middle of the room.

'For Christ's sake, Jack, have you got that American woman with you there?'

'The American woman? Tessa Wilson? Yes,' he said slowly, 'Mrs Wilson is just leaving. We've just done a session . . .'

'I don't want any dirty details, Jack. The woman's husband is going crazy. The Foreign Office is going crazy. *I'm* going crazy.'

'She's safe,' Abbeline said flatly.

'Okay, so far so good. But what's she doing in your flat at this time of night?'

'She has just opened up an important new line on the case of her missing sister. She'll phone her husband as soon as I deliver her to her hotel, *The Hallam*, here in Earl's Court. Which I am just about to do.'

There was a long silence. 'You're a smooth bugger, Jack. And thank Christ you are. An important new line on the case of the missing sister . . . that's really so?'

'That's really so, sir.'

'Right, I'll pass that on. It might help. My office first thing tomorrow morning, all the same. Nine o'clock sharp.'

Abbeline put down the phone. 'I think your husband, the British Foreign Office and my boss have effectively answered the question you were putting to me a moment ago.'

Tessa shook her head slowly and went out into the hall for her coat. 'Maybe,' she said. 'But I'll still be left wondering what the answer might have been without them.'

'So will I,' he said, as he helped her on with her coat.

CHAPTER TWENTY

The bell seemed to come from the very depths of the night, ringing in his head, ringing through the thick fog of sleep and alcohol. He rolled over and snatched the phone.

'Jack, are you there?' It was Jo's voice.

'Jo . . .' In the darkness he sat up naked on the side of the bed. 'What time is it?'

'God knows. I'm in Bangkok Airport and I haven't reset my watch. We fly on to Sydney in about an hour.' She paused. 'I thought I should call you.'

He felt a sudden flood of relief. He reached out and turned on the light. 'I'm glad you did,' he said.

'You've got no little bedfellow making pretty faces up at you?'

'Uh-huh.' He shook his head.

'I could have waited till I got to Sydney to call you. But I felt that would be a mistake.'

'I'm glad you called, Jo.'

'You told me that,' she said crisply.

'Listen, Jo we have a lot to talk about . . .'

'Jack . . .' She cut him off short. 'We've had plenty of time to talk. All this year. Now it's different.'

'What's so different suddenly?'

'What's so different suddenly is that Sepp Lander has asked me to marry him.'

He sat on the edge of the bed, the cold of the unheated room suddenly engulfing him. Sepp Lander, the producer of the programme. A darkly good-looking German, Jo had had nothing but praise for him since he had taken over the show the year before. 'When?' he said. 'When did this happen?'

At the other end she was silent.

'For Christ's sake, it didn't just happen there on the plane?'

'No.'

'No. So when was it?'

'A couple of days ago.'

'And you said nothing about it?'

'Jack, you were too screwed up about my ex-husband for me to start in on Sepp.'

'You said nothing for two whole days? You even said nothing about it at the airport?'

'No,' she said quietly. 'With you coming to Australia, I thought we had time to talk about it. Then suddenly you weren't coming.' She paused. 'But you know what I think is absolutely amazing, Jack?' she said quietly.

'No.'

Her voice rose. 'Stunning, in fact. And that is I told you a full minute ago that Sepp asked me to marry him and you still, *still*, haven't got round to asking me what I answered!'

'What was your answer, Jo?' he said quietly. 'What did you say to Sepp?'

There was a long pause. 'I didn't say no, Jack,' she said slowly.

'I see.'

'I told him I wanted to talk to you.'

'And you did,' he said, flaring angrily. 'In the middle of a press reception, with your ex-husband on one arm and your husband-to-be on the other. Not to mention thirty journalists and photographers circling like vultures. Great!'

'I can't talk to you like this,' she said. 'I shouldn't have called. Not in the middle of the night.'

'For Christ's sake, you're not going to hang up now?'

'Jack . . .' she said. 'It was a mistake to call. I'm sorry, Jack . . . I'll call you.' And the line went dead.

He tossed the phone on to the bed. Sepp Lander, for Christ's sake. Why in God's name hadn't he seen it coming?

At just after 8.45 Commander Keith Loverell grunted in reply to Abbeline's knock and put down his pen as the door opened.

'Come in, Jack,' he said heavily. 'Sit down.'

Abbeline took the upright armchair in front of the door and waited. He was feeling bad. His head ached; a wave of nausea swept over him every few minutes.

'Well, let's see,' Loverell said. 'Question one is whether that story you told me last night has any truth in it?'

'It has.'

'Yes, Jack. Stories, as we know, can be true or partly true. Quarter true, half true.' He paused. 'You were pursuing your investigation into the disappearance of Beth Naylor last night?'

'I was. Mostly.'

'Now come on, Jack,' Loverell said testily. 'Be a bit more forthcoming about this. At half-past one in the morning you're up in your flat with what I understand is a very attractive American lady. I know Jo's in Australia or on her way there and this American lady's husband is three thousand miles away. Squawking like a parrot, I may say, to anybody who'll listen. Luckily I fielded it. Now, you tell me, Jack. Are you humping her?'

'No.'

'Well, thanks. That must be at least word number five you've uttered since you came in here. All right, make me look a bloody idiot: are your intentions honourable?'

Abbeline smiled. 'Are you asking me to promise not to do anything you wouldn't do, sir?'

Loverell's face remained set. 'Okay, so you're not humping the clientele. That's all I wanted to know. But don't take it too lightly either, Jack. I want to warn you, you could endanger your job.'

'You're not serious?'

'I don't want any false innocence from you, Jack. You know bloody well I'm serious. Something like that gets out, it could be a tabloid nightmare. Even if we can keep the lid on it, the Foreign Office would be looking for your head. This lady's husband is prepared to call the Prime Minister if he's not satisfied.' He paused. 'Stay away from his wife, Jack. You know what I mean?'

'I know what you mean.'

'Now, between friends, *was* there an important new line? Or am I supposed to throw back my head and laugh – Har Har Har?'

Abbeline looked at him bleakly and Loverell quickly composed his face. 'Well?'

'There *was* an important new line, sir,' he said deliberately. 'Thanks to what Tessa Wilson told me last night, I had a dentist up at eight o'clock this morning comparing records with those of the dead girl we found in Cambridge.'

'You've identified her?'

'Yes.'

Loverell's face opened in a broad smile. 'Why didn't you tell me that's what you were doing last night, lad? I could have sent the Foreign Office off with a flea in their ear. Who is she?'

'Sally Marion Portal. A long-standing friend of Beth Naylor's and probably her half-sister.'

'Half-sister?'

'Quentin Naylor put himself about, it seems. Way back he had an affair with Sally's mother, Laura Portal. The week before Beth Naylor disappeared, the two women, Beth and Sally, were together in Cambridge.'

'At this time they did or didn't know they were half-sisters?'

They found out that weekend. Neither of them was very pleased.'

Loverell nodded, his face sombre now. 'Who else was told? Woodward, for example?'

'That we don't know, sir.'

'But a week later, Sally Portal goes up to Cambridge again. What for? Who did she see?'

'Woodward?'

'Is that the line you're running? She died playing sex games with Laurie Woodward? He realised what had happened, took off like a bat out of hell and crashed at that Granchester bend?'

'Something close.'

'And Beth Naylor?'

Abbeline pursed his dehydrated lips. 'There's the rub. The line doesn't go as far as explaining what happened to *her*.'

Abbeline left Loverell's office at just before ten o'clock and took the flight of steps down to his own floor. He was still feeling the effects of last night and sudden movements made his head swim. Throwing open the door of his own office, he at first thought it empty, until an extra twist of his head revealed Ken Russell stretched full-length on the black leatherette sofa.

Russell swung down his legs and began getting laboriously to his feet.

'I'm sorry to keep you, Ken. Loverell switched times . . . wanted to see me first thing.'

'So I heard.' Russell perched on the arm of the sofa.

Abbeline looked at him. 'You've been talking to his secretary again.'

'Only way to be kept well-briefed around here.'

Abbeline pursed his lips slowly. 'That's a liberty, Ken.'

'Sorry, sir. Bad joke.'

'You're feeling a bit scratchy because I've left you out on a limb with this Passmore case.'

Russell hesitated. 'That's about the size of it, I suppose, sir.'

'About last night, Ken. That was a combination of Jo going off to Australia and a new development in Beth Naylor's disappearance. Our meeting went clean out of my mind. Apologies.'

'Accepted. On my side, sorry to give you the moody.'

Abbeline nodded. 'So let's get to work.' He glanced at the file sitting on his desk. 'What have we got here?'

'The file in front of you is what we have to date on the Millennium Church – mostly what you'd expect from a fundamentalist group. They do a certain amount of real good here in Soho and King's Cross. Slightly loony maybe, but harmless in that side of the work. Underneath is a list of complaints I've collected from just within the Met area. Mothers whose sons and daughters have come under the influence. Sons and daughters whose old parents have handed over money. You know the kind of thing. Evangelical groups are a tough problem. First they may be completely genuine; second, genuine or not, they usually have a good front like these Soho, King's Cross Missions, third it's hard as hell to prove the money is actually extracted illegally from contributors. The case of the Passmore church is doubtful. They are definitely doing good works. But I've still got a whole sheaf of complaints – none of them approaching evidence.'

'Do we know what sort of membership numbers we're talking about?'

'No, I haven't been able to establish any idea of numbers in the

UK. In the States, of course, in the Mid-West anyway, they number tens of thousands. I've had a word over there and it seems there've been a dozen civil cases brought by parents against Passmore, mostly in Bloomington, Indiana. The full name of his outfit is the Millennium Church of Christ Reborn (Bloomington) Inc. It's a business, and as a business it relies on contributions from members. Some very young, some very old. So you have alienation of affection, undue influence, that sort of thing.'

'Any success?'

'Three have been settled privately, which sounds as if Passmore coughed up for his reputation's sake.'

'But no criminal case against him?'

'The evidence just isn't there.'

'So all sorts of mud but none that's really stuck?'

'That's about the size of it, sir.'

Abbeline was silent. 'I went to see Passmore, Ken. An invitation in response to my letter.'

'You've got your own ideas about him then?'

'Not really. That's why I let you run on. Very difficult man to come to a decision about. I think he's more than a straightforward businessman. I think he's a believer.'

'Any help if I were to tell you that he's not American at all? Or at any rate he's only naturalised a few years back. Born and bred in London, within a stone's throw of Ealing Broadway.'

'You mean the rich, ripe accent's a phony?'

'I suppose you could pick up an accent like that in nine or ten years. And it's not a criminal offence to be born in Ealing. Though it should be. What do you want me to do about him?'

'Rightly or wrongly the Home Office have got it in for him. They're thinking in terms of an example, to discourage any others coming over. I think they'd like to have enough for a deportation order. So keep prodding around, Ken. Just to satisfy the Home Office we're on the case.'

When Russell had left, Abbeline sat alone at his desk. His eyes were heavy. Whatever he'd said to Loverell, he wasn't feeling too happy about his own behaviour last night. A sense of guilt nagged at him. If he was in love with Jo, as he certainly was, what was he doing within a half step of getting into bed with Tessa? And he couldn't even give himself credit for refusing her . . . Loverell's call had done that.

He shook his head and it throbbed. He let his mind drift through the details of the Beth Naylor case. Sally Naylor was killed the same night Woodward came off his motorbike. Possibly even the same night Beth Naylor disappeared. Only the testimony of Mrs Taylor, the woman who rented out the parking space in Trumpington Street, put Beth Naylor driving off in her red Escort on the Sunday morning after Sally's death. After Woodward's accident. And Jan had done an interview with her and reported a basically solid witness.

He sat, as he often did on a case, and let his mind drift.

What was Laurie Woodward racing off to do in the middle of the night?

Had he just killed Sally?

Was he at that moment pursuing Beth?

Was it only the accident at Granchester bend that saved Beth Naylor?

Or was she already hanging in some barn or outhouse, killed in the course of Woodward's murderous sex games?

And if not, where was she?

He shook his head again, got the same aching result and scowled. He was still scowling when Ken Russell put his head round the door.

'You won't look like that when you hear this, governor.'

'How's that, Ken?' he said, letting his face relax.

'We may have what we're looking for. Norwich City Police are holding Leonard Passmore, United States citizen, on a charge of harassing a young American girl.'

'Trying to recruit her?'

'More than that, sir. Harassing as in harassing.'

Abbeline sat back in his chair. He was still thinking about Beth Naylor, about tattered bodies hanging in rodent-infested barns.

'This could be exactly what we're looking for,' Russell said.

Abbeline nodded. 'I think you'd best drive up to Norwich and find out exactly what's going on there, Ken,' he said, with as much enthusiasm as he could muster.

CHAPTER TWENTY-ONE

Inspector Ray Rose pursed his lips. He still found it difficult to believe that this girl in two inches of leather miniskirt and a punk haircut was of the same rank as himself, but she was sharp, he had to recognise that. And now he'd told her that forensic had just found traces of blood in the boathouse cottage, she had not pushed the point against him. He was beginning to think Scotland Yard were not so black as they were usually painted by his colleagues in the county police forces.

'So Sally Portal was hammered in the cottage and carried out and hung up in the boathouse?' Jan said, shaking her head. 'It's all got the mark of Woodward to me, Ray.'

He nodded. 'Which, unless we've got two killers running around at the same time, leaves Beth Naylor in all probability still alive – *if* Mrs Taylor's right about seeing her on Sunday morning.'

'Still alive, but where?'

He shrugged. 'Something else you might want to follow up,' he said. 'We asked the ski company Beth signed up with for full details and they gave us a printout of that tour. It appears she was going with Dr Butler from Pembroke College. Strange he didn't mention that when my sergeant went to see him yesterday.'

'I'm an old Poly girl, myself,' Jan said, looking round Will Butler's book-lined rooms with undisguised hostility. 'Although now they've renamed us we're all on the same level, aren't we? My Alma Mater was called St Cuthbert's Street Poly. Now we're the University of St Cuthbert. Neck and neck with Oxford and your lot.'

169

'How can I help you, Inspector?' Butler said, his head bobbing on his long neck. 'I'm afraid I've very little time. I have a plane to catch.'

'Going skiing?'

He looked startled. 'Yes,' he said slowly. 'I am.'

'What time's your plane?'

'I've a car coming up in half an hour to take me to Stanstead Airport.'

She nodded. 'Half an hour. That's okay.'

'I still have some packing.'

'Do it while I ask the questions.' She smiled. 'Or catch a later plane.'

He saw she meant it. 'Very well. How can I help you?'

She followed him as he went into the adjoining bedroom and stood, her back against the doorjamb. 'How well do you know Beth Naylor?'

'Quite well, professionally. On a personal level we are friends,' he said, packing shirts into a suitcase.

'Close friends?'

'I'd like to think so.'

'Well, since you've got so little time, Dr Butler, I won't beat about the bush. Have you ever spent the night at her flat?'

He stood up. Despite his strange short legs, he was an imposing height, his head almost brushing the beams of the low-ceilinged room. 'No, Inspector. And I object to the assumption behind the question. Beth and I are close friends. There is no further element to our relationship.'

'You had plans to go skiing together?'

He turned slowly to face her. 'You know about that?'

'I know you chose not to mention it to the Cambridge Police when they took your statement yesterday. Why was that, Dr Butler?'

He pulled at one of his overlarge ears. 'One doesn't like to make a big thing of being turned down.'

'Explain.'

'At the beginning of this term Beth and I had plans to go skiing together.'

'As a couple? Or in a group?'

He hesitated. 'As a couple.'

'And?'

'Later, perhaps at the end of October, she told me she would no longer be coming.'

'What changed her mind?'

'I can only believe it was meeting Woodward.'

Jan tapped around the room while Butler put his skis and cases on to the landing outside his rooms. 'What would be the appeal of someone like Woodward to a woman like Beth Naylor, Dr Butler?'

He put on a tweed jacket in a series of awkward, jerky movements. 'Like many artists, Woodward enjoyed the fact that his talents seemed to excuse his lifestyle.' His eyes glittered angrily.

'You mean Beth Naylor *knew* what sort of man he was?'

'Yes.'

'Knew he had a record? In detail?'

'In detail, Inspector, I assure you.'

'You made sure of that. You mean, you told her?'

'I did.'

'When was that?'

'A week or two after she met him.'

'Where did she meet him?'

'I don't recollect.'

'Try, Dr Butler.'

He looked quickly at his watch. 'Let's see. He, Woodward, was doing some woodcarving somewhere. I don't remember where.' He looked over the cases, counting them.

'But someplace she was associated with?'

'I suppose so.' The phone rang and he answered it. 'Yes, thank you, Baxter.' He put down the phone. 'That's my taxi,' he said to Jan.

She walked out on to the landing while he took his keys from his pocket, locked the inner black-painted door and swung the outer oak door closed.

'What reason did Beth give you for not going skiing, Doctor?' They stood between the cases on the narrow landing. 'Did she mention a new man? Did she mention Woodward?'

'Of course not.'

'What did she say? She must have given some reason.'

He began picking up bags, his awkward shape somehow accentuated by the cases he carried in each hand. 'She said a skiing holiday was no longer consonant with her religious beliefs.'

'Her religious beliefs? You mean she'd suddenly got religious?'

'I don't know how suddenly but I know that, during October, she was undergoing an intense religious experience.'

'Did you tell Tessa Wilson that?'

'I'm not given to irrelevant gossip,' he said tightly. 'Even to family.'

'So how was Woodward involved in this intense religious experience?'

Butler fixed her with his small eyes. 'Improbable as it may seem, Beth was attempting to convert him, Inspector.'

At King's porter's lodge they explained they had an appointment with Dr Grimes, arranged by Dr van Gelden from the Fitzwilliam. The porter in his cutaway coat pursed his lips. 'Did Dr Grimes say where you were to meet him, sir?'

Abbeline looked at Tessa. 'In his rooms, I imagine.'

'Yes,' the porter said darkly. 'Then it's just a matter of tracking him down. He's very restless, is Dr Grimes. Up to the library, down to the river, a trip over to the Market Place, then suddenly he'll stop in one place, stand stock still for an hour or more. Thinking, I suppose. Although sometimes you have to wonder.'

'Have you seen him yourself this morning?' Tessa asked.

'He's been back and forth past the chapel two or three times. Bit of work going on the stone face. Dr Grimes always gets very concerned when they're working on the chapel. Haven't seen him for the past hour or two. I'll see what I can do.' He ducked into his lodge, picked up the phone and tapped out two numbers. 'Albert, is that you? You haven't seen Dr Grimes down your way this morning?' He listened. 'Good enough. Thanks.'

He turned back to Tessa and Abbeline. 'He's standing on the bridge there.' He pointed down towards the river. 'Hasn't moved an inch in the last hour and a half.'

'When we find him he'll be frozen solid,' Tessa said to Abbeline. 'Are all these old dons like this?'

'Some of them have a reputation for eccentricity in their later years, yes,' Abbeline said judiciously.

Dr Grimes was unmissable. He was very tall and stood very straight, hands in his trouser pockets. He wore a long grey overcoat, open to allow him to sink his hands into his trouser pockets, and a pink scarf thrown across his left shoulder. He had pale, blond-grey hair, a lock of which fell across his forehead. He stood on King's Bridge looking out along the narrow River Cam in the direction of Newton's Mathematical Bridge.

Tessa turned up the fur collar of her dark green coat and kept step with Abbeline as they walked down to the river. She couldn't resist glancing around her at the panorama of stone buildings which lined the river bank. 'Pure escapism,' she said, 'but I can imagine, in summer, this would be the ideal place to float stretched in a punt, trailing my handkerchief in the water.'

'Cucumber sandwiches and white burgundy in the hamper?'

'Perhaps a little Paul Whiteman playing on the wind-up phonograph.' She smiled ruefully. 'Such thoughts. Thank God it's winter, with a wind cutting straight across from Siberia!'

He put his hand on her shoulder, squeezed it lightly and took it away again.

She looked at him. 'Thank God it's winter,' she repeated, to herself this time.

There was no one else on the bridge and their footsteps sounded loud enough to announce their arrival but there was still no movement from Dr Grimes. He stood immobile, his eyes fixed on some distant object.

'Dr Grimes,' Tessa said, 'I'm Tessa Wilson. Anna van Gelden called you this morning.'

'She did?' His head turned towards her. He had a deeply lined but once fine-featured face. 'You're perfectly right. She called me this morning. You are interested in the chapel?'

'This is Superintendent Abbeline. He's looking into the disappearance of my sister.'

'Abbeline?' Grimes was more interested in the name than in a lost sister. 'Not from Scotland Yard?'

'I'm attached to the Yard, yes, sir.'

'Abbeline. Autumn of Terror. 1888.'

'Yes, sir.'

'Remarkable. I think he got him, you know. I think the Ripper was that young teacher, Montague Druitt. Threw himself in the Thames immediately after that last murder, the awful glut at Miller's Court as it was called, the dismembering of Mary Kelly. Do you think it was Druitt?'

'Family legend says my grandfather did.'

'Fifty gold sovereigns in his pocket when they brought up the body. The final mystery – why did he withdraw it from the bank that day and then take it with him into the Thames? Did he plan to distribute it to the poor of Spitalfields? Perhaps. We shall never know.' Grimes turned back to Tessa. 'You must excuse me. How is King's Chapel connected with the disappearance of your sister?'

She had somehow assumed he was going to be absent-minded. 'We don't know that it is. She either received or was about to send a postcard just before she disappeared . . .'

Abbeline took it from his inside pocket. They stood on the bridge and turned to watch the afternoon dusk settle on the sweep of the narrow river, over the lawns of King's and Clare Bridge.

'Thirteen and fourpence,' he said, 'was the value of the old English mark. Until a few years ago undergraduates were fined in marks for any minor transgression.'

'But the red cross scrawled over the stained glass windows?'

'Put the two together,' Grimes said, 'and I would guess we're in the late-1640s. The chapel was considered an example of improper display, offensive to the Lord. A commission was dispatched from London, headed by a man named Smith, I believe, to break out the offending windows.'

'To destroy the stained glass windows?'

'The very windows you see today.'

'Good God,' Tessa said. 'They sent someone to smash the windows!'

'It happened all over the country. The God of the Puritans is just, but perhaps a little prudish too.'

'They're still there,' Abbeline said. 'What happened?'

'Mr Smith, if that was indeed his name . . . it's the name that appears, mysteriously, in the college accounts for that year . . . Mr Smith was bribed. By the Provost and Fellows of the college. One mark. "But for thirteen and fourpence," you see. It fits. But the tone of the postcard is one of regret that the glass survived.'

'Thirteen shillings and fourpence, less than one pound, to leave some of the world's finest stained glass untouched. Unshattered.' Tessa was shaking her head.

Grimes' strangely coloured hair lifted in the cutting wind. 'I think that's what your postcard expresses, Mr Abbeline. Regret that the work was not carried out.' He paused. 'Any other unusual aspects of your case?' he asked hopefully.

'Not unless you can tell us why a woman should be strung up with her ears cut off?'

Grimes nodded thoughtfully. 'Women, unusual. Men, of course, normally. Not at all uncommon.'

Tessa looked up at him. 'What do you mean, Doctor? Not uncommon?'

'I could quote you a dozen or so from memory, people like Bastwick and William Prynne, who had their ears judicially docked.'

'Docked?'

'It was a common seventeenth-century punishment for licentiousness, issuing or listening to blasphemy, sedition, any loose or overfree talk . . .'

'What was?' Tessa said in horror.

'Docking. The public hangman undertook the act. The ears were sliced clean.'

'Jesus . . .'

Grimes nodded equably. 'Normally that was the extent of the punishment. In certain cases one hears of the tongue being split as an additional flourish.'

They left him standing on the bridge and began to walk back along the gravel path. Tessa's face, Abbeline could see, was drawn.

The morning she had spent with Laura Portal before they drove back to Cambridge must have been appalling. Telling someone their daughter has just been murdered is one of the hardest parts of police work. There's no real training; nobody ever gets used to doing it. In the circumstances, Abbeline could only imagine what it had been like for Tessa this morning. But she had insisted on doing it.

They walked in silence for a while, past the Fellows Building, until they could see the pepper-pot screen in front of them.

'Add the postcard to what your inspector was told by Dr Butler this morning,' Tessa said slowly, 'and all this means that Beth has suddenly become a believer. Not just a believer but, like our mother, a passionate believer.'

'There have always been a few fundamentalist student groups in Cambridge,' Abbeline said. 'We used to get Cambridge undergraduates coming to London when I was a student, waving a book called *Who Moved the Stone?* They were naive fundamentalists, but I still don't think they would have favoured smashing King's Chapel's windows.'

'So who would?'

'We live in a world of violently held single issue beliefs, Tessa. The very young are particularly susceptible.'

'Beth isn't that young.'

'Maybe,' he said. 'How about lunch?'

She shook her head. 'I'm going back to take a shower and sleep for an hour or two. I have the feeling I have to let my life catch up with me.'

Jack Abbeline passed under the Tudor archway and stopped. He had asked Tessa to have lunch with him partly as a way of not thinking about Jo, he knew that. And though he didn't really think of Tessa as a Jo substitute, he did find he thought less about Jo when he was with Tessa. He stopped in the small courtyard. For the first time he really saw his surroundings. Wentworth Court. Low sixteenth-century brick buildings with mullioned windows enclosed a cobbled courtyard. Black iron lamps on bracket arms, still on at midday, spilled weak yellow light on to the snow. There were fewer and fewer places left in

Britain with an atmosphere like this. He thought he would like to show this to Jo, and that immediately triggered thoughts of her and Sepp Lander in Australia. She had asked Jack to marry her and he had refused. Wasn't that what keeping silent amounted to? So where did that leave them? Did they still have anything together – or had he dissolved that by his silence? If that was the way Jo felt about it he certainly couldn't blame her.

And why had he remained silent?

He knew of course. Jo had put it into words. Once, just once. It was the night before she'd been going to Austria for a few days on location at a ski resort. She had asked him, lying beside him in bed, if he minded her being away?

'I look forward to your being back,' he'd said.

'I'm not talking about when I get back. I'm asking, do you mind me going away?'

'It depends on what you're planning to do as après-ski?'

She had risen on one elbow. 'I'm planning nothing, Jack. But I'm asking if you'd mind if I were?'

He'd pretended it was a bizarre question. 'We're both free,' he said, 'at any time. I'm not tying you down.'

'Say I don't want the freedom, Jack?' she had said angrily. 'Okay, you give it me, but say I don't want it?'

'You never know.'

She had exploded with rage, risen naked from the bed. 'I don't want to be licensed to have an affair. Because I know what your licence is. It's another throwback to your damn mother. If you've said "Yes, that's okay, Jo" and I go ahead and screw someone, you've saved your precious pride. And that precious pride is more important to you than I am. That's it, isn't it?'

She was kneeling over him, naked. He had pulled her towards him and kissed her breast, then rolled her over until he lay half on top of her. 'That's it,' she insisted, 'isn't it, Jack?'

'That's it,' he said. But they had never spoken so frankly again.

At moments like these Jack Abbeline was not too fond of himself. The fuss he made about Leo Bannerman was a smoke-screen, he knew that. The truth was he was crazily jealous of any man with Jo. What he also knew was that, in a strange way, it was not a measure of what he thought of Jo herself. His jealousy was not the effect of loving – it was the desire for total, insanely exclusive, possession. Too frightening even to admit to himself. Far too frightening to admit to Jo.

He walked slowly across the court to find the entrance marked K staircase. It was low and the stairs he could see leading up were bare scrubbed oak. First floor, Jan had said. He climbed a flight and stopped before a heavy door. By the side a brass plate read *'Music Rooms'*. He knocked. The click of three-inch heels he would have recognised anywhere. He reached for the door as she drew it open. 'Welcome to your new offices, Superintendent.' Jan Madigan performed a miniskirted curtsey.

He walked past her into a beamed room, long, with windows on either side. Two small tables were arranged as desks with phones and a fax machine. A fire burnt in the stone fireplace, surrounded by several armchairs. 'This is the outer office,' Jan said. 'Phones will be permanently manned from tomorrow morning.' She opened the far door. 'Through there's yours.'

The second room had a desk, telephone, and two new filing cabinets. He walked over to the windows and stood looking down into the courtyard where the lamps were already lit in the December afternoon's gloom. 'I think we've been lacking a dimension here, Jan.' He turned and nodded to her to sit down. Quickly he sketched in the meeting with Grimes.

'Ties in with what Dr Butler told me about the reason Beth called off her skiing trip with him. He talked about intense religious experiences in the month before she disappeared.'

'That was the dimension we were lacking, Jan. Without the religious element we were looking at this case as a jig-saw. In fact it's more a Rubik's cube.'

Tessa let herself into Anna van Gelden's house. Going straight into the kitchen, she made herself a cup of coffee and sat with it at the table.

She had spent a harrowing morning with Laura Portal. Perhaps, she thought, the most harrowing morning of her life.

'They can't really be sure,' Laura had said over and over. 'Just tell me they can't be sure, Tessa?'

And Tessa had forced herself to face Sally's mother and say: 'A dental check, Laura. You know they made a dental check early this morning.'

The drive back with Jack Abbeline had steadied her. And the visit to Grimes had somehow diverted her from Laura's grief. Even from her own fears for Beth. Doctor Grimes' matter-of-fact seventeenth-century world, however brutal, was comfortingly distant, separate from today.

She stared down at the still swirling bubbles on the top of the coffee, and suddenly she couldn't maintain this separation any longer. Sally was dead, a hanging corpse held together only by the remnants of her clothes. Her ears savagely hacked at. Somewhere that could be Beth too.

She wasn't crying. Her shoulders were moving but there were no tears. She wasn't sure how long she sat there, but the coffee was cold when she thought to drink it.

When the doorbell rang, two or three long rings, and she opened it to Jan Madigan, Tessa found she could barely understand what the Inspector was saying. 'A garbage dump?' she repeated, shaking her head. 'You want to take me out to a garbage dump?'

There were too many big men in the small interview room at Norwich Central Police Station. The detainee, Leonard Passmore, was himself a big man, sullen and silent, wrapped in thoughts as dark as the shadow he cast under the bright light.

Inspector Bill Winter, although not tall, was barrel-chested and room-filling. His sergeant, in a grey houndstooth jacket, occupied a whole corner of the room. Ken Russell, overweight and heavy-shouldered, had been given a small chair to the side of the interview desk. A tape was running.

'I'm going to ask you again,' Winter said. 'What exactly is your interest in the American Air Force sergeant, Annabelle Wright?'

A faint jutting of the lower lip was the only indication that Passmore had heard.

Winter said: 'For God's sake, say something, Mr Passmore, even if it's only that you refuse to answer questions.'

The lip jutted again. For a moment Winter looked into the small eyes. Old eyes in a young face. 'I have nothing further to say,' Passmore said with deliberation.

Winter's sergeant leaned forward from his corner position, laying one large hand flat on the table. 'The inspector has asked you to answer the question. What is your interest in Annabelle Wright?' This time the lip barely moved.

'I just want to reiterate,' Winter said, 'that your silence could work against you if it came to a trial.'

Passmore's head dropped forward on his chest. 'I told your sergeant in the police car my purpose in talking to this young woman. I have nothing further to add.'

Winter leaned forward and spoke into the machine. 'This interview is suspended, 14.45, and will be resumed at a later time.' He punched the button, took out cigarettes and offered the packet to Russell.

Ken Russell shifted his bulk on the tiny chair so that he was facing Winter, his back half-turned to Passmore. 'You know, Inspector, I think our man's got something very special for pretty girls. God knows what he thinks the Lord's work means in *that* context.'

'Seal your lips!' Passmore brought his hand down heavily on the table in front of him. 'Even in the midst of my suffering, I will not hear blasphemy without countering it.'

'What suffering is that?' Winter asked him.

'Suffering beyond imagination,' Passmore muttered. He straightened, shook himself as if he were emerging from water. 'My work is the Lord's work. You have no cause to hold me here. I formally request you, Inspector, to charge me with an offence or release me immediately.'

Winter stood up and gestured to Ken Russell to follow him. Outside in the corridor he said: 'Did you get lunch?'

'Not yet.'

'Let's go and have something. I've got to release this one.' He grimaced. 'I don't like it. I've got bad feelings about him. But there's nothing to charge him with.'

'You've seen eyes like that before, haven't you? But you can't hold a man because he's got a crazy glint in his eyes.'

Winter held his glance, then turned to his sergeant who was coming out of the interview room. He sighed heavily. 'Go in and tell him he's free to go.' He turned back to Russell. 'You've had a wasted journey,' Winter said. 'Let's go and find a late lunch.'

CHAPTER TWENTY-TWO

Jan Madigan turned off the Ely Road about five miles out of Cambridge and almost immediately Tessa could smell the dump in the warm air drawn through the car's ventilation system. It was an acrid, chemical smell, not the stench of decay so much as a polluted sharpness in the nose and throat.

When they passed the screening stand of fir trees, Tessa could see that the area covered was not more than an acre or two of landfill. Fifty yards away, a pair of dumper trucks were spilling broken polystyrene boards on to a slope of rubbish. Closer to the road two police cars were parked, and blue and white tapes had sealed off a small area of the mound.

They got out of the car into the biting wind. Jan led the way, saying something Tessa couldn't hear to two constables who stood in the freezing wind, banging their gloves hands together. Within the sealed area four policemen in overalls were digging, turning over the rubbish with garden forks, occasionally lifting out a shoe or a remnant of clothing and placing it on a broad plastic sheet which had been pegged down to prevent the wind lifting it.

Abbeline stood next to Rose, staring out over the incredible diversity of the rubbish. Underfoot, he noticed with faint disgust, the compacted rubbish sagged under his weight.

Seeing Tessa, he turned and walked towards her, again feeling the sogginess underfoot unbalancing him as he trod. His eyes met hers. She looked pale and nervous biting her lip. 'It really is only clothes, isn't it?' she said quickly. 'It's not Beth?'

'It's just as Jan told you. I'm sorry to have asked you to come out to this place, but you're the only one.'

Jan lifted the tape for Tessa to duck underneath it.

Rose came forward. 'These items of clothing have been here several weeks, Mrs Wilson. They may have nothing to do with your sister.' He turned and gestured towards the plastic sheet.

Abbeline watched her force herself forward to half kneel in front of the plastic. She steadied herself with one hand on a broken wooden box and examined the items one by one. There were sweaters almost too stained and wet to reveal their original colour, several single shoes, a pair of torn jeans, several scraps of what had been stockings or tights . . .

'None of these items have American labels, or anything we can be sure are American labels,' Rose said. 'Except this one.' He pointed to a shirt, stained dark, the collar label exposed: 'The Gap. Made in USA'.

Tessa's stomach seemed to turn over. Had she seen Beth wearing a shirt like that? Green-checked . . .

'The Gap shops exists over here too,' Jan said. 'Most of what they sell is made in America.'

Tessa nodded. She was concentrating on the shirt. It was the only thing she thought she might recognise. After a moment she stood, using the wooden box to help her on the unstable surface. She shook her head. 'I don't think so,' she said. 'I thought for a moment . . .'

Abbeline nodded. The four policemen, leaning on their forks, looked disappointed.

Rose turned. 'Bring the lad out,' he said to one of the officers. 'Let's go down to the cars,' he said to Tessa.

She looked in panic towards Abbeline. 'We have one more thing to show you,' he said, walking with her down the slope of garbage. 'It was found here several weeks ago, apparently.'

A young dark-skinned boy in a tattered blue anorak was brought out of one of the parked police cars. He was carrying a cardboard box. Looking up at Abbeline and Tessa, the boy, fourteen or fifteen years old, ducked his head in embarrassment.

'Nothing to worry about, Billy,' Ray Rose said briskly. 'You were doing nothing wrong. And you may be of real help to us.'

'How often do you come here, Billy?' Abbeline said. 'The inspector tells me you live over in those caravans on the other side of the road.'

'I pop across here three, four times a week,' Billy said in a high, sharp toned voice. 'Most times for nothing much. Bit of lead, some cable, nice piece of brass sometimes.'

'And can you really remember when you found that?' he pointed to the box.

'Sure. Five or six weeks ago.'

'Show this lady what you found.'

The boy opened his box like a Levantine merchant. He drew from it a pale grey dress.

Abbeline knew immediately by the sharp intake of Tessa's breath. Her eyes were brimming.

'The label reads "*Jordans of Boston*",' Rose said.

'A big department store,' Tessa said, unable to recognise her own voice.

Abbeline put his arm round the boy and walked him a few yards apart. 'What made you phone the police, Billy?'

'This morning's paper said one of the colleges was offering a reward for information on that missing Yankee woman. In the paper I see she comes from Boston in America. And I remember the label.'

'How long has your mum been wearing the dress?'

'Since I found it. She give it a good wash first, a' course.'

'I'll do my best to see you get whatever reward's on offer, Billy.'

He came back to where Tessa was standing. She was staring at the dress which Ray Rose was putting back into the cardboard box. She reached forward and stayed his arm. 'That mark,' she said. There was a large darker grey stain across the breast. She seemed to gag on the words, then swallowed and began again. 'That mark. It's blood, is it?'

Abbeline took her arm and turned her back towards where the cars were parked. 'The dress has been washed,' he said.

'But *you* still think it's blood?'

He hesitated. 'It could be, Tessa,' his calm voice said. But her head was already down. Her gloved hand over her mouth muffled her sobbing.

In the Leather Bottle the second round of brandies was on the bar. 'How did I meet Jack Abbeline?' Winter said, lighting a cigar. 'I met him in France when I did an Interpol stint. Younger than me, of course, but at Interpol headquarters at Lyon, he was my senior inspector. When you see him in London, give him my best.'

'The story is he had quite a time there.'

'He did. But he nearly didn't stay the course. Nearly found himself returned to London before his year was up. Would have been a serious black mark against him.'

'I'm sure it would,' Russell said cautiously. 'What was the problem?'

Winter turned his brandy glass by the stem between finger and thumb. 'As you'd guess, it was a woman.'

'A wife?'

Winter nodded. 'Somebody's else's.' He paid the round. 'We'd better drink up.'

The two policemen left the pub and walked back to Police Central. As Winter pushed open the glass door he saw his sergeant moving quickly across the reception area. Winter looked at the younger man's face. 'What is it?' he asked him. 'Trouble?'

'It's the American Air Force girl. She's just been found dead in her apartment at Cathedral Walk.'

It was a more vicious attack than Ken Russell had seen for a long time. The mostly naked body of Annabelle Wright lay face down in the connecting doorway between the bedroom and bathroom of her apartment. The perfect smooth brown skin of her back arched over to the mass of bloody hair and tissue which was all that could be seen of her head. She wore a pair of white briefs rolled down to about the level of mid-thigh. One arm was still in a yellow bathrobe. The rest of the garment fanned out, bloodstained, in the bathroom.

Three or four specialist officers in blue overalls were working in the room. The doctor had just finished a preliminary examination. He motioned Winter into the small kitchen and spoke with him for a few moments before bidding Russell a quick goodbye and leaving.

'What does he say?' Russell asked.

'Death was the result of three heavy blows to the head. Time of death sometime late last night. Two to four o'clock in the morning.

Sexual interference is difficult to establish. Her dressing gown was pulled off, or was only halfway on when she was attacked. Same with her briefs.'

'You mean he may have been interrupted?'

Winter nodded. 'We'll get to talk to the tenants later. Let's go and have a quick word with the girl next-door.'

They left Annabelle Wright's flat and walked down the corridor. At the front door to the next flat, Winter stopped and knocked. 'It's the police, Captain O'Brien,' he said.

There was a long pause, then a rattling of a chain and bolts being drawn. A slender woman of about forty wearing an air force blue track suit opened the door. Winter showed his identification and Russell proffered his own card. The woman examined both carefully and unhurriedly then pulled back the door to let them in. 'Sit down, gentlemen,' she said. 'Can I offer you something?'

They both declined. She sat opposite them on a padded stool, her hands on her knees. She had short, almost black, hair and bright Irish blue eyes in a small face.

'You found the body?' Winter said, and when she nodded: 'That was at what time?'

'About an hour ago,' the captain said. 'I was just going out for a run. I noticed Annabelle's door was open an inch or two. As if she'd forgotten to close it properly.'

'What did you do?'

'I knocked a couple of times. Called her name. I don't know her that well, she'd just moved in this month from Germany . . . Called her name and when she didn't answer, pushed the door. I guess I made a couple of yards into the hallway and that was it.'

'Do a lot of American service people live in this block?'

'Sure.'

'Working all sorts of hours?'

She nodded. 'I got home at maybe two-thirty last night.'

'Did you hear anything unusual?'

'Is that when you think this happened, during the night?'

'Looks that way,' Winter said cautiously.

'Okay.' She thought, biting on her lip. 'There were certainly noises as I came up in the elevator. They might have come from this floor. By the time I reached here, they'd stopped.'

'What sort of noises?'

'We hear quite a few noises in this block,' the captain said. 'The Americans are mostly girls, mostly young. They have boyfriend trouble from time to time . . .'

'What sort of noises, Captain O'Brien?'

She sat forward, then lifted her head. 'I'm ashamed to say I did nothing.'

'What sort of noises?' he said again.

She leaned forward, forearms on her knees. 'You have to understand, it was very late. I'd just done a long spell. I'm in air traffic control. It calls for a lot of concentration.'

'You're saying when you heard these noises your reaction was anger?'

She lifted her head. 'Yes. I'd just done six hours on. A lot of air activity – we're holding a winter exercise with the RAF. Maybe you've heard the flights . . .'

'Plenty,' Winter said. 'So you were angry. Natural enough, Captain.'

'Maybe. But it doesn't feel good now.'

'What exactly did you hear?'

'I heard two, maybe three screams. When I think about it now, pretty desperate-sounding screams.' She shook her head.

Winter and Russell walked back down the corridor to Annabelle Wright's flat. Winter walked over to the lift and pressed the call button. He stood listening to the rumbling ascent. 'Pretty noisy,' he said. They walked across the landing to the dead girl's flat. 'As the lift, with the captain in it, came up, the noises stopped.' Winter nodded his head to himself. 'That may have been the moment he was disturbed. The ferret. Abbeline's word, right?'

'The ferret.' Russell's eyes roamed around Annabelle Wright's small apartment. He could see a light blue uniform skirt on the bed, and a uniform jacket neatly draped over a chair. 'Looks as if she had a few minutes then, between getting home and our man's arrival.'

'A few minutes. That's all.'

'So your people arrested Leonard Passmore less than a mile from here at just after two-forty-five last night? Fits like a glove.' Russell's eyes travelled back to the body and the bloody mess above the shoulders. 'What did he hit her with?'

'Upended lamp. It's bagged up ready to go.' He paused. 'There must have been another weapon though. One we've found no sign of yet.'

'What makes you say that?'

'Look at her head. The killer would have needed a knife of some sort. He seems to have made some sort of half-assed attempt to cut off her ears.'

CHAPTER TWENTY-THREE

They had spent nearly two hours in the freezing wind watching the officers digging on the rubbish heap. Each time some further piece of women's clothing was unearthed Tessa had come forward and crouched to examine it. But nothing more had been found that she recognised. And nothing of what she knew they were really looking for – a naked or near naked body.

It was dark and they were working under lights when Abbeline had suggested he should drive her back. The digging would continue. Any possible items of clothing would have to be brought back to Cambridge.

Tessa broke the silence in the car as they joined the road back to Cambridge. 'It's appalling to think of her lying somewhere under that vast pile of garbage.'

Abbeline took his eyes from the road ahead for a second. She looked drawn and tense but a lot calmer than when she'd stood at the dump. 'We've found a dress, Tessa. We haven't found a body.'

She was silent. 'You're going to turn over that dump. Or at least the whole area where the boy found the dress. I heard Inspector Rose giving the orders.'

'That's routine. Look, the dress might easily have been dropped in a dustbin somewhere miles from the tip. It might have been taken there by waste-truck. If Beth *is* dead, her body might well be miles away.'

'I suppose so.'

'What they'll be doing this evening is collecting and sifting the rubbish from the area around the place Beth's dress was found. This could provide us with addressed letters, newspapers with the delivery address still visible, something to track down the place the bag was thrown away. It could be a very long business, well into tomorrow before they turn anything up. If there is anything to turn up. Or of course the dress might have been, as you thought, abandoned directly on to the dump.'

She sat silently and as he glanced sideways at her he saw that she had closed her eyes. In the silence, against the humming of the car's engine, unwavering on the straight fenland road, he let his thoughts wander. They had found a dress. Perhaps the dress Beth had been wearing the night of 4 November. Perhaps the night she died.

But if she had died, had the killer taken the dress from the body? The blood on it suggested that. But if he intended to dispose of the body – why not leave the clothing on?

He looked uneasily at the silent woman next to him as if she might be reading his thoughts. He changed tack. The first thing was for Rose to get the dress to forensics. There was still no complete certainty that it was blood. The dress had not been washed in a washing machine so they would almost certainly be able to establish whether it was blood and, if so, possibly even the blood group. They had Beth's group from the University Medical Centre.

'I have to think of something else,' Tessa said from the seat beside him.

'It's not going to be easy.'

'No.' She was silent. 'Are you going back to London tonight?'

He shook his head. 'No. There's a college guest room next to the office in Wentworth Court. Jan tells me the deal she made with the Bursar includes using the room whenever I want it. She also tells me it has the scope and comfort of a monk's cell.'

'What will you do about eating?'

'I'll find something in the town.'

They had entered Cambridge and were travelling past King's, past Pembroke. The Fitzwilliam was on their right. 'Anna's out this evening,' Tessa said flatly. 'I was thinking it could just be my turn to make the omelettes.'

At Norwich Central Bill Winter came into his office carrying two styrofoam cups of coffee. He gave one to Ken Russell who was sitting behind the desk.

'Stay there,' he yawned, as Russell made to surrender his seat. 'I could do with a stretch.' He sipped the coffee.

'Any news of Passmore?' Russell asked, lighting the thirty-fifth cigarette of the day.

'None. Nothing at all. He left here, got into his old VW and vanished into thin air. It's a Satanic miracle. Maybe he's lying low somewhere in town.'

'The Millennium Church has a prayer centre somewhere not a million miles from here.'

'Is that so. Why didn't you say?'

'Because I've no idea where it is. East Anglia is all I know. What about the girl's boyfriend, the German lad, Karlheinz?'

'He's completely covered as far as alibi goes. He works nights at the Café Mozart. There's ample evidence that Annabelle left alone. The German boy stayed to work until the place closed at five then drank beer until nearly eight in the morning with a couple of language students who had stayed on.'

'You mind if I talk to him?' Russell asked.

'Be my guest. He's just leaving. Take it easy. He's a nice lad. Badly hit by all this.'

Russell got up and put out his cigarette in an ashtray full of broken, charred butts. Winter frowned. 'Why don't you take up cigars,' he said.

'Does it make a difference?'

'You still kill yourself,' Winter said. 'But with a lot more style.'

In the interview room Karlheinz Beck sat alone, a plate of eggs and sausage half eaten at his elbow. He was about twenty-five, wore jeans and a dark plaid shirt that made his fair hair look startlingly bright under the lights.

'What are you doing here, Karl? In England, I mean?'

'I'm an engineer. I'm doing a day course of English, working at the Café Mozart three nights a week.' He paused. 'And I was taking the chance to see Annabelle again. I met her first in Wiesbaden. She was posted there before she came to England last month.'

Russell nodded. 'Just a few questions,' he said.

The young German bubbled air through his lips. 'What do you want to know? I've told Inspector Winter all I can.'

'I know that.' Russell sat on the edge of the bolted-down metal table. 'When did Passmore first approach Annabelle?'

'I've told all this to Inspector Winter.'

Russell nodded. 'I know. But it'll help, I promise.'

Beck shrugged. 'She met him first a few weeks back. I think he approached her in the street. Hanging around her, trying to talk to her, you know.'

'And then?'

'Nothing more of him until the other evening. The time I told the inspector about.'

'What happened when he first approached her?'

Karlheinz shrugged. 'He was polite, friendly at first. One American to another, you know?'

'You weren't there?'

'No, last night was the first time I saw him. I knew immediately by his look that this was the man who had been . . .'

'Hassling her?'

'That's it, hassling.'

'Why do you think Passmore chose Annabelle? I know she was a very good-looking girl, but was that it?'

'He made a lot of Bible talk,' the young German said. 'Talk about the coming of the Lord and prophetic statements and so forth.'

'Prophecies – is that what he was interested in?'

'Mostly he was interested in Annabelle herself. Her family in America. Her upbringing. He was asking many questions.'

'About her family?'

'Yes, I think so.'

'About her background?'

'About her home in New York. The crazy man wanted to know all about her mother. Her mother's old – what is there to tell?'

'What was so special about her mother? Didn't he want to know about her father?'

'There was nothing to tell about him. Her father was out of Annabelle's life before she was born.'

'You mean, just walked out?'

'You know . . .' He shrugged.

'No. Tell me?'

'Annabelle's mother was a secretary at a television company in

New York,' Karlheinz said. 'Her father was one of the white married executives. Bang, bang, end of story.'

'What did Passmore want to know about Annabelle's mother, then?'

'Not very nice things. Did she sleep with many men? Questions you should not be asking about someone's mother, eh? Not even if you know that someone well.'

'Knowing she's dead, or feeling sure she's dead if you prefer, is a long way from thinking that this is the end,' Tessa said. 'No, in answer to your question, I'm not going back home, Jack. Not yet.'

'Until . . .?'

'I don't know. Until the body's found. Until you've established what happened. Established that Woodward murdered Sally, if that's what happened, and . . .' Her voice tailed off. 'Until I understand what the hell happened, I suppose. Until I understand how my nice, rather unworldly little sister got into all this.'

They were sitting at either end of a long sofa, coffee on the low table in front of them. 'Do you still believe she was that?'

'Believe she was what?'

'A nice rather unworldly little sister. It doesn't explain her connection with Woodward.'

'Nothing I know of explains that.'

'No,' he agreed.

Tessa was silent for a long time. 'Long ago,' she said, 'we had a family myth about what we all were. I was sensible, practical, all those doubtful virtues. Beth was the dreamer, the romantic. But it wasn't true. Beth was a go-getter. Vastly ambitious.' She paused. 'Astonishing how easy it is to slip into the past tense. Beth was, I suspect, quite hard. Certainly quite determined. Able to keep her emotions hidden. Unlike me.' Again she lapsed into a long silence.

'You're thinking of the letter she wrote to the man in Oxford?'

'Partly.'

'I had someone go round to his parents' home in London,' Abbeline said. 'Alan Waterman his name is, nothing more than an acquaintance of Beth's. He says that she was rather outspoken.'

'About me?'

'I'm afraid so.'

She was silent for a moment. 'Hurts,' she said. 'Hurts because I never realised. I thought of myself as the amiable mother-hen elder sister. A nuisance at times but what would she do without me? That sort of thing. Beth saw it differently, huh?'

'Yes.'

'What did she think of Carter?'

'Maybe she put you both in the same pot.'

'Whoops!'

'Best you know.'

She nodded. 'Best I know. Damn it, tonight I'm not taking any excuses.'

He raised his eyebrows.

'You're a hotshot detective. It shouldn't come as any surprise.' She stood up and carried her coffee cup to a table across the room.

His eyes followed her movements. She put the cup down and turned. 'Okay,' she said. 'I'll come clean. I lied to you.'

'What about?'

'Anna's not away for the evening. She's at a meeting in Oxford. Be back tomorrow sometime.'

'You shameless hussy.'

'Yuh.' She took a deep breath. 'What do you say?'

He stood up and put his arms lightly round her. 'Listen, Tessa, what's happening between me and Jo doesn't seem to be a good reason for spending the night with you.'

She looked up into his eyes. 'Good enough reason for me. If there's no other?'

He shook his head. 'You're not the sort of woman for a one night stand,' he said.

'Why don't you let me decide that, Jack? Or are you saying you're not the kind of man, is that it?' She leaned forward and kissed him. Not open-mouthed, but long. She moved her head back. 'I'm not making a big thing of this,' she said. 'I'm not laying down terms. It's all nice and simple. The way men are supposed to like it.'

'Jesus . . . You're play acting, Tessa.'

She clenched her teeth. 'It's the only way I can bear to plead with you like this.'

He tightened his arms round her until she pushed him away.

Picking up her coffee cup again, she took it through to the kitchen. He waited a moment then followed her. She was standing, her hands resting on the sink, her head hanging down.

He stood in the doorway.

'If you ever change your mind, as they used to say in the movies . . .' she said without looking at him. 'Make sure I'm the first to know.'

He came over and put his hands round her waist. She stood, still staring down at the sink.

'Listen,' he said, 'we're both at a pretty low ebb.'

'Maybe *that's* good enough reason to spend the night together,' she said, still not looking at him.

He moved his hands up until they covered her breasts. He felt the tremor go through her, heard the movement of air drawn through her teeth. She straightened slowly, moving into him.

'Yes,' he said into her hair as she turned. 'Good enough reason for me.'

She awoke before dawn in a tangle of sheets, charged with an elation she had never known. Beside her Abbeline slept turned towards her, one leg between hers.

She was not really experienced enough to be able to say how practised a lover he was, or how much more of a lover he might have been if she had not forced him to go to bed with her. There had been a few minutes when he had entered her and she felt his excitement growing with each thrust, when she believed it would all be good. She had tensed every muscle inside her, struggling to draw out of him those frenzied juices that could stand, for a moment, as an illusion of love.

Then he had kissed her, tongued her, lashing her to her own frenzy, short and almost frightening, the first she had ever experienced with a man.

Now they lay together, hand in hand. 'I must go,' he said quietly, breaking the silence.

'You know what they say about men who won't stay for dawn?'

He smiled. 'I have to see Loverell.' He lay back on the pillow.

She touched him, speculatively, dangling her fingers over him, but there was no response. She took her hand away. 'Hell,' she

197

said, 'a real woman would get up and make you coffee before you left.'

She stood at the open door as Jack Abbeline hurried across the pavement and opened the door to his car. For a moment he paused, lifting his hand. 'Go in,' he called across the few yards between them, 'you'll catch cold.'

She nodded, seeing the droplets of mist glistening on the top of the car as he got in and slammed the door.

She stayed, her blue robe wrapped tightly around her, until he drove away. The car, she noticed, had left a dry patch under the lamplight. She was about to close the door when she became aware of a movement, a man approaching.

'I must talk to you,' a voice said urgently.

She hesitated.

'I must talk to you about salvation.'

A tall figure in a dark trenchcoat stood by the gate. Had she heard an American accent?'

'It's five o'clock in the morning, buddy,' she said, emboldened by the distance between them. 'Even my salvation doesn't rate a doorstep sales pitch at this hour.' She began to close the door.

Through the diminishing crack of lamplight she saw him leap the gate.

The door banged against the catch and she heard him on the step. Large fingers hooked themselves around the edge. In the half second she had before he set his weight against it, she clipped in the safety chain.

The man's weight thudded against the door but the chain held the crack at no more than an inch or two.

'I have to speak with you . . .'

She looked round desperately. The fingers jerked and rattled the door.

'More immediate than your salvation,' the voice rose from behind the door, 'I have to talk to you about life itself. Your life.'

The fingers tensed. Under the weight of an invisible shoulder, the door shuddered. The brass screws holding the chain were wrenched sideways. She was screaming at him to go.

The shoulder heaved again and the heads of the brass screws

bent. On the hall table stood a Delft wine jug, of God knew what rarity or value. Tessa reached out, took it by the slender neck. As the fingers tensed round the door again she shattered the jug against them.

From outside on the step there was a roar of pain. And a moment later the fingers had gone, leaving a smear of black blood on the pale grey paintwork. She threw her weight against the door, heard it click closed and threw the bolt.

Turning, she ran up the stairs to the front bedroom window. The man was standing in the garden below, nursing his damaged fingers. For a moment his eyes seemed to roam across the façade of the house, then as an early-morning bus loomed from the direction of Hills Road, he turned away and walked off quickly into the morning mist.

In Police Central, Norwich, Ken Russell eased himself off the desk. 'Okay,' he said. 'Thanks for your help, Karlheinz. I think I have everything. Inspector Winter's giving me a copy of your full statement. He paused, half turning in the door. The young German had slumped forward on the desk, his head on his arms.

'One last question, Karlheinz?'

The blond head came up. Russell could see his eyes were red-rimmed. 'Sorry . . .'

'That's okay.'

'One last question, you said?'

'Did Annabelle mention hearing of any other American girls on the base that Passmore was talking to? These things travel fast. One girls speaks to another over a cup of coffee . . .'

'No. She never mentioned any other girl being approached by Passmore.'

'So it was just Annabelle, as far as she knew?'

'As far as she knew.'

Russell frowned, one hand on the door jamb. 'Does any of this make any sense to you, Karl?'

Karlheinz shook his head. 'Passmore was talking about salvation, about how he could save her . . . that's not so surprising for a preacher.' But . . .' He stopped. 'Small pieces come back to me that don't make a lot of sense?'

'What sort of small pieces?'

Karlheinz grimaced. 'Passmore had this story he was interested in her background. In her name, he said. Some men, you know, are very tricky.'

'Sure.'

Karlheinz nodded and fell silent.

'So he claimed to be interested in her name,' Russell prompted. 'In the name Annabelle Wright?'

'He said he liked history. Annabelle's name is famous, according to Passmore.'

'Is that so?' Russell frowned. He couldn't think of any famous Wrights in history, beyond the brothers. Abbeline would know. 'Wright's a pretty common Anglo-Saxon name,' he said.

'No, no. It wasn't Wright that interested him so. What so interested this Passmore was the name on her birth certificate.'

That sudden investigator's thrill touched Russell's spine. 'Her birth certificate name was *different?*'

'She was still Annabelle Wright . . .'

'But?'

The German shook his head wearily. 'Though Annabelle never saw her father, her mother still made sure she carried his name: Annabelle Naylor Wright.' Karlheinz enunciated slowly. 'Yes . . . I think that's what so interested this Herr Passmore – the middle name, *Naylor.*'

CHAPTER TWENTY-FOUR

'This one's like wading into a quicksand,' Commander Loverell said, pacing his office carpet. 'Two dead girls and a missing American researcher all have Naylor connections. But the prime suspect has no known connection with any of them except that he was hassling Annabelle hours before she was killed. And that he's probably the man who frightened the life out of Mrs Wilson this morning. What's going on, Jack? Have we got some sort of religious maniac on our hands?'

'Maybe,' Abbeline conceded. 'We're stumbling in the dark but there are one or two things we have to keep in mind.'

'What are they?'

'First Laurie Woodward's part in the whole business. What really made Beth Naylor get connected with him? Even stay connected? She couldn't have believed she could convert him once she began to suspect the sort of interests he had. Second, that the Naylor connection is at the heart of the whole business. Beth, legitimate child of Quentin Naylor, disappears in Cambridge. Illegitimate child of Quentin Naylor Sally Portal is murdered there. And another possible illegitimate child of Quentin Naylor is murdered in nearby Norwich.'

'Are there any other known or suspected offspring?'

'I asked Tessa Wilson but as she said, her mother protected them from any knowledge of their father's affairs when they were small children. As a precaution I contacted the FBI at Grosvenor Square. Quentin Naylor has an ageing sister in Bangor, Maine. The FBI are going to see if the old lady can produce any indiscreet details.'

'Family murders usually equal inheritances,' Loverell said.

'Not this time. Quentin Naylor left a modest pile to the two legitimate daughters. We've looked and we can find no sign of an inheritance to kill for, no sign of anybody in the family likely to be doing the killing.'

'What else?'

'The Millennium Church has a prayer centre somewhere in England. Almost certainly not too far from London. Perhaps even not too far from Norwich. Passmore's complete disappearance makes the prayer centre look a possibility.'

'You think he's hiding out there?'

'Odds on.'

'Surrounded by loyal followers. Surely we can find the bloody place before the press do? How about the helpers in the two soup kitchens? Somebody must have been to the prayer centre.'

'We've already drawn a blank there, sir. They use novices to work the soup kitchens and they don't get to know where the main hangout is until they're fully indoctrinated. I think that's how Passmore works it. The country place is a sort of retreat and its existence is kept quiet from the press. That means it's not going to appear in any local phone book or local authority record. But it exists and it's a good bet it's where he is hiding out at the moment.'

'So you're working two lines: Beth Naylor and a separate search for Passmore?'

'At some point those two lines are going to come together pretty quickly. Maybe they already have.'

For a few moments both men were silent.

'You know, Jack,' Loverell said, 'when I was a young detective working the streets, I kept a parrot.'

'On your shoulder?'

Loverell scowled. 'At home. I used to talk to this damn parrot whenever I was working on a difficult case.'

'Did you really, sir?'

'Don't smirk, Jack. It makes you look like a vicar who's just had his first wink from a favourite choirboy.'

'Sorry. Okay, the parrot.'

'Parrots, you see, question everything. It's their form of speech. Pretty Polly. *Pretty Polly?* I didn't do it. *Didn't do it?* They're natural doubting Thomases.'

Abbeline looked at him. 'I'm not quite sure what you're saying, sir?'

'Perfect to bounce your favourite theories off. What I'm saying, Jack, is if you need a parrot, don't hesitate to knock on my door.'

'No. Okay, sir. Thank you.' Abbeline smiled, getting to his feet. 'If I need a parrot, I'll remember.'

Loverell grimaced. 'Sod off,' he grunted. 'But before you go, Jack, let's have your thoughts on immediate action – without benefit of parrot.'

'My first thought is that we should offer Mrs Wilson some protection. She's part of the only common denominator we have in the case at the moment – she's a daughter of Quentin Naylor.'

'Protection?' Loverell grimaced. 'Expensive. I'd be happier if you could persuade her to pack her bags and go back home.'

'Passmore could as easily be in Boston as here. Almost as easily.'

'Someone else's worry,' Loverell said briskly. 'Now I'm not saying tell Mrs Wilson nothing from now onwards, but she's no longer central to your part in the case. We have two murders and a missing woman: Beth Naylor. We have good reason to fear the worst. We have a prime suspect in the form of Passmore who must be picked up as soon as possible. That's the situation I want you to take charge of. Mrs Tessa Wilson is no longer your primary responsibility. Go and see her, Jack. Have a word with her. Tell her it's time to go home.'

Tessa Wilson let her eyes wander round the huge bathroom. It had an Edwardian sumptuousness she had never encountered before with two bathtubs set at fingertip distance, floor-length gilded mirrors and tiling where satyrs pursued ample nymphs along the Delft blue frieze. She stood for a moment, the heavy white towel wrapped round her. Her thoughts were on her husband, Carter. She was avoiding his calls now. If she spoke to him she would tell him that their marriage was over. She'd say things that hurt, like: not so much over as not really ever begun. Vindictive things that she didn't think she really meant. But things to make him not want to patronise her with that cooing, understanding voice.

Yet she had to tell him. That much she had decided. She had no wish to hurt him more than was necessary but she knew he would simply not accept it unless she went on the offensive. He would find it impossible to believe that she had of her own free will decided to leave him.

So maybe she would just tell him she had been doing her damndest to get a man, the senior Scotland Yard man assigned to her case, to go to bed with her? And last night she had succeeded. She shook her head at herself in the tall gilt mirror and walked through the open door into her bedroom. More degenerate splendour. More mahogany and gilt. And a huge bed.

She began to dress, her thoughts on Abbeline now. He had been brisk on the phone, reporting the murder of the black Air Force girl in clipped sentences. Listening to her account of the man who had tried to force his way in just after he left and asking about her father in New York. Then telling her he wanted to see her as soon as possible. After last night did he think she'd make any difficulty about that? She had thrown herself at him, of course, and what good had it done? She paused, deliberately slowed her thoughts. It had done *her* good. She stood before the dressing table and brushed her dark-blonde hair until her arm ached. Then she tossed the brush onto the bed and put on the skirt and sweater she had laid out.

It was mid-afternoon and almost dark. She poured herself a brandy. Brandy in mid-afternoon. No matter, before Abbeline arrived she would take the bull by the horns. She would call Carter.

She threw herself on to the bed, stretching out a hand until it rested on the phone beside her. Again and again she rehearsed the reasons she would give: they had never really shared an interest in work or . . . she had come to the reluctant conclusion that she needed more lebensraum, more space as the young said now . . . to do what?

She picked up the phone and pressed the long series of buttons. Was morning a better time to deliver a 'Dear John' than evening? She guessed so.

The phone rang, the long tones of America. She saw Carter, in her imagination, crossing the room on narrow, bare feet. She saw him buttoning his faded red denim shirt. She saw him check the fall of his thinning hair as he always did answering door or phone.

There was a click. Carter's pleasant, civilised voice said hello.

She lay on her back unable to speak. Suddenly unable to speak. Carter, she wanted to say, it's all over, so there.

'Is that you, Tessa?' the civilised tones asked.

'Yes, it's me.' She sat up. 'A transatlantic hic. I could hear you, you couldn't hear me.'

'I could hear you,' he said. 'You were snorting like a rhinoceros.'

'Thanks.'

'A lady rhinoceros.'

'I feel better.'

'Tessa, I've been trying to call you. I think this nonsense has to end.'

'Agreed.'

'I think I must insist on your coming home right away.'

'Insist?'

A pause. 'Yes,' he said. 'Insist. It's time for me to take this whole thing in hand.'

She took the phone from her ear and rubbed it down her breastbone.

'Tessa . . .'

'You said, you insist I come home?'

'Today.'

'You also said earlier that this nonsense must end.'

'I did.'

'I agree, Carter. This nonsense must end.'

'You're coming home?'

'No. I'm not coming home. I'm ringing you to say I'm never coming home.'

'What?'

'I'm ringing to say this nonsense must end.'

'Have you taken leave of your senses?'

'No, Carter, I haven't. I'm agreeing wholeheartedly with you. *This nonsense must end.*'

There was a long silence on the line. She found it harder to imagine what he was doing. Was he looking down at his bare feet? Was he smoothing the thinning hair. 'Are you wearing shoes?' she said.

'What? No.'

'And your red denim shirt?'

'Yes. So what, for Christ's sake?'

'I thought so,' she said.

'Listen, Tessa.' His voice was lower, charged with threat. 'I'm putting down the phone now and I expect you to be home here in Boston sometime tomorrow. By evening at the latest. Can we be clear on that?'

She didn't answer.

'This is your husband,' he said, like an airport loudspeaker voice, 'asking you to come home. Can we be clear on that?'

She was sitting bolt upright now. 'Listen, Carter,' she said. 'Only one thing can we be clear about: our marriage is over. Probably never even began. I'm sorry, Carter but that is most definitely the way it is. With us,' she added for what she thought was appropriate emphasis. She knew she was making a mess of it. 'What do you say to that?' she asked, and regretted it instantly.

'This is not a call that takes me entirely by surprise . . .' her husband said slowly.

'It really shouldn't, Carter.'

'. . . but I want to say this,' he said in measured tones. 'In my opinion your conduct, your mental condition in the last few months, has rendered you incapable of being a wife.'

'I don't have to listen to this.'

'Incapable of being a wife,' he repeated. 'Incapable of being a mother.'

'What?'

'I'm simply saying this, Tessa, that in the event that you're pregnant again . . .'

'In the unlikely event, Carter. In the *very* unlikely event.'

'In the event,' he said firmly, 'that you are pregnant again, and in the event that this time you do *not* miscarry, I will assume control of our child.'

'Are you mad?' she screamed down the phone. 'We don't have a child. We are highly unlikely to have a child. And even if we did – there are courts to decide these issues . . .'

'There's no doubt on which side the decision of a New England court would fall.'

She found it difficult to breathe. 'Is that so.'

'That is so,' he said gravely. 'I've already consulted colleagues on it as a hypothetical case.'

'What?

'When you were pregnant and behaving very strangely.'

'You lowlife! Okay, you've consulted colleagues. Maybe they can tell you something about the law but they can tell you damn all about my body. I'm *not* pregnant. Got it?' She slammed down the phone. Her heart was pounding. Pregnant? She stood up. The man was mad! 'I'm not pregnant,' she shouted into the open room. 'I'm not pregnant by you . . .' She fell back on the bed. 'And,' she said in a lower voice, 'I'm unlikely to be pregnant by anyone else.'

CHAPTER TWENTY-FIVE

When the bell rang Tessa walked downstairs with a sense of foreboding. She had regained control. She was not pregnant. She put the thought aside and opened the front door.

Abbeline stood still for a moment before coming in, as if he were about to deliver his message there on the doorstep. She turned away and left him to close the door behind himself and follow her into the hall. For a moment they stood facing each other in Anna van Gelden's elegant sitting room.

'You've come to tell me everything's changed,' she said. 'That much I can guess. You haven't found Beth so it's not that . . .'

He shook his head. His hands were deep in his leather jacket.

'So what's happened?'

'I'm arranging police protection,' he said.

She shook her head slowly. 'I don't know what we're talking about but you're making a hell of a bad job of whatever it is. Let's start at the beginning. Why should I need police protection?'

'Let me have a drink, will you?'

'Scotch?'

He nodded and dropped down into one of the armchairs, stretching his long legs across the carpet. 'You need police protection, Tessa, as a precaution.'

She had her back to him, pouring whisky into two glasses. 'You mean one of my father's daughters has been murdered. One is missing with a pretty lousy prognosis. A third, if Annabelle Wright *was* his daughter, which seems pretty likely, is dead in a morgue in Norwich, poor girl. And I am the fourth known daughter of Quentin Naylor Esquire. Do you mean anything more than that?'

'It's enough. More than enough.'

'To win me police protection?'

'For me to suggest you go back home, Tessa.'

She handed him a glass. 'Your Mr Passmore hails from the United States, I thought you said.'

He drank. 'From Indiana. A long way from Boston.'

'This is your boss speaking.'

'Yep.'

'And you agree.'

He hesitated. 'I think so.'

'And if last night had worked out better for us, would you have thought differently?'

'Not about the need for protection, either here or in the States.'

'So, from someone you had orders to help, to cooperate with, I've now become something of an official liability. Potential liability. Is that it?'

He took a deep breath. 'Yep.'

'And honest Jack Abbeline has to deliver the message. That from now on Mrs Wilson gets no more information than the next woman. That from now on Mrs Tessa Wilson is to be left to kick her heels, albeit with police protection, until you track down Leonard Passmore. Better still that Mrs Tessa Wilson should fuck off back to the United States where her safety, if not her peace of mind, will be the responsibility of the Cambridge, Massachusetts, Police Department and no longer that of Scotland Yard's Embassy and Prominent Foreign Persons Squad. Jesus,' she exploded, 'I can see why all the world loves a policeman!'

Abbeline drove back to London slowly, trying hard to put a sense of guilt about Tessa from his mind. He'd been harder on her than he intended. And he knew why, of course. Because he'd allowed her to get closer to this investigation than, in fact, his instructions from Loverell had indicated. He'd allowed her to get closer to the investigation – and to himself. And he knew, if the truth were told, he blamed her for it. For being warm and attractive and available. So the cut-off was brutal. Was that, he wondered, the way all men were?

Weaving through sidestreets to reach Earls Court, he found it hard to throw off the feeling. He felt bad. But he knew he mustn't phone her when he got back, just to make it easy for himself. Best she thought him an unfeeling bastard. Best, as Loverell suggested, that she go back home. To Carter Wilson. He grimaced at the thought and slowed along the sidestreet, spotting a parking place outside his flat.

He braked and reversed rapidly, too quickly to see the woman who was swaying on the edge of the pavement. She stepped back quickly. He got out of the car to see his mother, Rhoda, shouting at him, words that weren't entirely comprehensible at first. Then she recognised him.

'It's you, Jack,' she said. Her tone changed immediately. 'I was just going to ring your bell.'

'Look,' he said. 'this is a busy time for me, Rhoda.'

'I've got trouble at the Sisters,' she said without preamble. 'Those women there are after my things. They've stolen everything.'

'The money I gave you?'

'Most of it.'

'Can you complain to the Sister on duty?' he said.

'I'm not going back there again. I couldn't. One of them tried to steal your letter.'

A letter begging her to come back that he had written as a small boy. For no reason he understood she had kept it, treasured it, was proud of it, despite the pathetic criticism it implied of her own actions at the time.

'If they'd taken that letter I would have killed them.'

'What about tonight?' he said. 'If you don't go back to the Sisters?'

'I was just coming round to ask you if you knew of any place?'

He stood looking at her, his stomach churning with a mixture of guilt and anger he had never been able to handle. 'I've no room in the flat,' he said. 'I've someone staying with me tonight. A foreign police official.'

She took the lie easily, for what it was, a drawing of lines. 'I was just wondering if you had any ideas,' she said. 'The thing is these women think they can do exactly as they please. They tell the Sisters to, excuse my language, fuck off . . .'

She wasn't after money, not in the simple sense of begging. She certainly wasn't even after love, despite the conventional wisdom. She wanted time. Somebody's time. She wanted to talk, and talk, and talk. To repeat a jumble of old complaints, to resurrect old bitterness. To talk. 'They've already stolen things from me. Sharon's a known thief. Done time in prison.'

'Listen,' he said. 'Let's get out of this wind.'

'I've been to the police and they do nothing. Now I wondered if you'd be able to tell someone to come round and see them.' She chuckled. 'An inspector. In uniform. That'd put the fear of God into them.'

She didn't want a police visit. She wanted someone there, standing in the wind on a street corner, sitting in a McDonald's, or best of all, a pub while she talked and they listened. Talked in infinite repetition of grievances a day or week or year old. The thieving, the rudeness of the Social, the refusal of doctors to treat her. The bullying, the women just out of jail and the Sisters . . . Gratitude played no role in her life and had little cause to. Even the Sisters she accused of stealing Marks & Spencer groceries to sell to people like her. 'A racket, she said, 'it's all a racket.'

He made a decision. 'In you get,' he said.

'Is this an arrest, or what?' she asked gaily.

'Or what,' he said. 'Have you eaten?' And when she grunted, always unwilling to reveal real details of her day, he said: 'We'll get some McDonald's, that suit you?'

Under the bright lights of the Earls Court McDonald's he could see how grimy her clothes were, how the make-up was applied, coat after coat, how her bright red fingernails were broken, the varnish chipped.

She swept back her grey-blonde hair with a graceful movement and smiled at him. 'This is fun, Jack,' she said. 'When I tell those women at the Sisters I've got a son in Scotland Yard, you know, they don't believe me.'

Abbeline looked at the family at the next table. The young mother didn't believe it either.

'We've got to get you settled for tonight,' he said. 'You can't sleep out in this weather.'

'I can't go back to the Sisters.'

'What I'm going to do,' he said, 'is take you back there and settle you in.'

'Oh no, Jack. I don't want to go back there. Any case, they lock the doors at eight o'clock.' She was wrapping half her Big Mac in a paper napkin and storing it in her handbag. 'Listen, if I just had the money for a place tonight, a hostel, I'd go to the Sisters tomorrow. I promise.'

'You know a place for tonight?'

'In Soho. Beak Street. Sharing three to a room but you can get a shower and do your washing there too. Extra of course.'

'I'll take you there,' he said.

'It's expensive, though.'

He stood. 'How much does this hostel cost?' he asked her when they were out on the pavement. He took out his wallet.

'I said it's expensive, Jack. It's thirty-seven pounds a night.'

Per person. Three to a room. Over a hundred pounds. Hilton prices for a doss house.

When they got into the car he gave her three twenty-pound notes. 'Soho,' he said, his policeman's mind working, 'do you still spend a lot of time there?'

She shrugged. 'I still have a lot of friends there.'

'Some of them who've fallen on hard times?'

'Inevitably. Why do you say that?'

'Have you ever heard of something called the Millennium Church?' They were driving round Piccadilly. He took Shaftesbury Avenue and turned into Soho at Frith Street. 'They have a Mission in Soho. Soup kitchen . . . a night stand at somewhere called the Old School.'

'I've heard of it,' she said vaguely.

'You have?' It was difficult to know with Rhoda.

She nodded, looking out of the window.

'Have you ever been there?'

'Not myself, no.'

'But friends, people you know?'

'Some . . .' Her voice trailed away.

'The Millennium Church. Can you remember that one?'

'Of course.'

'Okay. Now I want you to ask any friends who might have used it. Ask them what they know about the Reverend Leonard Passmore and the Millennium Church. Right? This is an investigation.'

'Is it?' She was immediately more interested. 'I've heard of the Reverend, I think,' Rhoda said as he stopped the car in Beak Street. He looked at her but she was frowning with effort, like a child wanting to be helpful.

'Ask anyway,' he said, and repeated the name. They have some place out in the country. Ask if anybody knows about it? Where will you be tomorrow?'

For a second, the hunted look.

'I'll meet you in the Wheatsheaf,' he said. 'In the afternoon. About five-thirty. Will you remember?'

'Not the Wheatsheaf,' she said hurriedly. 'In the café in Berwick Market.'

He nodded. 'You'll remember, won't you, Rhoda? Half-past five tomorrow.'

'Pull up here,' she said. The Wheatsheaf was in the next street.

Abbeline let himself into Jo's flat. Closing the front door behind him he crossed the hall and stood for a moment leaning in the doorway of the big sitting room. The faint scent was a potent reminder of her recent presence; a reminder too of his mother, of Rhoda, in other days when he had thought of her, dressed to go out, as having all the dazzle of a film star.

He peeled off his coat and threw it on the sofa. Jo's cleaner had bought all the newspapers covering her departure and left them in a stack on the desk. Abbeline stood for a moment, leafing through them. Photographs of Jo had always given him pleasure. But looking at these pictures of the press conference, Sepp Lander seemed everywhere, his arm proprietorially round her.

He dropped a copy of the *Mirror* on top of the pile and turned to pour himself a Scotch. Adding water, he carried the drink across to the phone.

Had he decided what he was going to say? He sat on the arm of the sofa sipping his drink.

The phone rang and he started in surprise then reached out and picked up the receiver. 'Is that you, Jack?' her voice said from the other side of the world.

'It'd better be,' he said. 'How are you?'

'I've called Scotland Yard. Your office in Cambridge. Your flat. And on a not too inspired guess I called here.'

'I just called in from taking Rhoda to Soho.'

'What are you doing there?'

There was something in her tone.

'I just thought I should keep an eye on the place while you were away. It's what you'd want, isn't it?'

There was a long silence, 'No, Jack,' she said slowly. 'It's not what I'd want. Not any more.'

'What are you saying?'

'I'm saying I don't want you to keep an eye on my flat, my life, me . . . not any more.'

He felt stunned. 'Does this mean you're going to marry Lander?' he said.

'It means I'm not going to marry you, Jack. You've made that clear enough yourself. I'm just making a few things clear for me now. Things I should have made clear long before this. What I decide to do about Sepp is up to me.' She paused. 'It no longer has anything to do with you at all, Jack.'

'Jo . . .'

'Don't tell me this isn't the time or place to talk about it. *Now* is the time and place. Leave the flat to look after itself, Jack. Post the keys in through the letterbox, please.'

Once downstairs, he ignored his car and began walking.

The snowflakes were heavy with water and were melting on the pavements, melting on the top of cars, almost melting as they fell, glittering beneath the street lamps.

He paid no attention to where he was walking. Dominated by the wild, churning in his head, he could barely have registered his own street. His mind played back a day for him, a month after his father had been allowed home from hospital after the shooting, after he had been reduced to a wheelchair for the rest of his life by a shotgun blast in a back alley. Jack Abbeline had been ten years old, sitting on the stairs in a cloud of scent that led down to where their voices rose from the sitting room. 'I said I'm going over to Mary's. So that's where I'm going.'

'You're just a bit dressed up for Mary's, aren't you?' his father's voice said mildly, not trying to provoke.

'I want to ask her about this dress. See how she likes it. I'm not sure about it myself.'

'Since when have you taken any notice of Mary?'

The boy heard the high heels clicking. 'Look, are you doubting me?'

Then a silence.

And his father's voice. The tone different, harder. 'Yes, maybe I am. I just don't think you're going to Mary's tonight, that's all.'

'All right.' His mother's voice was rising now. 'All right, I'll confess. I'll confess. I'll sign one of your fucking statements if you like. I'm not going to Mary's. I never had any intention of going to Mary's. I'm going out on the pull. I'm going out to pull a whole bus load of men, a whole station load of young coppers, I'm going to screw every man of screwable age in this whole bloody block of flats. Type that one up for me and I'll sign.'

'Where are you going?'

'It's none of your business.'

'Rhoda, listen. Sit down and we'll pour a drink and talk about this. I know things are different, have to be. It's not something of my making.'

He heard a sound from her. Could it really have been a laugh? 'None of it, none of it is any longer your business. Do you know what I mean?'

Then his father's voice. 'You're still a young woman . . . If you have friends from time to time – men friends, from time to time – I'll understand that.

At ten years old, nearly eleven, Jack Abbeline knew what that sentence meant. Vaguely enough perhaps, but from other arguments since his dad had come home again, he knew something of the trade-off that was taking place.

'Tell me it's anything to do with you! Tell me it's your business what I choose to do!' His mother's voice was a shrill challenge. 'And if you do, tell me what you propose to do about it, from that fucking wheelchair!'

Just one night. Not the worst. His father hadn't wept that night.

That would be later as she wore him down. Flaunting herself, then finally even flaunting her men friends in front of the man in the wheelchair. She had no mercy.

Walking through the night, Jack Abbeline was tortured still. What did his father want? What had he wanted? A steely chill crept over him. What his father wanted was to license her. If he couldn't forbid her, he could at least license her.

As he himself had sought to license Jo.

He stopped, very nearly physically sick. He was walking through a narrow park that ran along beside the river. With a start he realised that he must have walked in one vast circle. A few benches were occupied by old homeless men. It had stopped sleeting. He sat down on an empty bench and closed his eyes. He remembered writing the letter when she finally left home, a secret letter that he'd given to his aunt Mary. By then he'd hated his mother but his father was in anguish at her leaving. He was ashamed of the letter now, ashamed of the way he had revealed his father's secrets to bring his mother back. It was a rash, childish letter. Full of lies. And Rhoda treasured it still.

He fell asleep dreaming of Jo. You didn't need psychiatrists to deal with most of life. You needed what Jo had, a little honesty, a little common sense – and the good luck not to be born and grow up with a sackful of hang-ups.

A uniformed policeman woke him at five o'clock. 'Had a few too many, sir?' he asked, not unpleasantly.

'No,' Abbeline grunted. 'A few too few.'

'Don't suppose I have to run you in for vagrancy, do I, sir?'

'And find out you'd just arrested a senior officer at Scotland Yard?' Abbeline smiled as he stood up. 'Wouldn't exactly be your lucky day, would it?'

The constable stiffened uncertainly. 'You're not . . .'

Abbeline shook his head. 'No, don't worry. I'm a lunatic peer of the Realm. You're lucky,' he said, 'you've caught me on a good day. On bad days, I'm inclined to think I'm Napoleon Bonaparte.'

He walked back to the Yard, shaved and washed his face in the cloakroom and was letting himself into his office when the phone rang. He picked it up and gave his name.

The operator said: 'I have someone on the line who claims he's Leonard Passmore.'

'Where is he?'

'Won't say, sir. This is the third call in the last hour. Keeps each one short. He's just hung up now, sir. My guess is he'll call back in a couple of minutes.'

'Sure it's him?'

'American accent sounds real enough, sir. Refuses to talk to anyone but you.'

Abbeline grimaced. 'You're ready to trace the call?'

'All ready.'

'Okay, put him on when he calls again. Record the call.'

The phone rang again in a few minutes.

It was unmistakably Passmore's voice, but it was a voice cracked with exhaustion. 'Abbeline,' he said. 'Abbeline . . . I have no strength left. I have struggled and fought bitter battles with the Angel of Jacob and I am desperate to lay my head . . .'

'Tell me where you are, Mr Passmore,' Abbeline said evenly. 'I can send someone to pick you up in a matter of minutes.'

'Do you understand, I have been wrong, Abbeline?'

'Any of us can be wrong, Mr Passmore. In what way do you think you were wrong?'

It was as if Passmore had not heard him. 'Grotesquely, arrogantly wrong. I thought to found a church which would live forever. I thought to reveal a prophecy . . .'

'Why are you calling me, Mr Passmore?'

'Because I wish to surrender myself to you, Mr Abbeline.'

'Where are you?'

'Near Norwich. I tried to save her, Abbeline. I tried to save her but she would not hear my voice.'

'Mr Passmore, now I want you to listen to me . . .'

'I'm listening.'

'Go to your nearest police station. Go to Norwich Central.'

'Will you promise to be there, Abbeline? I want to talk to you. To you alone.'

'I'll be there as soon as I possibly can after I get a call to tell me you've arrived there. But one thing first, Mr Passmore. I must know. Is Beth Naylor alive?'

'She's alive,' he said, and the line went dead.

He called Winter at Norwich Central, then called Ray Rose.

'You're sure it was him, sir?' Rose's voice was heavy with doubt.

'It was him,' Abbeline said. 'But is he really going to come in? He sounded close to the edge. The only thing he sounded clearcut and positive about was the last: Beth Naylor is alive.'

CHAPTER TWENTY-SIX

As president of the Maskop (Cambridgeshire) Environmental Watch, Reginald Gummer's particular passion was the prevention of dumping in Maskop Quarry. A local beauty spot, the long-disused quarry had evolved into a lake with trees and bushes growing down its steep sides. Anglers fished it, sailboats used it and children swam in a carefully prepared section of the water.

It was Reg Gummer, beginning ten years ago, who had achieved the recovery of the old quarry almost single-handed. Rotten mattresses, building material and miles of abandoned War Office barbed wire had been dredged out. Trees had been planted and the sides of the quarry made safer. For his achievement at Maskop, Reg Gummer had received a special commendation from Cambridgeshire County Council.

At just before nine o'clock on the morning of Christmas Eve, Gummer had just finished his last phone call. His wife, May, had cleared the breakfast things and loaded the dishwasher. There was just time, they decided, to stretch their legs before the ritual of dressing the Christmas turkey.

They walked, their collie Jason running ahead, as they normally walked, towards Maskop Quarry.

The heavy snowfalls of the last week had been replaced by a thick grey mist which reduced visibility to little more than a dozen yards. But the weather did not daunt Reg and May Gummer; they knew every foot of the lane leading up to the quarry.

In their rubber boots they tramped, companionably silent, along the narrow road, turning on to Quarry Lane moments after Jason had skidded round the corner in search of something he might have heard.

A few steps into the lane Reg Gummer reached out a hand and stopped his wife. With his stick he was pointing to where a double track in the snow led up towards the quarry. 'Tyre marks.' They stood staring for a moment at the ribbed pattern in the snow.

'There's only one set of tracks,' said May.

'I know.' Gummer stood frowning towards the quarry. 'They're still up there.'

'It's not going to be a courting couple this time of year, is it?' She looked towards her husband, slightly nervous now. She had seen more than once how angry he could get when they had actually caught people dumping in the quarry. Two or three times he had been threatened by young builders. She pulled his arm. 'I don't want you to go up there, Reg.'

He shook his arm free.

'I mean it,' she hissed. 'I don't want you to interfere.'

'It's the way we made the quarry what it is,' he said, ' a decent place for people around here. Where's that dog?'

She stood beside him, suddenly aware that he was not anxious to go on. But aware too that he would have to.

'You go back home,' he said to his wife. 'I'm going to walk on a bit. See what's happening up there. Could well just be a couple driven up there after an office party or something. Bit of slap and tickle before they go back to their respective spouses.'

'Could be,' she said. 'But if you're going, I'm going with you.'

He grunted. 'We'll just take a quick look. Go as far as the gate. That should do it.'

They walked forward without speaking. At the gate they stood listening, leaning into the wall of greyness before them. 'I can hear someone moving about over there,' May whispered.

'It's Jason,' he said, his voice low and uncertain.

Then, as they peered up the slope where the tyre tracks in the snow disappeared into the mist, they saw the blurred lights of a car flick on. A sound carried to them, of wheels crunching over the snow, of small leafless bushes cracking as they were crushed. Then a car door slammed with that low unmistakable thud.

'They're running it into the quarry,' May said, aghast.

'You there!' Gummer shouted. Then stopped. The lights tipped, fell through grey space, and the invisible water suddenly erupted, a white ectoplasmic shape in the mist which faded into a low gurgle.

Gummer moved to open the gate but his wife's voice was firm. 'You're not going in there, Reg.'

'Somebody's dumped an old jalopy right under our noses!'

'Let's get back home,' May said urgently. 'Let's get home and phone the council.'

The phone was ringing. Tessa rolled over in the big bed and picked it up. She had slept late. It was already nine o'clock. She pushed her hair back and put the phone to her ear. Carter's well-modulated voice said: 'Tessa, I thought you'd just like to know . . .'

'Like to know what, Carter?'

'Like to know that this whole expedition of yours, this Stanlean pursuit of Livingstone, has been – not that I didn't warn against it – a complete and utter waste of time.'

'Carter,' she said carefully, 'less than eight hours ago we had a very important conversation on this line. I told you, with regret probably not sufficiently well expressed, that our marriage was over. Please, please don't call me now and speak as though that conversation never took place. As though nothing has happened.'

'Oh, something's happened all right,' he said. She could hear the smugness in his voice. 'Something's definitely happened.'

She waited.

'I just received a call,' he said. 'A call from England.'

'Yes?' She was frowning.

'A call from your sister Beth.'

'What?'

'Saying all was well . . . no need to worry. Away on vacation. Well earned rest after a heavy term . . .'

'Are you crazy, Carter? Tell me. Are you making this up?'

'Most certainly not, Tessa. Beth was in fine form. Enquired about you . . .'

'Where is she, for Christ's sake?'

'Didn't really say. Staying with friends maybe. I didn't ask. So come back, Tessa. Face up to it. You've made something of a fool of yourself but it's only me who knows the extent.'

'You *are* crazy. Did Beth really call, Carter?'

'Of course she called,' he exploded angrily. 'She's not *missing*.

Come back home, Tessa. I warned you you'd best not travel by yourself in your condition.'

Mostly now, they were worried about Jason, their dog. It was not too unusual for him to go out with them on a walk and disappear in pursuit of God knows what canine interest, but he would always be back before feeding time. And he had not been fed yet today.

But by eleven that morning Gummer had failed to raise anybody in the Environmental Department of the council and there was still no sign of Jason. At eleven-thirty Gummer had been up to the quarry and photographed, as best he could in the mist, the broken bushes and what was left of the tyre marks in the melting snow. There were still large patches of ice floating on the surface of the water and ducks standing immobile staring up at him. But there was no sign of Jason.

Returning to the house, he left an urgent message on the Environmental Officer's answering machine. They had worked together on several issues and the Environmental Officer would know this was not a storm in a teacup.

When he'd finished phoning Gummer walked back into the kitchen. When Jason returned from his forays it was usually the back garden path he chose. That way lay the fields and woods, and that way lay Maskop Quarry.

'Could it be gypsies?' May asked. 'They've been known to take a dog. A pedigree collie at that.'

'I suppose it's possible,' he conceded. 'But when did you hear of gypsies towing old vehicles up to the quarry? They just strip them and abandon them by the roadside.'

'They could have driven it up there.'

'Then why abandon it if it's still going?' He was sipping his mug of tea between sentences, peering out of the low kitchen window, hoping to see Jason come galloping, even limping, down the path.

'Why should *anybody* abandon it, if it was going?'

He turned from the window. 'You're right, May, of course,' he said slowly. 'Why should anybody take the trouble to take a car, a car you can still drive, up to the quarry and tip it in?'

He put down the mug of tea. 'You get a one track mind,' he said, 'dealing with environmental problems. This one's not for the town hall. It's for the police.'

'What have you got for me on the Naylor family?' Abbeline asked Jan as they drove towards Cambridge.

'Well, no vast sums of money flying around as I told you. So we're not talking *Kind Hearts and Coronets*. And I think we can rule out a vendetta against the Naylors as a family,' she said. 'It'd take a massacre to deal with them.'

'So it's a common enough name in the phone book?'

'One hundred and nine of them in London alone. Not to mention Naylers, who my genealogist says are essentially the same family. Hundreds more in the big cities all over the country. Thousands in the UK alone.'

'Not much help there,' Abbeline said. 'Both Beth and Annabelle Naylor Wright are American. Any light coming from that quarter?'

'Members of the Naylor family established themselves pretty early, apparently. They left England in the 1600s – no real dates, certainly not Pilgrim Fathers – but they settled in New England, mostly in Massachusetts. The family we're interested in, Beth and Tessa Wilson's family, goes back a couple of hundred years in the records. Doctors, small town lawyers, one state senator, that sort of thing. Made decent money in the nineteenth century as boot-makers. Nothing very special about them.'

Abbeline grimaced. 'There's somebody thinks there's something special, Jan.'

She glanced at him and saw he was frowning. 'What is it? The breakthrough idea?'

'No,' he said, 'I've just realised I'm not going to make it to meet Rhoda this afternoon in Berwick Market . . .'

'You don't believe it's true?'

Tessa shook her head. She was sitting with Anna in the bar of the Pelican Inn. 'After the miscarriage,' she said, 'in the middle of my breakdown, Carter seemed as steady as a rock. Good in a crisis, everyone said. But of course, I realise now that Carter and people like him are only good in *someone else*'s crisis. My troubles gave him the chance. What he was actually doing was building his own

225

self-esteem at the expense of my self-confidence. Not much of a deal.' She paused. 'The way I see him now is a sort of academic cuckoo. He can operate in his job, he's just not too hot in life. I think he made up the call from Beth. I'm damn sure he did.'

'Shouldn't you tell Jack Abbeline all the same?'

'No . . . I don't think he'd be interested in the sound of a breaking marriage.'

'You're sure that's all it is? You're sure Carter didn't get a call from Beth?'

Tessa nodded. 'I'm sure. I'm pulling free of his clutches and he wants me back. At any price.'

'And it's over for you?'

'It's one of the few things I'm sure of.' She smiled at Anna. 'Not a lot else I'm sure of just at the moment. Except the need to do something.'

'What sort of thing?'

'I'm not a patient mortal, Anna. I just can't sit around waiting for the police to hand me a few snippets of information. After I spoke to Carter this morning, I drove out to that awful garbage tip. The police are still there, but they didn't want to talk to me. It's as if I've suddenly taken a fall from grace.'

'Which you know is nonsense.'

'Not entirely,' Tessa said slowly. 'I've taken a fall from grace with Jack too. Personally, I mean.'

'You think so?'

'I think I pushed too hard.'

'Too hard?'

Tessa smiled regretfully. 'I asked him to go to bed with me.'

'Just like that?'

'I thought he wanted to. You know, drinks, soft music. In London we came very close. This time I thought I should make it easy for him.'

Anna smiled. 'The American way? I want it, you know I want it; you want it, I know you want it. Somebody had better damn well lay it on the line?'

'Something like that.'

'You're not telling me he declined the offer?'

'No,' Tessa said slowly. 'It was good. But we weren't really

226

making love. Come the dawn we both realised that.'

'Where does that leave you?'

'How about high and dry?'

'Even I can see he's a very attractive man,' Anna said cautiously.

Tessa looked at her. '*Even* you?'

Anna put her tongue in her cheek.

'Ah . . .'

'I've only had two love affairs in my life,' Anna said. 'One at school. One in the States when I was doing my doctorate at Princeton.' She paused. 'Both women. I don't suppose that comes as a total surprise to you?'

'No, not a total surprise,' Tessa said slowly. 'Not a *total* surprise.'

Anna nodded then leaned across the bar to order two more glasses of wine. 'What will you do then?' she said, as if the last conversation had never taken place.

'Here, let me get these.' Tessa fumbled with her purse and produced a five pound note. She laid it on the counter. 'I want to say something, but I don't know how. I guess it's that I really appreciate your friendship,' she said to Anna. 'You've anchored me through these extraordinary days.'

Anna nodded. This time it wasn't the barman who brought the glasses of wine but the publican, George Pringle. 'I thought I saw you, Mrs Wilson,' he said. 'I read about your sister being missing and thought I'd just come over and ask if there's been any word yet?'

'Not really,' Tessa said. 'The police have a few possible leads . . .' She let is rest there.

Pringle nodded. 'You've had a lot of people offering information, I expect? People like to get in on somebody else's troubles – as if they don't have enough troubles of their own.'

'There have been some,' Tessa said, anxious to continue her conversation with Anna.

He nodded. 'Did your American friend catch up with you?'

'A friend of mine? An American?'

'There was a young lady in the bar the other day. Asking if you were still staying here.'

'When was this, Mr Pringle?'

He paused, running his tongue over his teeth. 'Day before yesterday. Yes, must have been.'

'Definitely an American?' Anna asked.

'Definitely.'

'This girl,' Tessa said. 'How old was she?'

'Difficult to say. She was all wrapped up in a headscarf and complaining about the cold. And the wind had dropped that day. I asked her where did she come from, Sunny California?'

'What did she say?'

'To tell you the truth, she was a bit brisk. In – asked her questions – got her answers – out. Didn't even stay for a drink.'

'Tall, short . . . fat, thin?'

'Tallish like you. Fat or thin I couldn't say. Bundled up in a big coat, the headscarf halfway round her face.'

'What did you tell her?'

'I couldn't tell her that much. I knew you'd gone to stay with this lady here . . .' he nodded towards Anna '. . . because she came round to help you with your things. I remembered the lady worked at the Fitzwilliam, but I couldn't remember where you said you were going,' he added apologetically.

After he had moved away to the other end of the bar, Anna looked at Tessa. 'You think it's her?'

'Why should it be? An American girl . . . there are plenty in Cambridge. Beth must have known a few.' She shook her head. 'I don't know, Anna. No, how could it be Beth? Why wouldn't she come forward?'

'Fear of Passmore? She's a Naylor.'

'So am I.'

'Which is why there are two plainclothes policemen in a car outside.'

'What am I to do, Anna?' She knew she was close to putting her head in her hands.

'Go to Abbeline.'

Tessa shook her head. 'I couldn't. Not now.'

'Go to Abbeline,' Anna repeated. 'Or go home.'

'That's what everybody wants me to do. Carter . . . you . . . Jack and his unknown boss.' She paused. 'But I'm not having it, Anna. I don't know if I'm doing it for Beth or for me, but I'm not going to be pushed out of this.'

'What can you do?'

Tessa took a fierce gulp of her wine. 'I'm going to plunge in. I'm not going to be left here shivering on the edge.'

'How do you plunge? Where do you start?'

'I don't know, Anna.' Tessa said slowly. 'But I'm not going to be squeezed out by Jack Abbeline and chased off home to Carter. If Beth's alive, she's in trouble. She must be. I'm not going back while I think that.'

Once in their Cambridge office, Jan went out for sandwiches and coffee while Abbeline called Inspector Winter at Norwich Central.

'No sign of Passmore, sir,' Winter said. 'I've alerted all Norwich area stations. But when I think of the way he was when we questioned him here, I don't see him riding into town with his hands up.'

'You're assuming he killed the girl when you say that?'

'When I had him here, it was on a minor nuisance charge and he was as bold as brass. I didn't know there was a body lying in a flat half a mile away. Yes, I'm assuming he did. Don't you, sir?'

'I don't know,' Abbeline said. 'I'm trying to keep assumptions to a minimum.'

When he'd put the phone down he stood in the middle of the beamed room, thinking of Passmore's drained, exhausted voice. There was one sentence that kept coming back to him. 'I tried to save her but she would not hear my voice.' Was that just a biblical way of saying 'Despite all my attempts to save her, I had to kill her?' And was he talking about Annabelle Wright or Beth Naylor?

He called Winter back at Norwich Central. 'When you questioned Passmore, did he at any time offer any reason for talking to Annabelle in the street?'

'Not really, sir.'

'What does that mean?'

'Well, I could get you the transcript when it's typed up, but from memory he mostly kept quiet.' Winter paused. 'I think he began with some sort of talk about salvation. You know the sort of thing. He was offering her the chance of salvation.'

'Salvation? Did he actually use the word?'

'I think so, yes. He said what he was doing when he approached Annabelle Wright was trying to save her.'

'Not necessarily the same as offering her salvation, is it?'

'Not with you, sir.'

'You don't think Passmore was saying he was trying to save her . . .'

'Yes.'

'. . . from *someone*.'

'Christ! Never occurred to me, sir.'

'Let me know the moment he gets there,' Abbeline said, and hung up.

His eye ran over the room's proportions. These were probably the best rooms he would ever occupy in his career. He had twice been in the office of the Commissioner of the Metropolitan Police and left unimpressed. A bigger box, that's all it was. Whereas this room with its bulging walls, its mullioned windows, the dark, slightly twisted carved beams . . . '*I tried to save her but she would not hear my voice.*'

He threw himself into the chair behind the desk. He had decided not to contact Tessa, had decided all contact from now on would be through Jan, but he pulled the phone towards him now on an instinct. He wanted to see her. Dialling the number of Anna van Gelden's house, he hung up when the answerphone cut in.

So be it. Maybe he would call again later. Maybe not. For now there was the hard click of Jan Madigan's heels on the wooden stairs.

She carried pizzas and a bottle of Languedoc red. And behind her, in softer soled shoes, which was why Abbeline had not heard him, was Ray Rose. 'I picked him up on the street,' said Jan. 'I'm not sure if he's more interested in my mind or my pizza.'

Abbeline indicated a chair. While Jan found some glasses Abbeline pulled the pizza into three roughly equal parts, tore off pieces of wrapping paper and set it out on his desk. 'You look as if you might have something,' he said to Rose.

'I don't know, sir. It's that dress we found on the dump on the Ely Road . . .'

Abbeline swigged at the Languedoc, grimaced before the taste hit home, pursed his lips and looked at Jan. 'This isn't half bad.' He turned back to Rose. 'Go on.'

'First,' Rose said, 'how did the dress the boy found get there?

Was it delivered by truck with twenty tons of other rubbish, or was it dumped separately?'

'What do you think?'

'We picked over every piece of garbage in the area where the boy claims he found the dress. It's all reasonably local.'

'You're saying that the dress wasn't dumped separately?'

'I think it was shoved in a dustbin somewhere within twenty miles' radius of the dump.'

'Any progress on the stain down the front?'

'This is a lot more interesting, sir. Forensics say that if the dress was washed at all, it was a dip in cold water. They were able to establish beyond doubt that the stain was blood.'

'Anything more than that?' Jan asked cautiously.

Rose was enjoying the attention. 'Cambridge Medical Centre can confirm that it's not Beth Naylor's blood group down the front of her dress.'

'Not Beth Naylor's?'

'No, sir.'

'Could it be Woodward's?' Jan asked.

'The fatal accident record says no. It's not his either.' Rose pushed. 'It's a fairly common group so it's maybe not conclusive but I checked with Sally Portal's group. The blood on Beth Naylor's dress matches Sally Portal's blood.'

Abbeline nodded slowly. 'Well done, Ray. I think Rubik's cube is beginning to take shape.'

Doctor Grimes' rooms looked out at an angle to take in part of King's College Chapel, and at another angle to the eighteenth-century library that faced the Wilkins Screen across the Great Court. Abbeline stood for a moment then turned to Grimes who was busy pressing on Jan Madigan any alcoholic liquid that seemed even remotely appropriate for three o'clock in the afternoon. She settled, to Abbeline's surprise, for seed cake and a glass of hundred-year-old Madeira. Abbeline knew she would have much preferred a can of Red Stripe.

'What is it I can do for you, my dear?' Grimes asked. He was infinitely intrigued to meet a miniskirted Scotland Yard inspector – and made his fascination clear.

Jan sipped her Madeira. She glanced at the cake, broke off an edge with long red fingernails and stood, cake in one hand, eighteenth century cordial glass in the other, and grinned at Abbeline. 'This is the life.'

'You've got centre stage,' he said.

The grey-haired historian's eyes roamed happily from her legs to her prominent bosom as she elaborated on the deaths of Sally Portal and Annabelle Wright and Beth Naylor's disappearance.

'And the connecting link, if any, is . . .?'

'Beth's father, Quentin Naylor.'

'*London Calling*,' Grimes said. 'Yes, a very well-known wartime broadcaster.'

'He had an eye for attractive ladies.'

'Not so very reprehensible,' Grimes observed mildly.

'He was the father of Sally Portal.'

'Ah.'

'And very probably of Annabelle Wright. Her full name was Annabelle Naylor Wright. According to one witness, it was that Naylor element that interested Leonard Passmore.'

Grimes nodded and sipped his Madeira. Then he frowned off in the direction of his bookshelves. He seemed to be humming to himself.

'What is it, Dr Grimes?' Abbeline said.

'A thought only.'

'You see some sort of connection, Doctor?' Jan asked him.

'I might.' Grimes paused, aware of the theatre of the moment. 'When you came over to see me with Mrs Wilson, Superintendent, you were asking about the Chapel windows.'

'Yes.'

'And I told you the story of the bribe that saved them for posterity.'

'Thirteen shillings and fourpence.'

'It's in the very same decades, the 1640s and '50s,' Grimes said slowly, 'that the name Naylor first makes its appearance in history.' He seemed to pause. 'Jesus Christ,' he said.

Jan looked at him.

'No,' Grimes said. 'I mean Jesus Christ Naylor.'

Abbeline came forward. 'What?'

'Jesus Christ Naylor. A very prominent Puritan divine. Called himself, or allowed his followers to call him, Jesus Christ. Word spread that he had raised a woman named Dorcas Erbury from the dead in Bristol. Followers rallied to him. Not surprisingly he fell foul of Cromwell's government and was imprisoned. The restored Church liked him even less and he was executed shortly afterwards in the early months of the Restoration.'

'What happened to his family?' Abbeline asked.

Grimes frowned. 'Not usually considered of significance. wait a minute . . . A branch left for America shortly after his death. New England. Massachusetts.'

Jan grinned. 'Perhaps I could have a little more of that wine?'

'But of course, my dear. Inspector, I should say.'

'No. Just call me Jan.'

'All right, Jan. I'm Harold. Harry, to my close friends.'

They clinked glasses. 'Here's to you, Harry,' she said.

'A glass of Madeira, Superintendent?' Grimes brought the decanter over to him. 'What can all this mean?' the historian asked. 'Docked ears. Two Naylor women murdered. One missing. Is there anything I can add?'

'In what way was Naylor far out, Harry?' Jan said. 'Apart from the claim he was JC himself?'

'He professed to be no less than the Word of God, to have knowledge of revelation, prophecy, which would change the world. Which would make man see his fellow man . . .' he smiled at Jan '. . . and fellow women indeed, in a different light. He saw himself as persecuted because his message, his revelations, were, he believed, so deeply revolutionary. England, indeed the whole world, would never be the same afterwards. Some of those men were a lot more than radicals, Jan. They were the petty Lenins of their day. They claimed no less than to hold secrets that would turn the world upside down.'

They stood for a moment in the large room heavy with drapery, with gold-framed pictures, leather books and decanters on silver trays. Outside the daylight bled away. Abbeline thanked Grimes and shook hands. Jan gave him a hug and a kiss on the cheek. On the staircase outside, she stopped. She was smiling broadly.

'Don't say it,' Abbeline said.

'Jesus Christ Naylor!' she said. 'Fuck me!'

They walked on down the staircase and out into the great court. It had not snowed for twenty-four hours now but the freezing wind had left a crust of icing which sparkled yellowly under the college lamps.

CHAPTER TWENTY-SEVEN

Rod Keating of the US Embassy FBI was waiting in the Wentworth Court office when Abbeline and Jan got back. 'Pretty snazzy place you've carved out for yourself,' he said. 'I've been chasing you round half the police forces in England. I thought you should see this, and see it now.' He handed Jan a package. 'You put that on your video, darling. I'll make a few arrangements and we'll be ready to roll.'

'Where?' Abbeline said.

'You'll see. Don't rush me. I've sacrificed my last game of poker before the Great British Christmas holidays to burn up here. Be grateful.'

'I'm grateful,' said Abbeline. 'So what have you got?'

During the early evening a small police convoy made its way up the narrow lane towards Maskop Quarry. Reg and May Gummer and a group of people, mainly members of the Environmental Watch Committee, were waiting on a small rise, away from the edge where the car had gone over. Many of those waiting carried candles whose flames were swept out each time the wind rose, Captain Albert Forrest noticed, as he climbed out of his car.

It was not the first time Forrest of Norwich Fire Service had come up against Reg Gummer and the Environmental Society. He had for them a certain grudging respect. Who else would have pushed and pressured to get the vehicle recovery unit, police and divers up here, on Christmas Eve, to check out a car abandoned by gypsies?

He walked across to Reg Gummer and shook hands. 'I can't say I thank you for getting us out here tonight, Mr Gummer,' he said, not unamicably.

'If you'd responded when you should, it would be all over with by now.'

Forrest nodded. He didn't wish to get into an argument. He moved to watch the divers getting ready for a few moments before turning back to Reg Gummer and his wife. 'You saw the vehicle go in, you say?'

'We saw the headlights,' May confirmed. 'Sidelights more like, I suppose. They were moving down that slope.' She pointed. 'You can see where the bushes have been crushed.'

'And thinking it over an hour or so later, you decided you had reason to believe it might not be just an abandoned car?'

'That's it, Mr Forrest.' Reg Gummer stared back at him defiantly.

Forrest nodded. 'And your dog?'

'Still not back.'

'If it was gypsies,' Forrest said, 'they might like to pick up a pedigree collie.'

Gummer grunted. 'When did you ever see tidy gypsies, Inspector? If it had been gypsies that car would have been stripped of its battery, for one, and that would have meant no lights. For two it wouldn't have had any bloody wheels left!'

'You've got a point there, Mr Gummer.' He glanced over at the divers now, tall and black in their wetsuits. 'Okay, let's see what we've got.'

The two men lowered themselves into the water and disappeared with barely a ripple or bubble to mark the surface. Gummer and his wife watched as two powerful torch beams probed eerily, diffusing in the dark water, concentrating as they passed over the rock shapes.

Several onlookers afterwards claimed that they had been able to see the dark mass of the submerged car. Others, with hindsight, even claimed it had showed faintly red in the beam of a diver's torch.

To those watching above, through twenty-five feet of water the divers became no more than the moving torches in their hands. They came together and parted, waveringly circled a small area and came together again. Seconds later the lights began to ascend.

The divers' heads broke the surface a few feet apart. Two uniformed policemen offered their hands and, with a rush of water, first one then the other man was pulled out.

Forrest crossed towards them. The first man finished towelling his face. 'It's a red Escort,' he said. 'F120 NUL registration. There's a large air bubble but it didn't do any good. Whatever's in there is dead.'

'The dog?'

The diver nodded. 'And something else. *Someone* I should say. There's a body that's slipped forward from the passenger seat . . .' he described the movement with his hands '. . . and is huddled up in the footwell.'

'Man or woman?'

'Can't tell from any angle. It's very murky down there.'

Forrest was thoughtful. 'Thanks, both of you,' he said to the divers. He nodded to himself, thinking he must send someone across to tell Gummer about the dog. 'Can you bring the body up?' he asked the senior diver.

'Your decision, sir. Once we open the car door we'll get a rush of air to the surface that could suck up any small objects with it. Objects that might be useful in any enquiry. If it were an accident, we wouldn't hesitate.'

'But this one looks like suicide, you're saying?'

'Suicide or worse.'

Forrest stood rigid in the cold wind. A murder inquiry. As soon as that car number was circulated the enquiries, requests, demands would come thundering into his office. Goodbye Christmas.

The wind soughed across the hillside, biting at their faces. Forrest looked at the diver. His retirement was too close for him to take risks. 'If you're satisfied whoever's down there is dead . . .'

The diver nodded briskly.

'Then I don't think I should authorise you to try to bring them up ourselves. This one will have to wait for a senior police okay. You agreed?'

The diver laughed. 'In these temperatures, I couldn't think of a better decision, sir.'

It was Beth's voice. Even though strained and very strange, it was Beth's voice on the phone. 'Tessa, I need your help.'

'Beth, for God's sake! Where are you?'

'I've got to see you, Tessa. You've got to help me.'

'Are you in a call box or what?'

'A call box.'

'Have you got a car?'

'Yes.'

'Then get in it, Beth, and drive here straight away. You know the address?'

'I know the address but I daren't come there. Meet me, Tessa. Please. I don't have much time.'

The blood was thumping in Tessa's temples. 'Wait a minute. Why can't you come here?'

'I can't. You must come to me.'

'Where?'

'Let me think.' She paused. 'Laurie's place. The Old Boathouse.'

'No, Beth.' A chill ran through her.

'Yes. It's out on its own. It's safe.'

'Safe? Who from?'

'Please, please, Tessa! Just be there. Alone. Be at Laurie's place. At nine o'clock.'

'Beth, you're in trouble. I can hear it in your voice, dammit. Forget the boathouse. Let me get the police. Get in your car and drive straight here.'

'No.'

'Beth, where is Passmore? Is he with you?'

'No, Tessa,' she said quietly. 'He's no danger to us.'

'Let me get the police, Beth. They're outside the house now.'

'Outside?'

'I've been given protection. There's a squad on the doorstep.'

'Can you get away from them?'

'Get away? Why should I want to?'

'For me, Tessa. For my sake. Quickly.'

Her head was spinning. She tried to concentrate, to think. 'Why, Beth? Tell me why?'

'Don't ask me now. Promise me you'll come alone. To the Old Boathouse. Tessa, I desperately, desperately need your help.'

The phone clicked and purred.

Tessa put down the receiver and brushed tears from her cheek. Beth was alive. After all this, after all Tessa's certainty she was dead, her sister was alive.

238

CHAPTER TWENTY-EIGHT

Rod Keating put down the phone. 'Okay,' he said. 'Dr Hammond'll speak to you when we've seen the movie show.'

'Take it from the beginning,' Abbeline said.

'Bridgewater State Hospital. Ever heard of it?'

Jan looked towards Abbeline who nodded. 'It's a psychiatric hospital outside Boston. It treats, among others, the criminally insane.'

Keating nodded. 'Or whatever they call them these days. In the course of our search for Passmore we ran a check on Beth Naylor. Don't ask me why – it's the sort of thing we do.'

'You mean she has a record?'

'Detained by the Boston Police Department several times during the course of demonstrations.'

'In aid of . . .?' Jan said.

'She's a single issue lady. Animal rights. Palestinian rights. All kinds of Civil Rights.'

'What's a single issue lady?' Jan said.

'There's no gender attached to this one. The single issue personality from one point of view is someone who concentrates emotionally on one problem to the exclusion of almost anything else in their lives. In their heightened condition they can, and often do, act in ways most of society considers unreasonable and even dangerous.'

'They can take up different issues, of course,' Abbeline said. 'But they tend to be taken over by one at a time.'

Jan took out a packet of cigarettes. 'Anybody mind if I smoke?'

'I do, but never say no to a goodlooking girl. Goodlooking, despite the hair.'

'What a charmer.' Jan lit her cigarette and settled back in a swivel chair.

'This one was Animal Rights. After demo number three or four she began to cut up rough with the cops. Got herself booked. Got herself a recommendation from an unsympathetic court for psychiatric assessment.'

'Would Beth's family have known?'

'Probably not. Boston's a big city and the press have more to report than a slap on the wrist to a few demonstrators!'

'Okay. Bridgewater . . .' Abbeline said.

'And Dr Greg Hammond. Now I should put this to you straight, Jack. Dr Hammond would want me to. I've pulled in a lot of favours here, but Hammond's as concerned about professional ethics and confidentiality as anyone. None of this is public record. So nothing I have to show you, nothing he has to say on the line in ten minutes' time, is evidence.'

'Whoops!' Jan said.

'Your decision.' Keating got up and walked towards a television monitor and video in the corner of the room. Then he turned back to face Abbeline. 'You in on the movie or not?'

'In,' Abbeline said.

'Okay, this is what it is – interview five of eight half-hour interviews required by the court and taking place at Bridgewater, February twentieth. Enjoy.'

He hit the key and the screen began to jump and flicker. In fast forward were the figures of a tall, dark-haired man in a white jacket and Beth, taking off her outdoor coat, moving about, talking incomprehensibly at high speed, visibly agitated even in the frenetic movement of the fast forward.

Watching the digital seconds flick by, Keating waited, then pushed the key again.

A long silence held in the doctor's office. Beth sat in a neat white shirt and discreet plaid skirt, Hammond opposite her. The fixed camera point was somewhere high in a corner of the room. 'Is that a very painful question?' the psychiatrist said after a moment.

Beth turned her head away and stared out of the window. Abbeline was struck by how like Tessa in profile she looked. The same small nose, broad mouth and slightly heavy jawline, although the cap of dark hair immediately set her apart from her elder sister.

'I said, is that a very painful question to put to you?' Hammond asked again.

'You know very well it is. And unnecessary.' Beth's voice was crisp with disdain.

'Let me put it another way. You would think of such feelings towards your father as what . . . unlawful? Unnatural?'

Her mouth clamped tight.

'Which?' Hammond asked.

'Unnatural, obviously.' Beth turned her head to face him. 'I don't have to answer these questions, doctor.'

'No, of course not. But I remind you that you were the one who introduced the subject. I think you would probably like to talk about it. Am I wrong?'

Silence.

'I think I'm right, Beth, aren't I?'

The fixed camera had no dramatising or emphasising power. It stared unblinkingly at Beth's face – and recorded the extraordinary changes which began to occur.

She was full face to camera now, her cheek muscles flexing, her lipline thinning as she drew back her mouth. The eyes narrowed. Then the hands came up with an explosive smack to cover both cheeks. 'Oh my God,' she said. 'What I've seen I barely dare to tell. What I've seen her do, without shame, without remorse.'

The change was so complete that even Hammond's head rocked fractionally. Then he leaned forward again. 'What have you seen who doing, Beth?'

The hands came down. The face, if possible, hardened even more. 'Beth. Who's Beth? I'm Martine, aren't I?'

'Okay, Martine. And for the record, will you state your role in this matter?'

'Martine Mercullo, Investigating Officer, Moral Majority, Boston.'

'And what is that, Martine? Moral Majority, Boston?'

'We are empowered to expose examples of unseemly and immoral behaviour.' The voice was low, with a compelling intensity.

'Empowered by law?' the doctor asked.

'Indeed.'

'Can you tell me, for the record, who we're discussing.'

'Tessa Anne Naylor . . .'

'And the particular accusation?'

'On the death of her mother, Jane Naylor, the subject of our investigation, Tessa Naylor took it upon herself to move into her father's house. Using means about which I can barely speak . . .'

'You mean sexual means?'

'Yes. Using these means, she ingratiated herself . . .'

'You saw this yourself?'

'An old man, well over seventy. She's outrageous, disgraceful in her openness.' She exploded breath. 'She must be stopped. Punished!'

'Punished? How?'

'Does it matter how? These awful scenes must not be allowed to go on.' Tears were running down her cheeks now. 'It was awful. Wicked. My own sister.'

Dr Hammond sat without speaking. The camera showed his face in profile, unmoving. After a moment he leaned forward. 'Just rest . . . rest . . .'

Keating flicked off the video from his seat.

Jan formed an 'O' with her lips and blew a smoke ring. Abbeline scratched the side of his neck. 'We can rule out any form of hypnosis, I suppose.'

'Completely,' Keating said. 'I can take you back to a few minutes before that question about her father and you'll see the public Beth Naylor. Sparky, not exactly pleasant, but normal-aggressive for a student being forced to attend against her will.'

'And then this role-playing. The moral investigator,' Abbeline said. 'Almost a trance, you'd say. How long before she emerges?'

'Depends. Five, ten, twenty minutes.'

'You mean this happened several times during the interviews with Hammond?'

'Several times.' Keating nodded.

'And is she always the same personality?'

'The same name, Martine, but the role and personality change. She's pretty much always the investigator, the police, someone in an official position to condemn or judge.'

'Let's see another,' Abbeline said.

Keating pressed buttons. This time Beth lay back on the couch, face to camera. She wore very little make-up and her face looked calm, serene under the glistening short-cut hair. Her clothes were of good quality but not showy, a dark brown skirt, beige sweater and darker cardigan. Her shoes were dark tan and low-heeled.

Hammond's chair had been moved so that only the back of his head was visible. He was saying: 'There were a lot of stories at school?'

Beth shrugged. 'Natural enough. My father was very well known.'

'But what did you think of these stories.'

'Scuttlebut.'

'You weren't upset?'

'I knew it was all lies.'

'How old would you say you were at this time?'

Beth's head came up slightly from where it rested on the raised end of the couch. 'At what time?'

'At the time you began to realise that your father really *was* having affairs with other women?' Hammond said deliberately.

Abbeline watched in fascination as Beth's face very slowly changed. Again the muscles seemed to go rigid, the mouth become wider and thinner-lipped. She lay there without speaking for perhaps half a minute, then she sat up and with a vigorous, athletic movement, swung herself off the couch and stood in the centre of the room. Her hands were on her hips now as she looked down at the seated doctor, her tongue probing inside her cheek. She made several aloud mouth movements as if she were chewing invisible gum.

She walked across the room, even her clothes transformed by the arrogant movements of her body. 'Okay' she said and sat down at Hammond's desk. 'Okay.'

Watching, Abbeline admired the restraint of the doctor. He said nothing, never asked: 'Okay, what?' but waited, his eyes on her all the time, his notebook on his lap, waited for her to make the next move.

She leaned forward, the shoulders cocked aggressively towards him. 'The accusations brought against this woman are very serious, doctor.' The voice was harsh, the middle-class accent submerged.

'I think I'm talking to Martine again, aren't I?'

'You're talking to Detective Martine Mercullo.'

'And what are you telling me, Martine?'

'I'm telling you that the accusation against Tessa Naylor in the matter of her mother's death is serious. To the point of investigation.'

'How have you arrived at this conclusion?'

'We have a signed statement of evidence from her sister, Beth Naylor.'

'I see.'

'That statement establishes Tessa Naylor's intense jealousy of her mother. It details several occasions when Tessa tried to drive Mrs Jane Naylor from the marital home by imputations of her husband's infidelities with other women.'

'But surely Mrs Naylor was already aware of her husband's numerous infidelities with other women?'

'Not the details, doctor.' Beth's voice rose angrily. 'Not the detailed numbering of nights spent with this or that woman. Not their pleading, begging letters for more of what he had to give, read by Tessa Naylor to her mother. Not the details of illegitimate children spawned on black women all over New York City. Oh yes, Mrs Naylor suspected an occasional infidelity – but it was her daughter Tessa Naylor who nailed it down, who drove her to her death, with fact, fact, fact!'

She hammered the desk at each repeated word, her face flushed with fury. Then she sat back in her chair, glaring at Hammond, breathing heavily, her shoulders rising and falling as if she had just finished a desperately run race.

Keating clicked off the video.

The three of them sat silently for a moment until Abbeline slowly swung his chair towards Keating. 'I'd like to ask Dr Hammond what exactly we're seeing there?' he said, choosing his words carefully. 'What I saw was a woman who had seemingly moved out of one personality into another. What I'd like to know is how that could come about, in his opinion.'

Keating was punching numbers on the desk phone. 'Dr Hammond's ready for the call. We'll just catch him before he clears his desk for Christmas.' He held the phone up. 'Ringing now,' he said unnecessarily. 'Dr Hammond? Glad I caught you before you left. You were waiting? Well, thank you. I have Detective Superintendent Abbeline from Scotland Yard with me here. I've just shown him your material – under the conditions you stipulated. He'd like to speak to you.' He handed the phone to Abbeline who stood to take it.

They introduced themselves again. Hammond had a rich, heavy voice – the perfect psychiatrist's voice, Abbeline thought. 'I'm going to put you on speaker, Doctor, so that Inspector Keating and my deputy, Inspector Madigan, can hear. Okay with you?'

'Okay with me.'

Abbeline began by asking about hypnosis.

'No, no hypnosis was involved in any of our sessions,' Hammond assured him immediately. 'What you saw was one hundred percent engendered by Beth herself.'

Abbeline sat on the edge of the desk. 'Perhaps you can explain to me what that means? Does she remember, for instance, when she emerges from this other personality?'

'From Martine back to Beth? No, she remembers nothing. She has a strong sense of having lost time, so to speak. She will remember that at the onset she was seated in a chair perhaps, and on resumption of her own personality she finds herself standing at the window or wherever. After the longer periods of lost time she can often be made aware by reference to her watch or the clock in my office.'

'Okay,' Abbeline said slowly. 'Does she assume only one personality or have you seen several?'

'I've seen just variations of one. Martine. But I believe from clinical experience that the condition could produce a variety of personalities. That would depend entirely on how Beth Naylor is currently imaginatively adapting to stresses she is suffering.'

'This alternative personality is a recognised condition?'

'It's talked of as a fugue state. By definition, it's not a condition associated with mild disorder. But it is not uncommon in advanced mental disorders. And it's extremely well documented, Mr Abbeline, if you're having doubts.'

'No,' Abbeline said. 'What about causes?'

'Very broadly, religious and sexual disorientation.'

'Religious?'

'Beth's mother was a Protestant fundamentalist of the most unbending kind imaginable.'

'Is that enough to cause disorientation in a child?'

'It is if added to a father like Quentin Naylor. Of course Beth was aware of his infidelities from early teenage. But she was also deeply, perhaps dangerously, attached to her father. I've not, by any means, done enough sessions with Beth, Mr Abbeline, but I think you already have an idea of the psycho-sexual stress induced by her relationship to her two, very different, parents.'

'And this fugue state is a recognised result of such stress? She wasn't playing games?'

'No,' Hammond said slowly. 'I think that what we have here is a very real case of dissociative multiple personality disorder. It follows precisely the lines described in the textbooks. It's a disease, Mr Abbeline. A dangerous illness. Why other members of the same family, the sister Tessa Naylor, Tessa Wilson as she now is, do not suffer the same affliction would require more data than we as yet know how to process. But the facts are there. Beth Naylor suffers a severe personality disorder. She will adopt personalities as *she* sees the possibility of resolving her pain, her disorder, through the agency of those personalities. Am I going at this too hard and high?'

'No,' Abbeline said. 'I'm still with you. Let me walk through it, doctor. First she dissociates herself from her own persona, Beth Naylor. Her creation, Martine, then has free run through her life. In effect, she's using Martine to exteriorise all those concerns that shape Beth's life.'

'Yes.'

'And what would you say they are?'

'Her unnatural feelings for her father. Her intense, perhaps even dangerous, jealousy of her sister.'

'Could she kill?'

Hammond hesitated. 'Only if the background fantasy is strong enough.'

'Explain that.'

'When she was coming to me, I suspect the background fantasy – Martine – was not strong. The shifting nature of Martine's own role suggests that. But if she were provided with a background fantasy of real strength, then I think she would be capable of great violence. I also think, but this is speculation, that it would have to be a fantasy in which Beth would be able to function as herself.'

'You mean she would have no need of Martine? Even though she was in a fugue state?'

'Yes.'

'In the event you're describing, would Tessa Wilson inevitably be the target?'

'Ultimately, yes. I'm afraid that, from what Inspector Keating has told me, the arrival of this man Leonard Passmore on the scene has keyed in perfectly with Beth's childhood and teenage disorientation. Mr Abbeline, I think you've got a very angry and very dangerous woman on your hands. My recommendation would be to keep her sister Tessa Wilson as far from Beth as you possibly can.'

'Are you quite sure?' Anna asked.

'No doubt at all, Anna. It was Beth. She wants me to meet her.'

'At the Old Boathouse?'

'Yes.'

'Don't go.'

'What?'

'Just don't go, Tessa. Call the police. Let them handle it.'

'Beth asked me. Begged me.'

They stood facing one another.

'I'm going to need your help, Anna.'

The other woman shook her head. 'No.'

'Go down. Take the car. Drive it round the block and park it on the other side of the narrow alley . . .'

'You mustn't do this, Tessa. Call Abbeline.'

Tessa stretched out her hand. She knew she was acting unfairly. She let her hand slide down Anna's arm. 'Please . . .' she said.

There was a final hesitation. 'Scholars' Lane.'

'Scholars' Lane. Then come back here.'

Anna van Gelden stood immobile. 'I believe this is wrong, Tessa.'

'Will you do it?'

'If you really want me to?'

Tessa nodded. 'It's what I want. I want to do this myself. I don't want to go to Abbeline. I don't want to go to the police.'

Anna came forward and hugged her, rubbing her cheek against Tessa's. 'Okay,' she said, pulling back. 'Okay,' she said again. It was an admonition to herself.

She took the car keys from her bag and stopped at the door. 'Friend or not, I reserve the right to call the police, Tessa. If you're not back soon, I'll do it.'

'Put the car at the end of Scholars' Lane, Anna. Walk out of here so they're clear it's you, not me.'

Anna bit her lip. 'I reserve the right . . . okay?'

Tessa nodded and watched her friend go. Crossing to the window, she looked down. The unmarked police car with two men smoking inside was where it had been most of the evening.

A door slammed below and Anna came down the steps and headed for the BMW.

A lighted cigarette described a spluttering arc from the window of the police car to the tarmac. The engine was started, but the lights remained killed. They waited, watching the front door for Tessa to join Anna in the BMW. When the car took off with just Anna at the wheel, they relaxed. The engine was turned off. A few seconds later, Tessa saw another cigarette lit.

She stood in her coat counting to fifty. Then she walked quickly downstairs and stood, opening the door a crack.

She was breathing heavily, entirely caught up now in her desire to elude her escort, oblivious to anything that might lie ahead. She threw the door open, stepped out and pulled it to behind her. From the corner of her eye she saw the police car parked, facing in the other direction. Cigarette smoke, she noticed, curled from the driver's open side window. Taking the steps quickly she began to walk along Fitzwilliam Terrace towards King's.

She heard the car door open and immediately slam closed. Heard a half-suppressed curse. Heard the police car's engine start. Heard the quick, squealing bite of wheels as the car made a U-turn behind her.

But she had drawn level with Scholars' Lane. Before the police car drew up beside her, she had turned between the two Victorian bollards and was running down the stone-paved passage.

'Mrs Wilson,' she heard a voice calling from the car behind her.

By the time she reached the end, and the corresponding iron bollards, she could hear a car door slam and a man's footsteps entering the alley behind her.

The BMW was parked a yard or two away. The door was unlocked, the keys in the ignition.

CHAPTER TWENTY-NINE

From the lane Rose could see an irregularly shaped stretch of water, an untidy jumble of police cars, their headlights on, a scatter of tiny figures black against the residual whiteness of the melting snow – and a large yellow vehicle, part crane, part bulldozer.

As Rose brought the car through the gate, Albert Forrest crossed towards it, one hand holding on to his uniform cap. The wind, cold on his face as he had waited for the lifter to arrive, now tugged at the water on the quarry lake and flurried the snow.

He introduced himself quickly and led Rose over to where the yellow lifting vehicle was positioned. The two operators had already been briefed, divers had already drawn nylon nets under the submerged car. They were ready to go.

When Forrest gave the word, the arm of the lifter began to rise, the winch screeched and a cable tightened, leaping from the surface of the water.

Rose watched as the cable drew taut, took the strain, and the winch drum began to roll slowly. His eyes flicked across the edge of the quarry where the car had gone down. Red Escort F120 NUL was the registration circulated, Sally Portal's car. And there was a body already reported by the divers, inside.

The car broke the surface suddenly, awkward in its net, pouring water off the roof and over the bonnet. In the cold white arc lights Rose could see the dog bobbing in the back, the waterline a few inches above the base of the closed windows.

The lifter placed the net on the gravelled edge of the quarry and two policemen unhooked it so that it fell away and the red car gleamed and sparkled in the lights around it.

Rose and Forrest walked towards it. From a few points, thin jets of water sprayed out. A broad black puddle was forming underneath. Forrest shone his torch through the side window. The water level was dropping fast now.

He waited a moment longer then jerked on the driver's door and stepped back quickly. The rush of water came out over the sill carrying with it a woman's umbrella, a magazine, a slim leather note case. Water gushed over Forrest's shoes and the lower part of his trousers.

Rose was looking into the car. The body had been lifted by the rush of water so that the head hung out, upside down. For a moment he didn't recognise the slicked down black hair and narrow white face. Then he saw that it was the face of Leonard Passmore.

Rose bent and picked up the leather notecase. It was about eight by four inches and secured by a leather button clip. He stood for a moment looking down into Passmore's dead eyes, then opened the notebook. There was a thick wad of papers inside. Even the top sheet was too washed out to be decipherable. He wondered where, on Christmas Day, they would be able to find someone to deal with this.

Forrest stood beside him. 'Suicide, you'd say. Except for these.' He handed Rose a pack of photographs. 'Taken by Gummer from the local Environmental Watch a matter of hours after the car went in.'

Rose slid the notecase into an evidence bag and looked through the photographs. They showed a bleak piece of the edge of the quarry. Broken bushes where the car had rolled forward, tyre tracks and footprints beside them.

'He wasn't alone,' Forrest said. 'You can see the marks made by someone else clearly in the snow. By the size of them I'd say they were women's footprints.' He looked away from Passmore's staring eyes.

Rose grinned at him, turning Passmore's head with the toe of his rubber boot. The back of the skull was caved in. 'Suicide, except for the footprints . . . and the fact that someone took a bludgeon to the back of his head before they pushed him in.'

'At this time of night,' Lulu Mason said to Abbeline and Jan,' all good coppers should be tucked up in bed. Together.'

Abbeline looked down at Mason's plaster-covered leg. It was covered in crude graffiti, get well messages and the signatures of friends. 'Talking time, Mason,' he said. He stepped back into the shadow and nodded to Jan.

'You are in deep trouble,' she confirmed, standing at the bottom of the bed in a short Father Christmas anorak. 'You are up to your neck in sewage.'

Mason maintained his grin.

'Inspector Rose tells us you are making quite a fuss about getting your Mini-Cooper.'

'It's worth money.'

'That car was a write-off.'

'Sooner the car than me.'

'Not a point of view everybody'd be happy with,' Jan said.

'But I still want it back. I don't want it dragged off to some knacker's yard. There's spares there worth money.'

Jan came round and sat on the side of the bed. 'One of the coppers at Cambridge nick is a Mini-Cooper enthusiast.'

'And you've come round at Christmas to offer a price – no deal.'

She shook her head slowly. 'You're not fooling anybody, Lulu.'

He shrugged.

'Our man was looking over your old wreck and noticed you had some interesting features fitted.'

Mason's grin faded. He glanced quickly at Abbeline, saw only the shadowed face and looked back at Jan.

'Concealed door panel compartments. We haven't had time for a chemical analysis yet, but I'd say you deal. Cocaine, is it? Nasty. Strangely enough, though, that's not what interested us so much tonight.'

'You found the money?' Mason's face was set. He rotated his shoulders nervously. 'Look . . .'

'Yes. We found the money,' Jan said. 'Three thousand pounds. Exactly the amount Beth Naylor drew from the bank on the day she disappeared.'

Mason's head dropped. He gave a faint whimper.

'What do you have to tell us about this?' Abbeline said from the shadows.

Eyes still down on his hands, twisting in his lap, Mason shook his head.

'If you don't tell us, we draw our own conclusions,' Jan said reasonably. 'And conclusion number one is going to be that Beth Naylor paid you that money to kill Sally Portal . . .'

'No!' Mason's head came up with a shout of alarm. His teeth were drawn back.

'No?'

He moistened his lips. 'Charge me with theft, that's one thing. But just because Laurie's dead, you're not going to hang the murder on me!'

'Some of us are like that,' Jan said.

Silence settled on the room. Someone trundled a rattling trolley along the corridor outside.

'Well?' Jan settled herself more comfortably on the side of the bed. 'Let's start from the beginning. How did they meet?'

'Laurie had some wood carving work to do at their prayer centre.'

'Do you know where that is?'

'Not a clue. He worked all over the eastern counties. But that's where they met. Because at first, when Beth got all interested in Laurie, he thought she was trying to convert him.'

'But she wasn't?'

'No.' Mason hesitated. He looked from Jan to Abbeline. 'When I was in prison,' he said, 'at Leicester, Laurie came to see me. He said did I remember the American girl I'd seen him with once or twice? Of course I remembered her. Off her rocker about religion.' He took a deep breath. 'But Laurie says it's more than that. The girl's a double-dyed crazy. Belongs to some sort of cult church. Thinks she's a born again Jesus. No, *really* thinks this. That she's Jesus Christ reborn.' He paused. 'Or would have been if there wasn't someone in her way. Some girl she needed offing. So the reason she's been so friendly to Laurie comes clear. She's been cultivating him. She's offered him three grand to help her kill the girl. *Help* her, mind you . . .'

Jan glanced towards Abbeline's shadowed face.

'When they'd done it,' Mason said, 'and I'm telling the lot now, Laurie's job was to fetch the dead girl's car from somewhere in

Cambridge, load up the body and drive it out to some quarry Beth had found on the Ely Road. That's all I know.'

'You know more than that now,' Jan said. 'You know that, whatever Laurie told you, he agreed to do it. You know that Sally Portal's body was found in the boathouse. You know what happened to Laurie Woodward, the same night Sally was killed.'

'Yes. I know he came off his bike at that bitch of a Granchester bend.'

'On his way to Trumpington Street to pick up Sally Portal's car.'

Abbeline came forward from the shadows. He was speaking to Jan. 'So when Beth was seen by Mrs Taylor picking up a car from her parking space at Trumpington Street that morning, it was Sally's car. Same colour, same make. The car Woodward had failed to collect.'

'I want you to be clear about one thing,' Mason said. 'When Laurie came to Leicester and told me about this scam, we had a good laugh. It never, never, crossed my mind he planned to go ahead with it. I knew nothing about what had happened.'

'You went to Woodward's house . . .'

'That proves it,' Mason said urgently. 'I went there to see Laurie.'

'What happened that night, Lulu?'

'I got there thinking he might be expecting me. I'd left a message for him on the answerphone.'

'What made you go to the boathouse?'

'I heard something moving in there. I thought maybe Laurie was going to jump me as I passed. One of his tricks, you know.'

'So you looked inside.'

'Even then I thought it was part of a game. A dummy up there. Then suddenly that steady sort of musty stench hit me. And I knew it was for real.'

'I would have thought you'd have run for your life.'

'I did. I reached the car. Started up. Then sat there and thought it over. I thought if Laurie was hanging in there, it was some sort of party stunt that had gone wrong, turned nasty, whatever.'

'You never thought of the story Woodward had told you in prison? You never thought it might be Sally hanging there?'

'I swear. I just sat there in the car and thought Laurie liked it so weird that sometime it was going to catch up with him. And then I thought he'd got all this kit he'd not going to be wanting . . .'

'What sort of kit?'

'You saw it. CD stuff. Saleable. So I went in to help myself and I was there when the American woman came in, the sister.'

'Oh dear,' Jan said. 'There's one little matter you haven't cleared up, Lulu.'

'All right. Laurie had a place under the floorboards where he used to keep anything dodgy. I looked there and that's when I found the wad.'

'Where did you think it came from?' Jan asked.

'Laurie made good money sometimes. It was only when I was in the car and the police were on my tail that it suddenly hit me what the money might be.'

'It also must have hit you that the body in the boathouse was Sally Portal's. But when you were arrested, you kept up the pretence of thinking it was Laurie's.'

'I was out of my mind scared,' Mason said. 'If it was the girl hanging up there I could see the trouble I'd be in. The girl dead, Laurie done a long runner, and me holding the three thousand bloodmoney. I put my foot so hard on the accelerator the Coop nearly took off. And within minutes I had a cruiser on my tail. The rest you know. I went off the road, jumped out and made a run for it.'

Jan turned to Abbeline. 'Ready to go back to London, sir? Christmas Day and all that?'

'What about me?' Mason looked from one to the other.

'What about you?' Jan said. 'As I hinted to you in the beginning, Lulu, I think you're in deep, deep sewage.'

Tessa pulled the BMW into the side of the lane and killed the lights. For a few moments she sat there staring across towards where she knew the boathouse stood behind the trees. Then she got out of the car and stood, leaning back on it in the cold air.

The night was misty. Perhaps by the river at Granchester all winter nights were misty. The snow which had lain thick and white when she was last here on the dreadful night she'd found Sally's body, was now patched and blackened.

There was some light from the pale, cloudy sky, light borrowed perhaps from the lights of the village a few hundred yards distant.

In her hand Tessa held the BMW car torch, a heavy powerful flashlight Anna had insisted on her having. She kept it switched off for the moment, letting her eyes adjust to the darkness. Then, with an effort, she pushed herself off the car and began to pick her way, in darkness, along the path to the boathouse.

Before halfway she almost turned back. But it was the remembered strain in Beth's voice that forced her forward. She passed through the rhododendron bushes and shuddered as they rattled, then just beyond saw the dark outline of the place where Sally's rotting body had twisted on a rope, moved by the wind that night. The image brought sounds with it, perhaps in her imagination, she could not be sure. Sounds she remembered from that night, the slow squeak of the rope chafing on the beam. She found she was gasping with fear. Suddenly she saw that Anna had been right. She should not have come alone.

Along the creek, from the river itself, the mist eased and moved with every faint movement of air. She was no more than a few yards from the boathouse now and could see the outline of the cottage on her right. She stopped, the torch in her shaking hand rubbing against her leg. In the mist not more than twenty yards away, along the path towards the cottage, she was sure she saw a figure.

Her instinct was to switch on the flashlight, but she fought it back. She tried to imagine what the figure might see from its position, slightly higher, more exposed, than her own. Tessa's coat was dark and she stood still in the night shadow of the huge bushes. It seemed possible, even probable, that she had not been seen.

Then the figure moved. Just two steps towards Tessa, but two steps that left it almost silhouetted against the grey mist. It was a woman in a knee-length coat, a woman wearing a scarf tied under her chin. She was staring out towards the river but a wind-borne rustle of leaves made her turn. 'Tessa?' she said softly.

Tessa's thumb hit the torch switch. The beam cut through the mist and isolated the figure in a noose of light. 'Who are you?' she said.

The girl moved towards her anxiously. 'Please, put out the light,' she said, her hand raised to shield her eyes. She was slender, in jeans and a dark pea jacket. A pale narrow face and Mediterranean eyes.

'Where is she?' Tessa said, keeping the light on the girl. 'Where's my sister?'

The girl stopped a pace or two away. 'I can take you to her, if you want?'

She thrust a copy of a newspaper, that day's *Cambridge Daily News*, into the torch beam. Across the top of the headline, in Beth's handwriting, a message read: '*Tessa – Linda will bring you to me. I'm well. Just follow her directions. Desperately need you here. Beth.*'

It was a moment of decision, a second chance to call the police, but this slender girl, barely an adult, inspired no fear in her. 'The car's in the lane,' Tessa said and turned, sweeping light from the torch along the path and through the bushes.

Once in the car, she started the engine and pulled quickly away. 'Good,' said the childlike creature settling into the seat next to her. 'First we want the Ely Road.'

CHAPTER THIRTY

In less than half an hour it would be midnight, then Christmas Day. Abbeline walked, threading his way through the familiar streets until he reached Golden Square. There were a lot of people about, mostly young, mostly slightly drunk. One or two of the sex shops and peep-shows were playing Christmas Carols. There was a tree with lights in the middle of Golden Square. A few people were already settling down for the night, wrapped in blankets under coverings of wet cardboard or pieces of weatherproof tarpaulin. As he walked, he ran things through his mind. He knew the case was nearly at an end. He was sure now they would find this prayer centre, find Beth, in the next few days. Tessa was safe in Cambridge, watched over by a twenty-four hour surveillance team. Tomorrow he would phone her, somehow tell her Passmore was dead, murdered by her sister. tell her that Beth was probably responsible for Annabelle Wright's death. Responsible with Woodward for the first killing, Sally. Why? He didn't know yet. Some madness fed to Beth's already damaged mind by Leonard Passmore. Yes, tomorrow he would phone Tessa. She wouldn't be aching for the news he had to give. He wasn't aching to be the messenger.

Christmas Eve. Jo would be getting up now on Christmas morning in Australia.

And his mother was somewhere here among the derelicts. He wondered if there was really anything to be done for her. She wasn't the sort of alcoholic who drank until she dropped. She wasn't on drugs. But for practical purposes she might as well be. Somehow she no longer had a framework to live in.

He called in at two or three pubs he had heard her mention, but they were crowded with Christmas Eve drinkers enjoying the midnight extension, making it almost impossible to be sure he had not missed her.

At the Coach and Horses he managed to push his way to the bar. 'Has Rhoda been in?' he asked the young Irish barman.

'Gala night for all the friends,' he said. 'Rhoda backed an 11/2 winner at the Sandown meeting.'

'When did she leave?'

'About half an hour ago. She said she had to go down to the Old School.'

'The Old School?'

'They're pulling down an old school just off Lexington. There's a soup kitchen. Rhoda had some story she has to go and check it out for her son at Scotland Yard.' He looked at Abbeline. 'That's not you, is it?'

The light on a crane arm, sparkling like a star in the night, guided him through a series of narrow alleys, thick with the mud of heavy plant vehicles. Over a newly erected yellow hardboard fence, he could see the half-demolished school building. Within the perimeter fence Abbeline could hear voices: a man singing snatches of a Christmas Carol, women laughing. He walked the length of one alley and, following the mud trail from huge tyres, came to a place where two men were drunkenly helping each other through a hole in the boarding, smashed by a reversing digger. Abbeline waited until they had disappeared inside. He thought of what he was wearing, a black wool and cashmere overcoat, and considered for a moment removing his tie. But what good would that do? He approached the splintered gap in the plywood and stood for a moment without entering. He could now see that half the site was already demolished and the rubble had, for the most part, been cleared away. Shadowy figures passed back and forth in front of a big fire which burned in the middle of the site. Other smaller fires flickered in the darkness around it.

He passed through the gap and picked his way carefully over the rubble. A small shanty town was already coming into being. Low structures built of piled bricks and corrugated iron or packing cases with sodden cardboard roofing were scattered about the site.

Several of these dwellings had their own fire at the entrance. One or two had even graduated to a chimney.

It was impossible to guess how many people there were on the site. In an irregular-shaped area roughly sixty by less than a hundred yards long, there were, he could now see, several dozen small fires burning and figures moving about them. There were others singing scraps of Christmas songs or stumbling, laden with their bags, around the main fire. Perhaps there were yet others in the undemolished parts of the school.

While he wandered from fire to fire, the Christmas bells began to ring in distant churches. Near the main fire a group of people put up a ragged cheer and a few began dancing. Among the serious alcoholics, nobody seemed to notice that he was not dressed as they were, bundled in a drab padded anorak. He was struck by how friendly they were, how often he was offered a swig from the bottles they brandished. How many times he was invited to join a group, wished a Merry Christmas.

There were few drugs here, few introverted young people staring neutrally into the fire. Mostly it was a gathering of the middle-aged, often Irish in accent, with drink of all sorts as their pleasure.

After about fifteen minutes, a faintly donnish man with an orange juice jar attached himself to Abbeline. 'A Christmas drink, sir? A brew without subtlety but one that carries the guarantee of oblivion.' He stopped himself. 'But then, almost by definition oblivion can't be subtle, can it, sir?' He offered a taste of the orange drink and when Abbeline declined, stared out at the twinkling fires. '*And in their camp,*' he declaimed, '*the confident and overmighty French do play at dice . . .*'

'You were an actor,' Abbeline said. 'Or a teacher perhaps.'

'I was a civil servant,' he said, sipping from the jar, 'until a year or two ago.' He had a soft Dublin accent. 'I was hardworking, competent, discreet, and polite to ministers. I told no tales to the press and had no inclination towards small boys. But, sir, I was early retired at fifty-three. Why? Because a little IRA story was leaked to the press from my department. And Catholic, Dublin-born, I had to be the source did I not?'

'And were you?'

'I can no longer remember.' He smiled. 'And what's a gentleman and a scholar like yourself doing down here at the Old School?'

'I'm looking for Rhoda. Do you know her?'

'My heart leaps at the very mention of her name. She's not a kindly woman but she's beautiful enough to forgive.'

'Have you seen her here tonight?'

'She's about. Come along, sit by the fire and tell me the story of your life. You'll feel better for it.'

'I'm going to have to find Rhoda,' Abbeline said. 'If you see her, tell her someone's looking for her.'

'I will,' the man said. 'I surely will.' And sipping at his jar he turned away to stumble across the rubble, calling the name of a friend he may or may not have seen in the firelit shadows.

It had all happened too quickly. There was something unnerving about Linda, despite the fact that she was little more than a child. It was in the strange way she stared ahead, giving her directions in a dull monotone and refusing absolutely to talk further: about where they were heading, about Passmore, or most of all about Beth. A few miles down the road out of Cambridge, Tessa had had time to gather her wits. At a layby sign she pulled in the car and braked fiercely. Unclipping her seat belt, she turned to face Linda. 'Okay,' she said, 'this is as far as I go.'

The girl looked at her in astonishment. The first real expression Tessa had seen cross her face. 'What?' she said. 'What . . .?'

'You heard me,' Tessa said. 'This is as far as I go.'

There was suppressed panic in the girl's voice now. 'I don't know what you're talking about. We're going to see your sister. We're going to see Beth.'

Tessa shook her head. 'Not unless you're about to tell me a lot more than you have so far, Linda. I want to know what the hell's going on?'

The girl's dark eyes flicked from side to side as if seeking assistance from someone outside in the shadows.

'Just start talking, Linda. Start telling me what's going on.'

The girl fixed her eyes on Tessa. 'I don't know what you mean,' she said.

'Where are you taking me? We can start there.'

'It's a house. A big house. It hasn't got a name.'

'And who's waiting at this house?'

'Your sister Beth.'

'And Beth is okay? She's not being harmed?'

Linda looked genuinely astonished. 'Harmed? Why would anyone want to harm Beth?'

'She's there voluntarily? She's not being held against her will?'

'I don't know how you can even suggest that, Tessa.' There was a shocked sincerity in the girl's voice.

'Okay,' Tessa said slowly. 'Who else is at the house?'

'Some members of the mission.'

'Leonard Passmore?'

'No. The police are against him. Beth told me how careful we all have to be.'

'Beth told you?'

Linda nodded vigorously.

'Do you know Passmore is wanted by the police? Where is he now?'

The girl shook her head.

'I'm not moving this car,' Tessa said, 'until you answer me.'

She waited with something close to bated breath as the girl's face reflected her struggle over whether to say more.

'He's on his way back to America.' She was surly now, unhappy at having gone far beyond her remit. 'Can we go?'

'He's wanted for murder, Linda.'

'Goodness like his invites evil tongues,' she said. 'You do believe me, don't you?'

'Is this what Beth says, too?'

'Of course. And Beth knows. She has the Word. You must know that. Now I think we should drive on. Beth needs you with her.'

Tessa grunted uncertainly to herself. Searching the glove compartment, she found a packet of Anna's cigarettes and pushed in the lighter on the dash.

'I'd rather you didn't,' Linda said.

'I'd rather I did,' Tessa said, lighting the cigarette. She sat in silence for a few minutes, smoking, trying to think about what she was doing. She was certain that this strange girl beside her was telling the truth about Beth. That she was alive. That she had sent Linda to Cambridge. Tessa inhaled twice, felt the smoke burn, buzzed down the window and threw out the cigarette. And if she was telling the truth about Beth, she was probably telling the truth about Passmore too. He wasn't at the house. He was trying to get back to the States.

Unthinkingly she took another cigarette and lit it. She watched headlights approach and flash by. A car with four teenagers blasted music as it passed. Then the long road went dark again. She drew on the cigarette. This was her chance to help Beth. Nothing Linda said suggested she was being held against her will at the Mission. She was there voluntarily, convinced as many had been, as Linda was, by Passmore's rhetoric, by an atmosphere of prayer and saintliness. It was that all-encompassing appeal of the cult religion. Only we have the true Word. She drew on her cigarette and again threw it away, barely smoked. The resolution was growing in her. She could help Beth if she went ahead now. She put the car in gear.

Twenty-four hours ago, she thought, she would have found a phone and called Jack Abbeline immediately. But that wasn't the way she felt any longer. She sat with her hands on the wheel, staring ahead. Something like a sense of triumph was beginning to dispel her uncertainties. She could feel an excitement coursing through her veins. In a few hours she had pushed far beyond Abbeline. She knew Beth was alive; would soon know where she was. And if Passmore was on his way back to the United States, he would be picked up. Tomorrow morning, Christmas morning, she would phone Abbeline. Wake him up and wish him a Happy Christmas. And tell him that Passmore was flying into New York, that Beth was safe. But first . . . she moved the car back on to the road . . . first she must go to the house and find her. She must bring her back to Anna's house tonight, talk to her and then call Abbeline.

Tessa looked at the pale-faced girl beside her, the sense of triumph ebbing. A new weight of uncertainty driving it out. 'You promise me you don't know the name of this house, Linda?'

'We call it the Mission. Everybody there just calls it the Mission.'

'Okay,' Tessa said. If she brought Beth back to Cambridge, it would show Carter a thing or two as well. It would make up for the damage done by four years of being undermined, sneered at. Even Abbeline had patronised her when it came to the point: 'You're not the sort of woman for a one night stand,' he'd said. And how was he to know? He had gone straight back to London afterwards. How was he to know what sort of woman she *wasn't!* He'd been talking about his image of her as surely as Carter used and exploited *his* image of her. But let anyone try and patronise her after she had brought Beth back!

She knew she was pushing herself, fighting hard to regain that elusive sense of triumph. She glanced into the darkness of the rear mirror and pressed down on the accelerator. 'Okay,' she said to Linda, 'let's go.'

Jack Abbeline came across his mother nearly an hour after he had arrived in the Old School yard. In a dark corner of the site he heard voices raised. A woman's voice, accusingly. He headed for that side of the fire and saw Rhoda coming towards him, stumbling over the uneven ground in her high heels.

She showed no surprise at seeing him there. 'Jack,' she said, 'I waited for you in Berwick Street.' Her voice was accusing.

He looked at her. 'I'm sorry Rhoda. I just couldn't make it.'

'If you knew what a day I've had!' she said. 'The Sisters told me I couldn't go back for Christmas dinner tomorrow unless I went down to the Social. They're after the money for themselves, you see. So much for sweet charity!'

'Listen, Rhoda,' he said, 'you can come and have Christmas dinner with me tomorrow.'

'We'll see.'

They stood before the pile of old timber fifteen or twenty yards from the fire. The worst of the cold spell had passed on and with the heat from the fire on their faces, they stood in silence while Rhoda picked over the contents of her handbag.

'Did you ask about for me?' Abbeline said, staring towards the fire.

'I've been here all night asking questions while everybody else has been enjoying a Christmas drink.'

'Did you find anybody who knows the Reverend Passmore?'

She frowned, her head down now, checking through her bag again.

'Rhoda,' he said.

She closed her bag. 'Leilia knows about them. She told me she does.'

'Come on, Rhoda, I'm not here to chase fairy tales.'

'Leilia says she's heard of them,' his mother said indignantly.

He watched as she began yet again to rifle through her bag. He knew it was an indication of unease, disturbance, but beyond that he had no real understanding. Was she ever looking for something specific as she made these endless forays through her handbag. 'Rhoda?' he said gently.

She looked up.

'Where can I find Leilia?'

'She's here. Over there,' she said, as if surprised he had not seen and immediately recognised a woman as her friend, Leilia.

'Stay here, I'll be back,' Abbeline said. He stood up and walked over to the woman staring into the fire. Staring fixedly, rather than dreamily, Leilia was tall, no older than her mid-forties, dressed in an ankle-length black coat. Her hair was damp, greying, slightly curled. Her face, sharp-nosed, was what is called by a nation of dog-lovers, 'intelligent'.

'Leilia?'

She turned. 'I don't know you.' Her voice was crisp, like Rhoda's the product of good schools.

'I'm Jack Abbeline. Rhoda's son. You know Rhoda,' he added as an afterthought.

Leilia nodded, still staring into the fire.

'She says you've had something to do with the Millennium Church? They have a mission here . . .'

Her brief glance was arch. She swayed almost imperceptibly and he could smell the alcohol on her breath.

'I wondered,' Abbeline said, 'if you worked with them?'

She turned towards him. 'I have,' she said. 'On occasion. How can I help you? You're a policeman, Rhoda tells me.'

'I am, yes. And I'd be very grateful if you could help me.'

'One helps the police when one can.'

She left implied the idea that it was not often – and was in any case a pretty distasteful civic duty.

'We've had some complaints about them. Too pushy with their brand of salvation.'

She laughed. Her teeth were beautifully white though. Gapped at the bottom left side. 'Indeed. Many of my friends found the same. They probably originated the complaint.'

'Very probably.'

'You see, Mr Abbeline,' she said, 'they are inclined to misunderstand the position of some of the people here. Have you met Professor O'Dwyer, for instance?'

'I think maybe I have.'

'A distinguished civil servant. He's hardly going to fall for a banner proclaiming "The Wages of Sin is Death".'

'No. Where do they come from?'

'The Millennaries. Oh, they're a mixed bunch. Some have perfectly good backgrounds. Others are frightfully hairy round the hocks.' She laughed again. 'Shouldn't say things like that these days, I'm told. But some of them are terribly common.'

'I meant, where do they have their headquarters?'

She shrugged.

'Have you met the Reverend Passmore?'

'I heard the news on somebody's tranny. You're looking for him.'

'No longer. He's dead.'

She wrinkled her nose. 'An American. Quite persuasive. But not my type. I like my freedom too much.'

'What made you think he wanted to restrict it?'

'All Bible punchers do, don't they? Anyway, they asked me to go to their place in Norfolk.'

'Norfolk?'

'I said, God, no – the peasants there still hang the afterbirth of cows out at the crossroads.'

Abbeline raised his eyebrows.

'To protect themselves against the devil, werewolves, or whatever they imagine might be waiting there for them at the crossroads.'

Suddenly Abbeline felt his blood racing. He knew this woman could at any moment veer away, refuse to answer. She was talking to him on some kind of sufferance. Years of indoctrination had taught her to feel superior. Now, before a bonfire, among derelicts on a demolition site, it still sustained her morale. 'Did you go with them?' he asked.

'For a few days. They weren't looking for servants of the Lord, they were looking for servants of Passmore and his friends. Before I knew it they were expecting me to scrub floors and make beds.'

'Was there any attempt to make you stay?'

'No. I had to wait until they were doing the next trip to London, that's all.'

'They brought you back?'

'In their old van. Thrown about like cattle. It was a disaster. Rhoda hasn't stopped laughing yet.'

'Where was the house?'

'Ah,' she said. 'They made sure you never knew that.'

Abbeline felt his stomach drop. 'You couldn't see out of the van?'

'It was night anyway. There and back.'

'How long was the journey?'

She frowned. 'Four or five hours. All the way up to Norwich.'

'Norwich? Are you sure of that?'

'*Not* my part of Norfolk. My family home is Breedham, near the Rockingham house. Rockingham Hall. As children we use to play there.' She sighed. 'Old days, long gone. Passmore's place was nearer the coast, I fancy. A Yarmouth fish stall.'

'What?'

'The fish stalls. It's what my father used to call the houses sea-side to the broads. Some of them frightfully large fish stalls admittedly, but you still almost expected them to hang out the sign '*Frying Tonight*' on the drive gates.'

'So somewhere near the coast?'

She was silent. 'I don't know,' she said testily. 'I told you, it was night. They didn't want us to know where we were.'

'But Norwich?' he said, trying to keep the desperation out of his voice. 'You're sure of that?'

'Must have been. Just after we left the house, I leaned over the driver to get a light. Before somebody pushed me back I saw the cathedral. Saw the lantern tower. Superb, says I. But they're not very fond of cathedrals, of course. Plain worship's more their line.'

'If I showed you a map . . .?'

'Not really.' She shook her head wearily. She looked around. 'Where's Rhoda?'

He knew he was running out of time. 'But you'd recognise the house?'

'If I saw a picture I would, of course. Crumbling Edwardian. Queen Anne revival.'

'Would you be willing to come with me for an hour, across to Scotland Yard?'

Her head turned sharply. 'I don't want any trouble with the police.' Her manner had suddenly changed, from worldly arrogance to vulnerability.

'I promise you, Leilia, no trouble. And I'll have a car deliver you back here in an hour. In style, An unmarked car.'

She shrugged uncertainly.

Abbeline stood watching the firelight play upon her face. Beside her, a yard or so away in the shadows, were perhaps six or seven plastic bags. 'Will you be having Christmas dinner with Rhoda tomorrow?' he asked.

'We usually go to the Sisters.'

He nodded. 'There's a reward,' he said, 'for information.' He took two twenty pound notes from his pocket. 'I think you've earned it.'

She brightened. 'How very good of you,' she said. 'Believe me, most policemen would have tucked that into their own back pocket.'

When Inspector Ray Rose returned home from Maskop Quarry, Christmas Day was already over an hour old. The house was quiet. His wife and young daughter were asleep. He walked through the sitting room, past the unlit tree with the presents wrapped and clustered at its foot. He stopped and looked down. In the light coming from the hall he could see his daughter's name, Sara, on most of the packages. He felt a twinge of regret that he didn't know what a single one of them contained. This case . . . well, it was moving to its end. Passmore dead. The Naylor girl, according to Jan Madigan, some sort of religious psycho. They'd find her and a bunch of wall-eyed followers holed up in some house somewhere. Nobody could stay hidden for ever, and frankly it didn't matter now if they weren't dug out for a few days.

He was looking forward to Christmas. A couple of days with the family. A chance to see Sara open her Christmas presents. He walked through to the garage and stood looking at his classic XK 120. Since the discovery of Sally Portal's body at the boathouse he hadn't done one hour's work on the rust on the driver's door. He often thought of his relationship to the XK as that of a doctor to an old, rich and highly profitable patient. If allowed to fade away, the patient would be worth nothing. Every minute sign of ill-health had to be monitored and acted upon. Rust was like a cancer . . . He smiled to himself. A normally taciturn Yorkshireman, some streak of incurable romanticism was brought to the surface by these old cars.

He had enjoyed working with Abbeline although he knew that any credit that was flying about when the case was over would go to him. Scotland Yard attracted the newsmen, not Cambridge City CID. And what attracted the newsmen attracted the Chief Constables.

He left the garage and went through to the kitchen. His wife had left him something to heat in the microwave. As he picked up the plate he heard her step on the stair. He turned, 'Merry Christmas' on his lips.

Barbara Rose put her head round the door. 'Thought I'd better let you know, Ray, as soon as you got in. While you were out your surveillance team was trying to get in touch with you.'

CHAPTER THIRTY-ONE

There had been one last moment of doubt before she had entered this strange house. One last moment when she might have turned back. It was as she had braked and slowed into the gravel drive. She could still have thrown the car into reverse. Got back on to the main road and driven to the nearest village in search of the police.

But she hadn't done that. The sense of triumph was now something Tessa was holding on to in desperation. She needed this victory. Over Abbeline . . . over Carter. Most of all it was a victory she needed over her recent, wavering self. Snatch the credit, she said to herself. Take every ounce of credit that's due to you for having found Beth before Abbeline. Before the whole of the Cambridgeshire police.

If that, indeed, is what you *have* done, a small cautious voice warned inside her head.

There seemed to be no lights, but the moon silhouetted a large house against the sky. She could make out long sash windows on the lower floors, a line of bull's eye windows at the top, the whole thing bound together with a heavy, white-painted band of plaster dog-toothing.

She stopped the car in the drive. Linda jumped out eagerly and went before her up the short flight of balustered steps. As she approached, Tessa could see that thick ivy surrounded the door and a very faint light gleamed behind the fantail transom. She came slowly up the steps while Linda opened the door and held it wide for her.

She walked past Linda and stopped in the hall. 'Tell Beth I'm here,' she said. She was suddenly aware that she had dropped her voice, was whispering.

Linda spoke in a normal tone. 'I'll go and get her. You can wait in here.' She opened a small door to the right of the large staircase.

'I'll come with you.'

The girl had recovered something of her mettle. 'Only members of the church are allowed in the main part of the house,' she said firmly.

'Just go and get her, Linda.' Tessa walked through the door and Linda flicked a switch. They were in a bright, pleasantly furnished sitting room. Linda closed the door after her and Tessa walked into the middle of the Chinese circular carpet. There was a second door facing the one by which Linda had left. Tessa opened it and saw a small bedroom with a bathroom leading off it. She reclosed the door and came back into the sitting room. Thick velvet curtains hung undrawn on either side of a window that presumably over-looked the garden. That would be, Tessa thought as she approached the window, where the headlights of the BMW had picked up thick azalea bushes as they had driven in. To satisfy herself, she leaned forward and peered out.

With a sense of shock, she realised she was looking at her own face. The glass was darkened, vaguely reflective. There was no question of seeing through to the bushes outside.

Leilia exclaimed effusively in admiration of Abbeline's car but it was clear that what pleased her most was not that she was sitting back in the leather seat, being driven in luxury towards Scotland Yard, but that her friend Rhoda wasn't.

In the driver's seat Abbeline was trying to swerve past young revellers. Beside him Leilia was reflecting in lordly fashion on the unfortunates compelled to walk the streets on a bitter night like this.

Arriving at Scotland Yard, she looked up at the building and brushed back her hair. 'What a dreadful new building. My grand-father, you know was the Commissioner at the old Scotland Yard.'

Abbeline lifted her clutch of plastic bags out of the boot. 'Your grandfather was the Metropolitan Police Commissioner?' He wasn't sure whether to believe her or not.

'Old Scotland Yard. Well before the First World War.'

'General Sir Charles Warren?'

'Exactly,' she said. They walked to the entrance and past security into the main hall. 'I'm a Warren, of course. I expect Rhoda's told you that? Such a snob your mother is. Well, you must know. She loves to boast about her friends' connections. Sad, really, isn't it?'

Abbeline showed her into the lift, noticed the sole of one shoe clacking against the upper as she walked. He nodded agreement. 'Sir Charles Warren, when he was Commissioner, was my great-grandfather's boss.'

'Really?' She wasn't interested.

'My great-grandfather was senior officer on the Ripper case.'

'Really?' The lift of the voice told him it was of no consequence to her. The lift took them up five floors and the door opened.

'Your grandfather is reputed to be one of the few men who really knew the name of Jack the Ripper. It's said he claimed to have been given the name by the man's family.'

She nodded, not interested.

'There are no family stories you know of?' Abbeline pressed her. 'Nobody who claims to have known the real name?'

'The name?'

'Of Jack the Ripper?'

Her lips twisted in disdain. 'A man who murdered cheap tarts. Why should anybody be interested in that today?'

The lift doors parted and Abbeline heard Jan Madigan's heels clicking along towards his office. 'If these hours continue,' she said, 'my old man's going to divorce me. With any luck.'

'Merry Christmas,' he said.

'Merry Christmas. Give us a kiss.'

He bent over and kissed her on the cheek. 'This is Leilia . . .' Abbeline waited but she declined to supply her surname. 'What I want, Jan, is for you to find the best identikit artist we've got.'

'Tonight?'

'Drag him out of bed. Leilia's got something in her head that could put us on to Beth Naylor.'

'We need that,' Jan said, her face suddenly grim.

'What is it, Jan?'

'I thought I'd get my Christmas kiss in first. You've had an urgent call from Ray Rose. Tessa Naylor has slipped her surveillance. Anna van Gelden says she was on her way to meet her sister Beth.'

CHAPTER THIRTY-TWO

Tessa spun round at the sound of the handle turning. She started forward and stopped as the door slowly opened.

Her sister Beth stood in the doorway. Her hair was cut into a rough fringe just above the eyebrows. She wore no make-up. Below a long dress of a plain russet material she wore heavy shoes. There was something so totally changed about her that Tessa drew a sharp breath. She was neither fatter nor thinner; her face was, apart from the complete lack of make-up, no different. There were no new lines, no dark smudges under the eyes. Yet there was a difference, an angle of the head, a certainty, an imperiousness in her whole manner.

She was smiling, a chilling, patently empty smile.

'Beth,' Tessa kept her voice low, 'I've been worried out of my mind about you.'

The cold, meaningless smile didn't change.

'I was locked in, Beth,' Tessa said softly. 'What's happening here?'

Beth made no attempt to answer. She came forward into the room, took Tessa's hand and swung her round as if she were about to admire her sister in a new ball gown. 'Let me look at you, Tessa, You look so well! So completely recovered now.'

'What are you talking about, Beth?' She wrenched her hand away. 'Beth, you said you needed me. Needed my help. You must listen to me – Leonard Passmore is a dangerous lunatic. The police are searching for him . . .' She stopped at the expression on her sister's face.

'I am in no danger from Dr Passmore,' Beth said. 'The Reverend Leonard can be no threat to me.'

'The Norwich police don't think so. He's wanted for the murder of an American Air Force girl. Maybe for Sally Portal too. You do know she's dead, Beth?'

Her sister seemed to have heard nothing. She was studying Tessa with minute care. 'When I left you were terribly sick,' she said. 'Carter said you're better now. Fit physically. But still terribly fragile.'

Tessa looked at her sister in astonishment. 'What earthly difference does it make what Carter said? Why were you calling him when you knew I was in England? When you knew I was looking for you? Worried sick about you.'

'Were you, Tessa?' Beth gave her a quizzical, knowing look. 'I called Carter because there were things I needed to know,' she said loftily. 'Desperately important things.'

Tessa nodded slowly. She wanted to talk about Sally Portal, about Annabelle Wright, but those cold eyes and that frankly unbalanced smile made her hesitate. She had to get Beth out of this house. Get her to Cambridge. But she somehow sensed that she could not propose that yet. 'Beth,' she said in a steady voice, 'what's been happening to you? Why didn't you write? Why didn't you get in touch if you knew I was in England?'

Her head came up. Just the way it used to when she was a small girl and their mother offered criticism, but the expression was unchanged.

'Beth?' Tessa looked at her sister's blankly smiling face and swallowed hard. 'Why did you get Linda to bring me here?'

The expression was threatening. Despite the smile, it was threatening.

'It is Christmas Day,' she said. 'It is also the eve of the judicial murder of James Naylor, strung up like a common thief at the crossroads, his ears docked, his tongue split, not a hundred yards from this spot.'

'James Naylor?'

'A preacher of the Word. A prophet whose followers called him the Teacher of Righteousness, Jesus Christ Naylor, and who raised from the dead poor Dorcas Erbury in Exeter Gaol as witness to the power God had bestowed upon him.'

'I've heard Dad talk about him but this is hundreds of years ago,

Beth. You can't believe it has anything to do with us?'

'With *me*,' she said fiercely. 'Because the Word doesn't die. It resists all mortality. It lives on – waiting only to be spoken.'

'By you?'

'By the youngest living descendant of the prophet James Naylor.'

'Beth,' Tessa said in the silence that had fallen, 'I want you to tell me. I want you to tell me how it all happened? Leonard Passmore and his Millennium Church . . .' Somehow she still hoped to appeal to that other Beth she had known.

But the smile had faded. 'The Millennium Church? How did I come upon the Millennium Church? God led me here,' she said with devastating conviction. 'God led me to the historical discoveries of the Reverend Leonard.'

In Tessa's head alarm bells rang. She must take it slowly, very carefully. 'Where did you meet him, Beth?'

'He came to Boston. He first made himself known to me there, just before I left for England.'

'You didn't say anything about it at the time?'

'You were ill, Tessa. You'd just lost your baby. You'd become apathetic, withdrawn.'

'Beth, we're talking about *you*.'

'She nodded. 'It's painful for you to remember that time. Of course.'

'Why didn't you contact me here?'

'I myself, like every member of the church, am absorbed in God's work, Tessa. It's what comes first. To the exclusion of everything. There is no single matter that can be allowed to divert us from the path. No concern for ourselves. Or for others, no act of charity, nothing can be allowed to divert us from the path the Lord has chosen for us.'

'No concern for yourselves, you said? No concern for others? I thought that's what Christianity is all about?'

Beth's mouth tightened. 'I'm not talking about the masses. I'm talking about the *Elect*.'

'The Elect?'

'Those chosen of God cannot escape the call. Those chosen of God bear a terrible responsibility to carry out His will. You have to understand that. No, the Reverend Leonard was right. It's more than what comes first. It takes all our time, all our effort. It's a call to leave everything and follow. It's a call Christ has made to the chosen few since the church began. It is inescapable.'

'Is that why you gave up everything? Left Cambridge?'

'Of course.'

'Why you left the apartment at Market Place?'

'Exactly. I had spent all day praying with the Reverend Leonard. Praying to be relieved of my responsibility, praying that I was not chosen.'

'But Passmore knew you were?'

'He presented me with the truth, Tessa. The inescapable truth. He told me that the responsibilities I was assuming were awesome.'

'You could have turned away.'

'That night I came to see, as the Reverend Leonard saw, that my responsibilities were inescapable. He told me . . .' her voice rose '. . . he told me Jesus is hammering on the door. "*Jesus Christ, himself in his person, is hammering at your door. Let him in Beth, you have only to open the door, to let him in.*" '

For a second Tessa felt the wave of crude evangelistic power flowing from her sister, the power she remembered in their mother's voice when she read from the scriptures. But it was a call not to God but to madness. With her father's help Tessa had learned to resist it. Not so, Beth. Tessa knew that for her sister the words of Passmore had been delivered with a resonance amplified by childhood memories.

'Sally Portal . . .' Tessa said tentatively, aghast at what she now knew she would hear. 'Before you left, you asked her to come up to Cambridge?'

'There's no room for uncertainty on the Lord's path.'

'You mean you were not sure whether or not she was a Naylor? A Naylor younger than you. And Annabelle Wright the same.'

'There is no room for uncertainty on this chosen path,' Beth said. 'In the name of God you must understand that by now!'

A deep chill flooded Tessa as she stood there. But some need to know urged her on. 'And Passmore, Beth?' Tessa's eyes were on her sister's face. 'What about Leonard Passmore?'

'God leads people to us for a purpose. The Reverend Leonard was powerful in his conviction, strong in his love. He led me to a knowledge of who I am, whom I have been chosen to be. But he has served his purpose.'

There was an extraordinary coldness to her delivery that left Tessa in no doubt what her sister meant.

'Do you mean he's dead?'

'He was human and his will failed. At the last moment it failed.'

In the long silence Tessa knew she must make a move. 'I don't understand you, Beth,' she said slowly. 'But I believe we should talk a great deal more about all these things. I think we should leave here now. I'm going to take you back with me tonight. To a friend's house in Cambridge.'

Her sister's face hardened.

'You have to come with me, Beth. I don't understand, I don't pretend to understand, but dreadful things have happened.'

Beth looked at her with incredulity. 'I have made my decision for Christ. Can't you see that?'

'Listen, Beth, I'm not playing the interfering older sister I know you hate, but you must leave here. You asked me to come to help you . . . On the phone, you said you were desperately in need of my help.'

'I had you brought here,' Beth said, 'to forward God's purpose.'

Purpose. That word again. 'What can I do but help you get out of here?' Tessa said. 'Leave with me tonight. Leave now, Beth.'

'Leave now? When great things are happening. When I am central to the great events that are about to take place in this house.'

'Jesus Christ!' Tessa exploded. 'Great events! People have been murdered!'

The slap was delivered with tremendous force. Enough to rock Tessa backwards, to leave her cheek stinging fiercely. As she lifted her head she saw Beth was already at the door. Before Tessa could cover the five or six steps between them, it closed and the click of the key in the lock stopped her as she reached for the handle. Slowly she enclosed the brass knob and turned it. Pulled, pushed, only to rattle the locked door. There was no mistake. She stood with her hand on the ornate door handle without speaking, without crying out. She already knew there would be no point.

CHAPTER THIRTY-THREE

In Cambridge Police station on Parker's Piece Ray Rose had set up a large map of East Anglia. He had marked with red pins the principal locations in the case. The Cambridge and Norwich death sites of Sally Portal and Annabelle Wright. Maskop Quarry where Passmore was found. The rubbish dump on the Ely Road. And he had drawn a red thirty-mile radius circle round the city of Norwich, taking in the ports of Cromer, Great Yarmouth and Lowestoft. He was studying it when Inspector Winter from Norwich Central came on the line. 'This identikit picture,' Winter said, 'is it your idea, Ray?'

'Why, don't you like it?'

'I don't know. It's Abbeline's wheeze, is that it? Where does the information come from?'

'Some Soho baglady who was taken to the Passmore prayer centre earlier this year.'

'How long does Abbeline think we've got?'

Rose stared at the map and the number of villages within his red circle. He tried not to think of how many forgotten Edwardian villas might be hidden away behind a stand of trees. 'Not long enough to cover all this,' he said to Winter.

'You'll be all right, Ray.'

'It was my men that lost her. Lost Tessa Wilson.'

'That's what I mean. You'll be all right. If there's one thing Abbeline doesn't do it's to pass the buck.'

'Let's hope there'll be no need to,' Rose said doubtfully.

He put down the phone. There was no getting away from it, his surveillance team had lost her. By a simple run down an alley. And then had spent over an hour searching Cambridge for the car. They were his men after all. He walked through to the coffee machine in the silent entrance hall. He nodded to the desk sergeant, paid and drew himself a cup of black. Through the glass doors he could see the islands of melting snow on Parker's Piece. They'd never find her with just an identikit picture of the front of a house. And, whatever Winter said, it would only be human if Abbeline made sure he, Ray Rose, carried the can.

Jan Madigan slowed the Jaguar and took Rose's call. 'The boss is asleep at the moment. What's the problem?'

'I have this notebook thing. Belonging to Passmore. Has his initials on it anyway. It's a thick wedge of paper. The writing seems mostly washed away on the top page so I'm scared to try to lift any of the others.'

'We need it dealt with tonight, Ray.'

'I know. I could send it down by bike.'

Jan thought a moment. 'We don't have time to rush it down to London. Let's see, you've got a university there. Must be packed with experts in damaged documents.'

'If it is they've kept out of my way.'

'Grimes,' she said. 'Dr Grimes. King's College. Ring him.'

'You ring him,' he said. 'It's one o'clock on Christmas bloody morning!'

In the passenger seat, Abbeline awoke, rubbing his eyes. Dreamland. The word conjured up childhood, his mother feeding him huge mounds of pink candyfloss, his cousin, Sam, jeering at Jack because he wouldn't go on the Big Dipper. Because he winced every time it came swooping and screeching past them. Dreamland – the Fun Fair at Margate. Holiday time.

He glowered out of the window. They were passing by some small town, a mile or so away across the fields.

'Did I wake you?' Jan said.

'Not yet.' He yawned and sat up. 'Who was that?'

She told him about Rose. 'I just called my old mucker, Dr Harry Grimes. "Delighted to be of assistance, my dear. Only sorry you aren't bringing it round yourself." The dirty old bugger!'

'Where are we?' Abbeline grunted.

'Cambridge in twenty minutes.'

'You must have been doing a ton ever since we left London.'

'I've been doing better than that,' she said, aggrieved. 'Nothing on the motorway. Not a sign of the Old Bill.'

'You should be home with your husband.'

She gave him a sour look. 'He's been celebrating with his football mates. I called him before we left to wish him Happy Christmas. I even said I hoped next year might work out better than the last . . .'

He turned his head and saw she was biting her lip. 'What did he say, Jan? When you said you hoped next year would be better?'

'He said: "No chance unless Chelsea can afford a completely new defence." It wasn't a joke. The berk meant it.'

They passed through a village. Christmas trees glittered in the cottage windows. The village pub, on Christmas Eve extension, was finally closing.

'What about this American woman, Tessa? Has she put her head in the lion's mouth, d'you think?'

'She thought she was doing it to help her sister,' Abbeline said. 'But it still doesn't explain why she didn't call the police the moment she got the call to meet Beth.'

Jan put her foot down. 'Ray Rose says Anna van Gelden's now feeling guilty as hell. She knows she should have called the police the moment Tessa left the house.'

'Why the hell didn't Tessa want to?'

Jan glanced sideways at him. 'There are times, Superintendent . . .'

'What are you leering at? I asked you why Tessa refused to call the police?'

'Partly because Beth asked her not to.'

'And partly?'

'Because she was pissed off with you.'

'Christ, Jan!'

'Sorry, sir. Only repeating what Anna van Gelden said. Not word for word, of course. In any event, Tessa Wilson was pissed off. She wanted to handle this by herself.'

Abbeline nodded to himself. 'Anything else? From Anna van Gelden.'

They were speeding into Cambridge.

'Something else we didn't know about,' Jan said. 'Carter Wilson phoned Tessa yesterday and claimed he'd just had a call from Beth.'

Abbeline sat up. 'Why did she call Wilson?'

'Anna van Gelden says Beth had already been asking for Tessa at the Pelican. She needed to talk to Carter Wilson to find where Tessa had moved to.'

Abbeline puffed his cheeks. 'Why does Beth Naylor so badly need to see her sister?' he said slowly.

Jan was silent, concentrating on the driving.

Abbeline said, 'I think we have a matter of hours.' He paused. 'The identikits have all gone out?'

'Apparently the coppers on the beat are all complaining they've never had to show identikits of a *house* before.'

From shortly after midnight on Christmas Eve police cars had rolled into all the small market towns around Norwich. At Horsham, Dereham and Shipham, Roxham, Reedham and Aylsham, people on their way home from parties, customers in pubs on extension hours, publicans and bar staff, had been approached by uniformed officers carrying an artist's impression of a house, a turn of the century Edwardian red brick villa with a set of fine balustraded steps leading to the front door and a large stone crest set into the brickwork above a curved Queen Anne style portico. In car parks and as the rural Christmas Eve bus services picked up their last passengers for the night, travellers were asked the same question. *Do you know this house? Do you know any houses that look like it in your village?* Then: *Will you please look at it carefully – it could be a matter of life or death.*

CHAPTER THIRTY-FOUR

In Abbeline's Cambridge office the messages came in from car after car. None of the hundreds questioned in their homes, or in pubs and discos that night, recognised the identikit of the house. No estate agent in the Norwich area they had been able to question remembered seeing such a house in the last few years.

The inexorable conclusion was that they were looking in the wrong place.

'After all,' Jan said carefully, handing Abbeline a cup of coffee, 'the locating of this house in the Norwich area depends solely on one boozy old woman.'

'Okay,' he said. 'I accept that. But if Leilia is wrong, she made a mistake. It was not a deliberate attempt to mislead. Do we agree on that?'

'I never met the lady,' Ray Rose said.

'I go along with that,' Jan stirred sugar into her cup, tasted it and spooned in more. 'But how does that help?'

'It helps,' Abbeline said, 'because it probably means she's out but not *far* out.'

'It means we need more men,' Rose said. 'Except three o'clock Christmas morning is not the easiest time to be knocking up random punters to show a picture of a house.'

'It has to be done,' Abbeline said shortly. 'More men, and extend the catchment area around Norwich. Leilia specifically mentioned the cathedral.'

'She did to me too, when she was talking to the artist.' Jan was slipping through her notes: ' "We passed through quite a big town and there was the cathedral on my left, sticking up like a blunt thumb. I knew we had to be in Norwich . . . When I was a child et cetera".' Jan closed the book. ' "I knew we had to be in Norwich",' she repeated, looking at Abbeline.

'So let's keep at it,' he said.

Rose straightened up. His face was pale. 'Sticking up like a blunt thumb?' he said. 'Funny way to put it.'

Jan nodded. Abbeline's eyes were on him.

'Norwich doesn't stick up like a blunt thumb,' Rose said. 'Norwich has a spire.' His face suddenly showed the strain he was under. 'Crazy old bitch!' he swore. 'She couldn't have meant fucking Norwich!'

'Sit down, Ray,' said Abbeline. He stuck up his own thumb, looked at it and wagged it to and fro. 'Blunt thumb . . . spire . . .'

'She couldn't have meant Norwich,' Rose repeated bitterly.

'Where else?' Jan said.

'In East Anglia?' Rose let out a short bark of a laugh. 'Cathedrals? Peterborough. Ely, Bury St Edmunds . . . How far d'you want to go? And dozens of church towers that stick up like blunt thumbs. We could even be in the wrong part of the country altogether.'

'Take it easy, Ray,' Abbeline said. 'We use what we have. Everything points to East Anglia. The Norfolk/Cambridge border area. Within an hour or so of Passmore speaking to me on the phone he was being tipped into Maskop Quarry. Assuming he was killed by Beth Naylor, she didn't have time to drive across half the country to get rid of the body.'

The phone ringing made them all turn. Jan picked it up and punched the amplifier button.

A deep fruity English voice came over the line. 'Hallo, is that you, Jan?'

'Yes, this is Jan Madigan,' she said, frowning.

'Harry here. Terribly sorry to be calling you up at this bizarre hours of a Christmas morning . . .'

'It doesn't matter, Harry. It doesn't matter at all.'

'That notecase your Inspector Rose had delivered to me.'

'From the car at Maskop Quarry . . .'

'I've dealt with some pretty illegible documents in my time . . .'

Jan held up one hand, the fingers crossed.

'. . . but I've never come across anything with the instability of this modern ink. This is not a job for me, Jan.'

'It isn't?' Her voice fell.

'No. So I'm making arrangements for an old friend at the University Department of Criminology to look at it.'

'Harry, this is urgent, really urgent.'

'I understand that, my dear. He's on his way to his lab now.'

She had examined every window for a way out but in the bedroom and bathroom the same strange darkened glass within metal frames offered no indication that they were ever intended to open.

The bathroom window was smallest. Taking the bath stool, Tessa swung it at the dark glass, gritting her teeth for the crash and tinkle of shards on to the paving below. But the stool cracked against toughened glass and sprang back in her hand, rolling on to the bathroom floor.

Slowly she picked it up. A full sense of predicament was being borne in to her. She had made a desperate mistake, of course. Carter would say she had behaved with typical rashness, typical irresponsibility, typical . . . She hurled the stool against the window with all her strength, with all her anger.

This time it caught the glass at a slightly different angle – different but equally ungiving as the legs snapped and the top of the stool spun like a discus across the room.

In the silence, Tessa felt energy drain from her. She found it impossible to absorb what she now knew, on a different level, to be true: her sister's mind had undergone a monstrous sea-change. Something far more profound than ever before, something shaped by Passmore's unique conviction, unique ability to convey his faith. And Tessa herself was unable to summon help. Imprisoned in three rooms, with a reinforced door into the hall, and toughened glass, unopenable windows.

At what seemed a great distance but from within the house she could hear chanting, a swelling of voices in prayer. Then, as she pressed herself against the locked door, listening, a voice, a woman's voice, Beth's voice: '*Visit this place, Lord . . .*' And the rumbled response from unseen worshippers: '*Visit this place, Lord, with thy blessing.*'

'*Visit us this night . . .*'

'*Visit us . . .*'

She turned away and walked into the bedroom and sat down heavily on the bed. She thought again of Passmore. How was it that men like him were able to persuade, to convince? Of course she should have seen much earlier that it was in Beth's personality, that need to believe. It always had been. Just as Tessa herself was driven by a shaky need to be independent. Independent of the tailored, sanitised world-view of Carter . . .

Sitting on the bed, her back supported against the wooden headboard, she forced herself to believe that Jack Abbeline must have heard by now that she had evaded her surveillance unit, was already organising a search for her. Anna would have told the police about Beth's call. They would be alerted . . . But what did Abbeline have to go on? Certainly not the location of the house itself. She tried to think how he might possibly find it and her mind went frighteningly blank. Find it in time. In time for what? In time to save what from happening?

She knew she was in danger. She knew the danger came most directly from her sister. She knew her own danger was connected with the same single fact that had caused the deaths of Sally Portal and Annabelle Wright. But if some mad idea of Naylor ancestry was behind the murders, how could she be involved? The line had bypassed her. If it was true that her father was in direct line of descent from this seventeenth-century madman, James Naylor – then Beth was incontestably the last Naylor. Why had she, Tessa, been lured here?

Then suddenly it came to her so powerfully that she was forced to gasp. Suddenly she understood. Understood why Beth had called Carter. Suddenly she realised why Beth needed her here. Why she was being kept throughout Christmas night in these padded cells. She felt her palms moisten, felt sweat prickle her forehead.

She stood up in alarm. Uncertain whether she was propelled by fear at her realisation or, at that very same moment, by registering that the key had turned in the lock of the door into the hall.

Breathing fast, sick to her stomach with apprehension, she walked into the other room.

Linda was standing in the doorway. Her dark eyes stood out in a pale, frightened face. 'You must come,' she said. 'Quickly. It's Beth – something's happening to Beth!'

CHAPTER THIRTY-FIVE

The University of Cambridge Department of Criminology was deserted except for the single figure waiting in the hall.

Grimes shook hands with him and introduced Abbeline and Jan. 'Doctor Sampson,' Abbeline said. 'I realise what we're asking. I promise you if it hadn't been a matter of very real urgency we would not have got you out at this hour on Christmas morning.'

Sampson was short and bearded, wearing a sweater and corduroys. 'Of course,' he said briskly. 'Let's get down to it. Come into my lab.'

He led them down a narrow modern corridor and took out a bunch of keys to open an unmarked glass door. 'There's a rest room two doors down on the right,' he said. 'A coffee machine if you can stomach its regurgitations.' He stretched out his hand for the sodden notecase Grimes was carrying. 'Have the papers been examined by anybody other than Dr Grimes?'

Abbeline shook his head. 'The inspector who found them realised it was a case for expert help. It was passed late last night straight to Dr Grimes.'

As Grimes handed the notecase to Sampson, Abbeline saw that Passmore's initials were stamped in gold on the black leather. 'If the man in the car was murdered, wouldn't the murderer have taken this if it was in any way significant?'

'Life's not that tidy, Doctor, thank God. People under stress overlook things. We think the notecase had fallen unnoticed by whoever ditched the car. It came out over the door sill in a rush of water.'

'Is there any doubt about who did it?' Grimes asked.

'Not any more.'

Sampson nodded. 'So what sort of thing am I looking for? What sort of thing are you hoping to find?'

'Transcribe as much as you can, doctor. It's even possible Beth Naylor knew what was in these papers and didn't see them as important.'

'Or maybe didn't care any more,' Jan added. 'It's surprising how many times over-confidence does for them.'

Sampson raised his eyebrows. 'I'd like to talk to you about that sometime, Inspector.'

'After Christmas,' Abbeline said.

'Yes.' Sampson pointed. 'Try the coffee.' Pause. 'If you dare.'

Grimes and Abbeline, with Jan between them, walked along the corridor into a stark modern room with electric blue divans, without arms, positioned against three walls. Behind the door was a drinks machine. Abbeline stood in front of it, searching for coins. 'Do you dare?'

Jan nodded, dropping down on to one of the divans. 'Give me a black coffee with sugar.' From her bag she took a half bottle of Irish whiskey.

Abbeline looked.

She shrugged. 'Hell, it's Christmas Day.' She turned to Grimes. 'Harry?'

'As you say, it's Christmas Day. I'll take mine as it comes from the bottle.'

Abbeline fed in coins for one coffee and brought it over with two extra plastic cups.

While Jan poured Irish whiskey, Abbeline took a mobile phone from his inside pocket and dialled a number. 'Abbeline here,' he said. 'Anything?'

'Not so far, sir,' Ray Rose's voice said. 'We did a false alarm to a house in Reedham just outside Norwich half an hour ago. Two people had identified it from the identikit but it wasn't any more than quite similar. Perhaps if we knew what the stone coat of arms over the door was . . .'

'We do. Jan checked it with a member of the College of Heralds. It's entirely made up. The builder probably just put it together himself. It doesn't help. What we need is more men.'

'Norwich have given us nearly sixty uniforms. We've over thirty separate teams showing the picture. I don't want to be a defeatist, sir, but I can't help believing that if the photofit were at all accurate of a house in the Norwich district, we'd have the answer by now.'

'Keep going, Ray. See if you can wangle more men. That picture – however inadequate – is the only line we've got.'

He switched off the phone and sat looking at the skeletal head in a large reproduction of De Kooning's Woman I on the wall. Then, grimacing, he put away the phone and picked up the plastic cup of whiskey.

Tessa ran down the wide carpeted steps of the main staircase. In front of her Linda turned right through a smaller doorway and down again, narrower steps this time, to a basement level. In a small stone-flagged hallway, she stopped until Tessa reached her.

'Where is she?' Tessa quickly ran her eyes round the room. A long Victorian sofa occupied one wall. Copies of the Bible were piled on a side table. To one side an open arch revealed a boiler-room and woodstore. In front of her was a new carved-oak studded door.

'She's here,' Linda said. She opened the door and pulled it back for Tessa to pass.

She saw she was in a small chapel. Plain, without seats or pews. Darkness stretched beyond the guttering candles on the wall. At one end there were two stone steps and a table with a carved lectern beside it. Beyond the table Beth lay sprawled on the stone flags.

As Tessa ran towards her she saw that Beth stirred, that her hand clutched and relaxed again and again.

Kneeling beside her sister, Tessa took her shoulders and lifted, turning her on to her back. An extraordinary transformation had taken place in Beth's appearance. The face was bloodless. Her hair now fell wet across her brow; her cheeks were running with sweat. Her mouth opened and closed as words were forced out in scraps and half sentences: '*Visit me, Lord. Visit me, Lord. I am the of the seed, of the seed, Lord . . . Come down to me in love, Lord, in understanding . . . I am your servant . . . I am chosen . . .*' Between words she was breathing in deep fast gulps of air.

'Help me with her, Linda' Tessa said. 'Help me get her on to the sofa.'

'*The Gates of Knowledge are barred against me . . . I am denied my birthright . . .*' They lifted her to her feet, steadied her for a moment or two, then, both supporting her, guided her steps towards the small hallway and lowered her on to the sofa.

Moaning to herself, her face still pale but the eyes less fixed, the breathing less panicked, Beth dropped back among the cushions.

In the effort of concentration on Beth, Tessa was only peripherally aware that there had been other people in the chapel, figures that rose from the darkness and now stood in the door to the hallway, silently watching her.

She glanced again at Beth, saw that her breathing was fast but regular, and turned back to the chapel door. There were perhaps ten or a dozen people crowding the doorway. They were mostly in their thirties or forties, mostly casually dressed in jeans and sweaters. Mostly men but a few women. Some heads were dropped on their chests in prayer, others stared fixedly at Tessa with a look that was blankly but passively hostile.

She turned to look back at Linda. 'What the hell are you all on?' she said.

'It's nothing,' Linda said. 'A herbal cup before prayers . . .'

'She needs a doctor,' Tessa urged. 'We need to get the police and a doctor here straight away.'

A heavily built middle-aged man had taken the central position in the doorway. His eyes were running with tears. 'Brothers . . . Sisters . . .' he said. 'The Lord has turned His face from us.'

Others were shuffling uneasily. Many were weeping. A young man, his thin face a cliché of adolescent ordinariness, said: 'Without the Reverend Leonard we are a flock without a shepherd.'

The middle-aged man shuffled forward an inch or two. 'We must hold a meeting,' he said. 'The brothers and sisters must hold a meeting.'

Tessa looked at him. He was round-faced, overweight, astonishingly ordinary in his crumpled tweed jacket and khaki slacks. She looked past him towards the others. Did they have any idea, any of them, that murder had been committed in the name of their crazy beliefs? She felt no sense of danger to herself now. How could she, among these desperately ordinary people?

Instead, she felt in control. 'Hold your meeting afterwards,' she said peremptorily. 'My sister needs a doctor.' She turned to Linda. 'You know where there's a phone?'

'In the Reverend Leonard's study.'

'Call the police. Tell them we need an ambulance.'

The group had moved into the small hallway. They seemed only to move together, never as individuals. 'We are called to a meeting,' one woman said, her voice rising.

'We are called to a meeting,' the ordinary young man repeated to himself.

'The prophet has left us,' a young woman said. 'For our sins the prophet has left us . . .'

Tessa turned back to her sister as the group shuffled behind her out on to the stairway. Beth was muttering to herself, too softly, too indistinctly to be comprehensible. Linda, Tessa realised, was still standing in the doorway, her eyes fixed on Beth.

'The phone,' Tessa said harshly, almost as if to break a trance. She saw Linda hesitate, look again towards Beth. 'She's not going to be able to tell you what to do. She needs medical help, Linda. Go ahead – you know where there's a phone! Call the police!'

Tessa turned back towards her sister. Her face had the pallor of stone. Her eyelids were fluttering closed.

They had been sitting for over half an hour when a loudspeaker clicked into life in the rest room and an amplified voice said: 'Sampson here. If you'd like to come along the corridor to the lab, I can show you what I've got.'

The laboratory was long with several rows of benches. Sampson was working at the bench closest the door. The notecase stood open on the end of the white worktop. In front of him were six or seven large glass plates on which wet fragments of paper had been arranged and flattened.

They could read parts of a sentence or two: *And when the Teacher of Righteousness* . . . or . . . *arrested and taken to the Tower of London* . . . but virtually nothing else.

'It's not bad,' Sampson said. 'Certain modern inks wash away very easily and this can be a problem. But with a ballpoint we can go some way to reading not from the washed out ink but from the depression caused on the surface of the paper itself. Much of it is luck, of course. The heaviness of the hand, and so on. Now let's take the first page.' He sat in front of a keyboard and tapped in instructions. A white screen on the wall lit up and one of the glass sheets containing paper-fragments came into focus.

'This first one is clear enough. It's a receipt for a second hand Volkswagen. Bought in North London about five weeks ago. Is that of any interest to you?'

Abbeline shook his head. 'It's relevant but it's not what we're looking for at the moment.'

'What are you looking for?'

'If only we knew,' Jan said.

Sampson nodded. 'This is fairly clear.' He used a screen pointer. 'A letter from a man named Quentin Naylor to Leonard Passmore. Details of his family arriving in Massachusetts in the seventeenth century. Something of a family tree. Dates of birth, marriage details . . . All apparently the result of an enquiry by Passmore, the recipient of the letter. Date not clear but looking like June, perhaps three years ago.'

'That would be just before Quentin Naylor died.'

'Closer,' Abbeline said. 'But no help at the moment. He was looking at a large glass plate with several pages arranged on it. 'What's that one?'

'It's a handwritten copy of some sort of historical account book,' Sampson said. He stroked his beard. 'There were clearly other pages but this is the one of interest to our copyist.'

'I can't read a word of it,' Jan said.

'It's dated December 1660.'

'Very much our period,' Grimes said.

Sampson nodded. 'I'd say it was someone copying from a local public records office – something like that. You see the column on the left? A whole series of payments of five shillings.'

'To the people in the right hand column?' Jan guessed.

'No. To the public hangman for the execution of the people in the right hand column.'

'Christ! Five shillings. twenty-five pence a head.'

'What's the last item on the page?

'Yes, it's different,' Sampson said. 'First, as you see, it's six shillings and sixpence. Secondly it's paid not to the hangman, whose name was John Arbuthnot, but to a guard captain.'

'Does that help us?'

'I don't know if it'll help you, but I can explain how it happened. Take a look over here. Pages rather badly damaged, I'm afraid, but it gets better later. I think this explains the extra payment to our guard captain. The year 1660's significant, isn't it, Grimes?'

'If we're in December,' Grimes explained, 'the king, Charles II, had recently been restored. A tolerant man, but nobody had any time for far out Puritans any longer.' He nodded to Sampson.

'Let me try it for you.' Sampson began to read. The lines were awash with ink; barely four or five words were recognisable to Abbeline:

'During that morning the air was again thick with snow for upwards of three hours, rendering the road so nearly impassable that the company made but slow progress . . .'

Dr Sampson turned to Abbeline. 'Might this be of interest?'

'Let's try it,' he said. 'We've precious little else at the moment.'

'From scraps I can read of the next half page,' Sampson continued, 'the *company* appears to be an escort of twenty footsoldiers, under the command of a mounted captain.'

'Our captain?' Jan said.

'Not named but very likely, as you'll see.'

'What are they escorting?'

'A prison cart. A special prison cart. This one's transporting a condemned man.'

'James Naylor?' Abbeline said.

'That's the name that appears later. He has been condemned to death by the Bishop's Court, the hanging to take place within sight of the cathedral. So we could be on to something?'

'Let's go on, Doctor Sampson,' Jan urged him.

He adjusted his glasses.

'By eleven in the forenoon the company were still some miles from the cathedral square where the Bishop had ordained the hanging. And in that the Bishop's writ spoke of John Naylor's hanging that day at midday, the captain ordered that they should proceed no

further. And though they were still a distance of five miles from the city gate, the captain declared that they were nevertheless in sight of the cathedral and ordered that a gallows be set up by the roadside.'

Abbeline was following the reading from the text on the screen, his lips moving over those words he understood.

'Thus a gallows was erected for James Naylor, the Great Blasphemer, whose followers claimed that he was Jesus Christ come again and that his seed for all time was charged with the gift of great prophecy. And they further claim that one would come after him, of his seed, and on one Christmastide far hence reveal this most marvellous gift to the great betterment of this Earth and all the sinners thereof for the millennium to come.'

'The millennium,' Jan said. 'The Millennium Church!'

'Naylor's words are mostly obliterated but he clearly ended with some appeal to those who came after him to keep the faith, Sampson said.

'And so saying his tongue was slit and his ears docked and the gallows rope was affixed to his neck and the cart driven from under him.

'And so died James Naylor at the crossroad at Long Norton within sight of the Cathedral Church of Ely on the day of Christ's coming in the year of our Lord 1660.'

Jan was looking at Abbeline. 'Ely,' she said. 'Not Norwich.'

'We've had our men asking in the wrong county.'

Abbeline was already punching buttons on his phone. 'Ray,' he said, 'you were right about Norwich. Have you ever heard of the village of Long Norton, five or six miles from Ely?'

Sampson and Jan could both hear Ray Rose on the line. 'Long Norton? Yes, I know it. It's miles away from where we've been operating. It's the Cambridge side of the Norfolk border.'

'Get half a dozen cars over there right away,' Abbeline said. 'Jesus Christ Naylor was put to death there by an overzealous guard captain. Batter on every door in the village. Try to get hold of local estate agents. One of them's going to remember having sold a house like that in the last couple of years. The house is in an area somewhere between Long Norton and Ely. You can see the stump of Ely Cathedral from there, I guarantee it.'

'You drive.' Abbeline threw Jan the keys as they ran down the steps of the Department of Criminology. Catching them, she unlocked the door to the Jaguar. She slid behind the wheel, started the engine and had the car moving forward as he slammed shut his door. He was silent as she moved the car on squealing wheels through the deserted streets of Cambridge. Buildings of majestic beauty flashed past them as they raced down King's Parade, but Abbeline didn't turn his head.

He thinks it's already too late, Jan said to herself.

Roger Jackson came down in his dressing gown. The children were in the sitting room and were already tearing open presents. He looked at his watch. It was before eight o'clock. The front door was part open. His wife was turning towards him. From the stairs he could see that it was still dark outside and that the man on the doorstep was in uniform.

'It's the police,' his wife said, coming towards him.

'What do they want with us on Christmas morning?'

'They wanted to know if you were Roger Jackson, the estate agent.'

'Christ, the shop hasn't been broken into, has it?' He walked past his wife and pulled the door wider. A blast of cold rushed in.

There was a police car in the drive. The young policeman at the door held a clipboard. 'You're Roger Jackson, of Jackson Brothers, the estate agent's, sir?'

Jackson squinted at the clipboard while the man was speaking. 'Nothing wrong with my premises, is there?' he said. 'There hasn't been another break-in?'

'Nothing like that, sir.' The constable lifted the clipboard. Even before he'd smoothed over the picture with his hand, Jackson recognised the drawing of the old Simpson house, empty for nearly ten years before some scientific research company bought it last year.

CHAPTER THIRTY-SIX

Beth Naylor's breathing had slowed to something approaching normal. She lay on the sofa, her eyes closed. The twitching, the frantic pulling at her fingers had subsided. Her hands were still.

Tessa rose from where she had been kneeling beside her sister and stood looking down at her. This eerie house was now silent. Where just twenty minutes ago it had seemed full of worshippers, now it seemed empty.

For a moment Tessa stood, undecided. No distant police or ambulance sirens, nothing. At the sound of a step on the twisting staircase outside the old basement door, she looked up to see Linda.

Anger rose in her. 'Are the police on their way?' And when the girl's expression failed to change: 'Did you call the police?'

'They won't let me make the call,' she said.

'Make them! Or better still, take no notice of them!'

Linda stood silently.

Tessa felt a fury rise inside her. 'Tell that fat one to come down here . . .'

Linda shook her head. 'You don't understand.'

'I understand one thing, Linda, and that's that we need a doctor and the police here right away.'

Singing rose again from somewhere in the house.

'The meeting's over,' Linda said. 'They've decided.'

Tessa could hear the hymn clearly now, snatches of Blake's incomparable words: '*Bring me my spear, O clouds unfold! Bring me my chariot of fire!*'

'Decided what, for God's sake?'

Linda looked down at Beth, then gestured quickly towards the chapel. 'I have to speak to you, Tessa,' she said quickly. 'Now.'

Tessa walked ahead of her into the chapel. Two steps in, she turned to face Linda. With a sense of shock she saw that the wall-eyed blankness had gone. The girl's expression spelt fear.

'What is it, Linda?'

The girl took a half breath. 'At the meeting,' she said, 'a decision was taken.'

'What decision?'

'They're going to set fire to the house.'

'Set fire to the house? With Beth in it?'

'With everybody in it.' It was as if fear had cleared her mind. 'They're desperate. They've reached the end. They've been praying and fasting for days. They've left their families, sold their houses, everything. The Reverend Leonard has disappeared . . .'

Tessa looked at her in mounting alarm.

'And Beth failed them. Beth failed to deliver her prophecy,' Linda said flatly.

'Do they really mean to do this?' Tessa asked incredulously.

'They mean it.'

'Is there any way of getting out?'

Linda shook her head. 'They hold the keys.'

'No way out through the cellars here? Through the woodstore?'

Linda shook her head. 'Most of them would sooner die in prayer.' Tessa could see the exhaustion in the girl's face and felt sure it mirrored her own. She could feel the energy draining from her. She was on the verge of tears. She wanted Abbeline to be there. 'The phone,' she said. 'Somehow we must get to the phone.'

In her exhaustion she didn't at first understand what was happening. She saw the girl's face change, her head go up like a dog taking a scent, and only then did she understand. Linda had smelt smoke . . .

'Quickly!' Tessa said. 'We must move Beth.'

Tessa could smell it herself now. She watched Linda turn and open the door. She heard the singing of the hymn proceed relentlessly: '*Till we have built Jerusalem in England's green and pleasant land! Till we have built Jerusalem . . . Till we have built Jerusalem . . .*' The voices were building into a crazy crescendo.

The door opened wider now. Tessa felt a gust of warm, smoky air pass over her. In front of her, in slow motion, Linda seemed to ride forward, her arms rising, thrown wide like a preacher's. There was a cry, drowning the cadences of the hymn and the crackle of flames. Then the slender form crashed to the stone floor.

Behind her Beth stood with a wood cleaver in her hand, looking down at the sprawled ungainly body. The blow had struck her across the shoulder, biting through the collar bone. Unable to speak, Tessa watched the blood pump from her.

Christmas bells were ringing in the great cathedral of Ely when Jan and Abbeline approached the city. From the road they could see what the captain of the guard must have seen, over three hundred years ago, when he made his decision to erect a gallows by the roadside: the great cathedral, with Alan of Walsingham's central lantern tower, rising out of the fen snowscape. The huge mass of stone that supported it was a dark stump against the first early-morning light.

Somewhere ahead a car flashed its lights and Jan passed three police cars to pull level with Rose standing in the middle of the road.

Abbeline put his head out of the car window. 'Any luck, Ray?'

'First left,' he said. 'A local estate agent has recognised the house.'

'Use your radio,' Abbeline ordered. 'Get the Fire service on stand-by.'

Rose's tired eyes looked at him, bemused. 'The Fire Service?'

'Remember Waco, Texas,' Abbeline said. 'When people like this go, they can decide to take everything with them.'

'We have to get out, Beth,' Tessa said, her voice cracking in fear.

Beth was backing her into the chapel, pushing closed the door.

'We have to get out,' Tessa repeated desperately. Strange images and thoughts fluttered in her mind like captive birds: pictures of Beth as a child by the sea, of Carter's self-conscious, throaty laughter, of Abbeline . . . She could see no blood upon the steel, yet as it brushed Beth's rust-coloured skirt it wetted an outline of the long curved blade.

Reality returned. Tessa moved back a step. 'A purpose, you said,

Beth? You had a purpose getting me here. I know what it was now. But you're wrong. I'm not a threat to you. I'm no threat to your position as the youngest Naylor, *I'm not pregnant, Beth*. That's what you're afraid of, isn't it?'

Beth stood straight. The fall of candlelight glittered on the blade, outlined the shape of her leg, outlined the shape of the wetness of the blade. Her unsmiling smile was wolfish. 'You're pregnant, Tessa,' she said slowly.

'How in God's name . . .' She saw Beth flinch. 'How could I possibly be pregnant?' Tessa said quietly. 'My marriage to Carter is over.'

'There's been time since the miscarriage.'

'Don't be crazy, Beth.' Tessa bit her lip. She must be careful. She must watch her words. She had minutes only. She tried to speak neutrally, low key, but her voice raced ahead of its own accord. 'Beth, seven months ago I miscarried. There's time needed first for simple physical repair. Then, you know that things were bad for me. I wasn't well. I was sick. I wanted nothing to do with Carter, or a child by Carter. It's impossible, Beth.'

'He said you were pregnant.'

Tessa fell back in alarm. 'Carter said that?'

'When I called him in Boston, it was to ask him that. He said you were pregnant. He said you *must* be pregnant. By someone else!'

'Carter can't believe I would want to leave him for any other reason. But I'm leaving him because I don't love him, Beth. For no other reason.' Her voice croaked with tension. 'No other reason, Beth.'

Beth shook her head, once. Her eyes remained focused on Tessa. 'A man, Carter said, here in England.'

'Beth, *do* you know how long I've been here?'

'Someone you must have already known in Boston,' Carter said. 'A policeman. Abbeline. *That's* the reason you came to England.'

'This is madness . . . pure madness!' Tessa's voice rose in panic. 'There's no man. There's no pregnancy. I met Abbeline *here*, two weeks ago!'

Beth moved. The long rust-coloured gown shimmered the length of her leg. The point of the blade caught a thread then merged into shadow. Smoke curled lazily under the door.

'On this day, Christ was born,' Beth said. 'As dawn broke today, I stood ready to receive the gift of prophecy. The gift that's most certainly mine, Tessa. I am the youngest Naylor. The last Naylor in direct descent from James Naylor, who was destroyed here for the words he was about to utter. His ears were docked, Tessa. His tongue was split. He was hanged from a makeshift gallows.'

Tessa shook her head.

'And the revelation that was contained within him,' Beth said earnestly, 'is now contained within me.' Her shoulders straightened. 'I stood here and prayed, Tessa, I tore the strength to pray out of the very air around me. I prayed and begged God to infuse me with the power that was rightly mine . . .'

Tessa shifted back a pace, sideways, ready for a run at the door.

'But I failed, Tessa, because you stood in my way. I failed because that power couldn't be mine while you were pregnant. While you held the seed of another Naylor in your body.'

She saw the smoke, saw a new evenness to the curling rise of it, and knew she was lost unless she acted. 'No, Beth,' she said, moving another step, 'you failed to find the words. You failed this morning not because I'm pregnant, but because there *is* no revelation. James Naylor was a believer – but he might as well have been a charlatan because what he believed he was called to do was the product of a sick mind!'

The cleaver rose.

'A sick mind, Beth.'

'All our lives you took from me what was rightfully mine . . .' Beth said with the cold deliberation of a statement at law.

'Take *what* from you? What was rightfully yours?'

'A father's love. Isn't that a child's right?'

'Of course it is,' Tessa said desperately. 'And he loved you. He respected you for your achievements . . .'

'Except that you *intervened*. At every step you intervened in my life. You came between my own father and me.'

'Beth . . .'

'And now this. Don't you see, you're damned? The Lord destroyed your first child. Now, by your selfishness and lust, you've become pregnant again. It is God's will that your child should never be born.' She came forward.

Tessa stumbled backwards. Reaching to steady herself she touched the lectern, felt it rock under her hand. The Bible crashed from the stand and the long brass pole shuddered on its carved oak claw feet. It was a weapon of sorts. The smoke now rolling silently under the chapel door was settling around their feet.

As Tessa edged sideways Beth blocked her path. She had drawn up her hand now so that the blade of the cleaver was just visible in the half-lit chapel. Her face was set unmoving, as their mother used to say it would be if the Lord's name was taken in vain. Her eyes flared points of light, flared green as she came forward.

Tessa's hand reached out. She was finding it difficult to breathe. Smoke filled the room in thin grey layers under the candlelight. Her hand touched the lectern. The beaten brass reading hinge clattered to the ground. She grasped the pole and the heavy claw and ball feet swung upwards. 'If we stay here we'll both be dead, Beth.'

She gestured with the blade as Tessa edged forward. The flames of the pair of candles in the highest brackets dipped dramatically, revived, and dipped again until they were no more than a blue arc around the wick.

'You'll kill us both,' Tessa said. It was as if she stood outside the scene, watching the two sisters move like duellists, their eyes on each other.

Behind Beth, Tessa could see smoke pouring under the door. Perhaps it was lack of oxygen as much as fear because she seemed to see Beth's body moving, willowly through the smoke towards her. She saw Beth beating a dog they'd had when they were children, she saw the arm rise and the stick change to the wet gleam of steel.

And suddenly she was no more a third party watching the gavotte. Suddenly she was Tessa Naylor fighting for her life. Breath rasped in her throat. She darted her eyes towards the door. Under the edge, the pluming smoke was reddened with a tinge of flame.

She had no feeling for this woman in front of her. She knew she had to kill Beth to get out. To kill her sister. Without hesitation she swung the brass pole, struck Beth high on the arm, watched her stagger, saw the smoke puff and swirl under the door, swung again as her sister lunged at her with the knife, heard the crack of hard oak against Beth's skull.

CHAPTER THIRTY-SEVEN

The roof was already blazing, like a man with his hair alight. Silver arcs of water rose through the air towards it. Below roof level, in the bedroom windows, smoke masked the evidence of fire. On the ground floor, two windows had burst at one side of the house and black smoke was pouring out. But on the front ground floor the security windows reflected back the firefighters' lights, and smoke seeping slowly from around the front door was the only sign that this part of the house was connected with the blaze above.

At the back of the house, a team of firemen had already entered and were handing out limp figures to a waiting medical team. A young fireman was leaning against a fire engine coughing uncontrollably. A heavy-set man was handed out by four firefighters and immediately a medical team began working on him. Most of them knew he was already dead.

Red-faced, his cheeks glistening with sweat, the chief fire officer came running back to where Abbeline was getting out of his car at the edge of the drive. 'I don't know what we've got here,' he said, breathing hard. 'Some sort of mass suicide. Is that your information, sir?'

'It's possible,' Abbeline said flatly.

'It'll go any second,' the fire officer said. 'They've got toughened glass in the windows. They're holding for the moment but they've got to go under the heat building up inside.'

As if waiting on his word, the house seemed to shudder. Roof beams collapsed, showers of sparks rose into the air, windows burst open and smoke punched its way in long jets into the morning darkness.

The garden was overrun with vehicles. Police cars filled the drive, backing up behind fire engines, leaving a narrow way through for the ambulances which were just arriving. The wail of sirens from approaching vehicles, the crackle of radios, the shouts of fire and paramedics, filled the darkness around the burning house.

Jan got out of the car and stood beside Abbeline. For a few moments she stared, stunned by the enormity of the sight. 'I can't see anybody living in that,' she said.

He said nothing, the flame umbering his face.

'We've got one or two of them out from the back,' the fire officer said. 'The blaze seems to have started there. No survivors so far. There's just a chance for the front of the house. We're forcing the front door now.'

He gestured to where a team of firemen, blue arc lights on them, ran up the short flight of steps and began to hack at the locks on the front door. As they prised it open, smoke and sparks hissed and spluttered from the cracks. A second team had smashed through one of the toughened glass windows and a hose was now pouring thousands of gallons into the room beyond. Masked firemen clambered over sills to disappear immediately into the smoke and black-red flames within the house.

'The weird thing,' the fire officer said to Abbeline, 'is that up in the main room they're all lying in a circle. Roped themselves together like people in a lifeboat. Now I've seen suicide, but that's weird, don't you think, sir?'

When the fire officer had left them, Abbeline walked forward and Jan turned to join Ray Rose who was standing next to a police Rover angled on a bank. 'Is this where you and me, Ray, run in and drag out Mrs Wilson and her crazy sister unharmed?'

Rose shook his head. 'Not in real life, Jan.'

She nodded. 'Either way, that's it. It's all over. You can go back and enjoy your Christmas dinner in peace.'

The grey light of a fenland winter morning was stealing up around the scene. Rose shook his head. 'Shouldn't think about past mistakes at a time like this,' he said. 'But it was my surveillance team that let Mrs Wilson give them the slip. I should have given them back-up.'

Jan looked at him. 'Maybe. Maybe not. We're coppers, we're not fucking clairvoyants.'

'Does Jack Abbeline know that?'

Jan glanced at him.

'He's writing a special commendation of your work on this case.'

'I don't believe it.'

'Then you don't know my boss.'

They both instinctively looked towards Abbeline, standing alone, a tall bareheaded figure looking up at the blazing building. He was staring at a side window which the firefighters had broken open. There seemed to be less smoke coming from there than from the front of the house and somebody was being lifted over the sill.

He started forward, Jan a few yards behind him. They wove their way through the vehicles and reached a point close to the side of the house. An ambulance team was already there. They had placed Linda on a stretcher and were wheeling her away from the house. The girl was conscious, wide-eyed, smudged with carbon, her dress and hair soaked with blood and water. At the ambulance doors Abbeline bent over the stretcher. 'Are you Linda Mattia?' he said.

She didn't answer.

Abbeline knelt down so that he could bring his head closer to hers. 'You're Linda, aren't you?'

The girl nodded painfully.

'Was Tessa Wilson in the house with you?'

'Yes,' the girl said, her voice a croak.

'Where?'

'She was with Beth in the chapel. The chapel in the basement.'

At the side window firemen handed out a second figure, a woman's, and carried her to the grass verge where a doctor bent to examine her.

Abbeline joined him as the doctor straightened up, no longer concealing scraps of russet-coloured, fire-blackened dress clinging to burnt flesh . . .

Abbeline looked down at her. The short hair was singed but intact. Beth Naylor's heat-puckered nose and mouth he could just recognise from the photographs.

'She's gone,' the doctor said matter-of-factly.

★ ★ ★

'What they used as a chapel,' the fire officer said to Abbeline, 'lies in an extension of the basement at the back of the house. Right through here and then down.'

Jan followed a few paces behind them as they passed through a charred doorway. The stench of burnt wood and water was overpowering. Steam still rose through crannies of scorched brick, shreds of curtain hung from bent pelmet rods, a sideboard stood carbonised, an armchair reduced to blackened springs. Arc lights threw deep shadow against the blue-tinted haze.

'It looks bad but this is by far the most sheltered corner of the house,' the fire officer said. 'Rising heat drew some air through the ventilation system in the basement. A lot depends on how close she was able to get to it.'

They began to descend the stone staircase into the basement. The fire officer's enormous flashlight bit through the steamy darkness with a white beam. Jan saw the two men in front of her reach the bottom of the stairs and cross a hallway. Wet flagstones gleamed in the torchlight. She thought she saw Abbeline hesitate before he stepped forward.

She came down the last few steps. The two men had already passed through a heavily scorched oak door. As Jan arrived at the doorway she saw them in silhouette, the fire officer standing, two men in green paramedic's overalls, and Abbeline kneeling on one knee.

Jan stood in the doorway. The white light was held unwaveringly towards the floor. A woman in a black coat, and underneath it a once white shirt, lay on a stretcher. A woman whose face was not immediately recognisable, blackened, the hair scorched.

The paramedics lifted the stretcher.

'Is she the woman you were looking for, sir?' the fire officer asked.

Abbeline didn't answer. Jan came forward. 'Yes,' she said to the fire officer. 'She's the one.'

CHAPTER THIRTY-NINE

Standing there, only half listening to the flight calls and information announcements, looking down on the listless flow of people on the lower floor of the terminal building, Tessa Wilson tried to face the future.

'Did you hear me?' Abbeline said to her. 'We could take a look at Paris for a few days. Or Venice? This time of year it is cold but free of tourists . . .'

She shook her head.

'I have leave due. And you don't have to get back,' he said. 'You've told Carter it's all over between you.'

'No.' She was still staring down at the seemingly aimless movement of the people on the concourse below. 'I don't have to get back for Carter. I have to get back for myself. You can't imagine what it's like to be starting life halfway through your thirties.'

'Come to Paris, Tessa,' he said. 'Start life later.'

She turned to him, away from the drifting people below. Away from the newsstands where the tabloids carried front-page pictures of the marriage, in Australia, of Jo Saunders to her producer, Sepp Lander.

'You don't have to make up for anything, Jack. You don't have to make up for a night between us that didn't quite work out.'

He forced a smile. 'The next night between us might work out a whole lot better.'

'Uh-huh.'

'One night like that doesn't matter, Tess.'

She kissed him on the mouth. 'It matters to me, Jack,' she said. She picked up her bag. 'If you get to Boston this year, be sure to call me. You'll find me in the book – under *Tessa Naylor*'

THOMAS DRESDEN

TALKING TO A STRANGER

All of a sudden, Claire Garrison's world is falling apart. Her husband is having an affair. It looks like her closest friend is the woman involved. And trouble is brewing with her work as a researcher for her charismatic but volatile Russian father.

But Claire's problems have only just begun. When the bloodstained clothing of her young sister-in-law is found on the banks of the Thames, a chain of horrifying revelations comes to the surface.

And, as everyone around her seems to have become a stranger, Claire puts her trust in a man she has only just met. Although somehow she senses she's known him all her life.

'A chilling woman-hunt by a man with a nightmarish mind . . . a book you'll find difficult to put down'
Anthony Barwick, author of *Shadow of the Wolf*

HODDER AND STOUGHTON PAPERBACKS